Enchantress of Paris

Enchantress
of Paris

Marci Jefferson

THOMAS DUNNE BOOKS
ST. MARTIN'S PRESS
NEW YORK

THOMAS DUNNE BOOKS.
An imprint of St. Martin's Press.

ENCHANTRESS OF PARIS. Copyright © 2015 by Marci Jefferson. All rights reserved. Printed in the United States of America. For information, address St. Martin's Press, 175 Fifth Avenue, New York, N.Y. 10010.

www.thomasdunnebooks.com
www.stmartins.com

Library of Congress Cataloging-in-Publication Data

Jefferson, Marci.
    Enchantress of Paris : a novel of the Sun King's court / Marci Jefferson. — First edition.
        p. cm.
    ISBN 978-1-250-05709-9 (hardcover)
    ISBN 978-1-4668-6074-2 (e-book)
    1. Louis XIV, King of France, 1638–1715—Fiction.   2. Mazarin, Jules, 1602–1661—
Fiction.   3. France—Kings and rulers—Fiction.   4. Divination—Fiction.   I. Title.
    PS3610.E3655E53 2015
    813'.6—dc23

2015017353

St. Martin's Press books may be purchased for educational, business, or promotional use. For information on bulk purchases, please contact the Macmillan Corporate and Premium Sales Department at 1-800-221-7945, extension 5442, or write to specialmarkets @macmillan.com.

First Edition: August 2015

10 9 8 7 6 5 4 3 2 1

With love to my Prince
and our minions

The Italians

Cardinal Jules Mazarin—*chief minister to Louis XIV*
Geronima Mazarin Mancini—*sister of Cardinal Mazarin*
Baron Lorenzo Mancini—*her husband*

Their children:
  Victoire Laure Mancini—*married to Louis de Bourbon, duc de Mercœur*
  Paul Mancini
  Olympia Mancini—*married to Eugène-Maurice Savoy-Carignano, comte de Soissons*
  Marie Mancini
  Philippe Mancini—*later duc de Nevers*
  Alphonse Mancini
  Hortense Mancini
  Marianne Mancini—*later married to the duc de Bouillon*

Laura Mazarin Martinozzi—*sister of Cardinal Mazarin, married to Count Girolamo Martinozzi*

Their children:
  Laura Martinozzi—*married to Alfonso, Duke of Modena, daughter became queen of England*
  Anne Martinozzi—*married to Armand, Prince de Conti*

Dramatis Personae

French Royals

Anne of Austria, Queen of France—*sister to Philip IV of Spain, widow of Louis XIII of France*

Their sons:
    Louis XIV, King of France—*the Sun King*
    Philippe, duc d'Anjou—*later duc d'Orléans, known as Monsieur*

Gaston, duc d'Orléans—*brother of the late Louis XIII of France*
    Mademoiselle de Montpensier—*his daughter, known as Mademoiselle*

English Royals

Henrietta Maria, Queen of England—*sister to Louis XIII, widow of Charles I of England*

Their children:
    Charles II, the exiled King of England—*later restored to the English throne*
    James, Duke of York
    Henry, Duke of Gloucester
    Henriette Anne—*later known as Madame, duchesse d'Orléans*

House of Savoy

Christine of France—*sister to Louis XIII, married into the House of Savoy, known as Madame Royale*
    Charles Emmanuel, duc de Savoy—*her son*
    Princess Margherita Yolande—*her daughter*

Spanish Royals

King Philip IV of Spain—*brother of Queen Anne*
　　Maria-Thérèsa—*his daughter, later queen of France*
　　Don Juan of Austria—*his illegitimate son*

Courtiers and other characters

Marquis Angelelli—*friend of Constable Colonna*
Charles, comte D'Artagnan—*a musketeer*
Anne-Lucie de La Motte d'Argencourt—*encouraged by her father to flirt with Louis XIV*
Capita—*the jester*
Jean-Baptiste Colbert—*Mazarin's assistant, later minister of finance*
Pierre Beauchamp—*ballet master*
Isaac de Benserade—*poet, salon attendee*
Don Carlo Colonna, Archbishop of Amasia—*Constable Colonna's uncle*
Lorenzo Onofrio Colonna, Prince of Paliano, Constable of Naples—*Marie's suitor*
Louis de Bourbon, Prince de Condé—*French prince, enemy of Cardinal Mazarin*
Oliver Cromwell—*England's Lord Protector*
Ninon de l'Enclos—*courtesan*
Marie-Madeleine, comtesse de La Fayette—*maid of honor to Queen Anne, author*
Hugues de Lionne—*French statesman*
Charles, Prince of Lorraine—*Marie's suitor*
Jean-Baptiste Lully—*composer*
Armand de la Meilleraye—*nephew of Cardinal Richelieu, later duc de Mazarin*
Catherine Monvoisin—*the witch known as La Voisin, later burned alive*
Françoise Bertaut, Madame de Motteville—*Queen Anne's lady in waiting, author*
Molière—*playwright*
Moréna—*Marie's maid*
Madame d'Oradoux—*Meilleraye's cousin*

Dramatis Personae

Celio Piccolomini—*papal nuncio*

Don Antonio de Pimentel—*Spanish envoy*

Catherine de Vivonne, marquise de Rambouillet—*salon hostess*

Comte de Rebenac—*French ambassador*

Armand Jean de Vignerot du Plessis, duc de Richelieu—*great-nephew of Cardinal Richelieu*

François, duc de La Rochefoucauld—*salon host, author*

Rose—*nurse to the Mancini sisters*

Marguerite de la Sablière—*salon attendee*

Charles de Saint-Évremond—*writer, salon attendee*

Madeleine de Scudéry—*salon hostess, author*

Marie de Rabutin-Chantal, marquise de Sévigné—*salon hostess, letter writer*

Antoine Baudeau de Somaize—*secretary to the Précieuses*

Frances Stuart—*later mistress to Charles II of England*

Colbert de Terron—*cousin of Jean-Baptiste Colbert*

Christina Vasa—*former queen of Sweden*

Madeleine, dame de Venelle—*governess to the Mancini sisters*

Henri, vicomte de Turenne—*Marshall General of France*

Conscious that freedom is the richest treasure in the world and that a noble and generous spirit must stop at nothing to acquire it. I applied my efforts to obtaining it.

—FROM MARIE MANCINI'S MEMOIR,
   The Truth in Its Own Light

Enchantress of Paris

Madrid
1689

F ootmen threw open the front doors of my *casa,* my sanctum of peaceful exile in Madrid for near a decade, and a whiff of spices and the gleam of moonlight filled my front hall. Olympia brushed in, tall and fashionable as ever in black French silks and familiar diamonds, looking only half of her fifty years. Though she had come to Madrid for her own exile years earlier, I had not seen my older sister since her arrival visit. She took one look at my Spanish garb and frowned her disdainful courtier's frown. "Really, Marie, have you lost all sense of style?"

I kissed each of her cheeks. "It is good of you to come. What a beautiful gown."

She fluffed out her skirts and glanced about the hall, taking in the oil paintings and the Turkish carpets and, no doubt, appraising the price of each gilded candelabra. It did not worry me. She would recognize nothing to claim from our departed uncle's vast treasure trove. All of that had long been spent. "Yes," she said with a grin. "My dressmaker says the secret to making a gown beautiful is putting it on me."

I swept my hand toward the seats in my salon. "Then grace my divan and elevate my *casa* with the favor of your presence."

She caught the sarcasm. Her frown returned. "Did you summon me to exchange spite?"

"No." I marched into the salon in a manner that required her to follow. "What news from the Alcázar palace?"

She flopped down on the divan. "The court wears mourning for the Spanish queen." The Spanish queen had been a member of the French royal family in Paris, where Olympia and I were once the celebrated nieces of Europe's most powerful cardinal. France was no longer safe for Olympia, but in the Spanish queen's court, she'd led one intrigue after another. I no longer cared for courts or intrigue. Olympia went on. "In truth, nobody mourns her. The Spanish king had long tired of my old friend's daughter."

"Didn't you once try to steal that friend's lover?"

"The Sun King was my lover first, before *you* stole him from *me*," she snapped.

I gave her a look that told her she'd gone too far. "I tried to tell you potions wouldn't make a king love you."

She looked away. "Perhaps I should have listened. *You* merely have to whisper your desires and men obey."

On this she was wrong. There was one who had resisted my whispers. "Everyone talked about the extreme measures you took to get him back. I warned you to stay away from that dreadful witch in Paris."

She glared. "I never poisoned the king's mistresses. I just tried to replace them."

I hid my flush of jealousy at her use of the word *them*. "You managed to escape persecution in France, but you might not be so lucky this time. You gave the Spanish queen something to drink right before she died."

Olympia seemed stunned. "How do you know this?"

Some things I just know. "The Spanish king believes you're a sorceress, that you poisoned his queen. You will be accused before the Spanish Inquisition."

She dropped her head into her hands. "She complained of stomach fits and dizziness. I infused her milk with ginger and mint. To help, not to harm!"

I sighed. "I believe you. Flee Madrid or risk another witchcraft trial."

Olympia muttered, "How much time do I have?"

"Until dawn."

Her head jerked up. "This isn't fair. You were the one born under an evil star."

"I've borne my suffering, you know I have. Each of our sisters has had to pay the price of our family name." I walked to the window and gazed over the city. It wasn't always this way for us Mancinis.

Once, our uncle's power eclipsed everyone's. Once, his nieces were known as the Mazarinettes, and we were courted by kings and princes. And one king, the greatest monarch who ever lived, had loved Olympia. That is when everything changed. Because then his gaze fell on me, and France has never been the same.

CHAPTER 1

Palais du Louvre, Paris
December 1656

S ervants struggled under heavy black mourning velvet, draping it
across gilt-framed paintings and tapestries that adorned our uncle's
apartment at the Palais du Louvre in Paris. They worked their way around
the chamber until even the windows were covered, though they couldn't
dim the opulence. From candles twinkling in crystal chandeliers to the
incense of frankincense and myrrh wafting from a golden *brasier* to the polished marble floors, everything around us signified my uncle's power. For
such wealth stemmed from power, and my uncle was Cardinal Mazarin,
the most powerful man not just in France but in all Europe. In a chair
beside me, my sister Hortense eyed the mourning velvet and muttered,
"Mamma isn't dead yet."

I gripped my favorite novel tight. Our uncle had brought me into Paris
days earlier in case Mamma requested me. He would send me back to my
cold convent cell the moment she died. But what would he do with my dear
sisters?

Victoire, the eldest of the Mancini girls at twenty-two years, put a hand
on Hortense's arm. "The mourning cloth shows deference." Victoire's
marriage to the duc de Mercœur elevated her rank to princess of the blood.
Pregnant with her third child and adored by her husband, she brought
pride to our family. "But prepare yourself, for the physicians say Mamma
will not live."

Hortense turned to me with tears in her eyes. I was seventeen years of age, but this little ten-year-old sister was my closest, and perhaps only, friend. She was not only the prettiest Mancini but easily the prettiest creature I'd ever seen. It hurt to see her beautiful face look sad, and I pulled her into my embrace.

Mamma had been ill, as we had all known she would be, for months. Our uncle had moved her from Palais Mazarin to the Louvre for access to the king's physicians. Though busy as chief minister to King Louis the Fourteenth, the cardinal spared no expense trying to restore his sister's health. We came every day to see her, and every day Mamma called in one of my sisters or my brother. But not me.

Marianne, the youngest sister at six, eyed how I hugged Hortense and promptly started sniffling. Soft-hearted Victoire turned to comfort her. Marianne's sniffles amplified to sobs.

I myself was too fearful to cry, which seared me with guilt. *When Mamma summons me, I must seize the moment. I must beg her to convince my uncle to keep me at court.* God willing, my request wouldn't kill her. I patted my skirts to ensure the bottle of lung-wort syrup was still tucked safely in my hanging pocket. My astrological judgment of her disease suggested that lung-wort, ruled by Jupiter, might comfort her.

Hortense pulled away to study me. "Will His Eminence send you back to the Convent of the Visitation, Marie?"

Too many of my childhood years in Rome were spent in the Benedictine Convent of Santa Maria in the Campo Marzio, while my oldest brothers and sisters were permitted to live in Paris with Uncle Mazarin. When our father died and Mazarin summoned the rest of the family, my mother intended to leave me at the Roman convent. I'd begged her to bring me, pointing out Paris had convents, too. She'd brought me reluctantly, and I'd hoped my uncle would let me live at court. He had taken one look at me and declared I was too scrawny, not pretty enough. He put me in the Convent of the Visitation beyond the city walls, sending Hortense sometimes to keep me company. I'd spent two years there. The thought of returning to the convent, where life offered no color, no light, and where nuns with hairy chins woke me at all hours of the night for matins, filled me with dread. "He will not send *you* back because of how lovely you've become."

A blush rose on her cherub-pink cheeks. She had no idea how her loveliness had cost me.

The doors to my mother's sickroom opened. Cardinal Mazarin emerged, red watered-silk cassock swishing around him, waxed mustache curved perfectly upward at the ends.

All four of us scrambled to our feet. "Your Eminence," we said in unison.

He glanced over us. "Victoire, Hortense, and Marianne, your mother wants you."

She doesn't want me. Again. My heart grew heavy. My sisters proceeded through the doors.

But Hortense stopped short. "What about Marie?"

His Eminence did not look at me. "Your mother has not summoned her yet."

Hortense glanced back. "She'll be lonely."

Our uncle's face softened. "Stay. I will tell your mother of your generous spirit."

Hortense didn't mean to please, it just came naturally. A trait I had never possessed. The cardinal closed the doors, and Hortense returned to my side. But as soon as we opened my novel, the king's herald sounded in the outer chambers. "His Majesty the King!"

A row of pages in the king's tricolor livery rushed to line the walls. In walked King Louis wearing his austere frown. He had visited my mother's bedside before, but usually this antechamber was crowded. Now courtiers filing in behind the king encountered a mostly deserted room. One of the courtiers was Olympia, the second-oldest Mancini sister, and the king's favorite. King Louis had dubbed her his fair-lady and showered her with gifts. She wrinkled her long slender nose at me, which made the courtiers snicker.

King Louis looked at me. Even with his handsome aquiline nose and hooded hazel eyes, the king's frown always made him seem aloof. It was impolite to stare directly at a king, but as I struggled to overcome my nervousness, I studied him openly. That is when I recognized in that frown an emotion I often saw in my own looking-glass: loneliness. He studied me back, and for the first time, it felt like someone was actually seeing *me*.

I sensed it from the inside out. It swept my nervousness away like mist on the wind. He walked to me. "Mademoiselle Mancini, you hold vigil alone today?"

Hortense cleared her throat. "I am here!"

The king glanced. "So you are." He gestured behind him. "I haven't seen so many Mazarinettes in one chamber in weeks."

He meant us, the nieces of Mazarin. The courtiers chuckled graciously, and my female relatives cast smiles at each other. Besides Hortense, Olympia, and myself, our Martinozzi cousin Anne stood in his throng. The Martinozzis were fair of hair and skin where we Mancinis were dark. Anne had become Princess de Conti by marriage, and our uncle had already sent her sister, Laura, to wed Alfonso d'Este, the Italian Duke of Modena. Like us, they were part of my uncle's scheme to ally himself with powerful families. He had once tried to arrange a marriage for me. And now, with the king staring so intently at me, I became aware that the man who'd refused to wed me had entered with the courtiers. I wanted to run away. But Armand de la Meilleraye didn't notice me. He had fixated on Hortense, ogling her. My little sister was so beautiful that the man selected to be *my* husband had refused me because he loved *her*.

King Louis followed my gaze, and his expression changed. He leaned close and whispered, "Meilleraye is a fool. You're better off without him."

He understands. My face burned. Though the courtiers hadn't heard, they saw my blush and started whispering. I flushed all the more.

King Louis glanced at my novel, where my knuckles were white from gripping it. "What are we reading?"

I, the Mazarinette known for having brains instead of beauty, couldn't remember. I looked at it blankly. "It is *Gerusalemme Liberata*." He didn't seem to recognize it. "*Jerusalem Delivered.* An Italian poem fraught with magic and romance."

He grinned, a subtle crack in that royal frown. "You ladies with your love stories." His entourage giggled.

"There are battles." I held up the book. "The Crusades."

He seemed surprised. "Combat! That might be worth reading."

I extended it to him. "It may be why you start, but you'll finish for the romance."

The courtiers stared. Were they shocked that I would speak to the king?

Or at the daring way I'd spoken? King Louis took my book. *My precious book!*

He held it up, glancing at his retinue. "Wait until my tutors hear I've taken reading suggestions from a convent-educated girl." They tittered some more. He thumbed the pages. "The nuns let you read this?"

Hortense held a finger up to her lips. "Shhhhh!"

I grinned. "Amazing what you can get your hands on in a convent by bartering silk stockings."

Some of the courtiers pretended to look shocked. Most laughed. Olympia shot me a warning look.

Hortense didn't seem to notice. "Marie never forgets a word she reads. Go on." She pointed to the book. "Test her."

The king considered this, but Olympia spoke first. "Shouldn't Marie be reading prayer books while keeping vigil for our dear Mamma?"

King Louis nodded, never turning from me. "My sympathy. Has your mother improved?"

"The cardinal's physicians say she has not."

"I shall send my own physicians again."

I glanced at the curious faces behind him, not wanting to say too much. "What she needs is hope, for I'm afraid she's given up."

"That she must not do," said the king.

Hortense grasped my hand. "Mamma clings too much to our father's prophecy."

Olympia glared at Hortense and tried to change the subject. "Your Majesty, shall we go in to visit now?"

But the king looked into Hortense's innocent face. "What prophecy?"

Hortense must have been frightened by Olympia, for she moved behind me.

So I explained with a half-truth. "Our father predicted long ago, based on the alignment of the stars, that our mother would die before the end of the Year of Our Lord 1656."

He looked skeptical. "Who can trust the stars?"

But our father had used more than astrology to make such predictions. "Our mother's faith in the stars gives the stars power. Thus she robs herself of hope."

"How serious you are, Marie." He stared.

I didn't know how to reply, and there were no giggles.

Finally, he nodded. Hortense and I curtsied as he entered our mother's chamber. Olympia fluffed her skirts to the sides, blocking anyone from taking her place directly behind the king. The courtiers followed in step as if they were one body, slithering like a colorful, silken snake.

Hortense was asleep, head on my lap, when the king left with his train an hour later. Olympia insisted on waking her and taking her to a supper banquet. Olympia didn't invite me, and I didn't beg to go. I needed to wait.

I had fallen asleep myself when the summons came. My uncle opened the chamber doors and eyed me. "Marie."

Bleary-eyed, I leapt to my feet. Huge candelabra stood aglow in every corner, doing little to cheer the black-cloaked walls. My mother lay on a wide gilt bed. She stared at me, searching my face as she used to do, then held open her arms.

I rushed into them. "Mamma," I cried. *Why do you seem to fear me? Why am I always the last one you call?*

"My child," she muttered in Italian. She stroked my hair as I buried my face in her neck, breathing her scent. "You mustn't be sad for me. You mustn't cry."

But I would. "Yes, Mamma."

"When I am gone you must obey your uncle."

I sat up. "You must hope to recover."

"My time has come. Accept it as I did long ago." She glanced at my uncle. "You will be pleased at His Eminence's generosity."

I turned to him, almost hopeful. "Have you found another potential husband?"

He glanced at the maids. Without a word, they gathered their water basins and cloths and slipped from the room. The physicians followed, gripping their bloodstained tools. His Eminence leveled his glare on me. "Offering you to Meilleraye was merely my way of testing him. I counted on his refusal, and now he believes he owes me. I never intended for you to marry, but you shall have a handsome settlement."

All my dread of the convent returned.

Mazarin cleared his throat. "When your mother dies, you will not only rejoin the Convent of the Visitation, you will take holy orders."

"Become a nun? Please, no!"

Mamma put her hand on my arm. "It is the safest course for you."

"My heart breaks at the thought of leaving my sisters."

His Eminence said to my mother, "You must tell her."

She gripped my hands, and I listened intently. "Your father was a great oracle. Each of his predictions proved true, from your oldest brother's death right up to his own. He made predictions about you. They will make you understand why you must take holy orders." She rose on her elbow, breathless with sudden passion. "He drew up your horoscope the day you were born, then redrew it countless times, always coming to the same conclusion. He consulted the waters, he read the entrails of animals, even called on the spirits of the dead. Every sign confirmed it." She took a shaky breath, and I started to sweat. "You were born under an evil star. One day you will disgrace your family in ways no woman has ever done before."

My father hid my horoscope from me? "I would never—"

"When you grew up so headstrong, reading novels you shouldn't, acting so sullen, I didn't know how to handle you."

"If I was sullen it was because I saw fear in your eyes instead of love whenever you looked upon me."

She stroked my cheek. "This is the best way to protect you from your own destiny. Become a nun and counter your evil star."

"Your Eminence," I said, turning to my uncle. "You must not believe this prophecy."

"You Mancinis always carry the old superstitions too far. I am a Prince of the Church and cannot condone practices that border on witchcraft. But even Christ's magi followed the stars. I cannot discount what your father read in yours." He frowned. "Meilleraye must have seen what I see. You are different."

Different. Not charming like Olympia. Not beautiful like Hortense. Not angelic like Victoire. Not witty like Marianne. Each had potential where I posed a threat. I stood and hoped they wouldn't notice the bottle of lungwort syrup bulging in my hanging pocket. "You want me out of the way."

He looked aside. "It is something in your manner. You don't take correction. You have too much command of yourself, and others tend to follow commands you make."

The wary look on the cardinal's face reminded me of the time I had stolen fresh cannoli from the kitchens of Palazzo Mancini back home on Rome's Via del Corso. Cook had slaved over them. When she caught me with their sweet nut paste on my cheeks, she chased me outside to the courtyard herb garden and cornered me behind the rosemary hedge. She raised a hand to hit me. In my terror I did what came naturally. I pointed and whispered, *You cannot hurt me.* As she brought down her arm, she cried out. She cradled her hand, curled in an ugly cramp. *Strega!* she cursed. *You little witch!* She'd looked at me then the way the cardinal and my mother looked at me now.

"You are wrong." I thought of the charm in my pocket. "My sisters never do a thing I say."

Mamma fell back on the bolsters.

My uncle's words were a drop of honey in a bowl of vinegar. "We want to protect you."

I frowned at him. "You want to protect *yourself* from superstitions you claim have little merit."

They glanced at each other, and the pain in my mother's face made my heart drop. I had gone too far.

She closed her eyes. "This fuss is making me worse."

My uncle tried to usher me away, but I threw myself on the bed, kissing her hands. "Mamma, forgive me. I would never disgrace you. At least make His Eminence give me time!" My tears showered her frail skin, and I longed to give her the syrup. She cupped my face; I met her eyes.

But then she started coughing. My uncle jerked me back so hard I nearly fell on the floor. The physicians rushed in. The women reappeared, darting around, fighting fear and death with cloths and basins of water.

"Insolence," said my uncle, pushing me toward the door.

But I called past him, "Don't die and deprive me of my sisters, too!"

I heard sobs between coughs, and the door slammed before my face.

CHAPTER 2

I left the Palais du Louvre in a haze, throwing myself facedown on the seat in the cardinal's waiting carriage. I wanted to cry and scream, but there were no more tears. I needed my sisters. The cardinal's six horses made the coach fly down the rue Saint-Honoré. An extravagant number of horses for such a short distance, but His Eminence wouldn't have a Mazarinette ride in anything less splendid lest it reflect poorly on him.

They carried me past the gardens of the Palais-Royal, through the arcade of Palais Mazarin, and stopped in the court. I rushed into the hall. There was not one block of marble here, not one crystal sconce, not one painting worth less than a blacksmith's or a butcher's life savings. I'd seen Mazarin's coffers full of gold in the dungeons of the fortress of Vincennes when we'd stopped on our way to the convent two years earlier. My uncle had amassed wealth not only by ordinary landholding, like nobility, but also like a true Italian. He'd played moneylender, sold offices, and controlled the price of treasury bonds, buying them low and selling them high. How did I know his secrets? I glanced down the gallery toward his library, which housed more books than any other in France. In his adjoining study, where he hid the most important books, I'd stumbled upon Mazarin's private ledgers.

Might my father's papers be hidden there? I took a flickering taper from a sconce and tiptoed into the vast library and beyond, into the study. It swallowed up my small light, and I closed my eyes. I had explored this room every night since my return, devouring the philosophers on the shelves on the west wall, the mathematics on the southern shelves, and the explorers on the east side. But a locked case against the northern wall held the real treasures: forbidden books. Burned by ordinary churchmen, they were coveted by ambitious ones. Books about the stars, written in Arabic symbols that I couldn't yet decipher. Books on astrological medicine, with diagrams of the dissected human body's inner organs. Volumes on alchemy with colorful symbolic illustrations. Handwritten grimoires with spells to cure and to curse. And my favorites, the earthy-smelling herbals, which I felt contained the real magic.

Then there were the dangerous books, ones that once belonged to my father. The *Key of Solomon,* written by King Solomon himself, and the *Sworn Book of Pope Honorius* explained how to conjure and command demons. *Heptameron* was no safer, with its instructions for conjuring angels. Being caught with these would have condemned my father to burning at the stake for necromancy. Papa had been a respected Roman noble, too clever to get caught. Now my uncle kept them with *Picatrix* and occult books by Agrippa for purposes unknown.

I opened my eyes, stuck the taper in a candleholder, and snatched the key from beneath a marble bust of Julius Caesar. *If Mancini papers are anywhere, they are in that case.* I opened the glass doors, running a finger over worn spines until I touched a leather-covered casket in the corner. Always preoccupied with the books, I'd ignored it before. The lock gave easily, and papers spilled to the floor.

The first two dozen packets were letters with a unique seal: intertwined initials encircled by the letter *S* repeated four times. I scanned them. They seemed to be letters written by my uncle and the king's mother, Anne of Austria, Queen of France. They were . . . *love letters!* I took them to the taper, reading expressions of passion and affection, shaking my head in disbelief. I read whole passages of instruction, written by my uncle during the Fronde, on how the queen mother should guide the king *his son.*

I had heard the rumor. Every Parisian pamphleteer had circulated the claim that Mazarin was the king's real father, but nuns at my convent dismissed it as gossip. Now I thought through physicians' ledgers and other letters I'd read in this study that supported the story.

I stacked the letters with shaky hands and dug into the casket for the last item. A book more than a hundred years old titled *Strife of Love in a Dream* by Francesco Colonna. Had he been a member of the powerful Colonna family in Rome that had supported my uncle in his childhood? I flipped through the pages and caught my breath. The lettering was like none I'd seen, the woodcut illustrations highly detailed, the language Latinate Italian. It told the story of a man in a pagan dreamworld, encountering mythic gods as he strove to find the woman he loved. As I read, a folded parchment fell from its pages to the floor.

I picked it up, recognizing Papa's handwriting. *My horoscope.* Inside a great square were twelve triangular houses, and the symbols within explained each planet's position at the time of my birth. My eyes welled up as I read his notes in the margins. *A brilliant mind, but disobedient.* I admitted to both of those traits. Faint scribbles said, *A mysterious star in Libra suggests she will abandon her husband.* The star wasn't named. The last note shocked me. *Her gifts in divination may cause her downfall.*

Not if I could help it.

I held the parchment over the taper until it caught fire. I walked it to the empty hearth, remembering a time my father had stared into flames. He had carried me from my bed and bundled me in front of him on horseback for a midnight ride out of Rome. On an open hill beyond the city walls, he had scratched a magic circle into the dirt. He had warned me not to leave his side, uttered strange names, and thrown pungent herbs on an altar fire. I had been too tired to understand why the night shadows dancing beyond his flame seemed to gather together like phantoms, descending on us and terrifying me. I'd closed my eyes tight and remember nothing more. Had those spirits confirmed I would cause trouble?

My horoscope burned wildly, singeing my fingertips, ashes falling on the hearth.

M oments later I slipped into the apartment I shared with my sisters. They paused. Victoire held a brush over Marianne's head, Hortense looked up from her book, and Olympia turned from the fireplace and said, "Where have you been?"

"Mamma wishes me to become a nun."

Olympia shrugged and turned back around.

But Victoire beckoned me to the dressing table. She gestured for Hortense to take over brushing Marianne's hair, then unlaced my bodice. "What did Mamma tell you?"

With my laces undone, I took a deep breath. "One of our father's predictions. He said I would disgrace you all."

Olympia didn't look at us. "Oh, that."

"You knew?"

Victoire nodded. "We never thought much of it. You could never disgrace us."

Olympia snickered. "She disgraces us every day when she goes out in those convent rags."

I stared at my bodice, gray wool trimmed with black velvet, as Victoire tossed it aside. She helped me step out of the matching skirts. "I've had no need for court dresses."

Olympia stirred a pot hanging from a hook in the fireplace, making the scent of spices swirl through the air. She struck a fetching image in her lace chemise, but this was the sort of potion-making our uncle detested. "You slouch," she said. "You wear your hair too flat. Your neck is too skinny and your lips are too big. You wear no jewels."

I glanced in the looking-glass, where I now stood in nothing but my own chemise. I straightened my shoulders and tried to fluff up the tendrils hanging in bundles behind my ears. They fell back, limp and lifeless. "You took my only necklace, Olympia."

She grinned. *"Borrowed."*

"Then give it back. I want to look my best tomorrow."

Hortense poked me. "So you can flirt more with the king?"

Marianne gaped. "Did the king flirt back?"

Olympia lifted a spoon to her nose and sniffed. "Even if I give back your measly pearl necklace, the king will never flirt with *you*."

My face burned as Victoire sat me beside Marianne to brush my hair. "I want the pearl hair pins, too."

Hortense interrupted. "The king *was* flirting with Marie. I saw."

Olympia snatched a glass vial from the carved marble mantel and spooned golden liquid into it. "Well, he won't do it again."

"What's that you're making?" asked Victoire.

"Liquid assurance."

Victoire dropped her brush. "Not again."

I gasped. "Another love potion for King Louis? You shouldn't."

She'd concocted one the day I returned from the convent. Right when the king's carriage had arrived, she'd poured it into the brandy decanter in our salon. She ran away, planning on doubling back through the upstairs gallery to join the king as he entered the salon and then serving his brandy herself. But she tripped on the Turkish carpets and ended up under the stairs crying over a sprained ankle. I had to wrap it with dried St. John's wort to calm her down. King Louis drank the tainted brandy and promptly spent half an hour with the gardener's daughter in an alcove. Alone. Olympia was beside herself. The gardener's daughter had been sent away the next day.

Now Olympia frowned. "It is *not* a potion. It's just a . . . a little ginseng infusion to encourage his passions."

"What does that mean?" asked Marianne.

Hortense laughed so hard she clutched her middle. "It means that once King Louis drinks it, he will rub himself against Olympia until she finds herself pregnant."

"Quiet." Olympia plugged her vial. "I won't allow King Louis to do *that* until after I'm married."

Marianne jumped up. "I don't understand."

Victoire poured water into a silver bowl for me to wash my hands and face. "What Olympia means is, she wouldn't let the king . . . rub against her *until* she is married. So if she does get with child, society won't realize it's a bastard." Victoire scrubbed my face with a linen cloth a little too hard. "If our uncle catches Olympia making such potions, *she* will be the disgrace of the family and locked in a convent."

Marianne clapped. "Get caught, Olympia. I claim your bed!" She ran to Olympia's bed, the biggest, covered with more silk and gilding than the others. She bounced up and down on it squealing, "I claim your bed, your clothes, your jewels, and even the jewels you stole from Marie!"

Even Olympia had to laugh. Victoire kissed each of us and went home to the Hôtel de Vendôme, to her husband and children. We settled to our routine of rubbing almond oil into each other's nails and rearranging pillows. Olympia and I tucked Hortense and Marianne under their coverlets and pulled their bed curtains closed.

That's when I tried to warn Olympia. "Olympia, if King Louis cannot expend the passion you inspire, he will become frustrated."

"How do you know anything of men?" She took my brush and plopped herself before the great looking-glass, stroking her hair. "I will give him just enough to hold him in thrall until my wedding."

I decided not to tell her which books I'd read or how I'd gotten them. "You don't love him."

She waved this comment away. "Intimacy with the king is the loophole to power. He must tell his secrets and desires to no one but me."

"I don't understand."

Her expression changed. "You weren't here for the Fronde wars when Paris was a raging mob, burning, raping, pillaging, slaughter in the streets. Our uncle moved us just in time, plotting battles, buying loyalties, subduing the French nobles. He saved us. I *never* want to see that mob rise against us again. You would do well to follow his commands."

I didn't bother pointing out that French hatred for Mazarin's abuse of power was what sparked the Fronde in the first place, and it only ended because the French believed King Louis had come of age. "*Louis* is the one with the crown."

"So our uncle must know his private thoughts."

It made sense. The king's seal was needed to dictate state affairs. But our uncle was the one with the brilliance for making money. Which, I knew, he hoarded for himself. "Using the king thus is more reprehensible than anything I could contrive, yet *I* am being sent away."

Olympia held a bottle of beauty elixir aloft. Gold dust within it glittered in the firelight as she sipped it lightly. "If I could fully control the king, His Eminence would have made me queen. There is no potion for that. None that worked. At least as comtesse de Soissons I will become part of the Bourbon family, a princess of the blood! When I am married, I will have the freedom to bed the king. That will give me more power over him. His Eminence will reward me by making me his heir."

I was disgusted. "One of our brothers will be Mazarin's heir."

"Philippe is too difficult to control. Alphonse is too young to be useful. It will be *me*."

Control. Suddenly I understood my uncle's motives, and I hid my surprise by moving to my bed. Mazarin wanted me out of the way because he didn't think he could control me. To stay at court, I must somehow oblige him. There was as much chance of that happening as there was of Olympia handing over my pearl necklace.

Long after my sisters had fallen asleep, I slipped from silk sheets and crept to my *cassone*. Such Italian trousseau chests were meant for brides. Mine was half the usual size and secondhand, acquired hastily for my admission to the convent in Rome. The hinges creaked softly, but no one stirred. I shuffled linens and petticoats and opened the false bottom. I'd discovered this secret compartment during my first week at the convent. It had inspired me, for here I could hide my very own grimoire.

I'd bound the book myself from loose parchments and discarded leather, compiling charms I'd heard my father chant, listing from memory formulas to prolong life, and composing my own *oraisons*, healing spells that were half Latin Bible verses and half prayer. I jotted everything I'd overheard Papa say about the attributes of planets and astrological houses. When the nuns had assigned the pottage gardens to me, I'd subtly followed his lunar planting and harvesting times. I'd recorded my father's magical uses for herbs, making tinctures and teas, and testing them in my cell between convent duties. Since returning to Paris, I'd been memorizing passages from my father's texts in the cardinal's study on how to summon angels, then transcribing them while my sisters slept. Though it contained not a single curse or malevolent spell, my grimoire held knowledge that a girl with an evil star shouldn't possess. Especially one with a cardinal for an uncle. Altering a few herbal cures would turn them to poisons. My grimoire's mysteries would be misunderstood. A penchant for divinity had condemned me in my mother's eyes, but my grimoire would condemn me by law of church and man. I was not so bold as Olympia, and I had more to lose.

I closed the *cassone* and went to the fireplace, still crackling brightly, and stepped over a slave girl with ebon skin sleeping by the hearth. My uncle liked to keep Palais Mazarin warm and refused to bank the fires at night for safety. Instead, he appointed slaves to sleep on the floor to prevent flaming logs from rolling out onto expensive carpets. She was dispensable. Like me.

God help me cast aside old ways and blend in at the royal court. I tossed the book in, and flames leapt around it, twisting and dancing as my treasured pages curled, blackened, and turned to ashes. Sighing, I turned to step over the slave girl again.

Her eyes were wide open, bright reflections of my burning grimoire. We stared at each other a moment, saying nothing. Then I went back to bed.

CHAPTER 3

When I woke early the next morn, I knew Olympia would never return my pearl necklace, much less loan me the pearl pins. The maids crept about our chamber, fueling the fire and setting out our morning food. I made a decision. As I opened my bed curtains, Olympia arose.

"Maids!" she called, and chambermaids rushed to her toilette with focused attention. They stripped her naked, sponging her skin with an infusion of warm water and frankincense. They bustled about with curling rods, dress pins, and globs of face paint, and soon the chamber smelled of jasmine perfume. They tugged red and white striped Guernsey stockings up to her thighs and tied them in place with red ribbon garters. They helped her shimmy into a crisp white chemise and held her hands as she stepped into gray watered-silk taffeta petticoats. Her black velvet overskirt was lined with soft gray fur and trailed behind her even after bustling. They laced the matching bodice up her front and stitched a gray fur-covered stomacher into place over the laces. When the maids finally fell away exhausted, she studied herself in the huge Venetian looking-glass. She pulled on the corkscrew curls falling from the buns above her ears, then released them, and they bounced back into place. "Damn," she said with a frown. "Why did Mamma have to get ill? I look horrid in mourning colors."

She's going for jewelry next. "You should hurry," I said. "You wouldn't want to miss the king's early walk in the gardens."

It worked. She checked her backside in the looking-glass, then snapped her fingers. The maids brought a black fur cloak, tied it at her neck with a black satin bow, and raised the huge hood over her *coiffure*. Olympia turned on her black velvet high heels and left. I couldn't believe my luck.

The maids picked up discarded gloves and ribbons as they walked out. They would leave me with Rose, the old servant who had nursed us as children in Rome and knew nothing of *coiffures*. "Wait," I said quietly, and the slave girl with ebon skin stopped. "W-will you help me dress, too?"

Cardinal Mazarin had acquired many of her kind through business trades recorded in his ledgers, listed as the nameless, faceless tangible good called *female slave*. She'd never uttered a word in my presence. She grabbed my hand and squinted at my palm. Finally she dropped it, looking at me with guarded appreciation. "Are you a witch?" She gestured to the fireplace where my grimoire was lost in ashes.

"No!" I glanced, but no one was left to hear, and my sisters still slept. "I never made any pact with the devil and never shall. I merely practiced magic. But no more."

She almost seemed disappointed. "Very well, I'll help you."

I couldn't place the accent in her perfect French. "Did you learn palms in your homeland?"

She shook her head. "My mother and I were taken from Africa by Portuguese traders when I was knee-high. I never met the snake-god of my people, but my mother taught me our ways before she died, things that would scare you out of your skin. I learn a bit of magic from every household I'm sold into. Palms I learned from a diamond trader in Holland."

What might she learn from the Mancinis? "What did you see that made you want to help me?"

She thought before speaking. "Marks that indicate you'll live a liberated life. With you I'll have a chance at freedom."

I laughed. "Doubtful."

She seemed serious. "There are other signs, and they are stronger with you than with your sisters. If I help you now, you'll help me later?"

I did not see such marks or signs. "I always repay kindness."

She went straight to work, curling my hair and washing my face with rosemary vinegar. She pulled the laces of a black satin bodice until I was forced to stand straighter. She sprinkled me with a bottle of Olympia's best perfume and grinned.

I laughed again. "What is your name?"

"Moréna." She stuck the tip of her finger into a pot of Olympia's mix of special red containing cochineal and a secret ingredient I was determined to uncover. She dabbed my cheeks and lips.

I walked to Olympia's huge lacquered cabinet, a gift from His Eminence, and rummaged until I found my skimpy pearl necklace. I tied its ribbon behind my neck. We turned to the mirror, and I watched as Moréna placed the pearl pins in my curls. *Better.*

"Will King Louis visit your mother today?" she asked in a knowing tone.

"My efforts aren't for his benefit!" Or were they? I wanted to explain that if I showed Mamma I could blend in at court she might change her mind and convince Mazarin to let me stay. But part of me longed to see the king's frown turn to a smile again. Marianne and Hortense woke up, and I said nothing more, for it was time to return to Mamma's sickroom.

V ictoire met us in the cardinal's antechamber with her two sons. We played marbles on the floor until our brother Philippe arrived with the shadow of a beard on his face. At sixteen he was taller than most men, yet hadn't learned to shave like one. He put his hands on his hips. "Did you miss your brother?"

Marianne scoffed. "We saw you just yesterday."

Philippe shook his head. "I've brought your *other* brother Alphonse from school!"

A scrawny boy just taller than Hortense entered with a wide grin. Oh, how he'd grown!

We all jumped up to embrace him. We kept our voices hushed, retelling old stories from Rome and sharing new ones of schools and convents. Physicians came and went, ignoring us, shaking their heads, arguing over which emetic to give Mamma. Victoire's children fell asleep on the padded benches while Philippe and Alphonse took to editing one of Philippe's poems, spreading parchments on the floor. Finally, in the late afternoon, King Louis arrived, as I'd secretly hoped he would. I'd smoothed my skirts and thrown back my shoulders before I even noticed the pulse of excitement coursing through me. He searched the room and found my face. And smiled.

I curtsied alongside my family, trying to think of something clever to say.

He nodded toward the stack of books by my chair. "Ever the reader, Marie Mancini."

Say something! "You read my book?"

"A few pages. Enough to meet Rinaldo, our valiant hero."

"What do you think? Will he give up his quest for Armida?"

He frowned. "Her part confused me. I had to skip to the end to—"

"Don't do that," I interrupted. "Read it properly!"

Behind him, Olympia stared daggers at me. The courtiers gasped. I pressed my lips shut.

But King Louis just grinned. "Very well. Give me one week." Then he turned serious again. He moved to my mother's chamber and the doors opened to admit him.

I smiled as he passed. I doubted he would read another page, much less finish in a week.

Olympia stepped out of his train, eyeing my pearls. "You used my special blend of red."

"Don't begrudge me a little pleasure before His Eminence sends me to rot in a convent. You forgot this." I handed her the little vial of yellow potion.

She glanced around to be sure no one was watching and slipped it into the hanging pocket beneath the folds of her skirts. "He isn't for you." She hurried to her place behind the king.

They weren't long. King Louis left quickly with just a nod in my direction. Physicians ran in and out. Mamma's maids ordered more hot water from the footmen in the antechamber. One woman ran out only to return moments later with a jug, sloshing milk out onto the marble floor in her haste.

Finally the cardinal threw open the doors. He stood sentinel and called my sisters one by one to Mamma's bedside. Victoire went first and returned holding her pregnant belly as if she needed to lie down. Marianne went next and came back crying, which made Hortense cry as she went in. Philippe and Alphonse went in together. My nails had cut deep slits into my palms when they finally came out and His Eminence signaled for me. I rushed forward, but a woman screamed from within, "She's breathed her last!"

My uncle turned, his great scarlet silks whipping my skirts as we ran to her side. Ashen, my Mamma wouldn't look at me. Her eyes were fixed to a spot above her bed. "No!" I cried, and fell beside her. My sisters were behind me then, wailing. The women covered their faces with their aprons and the physicians argued and the cardinal chanted prayers. Mamma's life was over. And so would mine soon be.

CHAPTER 4

Never had man manners so courteous in public and so harsh in his own house as
Cardinal Mazarin.

—HORTENSE MANCINI'S MEMOIRS

Days later I descended the stairs of Palais Mazarin with Hortense and Marianne for our mother's funeral, so bewildered by grief that I hardly noticed the man waiting in the great hall.

He stepped to me as we reached the door. "Mademoiselle Mancini."

"Yes?" I let my sisters step out to climb into the first waiting carriage and lifted my black lace mourning veil. It was King Louis, dressed simply in a gray satin doublet and petticoat breeches, without jewels or even his ceremonial scabbard. I fell into a curtsy. "Forgive me, Majesty. I didn't recognize you without your heralds and pages."

He glanced at his attire. "Moving about incognito allows me to be unobtrusive. Kings are prohibited from attending funerals, so I shall make this visit brief."

I stood, feeling foolish for not understanding the ways of his court already. "Olympia is still upstairs. She is waging a minor war against our old nurse about appropriate mourning attire."

"Actually, I came to see to you." He took off his hat. "Knowing you would lose your mother cannot have lessened the blow."

Tears burned my throat. "Sire, your kindness is touching." Even without royal trappings, majesty still resonated in his dignified bearing. I reminded myself of Olympia's warning. *He's not for you.*

"You and I are both serious by nature. I understand how you scrutinize your own pain. I, too, lost a parent."

His perception seemed uncanny. Something else occurred to me. *He must not know about his real father.* I had to look down.

He took it as sadness. "I should leave you. When your mourning concludes, I hope to see more of you at court." He smiled softly, warming his features. "You're not like other girls."

"Me?" I felt breathless. Could it be that what made me different from my sisters actually gave me merit in the king's eyes? I longed to receive that soft, unexpected smile every day. "I won't be at court, sire. My uncle will send me back to the convent."

He seemed surprised. "No. You'd be wasted there. Shall I speak to your uncle about this?"

Just then my uncle cleared his throat from the center of the great hall. I hadn't heard him enter. His eyes darted from me to King Louis. "Sire, it's good you've come. I have papers for you to sign before I leave."

The king nodded to me, then disappeared with my uncle. I went out to the carriage harboring affection for the king my family used so badly.

Wearing nothing but black, my sisters and brothers and I held one another quietly, tears spent, at the Church of the Augustins. Victoire looked pale and held her stomach continuously. I held the hands of Olympia and Hortense through the bishop's eulogy and watched Cardinal Mazarin make a great show of wiping his eyes before the dukes and princes in attendance.

After the requiem mass we lined up to exit the nave, and Mazarin said to me, "Kiss your brothers and bid farewell. Say good-bye to your sisters and prepare your things. You take leave on the morrow."

Victoire suddenly leaned on my shoulder, steadying herself.

The cardinal looked alarmed. "Are you unwell?" he asked her.

"I must return to the Hôtel de Vendôme. Please don't take Marie from me so soon after God has taken my mother."

He pressed his lips together. "Very well, I entrust your three youngest sisters to your care. Marie mustn't go to court. She must obey you in everything, Victoire. And as soon as that child of yours is born, Marie goes."

And there in the midst of my mother's funeral, I felt elation. *God forgive me.*

Philippe took our tearful little Alphonse back to the Jesuit College at Clermont. Victoire took Hortense and Marianne. The cardinal, Olympia, and I rode alone to Palais Mazarin. We sat opposite her, and she pouted while I planned what to pack.

Guilt forced me to keep from looking too happy. "I'm going to Victoire's at the Hôtel de Vendôme. I'll be taking my pearls with me."

Olympia shrugged. "You'll have no better use for them than I. We must seclude ourselves in mourning."

"Victoire will have many visitors."

"I don't need visitors, I need the king." She kicked our seat.

Surprisingly, our uncle didn't grow angry. "You may return to court after a few weeks."

"King Louis could replace me in that amount of time, and you know it."

Mazarin showed no emotion. "You should have wept more during your mother's illness. Then he would have reason to believe you need consoling now. Think of how you might have taken advantage of a king's succor."

"Lift our mourning restrictions," Olympia said. "Let me perform in the ballet tonight."

He gently tugged the fingertips of his red leather gloves, one by one, inching them off. "That would expose you to ridicule."

"At least let me watch. I must see for myself which of the simpering court brats throws herself at the king's feet."

Even I, one who rarely went to court, knew the answer to that. "They all will."

Our uncle was unmoved. "Olympia," he said, not looking up, "you sound like a woman who doubts her powers of seduction. It's that fool witchcraft of yours. You can't win a Frenchman with potions."

I gasped. He cast me a sidelong glance that made me want to scoot away.

"It worked for Catherine de Medici." Olympia threw out her hands. "She was Queen of France for years."

I had to interject. "She only succeeded in making the French hate Italians."

Olympia ignored me. "The only way I'll be able to control Louis is if I lie with him. Move up my wedding."

Our uncle bent his arm and lunged at Olympia, bringing his gloves down on her cheek so fast she had no chance to move. The leather made a horrid *slap* against her skin. She cried out. I backed into the corner of the carriage and balled my hands into fists.

"*Never* command me." He settled back in his seat, unruffled, as if nothing had happened. "Keep your hold on the king or be replaced. A campaign in Flanders is forthcoming. I want the king to sign for troops and ride to the front himself. Ensure he is amenable or I will send *you* to a convent, too, as far from Paris as I can find."

She put her hands down, cheek glowing. "As you wish, *Your Eminence.*"

Our uncle started replacing his gloves. He'd planned to strike her all along. "Come down from the ceiling, Marie. As long as you obey, you have nothing to fear."

I hadn't realized I'd climbed the bench in my attempt to distance myself. I sat back down and pressed my face against the wall of the carriage. I felt the jerk and dip of every broken flagstone in the street.

Watching me, Olympia let out a sinister laugh. "Are you certain you don't want to go back to your convent, Marie?"

"What has happened to you all?"

Our uncle ignored me.

Olympia snorted. "Welcome to Paris."

At Palais Mazarin the cardinal's chief minister, Jean-Baptiste Colbert, was waiting. We followed them into the front hall, where they turned directly into the library and shut themselves up for what might be hours of fiscal discussions. Olympia grabbed my hand and pulled me back out. "Come to the Palais du Louvre with me."

"To see the ballet?"

She nodded. "We can make fun of the bourgeoisie who attend in second-rate satin, striving to imitate nobility's fashions." Winter wind blew back her hood. Her hair blew wildly. "I know what you are up to with your little pearls and face paint."

I held my hood so my carefully placed curls wouldn't get ruined. "You don't know what it's like in your shadow."

"If you want to remain at court, you have to know which men have the money, which women spread their legs, and who needs the most favor. I can show you."

She was right. All I knew of the French courtiers I'd learned from reading my uncle's papers. "No tricks?"

She dragged me down the steps and waved to the carriage driver, a wrinkled old man, just as he started unharnessing the horses. "To the Louvre!" she called. He looked skeptical. Everyone knew we were in mourning. She flashed her dimples. "Please?"

The old man actually blushed, and he shouted toward the stables. In moments, coachmen and equerries swarmed the carriage, and we were rumbling down the road again. Olympia reached behind a red velvet cushion and produced two black vizard masks. "You planned this," I cried as she tied mine into place. She only winked.

The men helped us alight at the Louvre, and with hoods pulled over our hair, we slipped in through a side door. Olympia led me upstairs, through a few chambers, and finally into a gallery box. A handful of people turned to watch us enter, but we stepped aside.

"There is Colbert de Terron," she said, pointing to a man in the hall below. "He is Jean-Baptiste Colbert's cousin. Ambitious, but easily bribed."

A woman in the gallery studied us with discontent. Olympia snapped open a fan to hide our mouths, and she whispered, "That sour thing is Madame de Motteville, the only woman who sincerely likes the queen mother."

A minor commotion sounded below, and Olympia pulled me to the railing. "Ah," she said. "And now we have King Charles the Second of England, here in exile since their parliament executed his father. Look at that swarthy complexion and black hair, don't you just want to taste him?"

I elbowed her.

"He may have no kingdom, but he *is* still a king. Look, it's his mother, Henrietta Maria, aunt to King Louis, and his sister, Henriette Anne. Isn't she deathly thin? Their shabby English retinue have taken over the Palais-Royal and live off our scraps." She looked at me pointedly. "Is this a family you should ally with?"

I understood. "Stay within their good graces because they have the king's favor, but don't pander because they have no power."

She grinned, proud, then pointed to the audience below. "Note who to avoid based on who is absent. You do not see Gaston, duc d'Orléans, uncle of King Louis. He and his daughter disgraced themselves by siding against the crown in the Fronde. Same with the Prince de Condé—that Bourbon cousin was the master behind the Fronde." She tipped her head toward the stage. "Endeavor to please those closest to the king. The ones he chooses to dine with, to gamble with, to dance with."

The violinists in the opposite box began to play, and the violas and *basse de violon* joined in the overture. I hadn't participated in a *ballet de cour* since my brief introduction to Paris years earlier. Now, hearing the music again, I gripped the rail and let the melodic chords flow through me. Onstage, lovesick Cupid languished upon a bed. The Sun King himself danced into view, dressed as Apollo. Nine muses twirled around him, our Martinozzi cousin, the Princess de Conti, among them.

"I should be dancing," Olympia muttered. "Look how Mademoiselle d'Argencourt eyes the king. She'll let the shoulder of that skimpy Grecian costume slip off. She'll snare him."

"Didn't you use the new potion?"

Olympia shrugged. "The damned things don't seem to have lasting effect."

"Beyond the heat of the moment, you mean?"

She frowned. "The cardinal is wrong. The king will come to console me. I'll have to do something drastic."

I paid no attention, just let myself fall into the dotted rhythms and upbeat flourishes of the music.

Back at Palais Mazarin, the cardinal was nowhere to be found. Moréna had my sisters' things packed in a trunk beside my *cassone*. "I'm going with you."

"Moréna, you belong to Mazarin."

"Can a man really own a woman?" Her voice had a determined edge.

"I don't have the power to free you."

"You need a maid. Tell Mazarin you've merely borrowed me to keep logs in your fireplace at night."

I shrugged. "Then let us away."

We left Olympia hunched over a mortar and pestle, grinding walnut shells for a face scrub, and set out for our new adventure.

CHAPTER 5

Hôtel de Vendôme

January 1657

"How do you like your rooms?" asked Victoire from her silver gilt bed, where physicians insisted she spend the remainder of her pregnancy. Her belly was surrounded by fluffy down pillows and lacy Dutch linens. She extended her hands, and I kissed each of her cheeks.

"Far enough that I cannot hear Marianne's fits when the governess makes her go to bed, and close enough that Hortense can find me if she has bad dreams."

Victoire laughed. "I banish bad dreams." Her eyes glittered. "Help me entertain visitors."

This stunned me. "Me?" With my skinny neck, my big lips, and my pagan ways? "I don't fit in with the nobility of Paris."

She made a *tisk* sound. "Noble blood doesn't make a person noble at all. I've invited the finest Parisian women so they can see how bright you are. Make a favorable impression and the cardinal might be persuaded to let you stay."

I grinned. "Everyone who comes simply must stay to dine."

Victoire's husband, the duc de Mercœur, walked in. "And gamble." He kissed Victoire. "Offer gambling and the husbands will stay for hours."

"Which means Marie can converse longer with the ladies." Victoire turned back to me. "Start your own salon here. You will be like our father leading the Accademia degli Umoristi!"

I had clear memories of Rome's most distinguished literary minds assembling at Palazzo Mancini for readings. And I'd heard of Parisian salons where the witty, the elegant, and the most refined excelled at conversation and exchanged new ideas. Hadn't King Louis suggested I had merit? "You think I could?"

Victoire smiled. "You could shine!"

I raided the Hôtel de Vendôme over the next week. I ordered the servants to carry tables upstairs to Victoire's rooms for gaming. We moved carpets and paintings and half a dozen candelabra. I sent up the library's best books on philosophy. I went to the kitchens, where hams and bundles of herbs hung from the rafters, and women pounding pastry dough in great wooden bowls worked in clouds of flour.

"The duchess directed me to order suppers," I said to the cook sweetly. We drew up menus featuring oysters, foie gras, and poached pears and ordered cases of wine from d'Arbois.

I instructed the servants. "You must never let the fires die. Never leave a wineglass empty." They nodded with anticipation.

On the night of our reception, Moréna laced me in gray silk and poked my ribs. "You should eat more." She pinned one bundle of black silk flowers in my hair and another at my décolletage, then tied a simple black ribbon around my neck. "You'll need new dresses."

But I was too nervous. "They may not even like me."

At last a carriage pulled into the court with our first arrival. The footman muttered a name as she stepped out. Madeleine de Scudéry, the author. *This is my chance!*

I greeted her in the front hall with a deep curtsy. "I owe you a debt of gratitude."

Scudéry seemed confused. "What have I done to deserve such thanks?"

"Your novel *Clélie* provided hours of entertainment at the Convent of the Visitation."

She beamed. "I had no idea they read my work in the convent."

"Oh, yes. And they always shall." I winked at her. "As long as we don't tell the abbess."

Scudéry laughed all the way upstairs, where Victoire insisted I entertain them with dramatic recitations of *Clélie,* and we laughed and supped into the night.

The next week Scudéry brought another writer. Comtesse de La Fayette, seasoned courtier and matron of honor to the queen mother, studied me up and down. They supped with us, then sat around Victoire's bed, politely debating the merits of marriage.

"Marie," said Scudéry, "what say you?"

I hesitated. "I would rather not subject myself to a husband. I long to embark on sweeping adventures to distant lands and live on my own terms."

La Fayette eyed Scudéry. "She speaks her mind."

I tried to make a joke of it. "Blame it on my too-big mouth."

Scudéry ignored me. "Yet I sense restraint. She lacks flair. She needs to visit *her.* We must take her to a rare meeting at the Hôtel de Rambouillet."

The others nodded in agreement. I felt like some doll they were about to toy with. "To meet the Précieuses?"

Victoire smiled triumphantly. "The most famous salon of all."

CHAPTER 6

Those things that cannot naturally bring about the effects for which they are employed are superstitious and belong to a pact entered into by devils.

— JACOBUS SIMANCAS,
Institutiones Catholicae

A few weeks later I stood on the rue Saint-Thomas with Scudéry on my right and La Fayette on my left. The Hôtel de Rambouillet's red brick, stone facing, and steep roof matched the other houses between the Tuileries and the Louvre. They took me straight in and directly up a circular staircase. I gripped the wrought iron balusters, suddenly anxious.

La Fayette took my hand. "Be at ease. We aren't ostentatious or crass like courtiers at the Louvre. You'll find in us the quality of *honnêteté,* restraint and decorum."

But what will they find in me?

We passed through a dining room, a bedchamber, then entered a grand salon. Walls of robin's-egg blue matched blue and gold tapestries hanging between bright windows that stretched from floor to soaring ceiling. The famous *chambre bleue.* It was like entering a new world.

A woman arranging hothouse flowers in a crystal vase turned to study me. Catherine de Vivonne, marquise de Rambouillet. Bright eyes suggested a sharp mind despite elderly age. "This is the Mancini you claim is worthy?"

La Fayette nodded but didn't curtsy. Scudéry pulled me into the small gathering of men and women, but there wasn't time for introductions. Rambouillet swept her hand over the red-covered divans, stools, and armchairs, and her guests seated themselves. Scudéry sat beside me, whispering the names of people who spoke.

The first was a shabbily dressed actor known simply by the name Molière. He held out a roll of paper. "I would like to discuss a new play. A comedy to take Paris by storm."

A self-satisfied-looking man, Isaac de Benserade, shook his head. "Poetry and tragedy are the order of the day."

Molière looked defeated, but Rambouillet ignored them both. "Today we will discuss palm reading. Is our destiny to be found in our hands?"

I froze. Of all topics! Did Rambouillet know about my family? My father's prophecy? My gift for divination?

Marguerite de la Sablière, a Protestant, answered first. She held out her hand and spoke in a soft, elegant manner. "Only simple country people still practice such things. Brittany women sweep dust from the church to their homes for luck. Autun villagers sacrifice bulls to the Virgin Mother to protect against plague. Every French farmer has a horseshoe over his door and a rabbit's foot in his pocket. These are not the ways of nobility."

The widowed little marquise de Sévigné seemed surprised. "Members of high society merely practice different arts. Some buy potions from a sorceress named La Voisin off the rue Beauregard outside Paris." Everyone stared at her. "Not me, of course. But I know courtiers who buy charms for health, wealth, beauty, and love."

"La Voisin is no mere sorceress," said François, duc de La Rochefoucauld, an old noble who had fought against my uncle in the Fronde. His presence made me even more nervous. "She's a witch in league with the devil, performing black masses sanctified with infant blood. Pay renegade priests to consecrate your charms instead. Everyone knows the miracle of the mass activates certain spells."

I could name a dozen such spells. Molière looked bored to tears. Benserade seemed to be sleeping.

Sablière tipped her head in thought. "From what I know of your Catholic faith, that is sacrilege, treason against God, a capital crime. Such priests could be put to death."

An old man named Charles de Saint-Évremond said, "Priests are consecrated to mediate between visible and invisible realms. But take heed. Merely inverting the technique turns curative spells into curses, turning superstition into dangerous magic." He had a bulbous protrusion of flesh between his eyes, but it didn't detract from the wisdom in his words.

Rambouillet turned her bright old eyes to me. "What say you, worthy Mancini? Is our destiny to be found in our hands?"

I fought the urge to squirm and tried to seem relaxed like them. "The ecclesiastical nature of my uncle's office prevents me from engaging in any such pagan practices." They stared blankly, still waiting. I cleared my throat. "But I agree in a sense. We *use* our hands to forge our own destiny."

The women broke into smiles, the men nodded their appreciation, and I felt a rush of relief. Antoine Baudeau de Somaize, fingers smeared with ink, glanced at Rambouillet from the table where he'd been recording our conversation. "It seems we have another cunning Italian blazing her way into French society."

Rambouillet is Italian? I stared at her in surprise. She winked and changed the subject.

An hour later, we made farewells at the front door, and even the unimpressed Molière dismissed himself politely. On the steps Rambouillet muttered to me, "You are surprised that I, too, was born in Rome."

"How did you rise to influence the French?"

"There is no end to what woman is capable of when she aspires."

I thought of those words all the way back to the Hôtel de Vendôme. *What might I be capable of?*

Conversation in the salons of Scudéry and Sévigné moved to safer subjects like Homer, Virgil, Plutarch, Philostratus, and Plato. For the first time in my life, I knew the simple joy of friendships and society. A month passed in a flurry of salon engagements, and Victoire finally insisted I spend an evening with her.

She propped herself on plump velvet bolsters for a game of chess while the governess, Madeleine, dame de Venelle, from an educated Provençal family, read aloud. Within an hour Victoire put me in checkmate, clever girl, and the next moment she fell back in a faint.

Venelle and I jumped up and threw back the chess table, and the duc de Mercœur ran to fetch physicians. I held my sister's hands and said a prayer to the Virgin Mother. Those foolish old physicians in their black robes came in, muttering incomprehensible jargon, peeling back her eyelids and prodding her belly.

She woke before they could make a pronouncement. "The baby is coming," she said. "And fast."

"Hortense and Marianne, go wait in your room. Moréna, find clean linens." I flew to the kitchen and ordered vats of hot water, snatched dried witch hazel and yarrow from the rafters, and bundled them into cheesecloth pouches. Papa had made similar pouches to stanch Mamma's bleeding after Marianne was born, but he'd assembled his under a full moon and cinched them closed with strands of Mamma's hair. I glanced to be sure no one was watching, put a hand over the pouches, and silently implored the Virgin Mother to make them potent. Surely there was no harm in such a prayer.

Venelle propped Victoire up, and Mercœur held her hands. My sister grimaced as she pushed, and the physicians leaned in so far their heads disappeared between her knees.

"Stay strong, Victoire!" cried her husband. But she looked so pale, so tired. Her chemise clung to the sweat on her chest. She grunted with pain, and we urged her to push. The maids prepared basins, the wet-nurse arrived, and I held the linens ready. At long last, the baby slipped out in a rush of bloody fluid. The physicians handed it to me and turned their attention to the cord. "A boy!" I cried.

But Victoire didn't look right. The left side of her mouth drooped. "I can't move my arm."

Mercœur took his newborn son from my arms, cooing, and I moved to Victoire's side.

"I'm so tired," she said.

"Lay her down," grumbled a physician. "Clean her up and let her rest, and soon she will mend."

I positioned her limbs, arranged her infant in the crook of her arm, and went to work cleaning blood and pulling soiled quilts from beneath her. So much blood, and when I pushed on her belly to help shrink her womb, more trickled out. I pressed the herb pouches on the tear between her legs.

In the morning we couldn't wake her.

Mercœur sat by her bed and bawled.

"Is it apoplexy?" one physician asked another, who replied, "We must cup her."

I interrupted. "She's lost enough blood—"

They glowered so fiercely I feared they'd send me away. "Set up the table."

I made Mercœur leave and used the chess table to set out their gruesome knives and glass bowls.

One used tongs to hold a bowl in the fireplace until it glowed red-hot. The other barked, "Hold her still." He rolled Victoire to her stomach, yanked the back of her chemise up, then sliced her lovely skin. Her lids flew open. She cried out in pain. Blood poured forth. The other physician put the hot bowl over the cut, and my sister screamed. The bowl filled with blood, a grotesque sight.

Victoire clung to me and wept. "Stop!"

One physician smiled. "She is alert. It worked."

Victoire stared, distant and helpless, and I knew it hadn't. I turned to Moréna. "Get Mercœur. Wake their sons and my sisters. Send messengers for Olympia, Philippe, and my Martinozzi cousin." I turned to Venelle. "Find the cardinal."

"Please don't let them cup her again," I begged the cardinal when he arrived. Our entire family gathered in shock.

The physician interjected, "Cupping saved her. She is in no danger."

The cardinal frowned at me. "Don't interfere with the physicians. We must all pray."

Olympia and I glanced at each other. I'd shown her the healing laceration between Victoire's legs. She'd felt the shrinking womb herself. She agreed Victoire's weakness was caused by a problem in the brain and cupping wouldn't help. Nevertheless, we fell to our knees with the rest of the family, and His Eminence made the sign of the cross.

They cupped her. She cried out. Victoire's sons wailed at the sight of their mother's bloody back. Marianne sat in the corner with her face in her hands, yelling, "Make the physicians stop!"

Finally, Mercœur put his ear beside his wife's lips as she whispered, and his face crumpled with grief. With her good hand, she gestured for her sons. The light around her seemed to fade, as if her life were draining. *She is dying.*

We positioned her with the baby cradled in her good arm. Philippe and each of my sisters knelt for a final kiss. I started to approach, but the cardinal ordered the last sacraments. A priest drew wine and lit incense while Mazarin spilled a litany of Latin. Victoire took a crumbled bit of communion wafer, but it fell from her lips. *Rumors be damned! Why hadn't I followed Papa's example and hung a protective amulet over her bed?*

I stepped in front of the cardinal and put my lips to Victoire's cheek.

Her eyes met mine. "Live well for my sake." Her next whisper came out in a rush. "Wherever it leads, your star is your own. Let no one conceal its brilliance." She didn't draw another breath.

Cardinal Mazarin shook her. She was limp. Olympia started wailing.

"She's gone?" asked Marianne between sobs.

Hortense clung to one of my hands, and I put my other in Olympia's. We stared in disbelief. The angelic one was gone. I felt an abyss of grief, yet it slowly filled with the command in her whisper. A Mancini whisper. Last words of the dying hold power, and she'd uttered hers for me. *It is time for me to live.*

The wet-nurse took the baby, Mercœur took his other sons into his arms, and servants covered Victoire. Olympia looked at me with tears streaming down her cheeks.

I whispered, "I have had enough of death."

Mazarin heard. "Get your sisters and brother," he muttered to me. "The Mancinis must come to Palais Mazarin."

We backed out of the room together, slipped out of the Hôtel de Vendôme, now a house of mourning, and piled into the cardinal's coach.

I was the first to speak. "Without Victoire, we Mancinis have no alliances. Olympia must wed."

Mazarin nodded. "Olympia will marry within a fortnight."

Olympia quieted at that, but Marianne and Hortense continued to cry softly. Philippe put his arms around them.

Mazarin studied me. "The king inquired after you. He thinks you should stay at court." He went on before I could question him. "I intended to send you away after the birth. But now . . . you will help Olympia prepare for her wedding. Give orders to the cooks, request my carriage if you have need, and for God's sake try to dress better."

King Louis spoke on my behalf! "No convent?"

The carriage halted, and he narrowed his eyes. "I'll hire dame de Venelle to help you return normalcy to Palais Mazarin. *Then* you'll go. Be on your best behavior. Be eyes. Be ears. Bring me something useful to solidify your place here."

It made my stomach turn. I thought of his finance papers. His accounts, his notes, the lists of people he took advantage of by gaining such useful information. "Anything to serve you." I couldn't believe how easily the lie leapt to my lips.

CHAPTER 7

A person often meets his destiny on the road he took to avoid it.

—JEAN DE LA FONTAINE, *Fables*

The morning after Victoire's funeral, the cardinal had his table placed in the middle of our shared chamber. "Dress!" he commanded. Hortense, Marianne, Olympia, and I hid behind screens to be washed by maids while he rifled through a pile of letters.

We'd barely slipped on chemises when Philippe marched in with more parchments for the cardinal to read. "You're like a bunch of soldiers waiting for battle armor," he teased.

Marianne stuck her tongue out at him. "Go find a razor and shave for once."

We Mazarinettes laughed at this, but the cardinal barked instructions. Philippe scampered from the chamber. He collided with a dozen seamstresses at the door. They streamed in around him carrying piles of fabric, baskets of lace, boxes of thread and pins and spangles and tassels and feathers of every shape and color. Seamstresses laid siege to each of us, wrapping us with silks and taffeta, piling on velvet trim or bright silk flowers, calling for the cardinal's attention. He glanced up. If he shook his head, the seamstresses stripped the pieces away and started over. If he nodded, an artist pulled out paper, sketching a bodice, an undress gown, a petticoat, an overskirt. A spectacled man scribbled notes about fabric, color, trim, and cost. They ran to the table with finished designs. The cardinal's signature, a commitment to pay, made them skip back to us with glee and begin again. We were stripped and redressed all day.

The next morning jewelers arrived with designs for headdresses, necklaces, earrings, and rings. With a "No" from the cardinal, a career was dashed, but "Yes" made a man's fortune. Some came to the cardinal on bended knee, kissing his ring, holding up caskets overflowing with precious stones in every color. The cardinal signed receipts. He buried his hands into a box of diamonds, pulling out fistfuls, letting them spill between his fingers, smiling euphorically. The next day, the jewelers returned with a bouquet of pearls for Olympia's hair, long silver diamond earrings, and diamond pendants stitched onto a stomacher so dense I couldn't see the fabric underneath. The necklace they presented held Mazarin's largest diamond, the Mirror of Portugal.

When a jeweler arrived with a casket of diamonds set in lace-patterned silver buttons, the cardinal gestured to a dressmaker. "Don't leave this room until these adorn Olympia's silver gown." The dressmaker trembled, either with fear or excitement. She sewed for the next twenty-four hours straight, even while we slept, until the gown was covered.

She whirled it over a dress form. The skirts fell in a silver bell-shaped cascade. It glittered with diamonds from neck to hem, the most spectacular dress I'd ever seen. Olympia threw herself on our uncle, hugging his neck until he actually smiled. Not only would Paris be unable to doubt the cardinal's wealth, Paris would be dumbfounded by it.

"How much do you suppose that gown is worth?" asked Marianne.

"A palais at least," said Hortense.

The cardinal would never let her keep it.

On the morning of February nineteenth the Mancinis rose to be curled, powdered, and bejeweled. Moréna studied my new rose watered-silk gown and cross-shaped ruby necklace. For once she gave me an approving smile. She knew my sister's wedding also served as my first real appearance at court. "Make the most of it," she whispered.

We rode in a procession of gilded carriages to the Louvre. Courtiers stopped to watch us alight. The cardinal led Olympia in her silver diamond gown and stunning diamond necklace straight into the king's apartments.

I followed with my sisters close behind and caught snatches of courtiers' comments as we passed . . .

"The cardinal's nieces could feed the army with those jewels."

"I'd rather feed the cardinal himself to the army."

I tried to stay focused. For the sake of my sisters, I had to learn to maneuver at court.

Inside, soaring, gilded walls met muraled ceilings, making me feel small. Then the king appeared. I hadn't seen him since the day of Mamma's funeral. His eyes found mine, and *he smiled.* At me! My heart fluttered wildly. Olympia noticed our exchange, but she had no time to intervene. Eugène-Maurice of Savoy, newly made comte de Soissons, entered. He glanced at Olympia, then took quill in hand and signed the marriage agreement.

The king's brother, styled by the simple honorific Monsieur, poked his elbow in my ribs. We hadn't spoken since I left for the convent two years earlier. "What have you done to your skin? It's more radiant than that gown."

I grinned, catching a whiff of his expensive perfume. "That is the flush of excitement, Monsieur."

"Bottle it for me." He arched one perfectly plucked, clove-darkened brow. Monsieur wore feminine beauty elements better than most females. It made him unusual, and made some uncomfortable, but I was unusual, too. "Better yet, how about letting me borrow the gown?"

I whipped open my fan, painted side out, as the salon ladies always did. "Only if you promise to come to my fête at Palais Mazarin."

"Can I bring my friends?"

"All the better."

The cardinal poured hot red wax on the marriage agreement and stamped it with his seal. He led the wedding party the long route through lofty chambers to the queen mother's chapel. Everyone at court, Mazarin's enemies and heads of noble factions, was forced to bow until we'd passed.

In the queen mother's chambers, attendants greeted us with silver goblets of wine. I spotted Somaize, my ink-fingered friend from the salons, and kissed his cheeks.

"This wine is delicious," I said.

"It's from Burgundy," Somaize said. "The king's favorite."

"You simply must bring some to Palais Mazarin for a fête next week. Monsieur will be there, you know." His eyes widened. "Bring some friends."

The queen mother appeared and we bowed low. She took the cardinal's arm and led us into her private chapel. Olympia spoke her vows with surprising solemnity. A show. I wondered what the king thought of it and glanced at him. He winked at me. I had to press my lips together to keep from giggling like some maiden in a fairy story.

From there we proceeded to the cardinal's apartments. Crystal chandeliers hung above a long table where gold cloth set off the gleam of gold plates. Footmen in the cardinal's green livery stood behind our seats. Holly boughs and evergreen sprigs were tucked among the candelabra topping the table, but their fresh scent was replaced by that of onion soup. Six servants rushed in carrying roasted peacocks on giant silver platters, their feathers splayed out fancifully over the succulent meat. A collective *ahh* went up when they brought in dishes of créme brûlée and towers of marzipan fruits.

King Louis held up his golden goblet. "For the newlyweds, a gift of music."

Giovanni Battista Lulli, an Italian who'd changed his name to Jean-Baptiste Lully to adapt in France, entered playing his violin. His best players followed, pulling a lively tune with their bows. Olympia held her goblet toward the king in thanks.

When we'd eaten our fill, and perhaps drunk too much, the violinists followed us to the bedchambers. Mamma's old rooms. The queen mother blocked the men. "Back, beastly men," she said with a laugh. "The bride's sisters will prepare her."

Moréna slipped out as we walked in. *What's she doing here?* There was no time to ask. Hortense and Marianne helped me cut the stitching around Olympia's diamond stomacher. She slipped off the bodice and stepped out of her skirts. I wrapped the precious gown in linen, placed it in a chest with the mesmerizing Mirror of Portugal, and locked it with a key my uncle had given me.

Olympia hiked her lacy chemise up around her waist, then lay upon the bed. "Marie, reach behind that cabinet."

Confused, I did as she asked. I felt around until my hand touched a cold glass jar. I pulled it out, took one look, and threw it on the bed. "What is that disgusting thing?"

"*That* is my salvation."

"A chicken's bladder filled with blood, by the looks of it," said Hortense with fascination.

"What are you going to do with it?" asked Marianne.

She bedded the king! "You don't want to know," I replied angrily.

Olympia bent her knees and spread her legs, a sight I could have done without. "Put it in," she said to me.

Hortense gasped, then bent down to whisper in Marianne's ear. Poor Marianne went pale.

I crossed my arms. "I will not."

"I must give my husband proof of virginity."

"That isn't proof, it's fraud. If Soissons discovers it, he'll be furious."

She grabbed my wrist. "Then help me get it in deep."

I opened the jar and held it out to her. "Shove it in yourself."

She did it, and I thought Hortense and Marianne would throw up right there. Olympia held out her bloody fingers, but I couldn't find a cloth to wipe them. I had to rip my inner silk petticoat and use spit to clean blood-stains from her inner thighs and fingers. I packed the cloth into the jar.

"Get rid of that," said Olympia. "And you two," she hissed at Hortense and Marianne, "keep your mouths shut about this." She straightened her chemise and pulled the silk sheets up to her neck.

I dropped the filthy jar into my hanging pocket so it was good and hidden beneath my beautiful gown. "God protect us all if you get caught." I threw open the doors. "The bride is prepared."

The cardinal shot me a look as if to ask, *What took so long?* The men had stripped the comte to his long linen shirt, and they escorted him to the bed in his bare feet. The cardinal blessed the union and made the sign of the cross. We pulled the bed curtains closed on their anxious faces and slipped out.

"It is over," said the cardinal. He turned to go, snapping his fingers. "Come, girls!" Our signal to follow him like little ducks.

"We'll be celebrating your wedding next," King Louis said as I passed.

"Not likely," I said, irritated at the tender feelings I'd been having for him. *Why does he bother winking and smiling at me when he has Olympia?* "You've had my book more than a week, Majesty."

He actually blushed. "I haven't quite finished reading it. Next week."

* * *

At Palais Mazarin I marched into the servants' quarters and dragged Moréna from her bed. "You assembled the chicken bladder for Olympia."

"In my homeland a bride would be returned to her family if she didn't bleed on her wedding night. Besides, Olympia paid."

"It will cost infinitely if you are caught. If that thing stays inside her too long, she'll get sick. From now on, you work only for me."

"I *was* working for you." She wrenched her arm free. "The fates say your star won't rise until Olympia's sets. How will you shine if she is your eclipse?"

"If you mean Olympia is to be harmed I will—"

She held out her hand as if she feared a beating. "I mean you will distinguish yourself. As the eldest sister in residence *you* are the lady of Palais Mazarin."

I paused. "That is true." It would be luxurious. While it lasted.

She lowered her hand slowly. "Consider what you might make of it. Especially now that you've caught the king's eye."

I frowned. "That part isn't true." And I left before she could sense my sadness.

Early the next morning we returned to the Louvre, where we gathered with the royals, the Martinozzis, and the Soissons family outside the marriage bed. I did my best to ignore the king. The queen mother parted the bed curtains. Soissons was still asleep. Olympia whipped back the coverlet and pointed to the bloodstained sheet. A murmur of approval went up. I gave Olympia a questioning look, and she eyed the nearby closestool. She'd hidden the nasty thing in the night soil. I sighed with relief.

My sisters and I dressed Olympia, then stood behind her like ladies in waiting behind a queen while she and Soissons received visits. Courtiers lined up to congratulate them, not for their own sakes but to please the cardinal. They bore gifts—a jeweled brooch, goblets cut from alabaster, a looking-glass, a purse of silver, and even a great green parrot.

In the afternoon, Notre Dame Cathedral gave a special mass. My younger sisters and I rode through Paris with our uncle in a long procession of carriages. Hortense and Marianne watched a boy carrying a sheep slung across his shoulders as he led a mule harnessed to a wagon full of pigs. From an upper window, a woman dumped piss from a chamber pot, splashing the mule. Startled, the mule slipped in a pile of steaming horse dung in the street, jerking the wagon and setting the pigs to squealing and oinking. A passing gang of Gypsies whooped with laughter.

"Your Eminence," I said, taking my opportunity with measured confidence, "I've planned a small fête at Palais Mazarin."

"You are the temporary lady of the house." He hardly looked at me. "But if one distasteful rumor is uttered, you will be gone before the gossips draw their next breath."

I nodded, suppressing my smile.

He turned his attention to homes along the quay. Even the most stately had mud and garbage littering their doorsteps. "Look how the bourgeoisie merchants climb into their fine carriages wearing gold cloth when they know only nobility are permitted to wear it." He made a *harrumph* sound. "Looks like they can afford new taxes."

We turned onto the wide Pont Neuf toward the oldest part of Paris, the Île de la Cité. The great cacophony of Parisian life on the Pont Neuf, as much an open street theater as a bridge, echoed around us. Vendors called out such goods as oysters, wooden legs, cakes, or glass eyes. Charlatans yelled louder, selling phoenix fat, dirt from the Holy Land, and water guaranteed to extend your life by one hundred years. A singer dressed in an exotic costume from the East belted out a song about a murder that had taken place on Pont Neuf a week earlier. Beggars and rowdy drunks clustered under the statue of Henry the Fourth to watch a burly man yank a tooth out of an older man's mouth. Pickpockets darted among the crowd while prostitutes scanned it for randy customers. While I watched this in wonder, a thud sounded against the carriage wall. Mud spattered on the cardinal's scarlet robes. I sat up in time to see a man in a butcher's apron hurl another great handful of mud at us. "Death to the Italian!" he screamed over the racket. A cheer went up on the bridge and along the quay.

Our driver whipped the horses, and we coursed across the rest of the bridge. I fell back. Mazarin wiped the mud off with a handkerchief as if it were nothing.

They hate him. The poorest peasants, the middling bourgeoisie, merchants great and small, minor nobles, and the elite closest to the crown—they all harbored the same hate for Cardinal Mazarin. They screamed it on street corners, printed it in pamphlets, and probably begged it in their prayers: Death to the cardinal who wallows in their money and seems to control the king by magic.

We arrived at Notre Dame Cathedral, where bells pealed and birds scattered as we halted before the Gothic doors.

Marianne pointed to the fanciful gargoyles overhead. "Aren't they adorable?"

"They're supposed to be frightening," I said as we entered. "To ward away evil."

"They don't work because Olympia can get in. And look—" She stuck out her tongue and crooked her fingers atop her head to mimic the devil's horns. "So can I!"

I shushed her, but she'd been heard. Someone behind me said, "Those pagan Mancinis!" My cheeks burned. I wanted to turn around to see who it was, but something stopped me. This was the way of courtiers. *I don't have enough standing to condemn their spite.* So I kept walking.

By the time we returned to the Louvre I was sick of uppish courtiers and tedious ceremony, sick of wondering if the king would try to talk to me again, and sick of worrying how I'd respond. When the best carriage arrived to escort Olympia to the Hôtel de Soissons, I was overjoyed.

"Can we go home now?" begged Marianne.

I scooped her up and took Hortense by the hand. "Home, where a new life awaits."

CHAPTER 8

God must needs have given free will to man. God's foreknowledge is not opposed to our free choice.

—SAINT AUGUSTINE

Weeks later I stood at the top of the stairs of Palais Mazarin to welcome my guests while one hundred blazing torches lit the courtyard. My friends from the salons alighted from carriages. Molière kissed my cheeks, and Lully brought his violin. My brother Philippe, who had finally had the decency to shave, showed them inside.

Then Monsieur finally appeared, the prettiest of all with extra pink ribbons on his doublet and matching pink hose. "Cousin," he said to me with a kiss. He and the king had always affectionately called the Mazarinettes cousins, and we'd thought nothing of it. I remembered the love letters I'd found in Mazarin's casket. Did Monsieur and the king realize the cardinal was their father, that we were *truly* related?

I stuffed down the thought. "Welcome."

Monsieur gestured to his carriage. "I brought my other cousins."

Out stepped the exiled King Charles of England wearing a broad grin. "Hope you don't mind."

His brother James, Duke of York, a copy of Charles with lighter skin and hair, and their youngest brother, the Duke of Gloucester, alighted next.

I could hardly believe it. I curtsied. They bowed in return. *Royalty at my fête!* "Gentlemen, don't think I'm dazzled."

"Our titles aren't illustrious enough for you?" Monsieur offered his arm.

I crooked my arm into his. "Each of you is merely another dance partner."

King Charles took my other arm. "Well, it's a good thing we wore our dancing shoes tonight, eh, brothers?"

The five of us entered the palais together. Footmen threw open every set of doors on our way to the dining hall. Eyes widened at the sight of my escorts, and servants scrambled to ready additional seating. Violinists serenaded us through dinner while the Stuart brothers and Monsieur compared the English Civil War with the French Fronde.

"Is there hope of regaining your kingdom?" I asked King Charles at a moment when everyone else was engaged.

He grinned. There was something handsome in the ease of his smile. "Every fresh hope has led to renewed disappointment. Your uncle isn't making it easier."

"You mean the cardinal makes life difficult for those other than myself?"

He shrugged. "He's forming an alliance with Oliver Cromwell, the man who executed my father, led his army against me, and rules England in my place."

"Blame the Prince de Condé, my uncle's greatest rival during the Fronde. When Condé lost, he sided with Spain in the endless war for territory. It is bad enough that France is at war with Spain. Condé was starting to gain support in London. Mazarin couldn't allow that."

"Mazarin has a chance of finishing the Franco-Spanish wars for good with Cromwell's troops on his side. It will force me to leave France."

"If only you could raise your own army for my uncle."

He glanced around. "This new alliance makes the King of Spain nervous. He may give my brothers and me our own regiments."

I gasped. "You would side against your own cousin King Louis?"

"Against your *uncle*." He spoke softly. "Louis may be king, but he will never rule France until he is free of Mazarin."

So it was obvious to all of Europe, too. Poor King Louis.

Our party moved to the great hall, wineglasses in hand, where King Charles quietly studied works of art by the old masters. I realized with a pang of guilt they were part of his slain father's collection, which Mazarin had purchased from Cromwell. Clarinet players joined the violinists by the virginal and struck up chords for the opening branle. King Charles whispered to me, "Some have said Louis will never cast Mazarin off because he is his real father. Do they call you cousin as an endearment, or are you cousins by blood?"

I turned to him. This king without a throne, so affable I'd made no pretenses, was too sly. He wouldn't get secrets that would damage King Louis from *me*. "I may not love my uncle, but I will be sorry to see you take arms against him." I smiled sweetly. "My uncle *will* learn of it eventually. Now. Let me see your palm, and I shall tell you whether you'll rule England again."

He laughed, opening his hand to me.

I glanced at it quickly, before anyone could accuse me of witchery. Fractured at the beginning, his solar line deepened, then ran long. "Stay your course, sly king. You will soon be restored." I took a sip of wine.

He grinned. "Keep my alliance with Spain a secret?"

Agreeing would be siding against my uncle. I couldn't help it. I nodded. "You should give the cardinal your word that you will ally with France if you regain England."

King Charles nodded his agreement. He lifted his glass, and I clinked mine against it. "Clever girl. I don't see why King Louis spends so much time with Olympia."

What could I say? *Olympia uses love potions to keep the king entranced.* "People call her the charming one."

He turned to watch Hortense spin gracefully on the dancing floor. His admiration was plain. "And is Hortense clever and charming like her sisters?"

"She is both." I had to smile at his obvious fascination. An idea struck me. One that might get Hortense a crown. "And she will be of marriageable age in little more than a year."

He nodded appreciatively. "Is it true Cardinal Mazarin intends to make her his heir?"

Is that what people are saying? "She is his favorite. To marry her would secure an alliance with France."

Just then I spotted my uncle, watching us from the corner of the chamber. He curled one edge of his mustache and moved toward us. Women stopped dancing to curtsy as he passed.

"Your Eminence," I said.

King Charles bowed to him, a mere courtesy since he wasn't Catholic. "The Eminent Mazarin. Might we have a private word?"

My uncle gestured toward the farthest door, toward his library and private study. "Just what I was hoping for."

I watched them leave. *God, don't let Charles betray me.*

Monsieur muttered at my ear, "What have you done, cousin?"

I'd proven myself either a liability or an asset, all depending on what Charles told my uncle.

We drank wine and played basset long into the night. Venelle insisted on putting Hortense and Marianne to bed early. It was after midnight when I escorted the last of my guests to their carriages. The servants doused the courtyard torches, and I turned to find my uncle waiting on the front steps.

"You made an impression on King Charles of England."

"So did the lovely Hortense." I held my breath.

"But what did he tell you of his plans?"

Had King Charles told him? Was this a test? *My future could depend on my answer.* "Political shifts may force him to fight for Spain, but he will remember your generosity when he regains England's throne."

He nodded. "That is what my spies suspected."

I held my breath. "Did he mention Hortense?"

"I couldn't marry Hortense to anyone who'd side with Condé against France."

I felt sick. I might have passed my test, but I'd betrayed a king *and* spoiled my sister's chance at a crown.

"Carnival season is almost over. When Lent begins, people will take to salons instead of balls and fêtes. They will blabber until the summer war campaigns begin. They may discuss things I need to know." He walked up the steps. "You can expect invitations."

"And . . . the convent?"

He didn't turn back. "Not until the summer war campaigns begin."

CHAPTER 9

I took the cardinal's best carriage to the best quarters in Paris in the next months. At Scudéry's, women of rank mingled with the wives of playwrights. They kissed my cheeks, studied me up and down, and I pretended I didn't hear them whisper about me behind their fans. At Rochefoucauld's house, he tried to get us to exchange witty maxims. But the gossip on everyone's lips was the cardinal's alliance with Cromwell.

"King Charles left France."

"Not without asking to marry one of the Mancini girls so he wouldn't have to go. Is it true, Marie?"

It was. "Every man adores Hortense."

The women were all atwitter.

"Well, I heard the cardinal let King Charles down easy, saying it would do the Mazarins *too great an honor.* Can you believe it?"

Everyone laughed, but it was exactly what my uncle had told Hortense.

The next gathering at Sévigné's was no better. She brought out her astrolabe and insisted we discuss astrology. Instead, everyone turned to me and asked about Olympia. "What is the secret to her hold on King Louis?"

Before I could think of a clever response someone said, "He visits the Hôtel de Soissons nightly."

Another woman threw her hands in the air. "They spend hours together in her room *alone.*"

"Her new husband will get angry," someone insisted.

"And risk losing royal favor? Never!" insisted someone else.

My friend Somaize finally spoke up, "It's not *royal* favor her husband has to worry about, it's the *cardinal's*." Everyone turned spiteful eyes to me.

I shrugged. "Don't we all?"

They laughed, and I felt myself relax. *If my uncle thinks I'll glean secrets from these gossips, he is mistaken.*

Weeks later the gossip was entirely different. An excitable young woman fluttered her fan so hard I thought her wig would blow off. "King Louis only goes to the Hôtel de Soissons out of courtesy now. Last night he invited Anne-Lucie de La Motte d'Argencourt to dine with him, and they played cards for money late into the night."

Another lady rolled her eyes to the heavens. "You call that juicy *on-dit*?"

The young woman put down her fan. "When she ran out of money, Mademoiselle d'Argencourt bet her partlet and *lost* it." A collective gasp went up around the salon.

Mine may have been the loudest. Modest ladies and old-fashioned women wore such collars from neck to décolletage. "Did King Louis actually *take* it?"

The woman shrugged. The ladies placed wagers of their own. Most bet d'Argencourt would be in the king's bed before Lent was over.

Later that night, I crept into the cardinal's study. "We have a problem named d'Argencourt."

He rifled through a casket of papers and waved me away without a word.

But the next week, when I returned to Palais Mazarin from a salon one evening, the cardinal met me in my antechamber. He handed me a tiny pearl ring. "Take this to Olympia with my compliments. Tell her I said to make the king forget d'Argencourt."

"I tried to warn you."

He frowned. "D'Argencourt's mother made it clear she would allow the girl to become the king's *maîtresse-en-titre*. In exchange for a fortune."

I cringed. "How far has it gone?"

"That's what you're going to determine."

Moréna peeped out from the front door, and I signaled her to join me. In the carriage she freshened my rouge and dotted perfume to my wrists and neck. At the Hôtel de Soissons, Olympia had spared no expense on entertaining the king. A great bonfire burned in the middle of the courtyard, and liveried footmen lined the stairs to the front entrance. The cardinal's page announced me to the musketeers guarding the front hall, and they broke rank for me to pass.

Olympia sat in a chair by the fireplace in her state bedchamber, arms crossed. King Louis had his elbow propped on the mantel above her. Soissons stood nearby wearing a purposefully indifferent expression.

King Louis looked thoroughly bored, but smiled when I curtsied. "Have you come to demand *Jerusalem Delivered*? I confess I haven't finished reading it."

"Next week," I said with a wink, and he laughed. I presented the ring to Olympia. "A gift from the cardinal."

She frowned at it, then caught my eye. She knew she was in trouble. "What news? Is the old cardinal's gout worse? Or did my spell to make it worse fail?"

"Olympia!" I glanced at King Louis. "You don't know spells." I couldn't believe she would say such a thing in front of him.

"Oh, I was jesting." She tossed the ring aside. "Give him my thanks and my love and whatever else you think he wants."

King Louis cleared his throat. "I will allow the two of you time."

"You just got here." Olympia sounded angry.

Soissons backed from the chamber. I felt sympathy for Olympia's cuckolded husband.

The king looked torn. "There's gambling at the Louvre."

"What are you going to do? Try to get that d'Argencourt girl to wager her skirts this time? She's not so stupid that she'll drop them for less than half your kingdom."

I wanted to clap a hand over Olympia's mouth.

"If you degrade her, I will leave."

Olympia turned away. "Go, then. You'll be begging to get up my own skirts again soon enough."

He rolled his eyes to the heavens, then bowed to me, an honor he wasn't required to bestow. "Next week," he said, and slipped from the chamber.

Olympia frowned. "What is this *next week* nonsense?"

"He's been returning my book *next week* for several months now." I paused. "His Eminence will be angry."

"I should be angry. That paltry ring was meant as a reflection of the job I'm doing."

"What is wrong with you today?"

She rushed to a potted orange tree and vomited in the soil. Her voice softened. "Tell our uncle I'm sorry. I will of course be more attentive to the king when I'm feeling better."

"Olympia—"

"Tell my maids I need them on your way out."

In the carriage, Moréna grinned. "What ails your sister?"

"Stomach gripe. I'm worried."

She shook her head. "Olympia stopped bleeding."

My breath caught. *With child!* Was it Soissons's or the king's? "Say nothing. His Eminence mustn't find out yet."

"He needs to know *now*. To replace her."

"With some slut we don't know?" The idea made me cringe. If I had to see my king with anyone, I preferred him to be with my sister. "At least with Olympia I can intervene if she mistreats the king. Give her a chance to recover."

Moréna looked smug. I didn't want to know what she was thinking.

CHAPTER 10

Marie Mancini is ignorant of nothing, has read all the good books, writes with an ease that cannot be imagined.

—ANTOINE BAUDEAU DE SOMAIZE, *Dictionnaire des Précieuses*

L ater that week, for the first time since my return to Paris, I received a summons to attend the queen mother at her morning toilette. The guards at her Louvre apartments admitted me, and I crept through the cavernous marble rooms. In the state bedchamber, high-ranking princesses of the blood stood closest to the queen, handling her clothes, shoes, pins, ribbons, a handkerchief. Duchesses and countesses stood behind them, passing clean clothes to the princesses or waiting to discard a dirty gown. My cousin Martinozzi, a princess of the blood by marriage, stood near the queen. I stood in the *very* back. Which suited me fine, since that's where wisps of gossip flew freely . . .

"King Charles is in Madrid, that traitor."

"I was sorry to see King Charles go. He was *so* good in bed."

"Oh, kings make terrible lovers."

One of the gossips poked me. "Now that our own king has cut his teeth on your sister, he's taking a bite of Mademoiselle d'Argencourt. You Mancinis will fall from favor yet."

I did not respond. The princesses of the blood had parted, and the queen mother stood listening. I glanced at her. The gossips turned around. They realized their scathing words had been overheard. They curtsied.

The queen mother ignored them. "Marie. Walk beside me to mass."

I knew this mark of favor would infuriate the gossips. *Good.*

She cut a path through them, took my arm, and we fell into step together on the way to her private chapel. The princesses kept a respectful distance, and the queen talked softly. "I didn't want to believe any of it. But they are quite right, I'm afraid. My son, the king, has dined only with d'Argencourt this entire week. Your uncle and I are beside ourselves."

"How is this any different than the way he behaved with my sister?"

"D'Argencourt puts on airs when she comes to my chambers. Making shallow curtsies, wearing a superior expression, laughing with haughtiness. I cannot allow her to gain influence over my son."

"The king respects you and follows my uncle's advice in everything." We reached the queen's chapel and stepped inside. Hundreds of candles glittered against motifs of gilded *fleur-de-lis*. Cherubim and seraphim frolicked amid clouds in murals overhead.

The queen went on. "D'Argencourt is the pretty face before a grasping, greedy family. She is filling his head with spiteful rumors. They use her to seek power and position that your uncle and I are not willing to concede."

Yet they used Olympia in the same manner. "Surely your son rules his own mind."

She glanced sidelong at me. "I hope not."

That made me uneasy. *They treat the king like a child!*

At her pew she waved other ladies away. "Olympia is with child. She is ill and is clearly losing her grasp over the king. It alarms me. I am sending him away. I shall speak with your uncle about what should be done with you upon the king's return."

They must have spies everywhere! "Me?"

"If your sister has been thrown from the saddle, perhaps you can take the reins."

The liturgy began. It kept me from snapping back that I would *never* serve as her spurs.

Later that night, Moréna made me rinse my mouth with rosemary and myrrh water, brushed southernwood oil into my hair, and was about to apply a mask of egg whites and almonds to wear on my face overnight, when Jean-Baptiste Colbert entered my bedchamber unannounced. "You're summoned to the queen's."

Moréna cursed him for scaring us, then hurriedly dressed me in a simple bodice and gown. Colbert's carriage driver made haste. When I reached the queen mother's doors, they burst open.

The king started to walk out but stopped when he saw me. He pointed at me and turned back. "And another thing," he said, his voice tense. "I have had Marie's book for months. Months! Yet my readers, whom you appointed, will not read it to me because *you* don't allow it."

My uncle, standing beside the queen in her bed, put his hands out. "We choose readings that are edifying to Your Majesty."

"I will give up the lover that you so vehemently disapprove of, but you will appoint a reader of my choice."

My uncle nodded. "Your Majesty is wise in avoiding the d'Argencourt family."

King Louis frowned. "I'm leaving for the Château de Vincennes in the morning for a week of hunting." The queen mother started to speak. "Don't follow me. I want only a small retinue and musketeers."

I grinned, not moving out of his way, and whispered, "There is nothing like a little reading after a long day of hunting."

He actually laughed. Cardinal Mazarin and the queen mother leaned toward us.

I kept my voice low. "Forget the readers. Make use of those royal eyes and read the book *yourself.*"

He nodded deeply to me and said, "Very well, Marie. Next week." He marched out. I fought the urge to follow him.

"Marie," called my uncle, "close the doors."

I walked in slowly, pulling the doors closed behind me. They glanced at each other.

"Why did he laugh?" asked the queen mother.

I shrugged. I certainly wouldn't tell.

The queen mother shook her head. "What do we do?"

"Don't fear, my love." The cardinal stepped to me. "A week at Vincennes will do him good. When he returns . . ." He stroked a long, shining curl resting on my shoulder. "This niece has developed into a promising candidate."

"Marie and Hortense are the *only* candidates now."

I stifled a gasp.

"Can you trust Marie?" she asked.

The cardinal gave me a pointed look. "Can I?"

They couldn't use little Hortense! "Have I ever been dishonest?"

My uncle crossed his arms, hands disappearing in the folds of his long sleeves. "Do you understand what we want?"

"You want the king to attach himself to me."

The queen mother smoothed her coverlet. "We shall host a ball. She must prepare."

My uncle turned to the queen. "She shall have new gowns, new jewels, and I will grant her apartments at the Louvre, close to the king."

"She will attend my toilette, showing herself at court every day." The queen counted each item off on her fingers. "She must have a fine carriage, invitations to banquets, her own servants. Come summer, she must follow the court to Fontainebleau." She paused. "Will he like her?"

My uncle's smile mirrored his upturned mustache. "He already does."

My breath caught. All this time I hadn't allowed myself to hope. If anyone knew the king's secrets, it was Mazarin. *The king does like me.* I curtsied, took three reverent backward steps, then left. I took Colbert's coach home in a haze of joy. I forgot Olympia. I didn't give much thought to what they were *really* asking me to do. *The king likes me!*

CHAPTER 11

Palais de Louvre

Spring 1657

Moréna built huge fires in my hearth and made me soak in milk baths in a great copper basin each day. Gradually my skin grew soft and luminous and pale. She delighted in making me eat creams and pastries, cakes and confections.

"I cannot eat all of this," I grumbled.

She grabbed my breasts. "You must fatten up!"

She sat before me with pincers and plucked a hair from my eyebrow.

"Ouch! No more."

"Sit still," she said. "If you want the king to see the beauty of those black eyes, let me frame them with pretty arches."

So I endured it, pluck by pluck.

Yellow narcissuses and buttercups burst from the earth, and I itched to plant a pottage of healing herbs and sprinkle it with holy water on the spring equinox. But the king would soon return, and I *did* want him to see me at my best. So I spent my days with the cardinal's dressmakers. They created splendors of gold and silver gowns for suppers at the Louvre, purple and red silk ensembles for balls, rose and blue satin day dresses, a red coat cut like a *justaucorps à brevet,* and riding costumes. I had a dozen new pairs of gloves, from long satin creations that covered my forearms to the softest kid leather for riding to the toughest leather gauntlets for hawking. They delivered so many new *pantoufles* and boots and high-heeled mules in every color and fabric, I might never wear the same shoe twice in a season.

At the end of the week the cardinal came to my chamber with Colbert, who was carrying a velvet tray. He threw back the cover to reveal a *parure* of diamonds. The set included earrings, bracelets, rings, a great necklace, hair combs, and hair pins. Some were so large they had to be from Olympia's wedding gown. *She will be outraged.*

"Thank you, Your Eminence."

Cardinal Mazarin took my arm and began walking me downstairs. "Do you know why I worked so hard to secure a marriage between my sister and your father?"

"Because he was a nobleman," I said, repeating what Mamma had explained.

Mazarin spoke softly of something our family rarely discussed. "My father was a pauper from Sicily, elevated by the position he won as steward to the powerful Colonna family in Rome. The Colonnas did much for us, but we grew up merely one step ahead of poverty. The responsibility of improving our station fell on me. I've spent a lifetime promoting my family, striking business deals, bargaining for offices, arranging marriages. Do you have what it takes to help me maintain the prominence we've achieved?"

I am nothing like you. We reached the courtyard. There, led by six white horses wearing fluffy white plumes, stood a whitewashed carriage gleaming in the spring sunshine. Silver curtains hung in the windows. The driver and postilions bowed to me. A white-liveried footman opened the door, and I touched the white velvet benches. "Generous, most eminent Uncle, there is one thing I've been meaning to ask for."

He waited.

"I can't curl my hair properly without the slave girl Moréna, and I've grown quite dependent on her. Might you grant her ownership to me?"

"Moréna belongs to me and to Palais Mazarin. But as long as you are in my service, she may serve you."

Not the answer I'd hoped for. Just then an equerry rode a huge white stallion into the courtyard. Silver ribbons were braided into the horse's thick mane and tail. Pearls encrusted the pommel on the gray leather saddle. Muscled and elegant, the animal pranced and bowed at the equerry's command, hoofs clopping and bridle clanking. I couldn't resist stroking the animal's neck. I kissed his soft muzzle, and he nudged my shoulder.

"Andalusians are hard to find," said my uncle. "Strong and fast enough to keep up with the king's best war horses."

In other words, don't fall behind. "I cannot thank you enough."

"King Louis mustn't give another thought to d'Argencourt."

Deep within, the thought of helping my greedy uncle turned my stomach. But if I didn't perform, he might make sweet Hortense his marionette. Could I find a way to shield the king from Mazarin's fierce control?

My uncle said over his shoulder as he went back inside, "You are mine. By making the king yours, *he* will be mine, too."

The equerry tossed me an oat cake. "Can you handle so powerful a creature?"

It took me a moment to realize he meant the horse. "My father taught me to handle the most spirited horses." The horse ate the oats from my hand. "What is his name?"

"Trojan."

I laughed. "Does my uncle know that?"

The equerry shrugged.

So my uncle had gifted me a Trojan horse. Well, I would certainly be on guard.

I ordered all six horses to be harnessed for the brief journey from Palais Mazarin to the Louvre on the night of the king's return. More than required, and just enough to make a statement. Moréna and Philippe rode with me. Candlelight from the crystal sconce flickered over her new white turban and dress. She pulled a vial from her hanging pocket and extended it to me.

My brother pushed it away. "No love potions."

She pulled out the cork and put it under my nose. "It's just a tincture to give her strength."

I took the vial. "No magic?"

"You stopped believing in magic the night you burned—"

I shot her a warning look. The tincture smelled of cinnamon, and I downed it in one gulp.

We rolled into the eastern corner of the Cour Carrée, passing crumbling towers from the Middle Ages on our left. Construction on the Italian-style wings to our right had begun during the last king's reign but stood unfinished. The Louvre remained an incomplete mix of styles because my uncle focused funds elsewhere. No carriage in the court compared to mine, and the others made way. Philippe peeped around my silver curtains and pointed. I saw d'Argencourt standing with her father between carriages.

She seemed angry, and her voice carried. "All the king told me is that Mazarin hopes to ally with Oliver Cromwell."

Her father frowned. "To use his supply of soldiers?"

"I won't have a chance to find out because I'm not doing this anymore." She turned from him.

He grabbed her arm. "You must to secure your family's position. Tonight may be your last chance."

Philippe and I exchanged a knowing look. My footman opened the door at that moment, and d'Argencourt and her father hastened inside the Louvre. I stared at the creamy limestone of the Lescot Wing. How many times had I entered without seeing the white stone oculi, the oval marble plaques, cartouches, and lintels? I had always rushed past, in the anxiety of moving to a new country, the grief of my mother's illness, or the flurry of Olympia's wedding. The Mazarin apartments were here, most rooms now appointed to me. I could now come and go as I pleased. I balled my hands into fists and then loosened them. Tonight I entered for *myself.*

Moréna stepped from the carriage behind us, carrying my train as I entered the Salle des Caryatides. She slipped away at the door, not to be seen again until needed.

A footman announced us. "Monsieur Philippe and Mademoiselle de Mancini!" My name echoed in the marble and stone great hall where courtiers danced to Lully's violins. No one took note. At least, they pretended not to.

Philippe gave me a worried look. Our uncle had instructed him to stay out of my way. "Good luck, sister." He slipped into the crowd.

To the south, the raised Tribunal sat empty. Neither the king nor queen mother had arrived. I snapped open my fan and walked to the north end, sidestepping clutches of courtiers. They glanced, promptly turning back to their groups. I told myself they envied my diamonds, my silver gown, the elaborate painting of Diana on my fan. I passed the d'Argencourt family unseen. I stopped behind the row of carved armless caryatids supporting the musician's gallery. A herald ran down the stairs calling, "Their Majesties King Louis and his mother Queen Anne!"

The music stopped. The dancers cleared the floor, and the entire assembly bowed and curtsied. Colorful Swiss Guards marched down in two rows, staggering themselves along each side of the staircase. I hid behind my marble caryatid and watched the royals descend. The cardinal followed them. The musicians resumed, and courtiers rose, watching the king open the dance with his mother. She didn't move gracefully, and the ceremonial opening was brief. The royals moved to the Tribunal, where the king struck up conversation with Colbert.

From my place behind the caryatids, I saw d'Argencourt's father nudge her. She frowned. He gave her a scathing look.

D'Argencourt heaved a sigh. She took a step, threw back her shoulders, then walked right through the empty dancing area. I left my post and slowly circled the hall, keeping behind nobles and courtiers, listening to the flurry of whispers that rose in her wake . . .

"She'll either make her family's fortune or ruin herself."

"I bet ten francs the king refuses her outright."

D'Argencourt reached the king and curtsied low. He hesitated. To my dismay, he led her to the floor to dance a sarabande. I continued toward the Tribunal, listening to the gossip fly . . .

"You owe me ten francs."

"Look at the king flush. He's enraged."

The melody rose to a high note and ended as I reached my uncle's side. He took my hand upon his arm.

The king bowed politely to d'Argencourt, then marched straight to Mazarin. "See to it that she has no opportunity to impose on me again."

My uncle bowed his head. "I have already informed the abbess at the Convent Sainte-Marie at Chaillot. D'Argencourt shall be installed before dawn."

Convent exile. The thought made me shudder. The cardinal backed away, offering my hand to King Louis.

The king took it. "Marie."

"You've had an eventful evening."

"I . . . I cannot allow a woman to use me for her own gains." He studied me.

"There isn't a woman alive who is worthy of you."

He laughed a little. "What is different about you tonight?"

I shrugged. "The cardinal poured Olympia's old diamonds on me."

The king looked me over, pausing on my décolletage a moment too long. "I never noticed before, but your eyes, they sparkle like the night sky."

My heart nearly thumped out of my chest. I had to look down.

"Dance?"

I answered by looking back up, and he led me out. Flutes and clarinets in the gallery played the opening chords of a minuet, and violins joined the melody. We stepped in time. Along the perimeter, painted faces looked astonished, and powdered heads tipped together to chatter. I couldn't care less.

"I can finally face you without shame," the king said. "I finished *Jerusalem Delivered.* Rinaldo was a lucky man."

"Lucky?" I said, feeling flushed from the cinnamon. "He was bewitched by Armida until he looked into the mirror!"

"Armida loved him deeply. Every man should be so lucky."

"Perhaps luck is what I need."

"Why does a lovely creature like you need luck?"

I took a breath. "To make you realize my eyes sparkle like the night only for you, that you might look inside them to find an Armida who loves you already."

The violins ceased, and the flutes brought the melody to a gentle close. *Why did I say that?* I began trembling so badly I was sure everyone could see. I started to leave.

But the king grabbed my hand, bowed, and kissed it. "Forgive me for having failed to see before."

He doesn't mean it. With a quick curtsy, I slipped my hand from his and stepped back. I turned, looking at no one. The wall of courtiers parted, and I flew to the door. Moréna appeared and called my driver.

My carriage met us in the middle of the Cour Carrée. "Home," I ordered, climbing in.

"Were you bold?" asked Moréna in the guttering light of the crystal sconce.

Too bold.

She grinned all the way back to Palais Mazarin.

CHAPTER 12

It is the public scandal that offends — to sin in secret is no sin at all.

— from MOLIÈRE's comedy *Tartuffe*

That night, unable to sleep, I paced before my empty fireplace, watching a lone candle burn shorter and shorter. *What if he never wants to see me again?* I couldn't decide which was worse, having to return to the convent, failing my sisters, or displeasing King Louis.

The cardinal stepped noiselessly into my bedchamber well past midnight. "You left early."

"Your Eminence is light of foot," I said, startled. "I had been too forward. It won't happen again."

"It is a good tactic. Be the prey to his hunt. Let him pursue you."

I dared not confess I hadn't developed this tactic on purpose. "Shall I wait on the queen tomorrow?"

"Leave the work of the toilette to other women. Go when they are at leisure, for cards and music. That is when Louis visits." He quietly appraised me. I crossed my arms so he would not see the shadows of my nipples under my thin silks. "You look lovely."

I wanted to jump into bed and tie the curtains closed. I tried to jest. "Even without my jeweled bodice and diamonds in my hair?"

He smiled a little. "Proof of true beauty."

I didn't know what to say. No one had ever called me beautiful.

He took a step toward me. "Make the king love you, and he might do more than share secrets."

I leaned back. I couldn't imagine King Louis loving me. "More?"

"What do men do when they love deeply?"

"Your Eminence, bedding the king didn't serve Olympia well—"

"Olympia lusts too much. She gave herself too readily. But you fled when the king's interest was piqued. Let him think he must own you before he can bed you."

"Own me? If you mean marriage—"

He held up his hand. "Do not speak of it. Just be the prey."

He slipped out, and I was too dazed to go after him. The candle finally died, and I stood alone in the dark. God help me, I laughed! I clapped my hands across my mouth, but the thought of the king marrying *me* was nonsense. D'Argencourt had failed without aspiring so far. And she would be in a convent by dawn. *I am doomed.*

I rose at midmorning and found a slip of foolscap on my pillow.

> If a man who once waged war against me wishes to return to my king's favor, that man must first pay me homage, and an attempt to circumvent me by way of the queen will lead to his destruction.

It was Mazarin's writing. An assignment. I ripped up the paper and threw the pieces into the cold fireplace. "Light it," I said to Moréna.

"But it's a beautiful spring day."

I didn't even understand the note, but I wanted no visible trace of my uncle's command over me. "Tell my driver I go this evening to the queen's."

The sentinels at the queen's apartments admitted me without hesitation. My new high-heeled mules click-clicked on marble floors as I moved past pillars and sculptures in the vestibule, the anteroom, and into the salon where the queen mother played cards with three other women. I curtsied before her table. She nodded without looking up, and I took my place standing between a window and a candelabra.

My Martinozzi cousin Princess de Conti approached, gold hair shining in the window's evening light. "D'Argencourt departed for the convent at Chaillot."

"Poor girl."

"The court is abuzz, wondering if Mazarin did it on *your* account."

I laughed and hoped it sounded convincing. "I imagine I'll be following in d'Argencourt's wake soon."

"Look," she said, gesturing to a man carrying papers. "Here is the new secretary our uncle appointed for the queen. You know what happened to that older secretary who served her faithfully for decades?"

I watched the new man present himself to the queen. "What happened to him?"

"Our uncle happened to him," she said.

"He must not have been trustworthy if our uncle dismissed him."

She shrugged. "He dismisses anyone he can't control. Be wary."

I glanced at her.

"He's using you. And *you* are not one to be controlled."

When we'd first come to Paris, right after her wedding to the Prince de Conti, we'd danced in a ballet, *The Marriage of Peleus and Thetis*. She'd played a goddess, and I'd played a musical muse. From backstage I couldn't see the king dancing as Apollo. She ordered me to stay behind a backdrop while she looked for Conti. But I'd climbed up the cranks and pulleys of mechanical clouds to get a peek onstage. When she couldn't find me, she panicked and begged Conti to organize a search party. I'd started laughing, and they spotted me. *Say you're sorry,* she'd commanded. But I wasn't. I'd seen the Sun King dance!

Now I touched Martinozzi's arm. "He'll send me to the convent if I fail."

She sighed. "Don't try to fool him, you wicked girl. He'll make you beg for the convent."

The king's herald called from the antechamber, "His Majesty the King!" and we curtsied.

King Louis went straight to his mother and kissed her. He looked at her cards, then rounded the table, checking everyone's hand. "I'd slip Madame de Motteville a spare ace, but that would give her away." He paused to absorb their chuckles. "So instead, I'll sweeten the bank." He tossed a golden coin on the table, where it clinked among the silver. Then he turned to me. "Marie!"

Martinozzi backed away as the king approached.

"You don't play cards?" he asked.

I glanced at the table, where I had not been invited to play. "I'm afraid I'm no better at dealing with card players than with politicians."

He looked confused.

I grinned. "I never know when they're bluffing."

He laughed heartily. So did the queen's ladies.

"Marie," cried the queen, "you're such a wit!"

"Pray don't tell my uncle," I said. "He'll either ship me to a convent or rent me out as a royal jester and pocket all my profits."

Everyone roared at that, and I prayed they really *wouldn't* tell my uncle.

The queen mother dabbed her eyes and gestured to a tufted bench. "Please, Marie, sit when you talk to the king."

To be allowed to sit in the presence of royalty was rare. Everyone watched us sit together, and I didn't have time to worry what they thought.

King Louis reached into his doublet and pulled out my book. "There was a reason for the delay. I . . . I had to learn Italian."

I was stunned. "You learned Italian—for me?"

"Your sisters say *you* read in every language."

"Not every. Greek, Latin, English, Italian, French, Spanish."

He laughed. "I confess, I struggled with some passages." He flipped through the pages to canto fourteen. "Here. What's Armida doing?"

I looked. "Ah, the best part. She's just enchanted Rinaldo."

"But why does she fly him to her magic castle?"

"To keep him for her pleasure." My cheeks burned. "But it doesn't last."

The queen mother looked our way. "Read aloud, Marie."

"She doesn't have to read," said the king. "She knows whole cantos by heart."

The queen's eyes widened. "Then recite!"

"Yes," said the king. He searched the pages. "Here. Recite your favorite verses from canto sixteen, and I will see if you get them right."

I resisted the urge to wipe my palms on my silk skirts. I began to recite the canto in Italian.

> "Her veil, flung open, shows her breast; in curls
> Her wild hair woos the summer wind: she dies
> Of the sweet passion, and the heat that pearls,
> Yet more her ardent aspect beautifies:

A fiery smile within her humid eyes,
Trembling and tender, sparkles like a streak
Of sunshine in blue fountains; as she sighs,
She o'er him hangs; he on her white breast sleek
Pillowing his head reclines, cheek blushing turn'd to cheek."

Aware of the furious blush in my own cheeks, I glanced at the king. He rifled through pages. "Yes! She got it."

The queen and her ladies applauded, murmuring to each other. *They have no idea it is a love scene!* I bowed my head.

King Louis handed the book to me. "Alas, I promised my brother a game of billiards." He stood to go. "Will you join us for a game tomorrow?"

"As you wish."

The queen mother called to him, "I almost forgot! I received a letter from your uncle Gaston, duc d'Orléans. He asks permission to pay us his respects."

Gaston. One of the leaders of the Fronde! Mazarin's mysterious note came to mind. *That man must first pay me homage.* I held my breath.

King Louis considered it. "He hasn't been to court since he surrendered. How many years?"

The queen focused on her game. "They say he now lives a life of piety."

"Send the note to my chamber and I'll answer it," he said as he walked out.

Oh no. What should I do?

As expected, the cardinal came to my room that night. He opened my bed curtains. "Gaston thinks he can sidestep me. You cannot allow it."

There was no use feigning sleep. "He wants to pay respects to the king and queen."

"If Gaston doesn't show reverence to *me*, Condé will never fear me. Condé is massing his troops for the summer. He will strike again in the north. France is weary of war. Help me make it stop."

I clutched the coverlets. It was more than that. Mazarin needed to prove to every last footman in Paris that *he* was in control. "I will do what I can."

* * *

The next evening, my carriage arrived at the Pavillon du Roi at the Louvre. Musketeers stood aside. I'd asked Philippe to escort me, but Mazarin said I had to work alone. So my page walked before me while Moréna carried my ivory satin train. I went straight to the king's quarters, my gold silk shoulder drapery fluttering as I passed marble pedestals and sculptures. The footmen announced me and opened both doors to the king's apartments.

Tapestries, paintings, or murals covered every inch of space. Dozens of the finest candles lit a green-covered table and smelled faintly of honeybee wax. The far windows looked across the Seine to the Île de la Cité, with its fetid alleys and crooked streets.

The king himself stood to greet me. "Marie." He kissed my cheeks. Like a cousin. Or perhaps more.

I looked around. "Who is brave enough to teach me billiards?"

Monsieur called, "Not me. I'm wretched."

"King Louis is the best," said the Prince de Conti. Though he was Condé's brother, he'd submitted to my uncle after the Fronde. His marriage to my Martinozzi cousin was a triumph for Mazarin. Conti could be an asset. He leaned over the table and used the wide end of his mace to strike the balls, making a fantastic racket.

King Louis grabbed a mace. "We play King and Hoop. We each have three balls." He positioned me at one end of the green-upholstered table and pointed to six side pockets. "Keep them from falling in the hazards." Then he indicated a hoop rising from the tabletop. "Whoever moves all their balls through the hoop first wins." He put my hands on the mace and positioned my arms. "Try."

I pulled the stick back, aimed, then struck the ball. It whacked the others, missing the hoop and the hazards.

"Très bon!" said King Louis, and he stalked to the other side. "Knock your opponents into the hazards if you can."

"So, the mace is the king of the billiards table," I said.

Conti nodded. "It commands the subjects."

Monsieur laughed. "The subjects don't always move through the hoop like they're supposed to."

"Maybe not for you," said King Louis. With that he struck, and a ball rolled through the hoop. "The king must be skilled."

Monsieur elbowed me. "My brother doesn't have to be skilled while your uncle is around!"

The king struck and missed. "My subjects will follow commands when I issue them."

I lined up. "Who was it your mother said wishes to return to court?"

"Gaston," said Conti from the corner. "And he ought to be forced to crawl back."

I struck, sending a ball through the hoop. "Didn't he defy my uncle in the Fronde? You should test your skill on him. Command Gaston to first visit Mazarin." I rounded the table, lined up to strike.

"Yes," said Conti, to my relief. "He wanted to kill Mazarin."

King Louis thought a moment. "If Marie puts her next ball through the hoop, I'll order Gaston to fall on his knees before Cardinal Mazarin."

Conti glanced at me. Monsieur laughed. I struck the ball hard. Straight through the hoop.

Conti applauded.

"Well done," said the king, beaming at me with evident pride.

Monsieur lined up for his turn. "The cardinal will be thrilled."

The thought that my king might realize I'd been maneuvering for this very thing made me sick. But I threw back my head and laughed. "Just don't tell the old bird I had anything to do with it."

I stood behind our uncle with my brother and younger sisters in the great hall of Palais Mazarin weeks later, watching the entourage of Gaston, duc d'Orléans, clamor into the courtyard. The old prince who had caused my uncle and my king such trouble entered alone, limping with gout, leaning on a gold cane. He reached the cardinal and, grimacing, eased himself to his knees. He kissed my uncle's red cassock and white lace rochet. He begged forgiveness. My uncle extended his hand, and Gaston kissed his fingertips. Thus, through me, Mazarin's power over the French and the king was enforced. I hated every moment.

Gaston left for the Louvre, and my uncle turned to me. "I'm not sure whether it is your fear of the convent or your love for the king that has made you useful."

"I did it out of love for *you*, Uncle," I lied.

"Next to beg my forgiveness will be Condé. I am moving our troops to the north. We must leave nothing to chance. You must convince King Louis to join them."

"Why put the king so close to battle?" It didn't seem a fatherly thing to do.

"To inspire troops who are sick of war to fight with all their hearts."

According to Parisian pamphleteers, the whole country was sick of war. But Mazarin's private ledgers showed how he profited by provisioning the army and controlling its budget. *Oh, how little lives are worth when there's money to be made.*

He watched me carefully. "Perhaps you're wondering what's in it for you? The King of Germany is dead."

I shrugged.

"Ferdinand the Third was also the elected Holy Roman Emperor, which forced the imperial countries to help him when he sided with Spain against France. Imagine what Louis can do if he wins the next election."

"It would help us defeat Spain and Condé."

"I've sent emissaries to bribe the Electors and will go to Metz myself for the vote. The king should come with me. As Holy Roman Emperor, King Louis could marry anyone he wants. Even the mere niece of a cardinal. Suggest it. Make him think it's his idea."

An opportunity to end the war *and* marry the king? I retired to my rooms not knowing what to believe.

CHAPTER 13

Summer 1657

S ummer's sun warmed the countryside, trees and fields blossomed with bounty, and two countries took up arms to resume a war that had been ongoing for thirty years. The court traveled to Sedan to be closer to the fighting. The journey took days. Regiments of musketeers, companies of gendarmes and light horse, cavalry regiments, and royal carriages followed the kettledrums and trumpets, winding north through vineyards swollen with juicy grapes and past lavender fields glittering with purple. We converged on towns at night, where troops put the great houses under arms and sweaty courtiers descended from carriages to collapse in assigned lodgings.

Hortense and I rode in the queen mother's carriage as part of her household, since Venelle stayed behind in Paris with Marianne and Olympia, whose belly swelled with child. We were trapped, reading aloud from boring prayer books, jostled over broken pavers, the heat exacerbated by our voluminous skirts. Moréna fared worse, sitting atop my *cassone* in a wagon, baking in the sun. I envied the king, who rode horseback most of the way.

When we reached Sedan, Mazarin, King Louis, and Monsieur closeted themselves to review plans to attack Montmédy. Hortense and I shuffled to our room in a château designated as the royal lodging. Moréna arrived with our belongings, and we stared at each other.

"Why are we here?" groaned Hortense.

So the cardinal could use King Louis. "So the king can receive updates and issue prompt orders."

"So the *cardinal* can issue orders," Hortense replied.

Indeed. Moréna drew curtains over the windows. We all stripped naked and collapsed on the bed.

The most favored French female courtiers gathered daily in the queen mother's makeshift presence chamber, jostling for position near open windows, fanning themselves rapidly. Hortense stood in a corner, reading aloud, and I sat nearby playing the guitar. The queen mother played cards with my friend from the salons, the comtesse de La Fayette. Even our guards seemed about to melt with boredom. They stood at every doorway, surrounded the château, stood at every city gate, and blocked every street. I eyed their harshly gleaming muskets and fat pouches of gunpowder. They reminded me of danger. We were at war. And Mazarin wanted my king near the fighting. *Well, I don't.*

The cardinal, the king, and Monsieur arrived.

"Sit. Have some black-currant wine," said the queen mother. "Marie, play something more lively."

I plucked out a quick melody while servants distributed glasses.

"Where are the dispatches?" asked King Louis in a huff.

"My brother is anxious to distinguish himself on the battlefield." Monsieur tugged the lace of his cravat. "And I wouldn't mind showing myself on the battlefield in this fine uniform."

The ladies giggled. Just then a messenger arrived, and I stopped playing.

The cardinal read silently, then stood. "We are laying siege to Montmédy. The moment is crucial." The king sat up. My uncle glanced at me. A signal.

I took a swig of black-currant wine, buying time, studying the king. He seemed so . . . excited. *He wants to go.* He was on the verge of saying so himself. What would a little prompt harm? "Ah, I'm reminded of Rinaldo marching bravely into Jersualem before his glorious triumph."

The king beamed at me. "Brother, ready your horses. We leave immediately for Montmédy!"

The three of them bid farewell to the queen and were gone.

Had he really been waiting on my approval? I felt terrible dread. *What have I done?*

A furious chatter rose among the ladies. They must donate to the king's fund for arms, they must go down to watch the king depart, they must lift up prayers for the king's safety.

"*Pardon,*" I muttered, and fled without proper dismissal. I ran to my chamber, trying to remember my father's quickest charm for protection.

"Moréna, I need rue," I said, out of breath. But she wasn't there. She was likely in the kitchens preparing our supper. I opened my little casket of medicinal herbs, but rue wasn't an herb we had much use for. Known to ward off evil, it also blistered the skin. I grabbed a pewter vial of holy water and an empty white jewelry pouch and ran out to the gardens. Beyond the ornamental *parterres,* I found the kitchen pottage garden and searched for the yellow blooms of summer rue. At last I spotted some, neglected along a fence, and ripped off a handful. Kettledrums and trumpets sounded at the front of the château. I ran, pouring holy water over the rue, stuffing it into the pouch, and reciting powerful Latin, "*Ihesus autem transiens per medium illorum ibat.*" If I could just get it to the king in time I would hang it from his neck, stuff it into his pocket, slip it under his saddle. But as I reached the courtyard, the king's retinue galloped away at full speed, dust rising in their wake. I crushed the charm in my hand. Rue and holy water dripped between my fingers and splattered my silk skirts.

The cardinal found me crying in my room. "I'm going to Mardyck to be closer to Montmédy," he said. "Get up. Stay near the queen mother. Mademoiselle de Montpensier is coming, and I want you present."

I wiped my face. "The duc d'Orléans's daughter? Didn't she fight alongside him during the Fronde?" She'd fired the Bastille's cannons at Mazarin's army, wounding my oldest brother, Paul, and making it impossible for Mazarin to enter Paris. It took Mazarin a whole year to regroup. Paul had died.

Mazarin sensed my shock. "I stripped her of many lands and bonds, but she's still the richest woman in France. I can't let her marry, lest her husband use her wealth to raise another army. Letting her back to court will give me more control over her. She has an eye to wed King Louis."

I put a hand to my head.

"Ah, I see the notion doesn't please you either."

CHAPTER 14

I obeyed. I went with the queen mother to mass, to prayer in her chambers. I waited behind her at supper, where she talked of nothing but the king's safety. We prayed in the morning, we prayed at night, we never missed a mass. Day after day, my prayer was the same. *God keep him safe, and I'll never subvert him again.*

Within a week the queen bid us accompany her to meet Mademoiselle de Montpensier. Moréna laced Hortense and me into our best day dresses.

"It's too hot for this. We'll sweat and ruin the silk," complained Hortense.

"You want to look frumpy in front of one of the richest, highest-ranking women in France? You want her to think you are nothing and nobody?" Moréna slathered perfume on our necks. "You'll wear it and your jewels, too."

The queen ordered half the guards and three carriages to carry us to a meadow outside Sedan. We arranged ourselves behind the queen mother and heard the sound of trumpets. Mademoiselle's gendarmes and cavalry broke from the distant woods and dashed into the meadow, followed by her own carriage. Her troops formed a path between her carriage and the queen, and she stepped out. As tall as King Louis, blond and dressed modestly, she wore no jewels. She walked the twenty paces to the queen and fell to her knees. She kissed the hem of the queen mother's gown.

The queen mother hesitated. "I don't blame you for obeying your father's orders." She seemed to tense. "But for firing that cannon . . . I could kill you with my bare hands."

Part of me wanted her to.

Mademoiselle kissed the queen's fingertips. "I deserve it."

Finally, the queen pulled her up and embraced her stiffly. "Let us start afresh. You haven't aged in six years."

"I've been so unhappy while deprived of your court that some of my hair has grayed early."

The queen laughed and fell into a conversation about hair powder. Mademoiselle joined us in the queen's coach, and they didn't stop talking—about hair and what they'd been doing for six years and the royal salute from the King's Gendarmes that the queen had arranged to welcome her as we entered the city gates. Hortense and I glanced at each other. Mademoiselle didn't say a word to us. *I am no one to her. But she could take everything from me.*

Inside the city gates a courier from the cardinal chased down the royal carriage.

The queen ripped open his missive. "We've taken Montmédy!"

"And the king?" I asked, trying not to sound breathless.

"He returns tomorrow. For dinner."

I rubbed the blisters between my fingers caused by the rue. *Praise God.*

When we left Mademoiselle at her lodgings and were alone in the carriage, rolling back to the château, the queen eyed me. "What did you think?"

"She is a regal woman." I hated to admit it.

Mademoiselle went with us to mass, then followed us to the queen mother's rooms. The queen showed off her jewelry, plied Mademoiselle with sweetmeats. "Why do you wear your hair in the old style?" the queen mother asked her with a sickening smile. She promptly rearranged Mademoiselle's hair herself. She insisted on playing *piquet,* and when the card game was done she made Mademoiselle list every single property her father had forced her to relinquish after the Fronde. She seemed to relish Mademoiselle's torment. "It's a shame you weren't clever enough not to sign so many documents."

In truth, the cardinal made Gaston take property from Mademoiselle as a condition of returning to court, and the queen knew it. Mademoiselle just nodded, bearing royal punishment like a true princess.

We heard the kettledrums and trumpets at the supper hour. *The king.* I flew to the window. He galloped into the courtyard, tall in the saddle, his shiny black boots and gray riding habit covered in mud. I breathed a sigh of relief.

The queen snapped her fingers. "I will reintroduce Mademoiselle to the king alone."

I followed the other women to the antechamber, where they watched the return of the troops from the windows. I stayed by the door. The king marched in. We dipped low, and he winked at me as he passed. I couldn't remember being happier in all my life.

I overheard the queen tell him, "Your cousin Mademoiselle swears to be good in the future."

The king laughed but didn't offer forgiveness. "My brother will arrive shortly. He took his carriage rather than muddy himself up on horseback like me. He heard you'd be here and wants to impress you."

I chuckled. If poor Monsieur thought he could brace up his finances by marrying Mademoiselle, I would have to warn him of my uncle's plan.

The king went on. "I wouldn't be such a mess if not for the assassins. We were shot at from the woods. They killed my coachman, but we chased them down."

"Good God!" cried the queen.

I clamped my hands over my mouth. *Condé.*

"We captured twelve Spanish gunmen. Two with fresh gunpowder on their hands were executed on the spot. The rest are prisoners."

Monsieur's carriage stopped before the château, and he rushed through the antechamber. I barely heard the queen mother introduce him.

I walked alone and in silence to the king's lodgings. I stood against the wall of his antechamber, empty but for two guards at the door and another pair at the entrance to his bedchamber. It didn't take long.

The king marched in by himself, dripping mud with each heavy step. He didn't spot me until the moment he passed. He looked up. Smiled. "Marie!"

I shoved him as hard as I could. He fell back a step. All four guards advanced. The king held up his hand, and they halted. He glared at me,

Marci Jefferson

astonished. I balled my hands into fists and went after him, pounding his shoulders, his chest, and then his hands as he fended me off.

"How could you?" I cried.

He grabbed my fists. "What is this rage?"

"You're a damn fool chasing those gunmen." I tried to break away, but he pulled me close. "You should have left it to your men."

"I'm unharmed!"

"If you haven't a care for yourself, you should have considered *me*. What would I do? I—I think I would die if you died."

His face softened, and I burst into tears. He glanced over his shoulder, and the guards scrambled back to position. The king pulled me into his bedchamber and wrapped his arms around me. I thought I would melt into a puddle, but I couldn't stop crying.

"Hush now." He wiped my face with his muddy fingers. "The Spanish are in retreat, and the fighting is over for the season. You have nothing to fear."

In retreat. Not beaten. I put my hands on his, savoring the feel of his palms on my cheeks. "You're the only one who's ever seen me cry."

"You surprise me, Marie."

I looked into his eyes. *What am I doing?* I took a step back. The king stepped with me, and lowered his lips to mine. I stiffened, surprised. But his kiss was a gentle caress, tentative. In a flash as fierce as my fury, I kissed him back. Something hidden and hungry within me rushed forth. He pressed against me, tilting my head back, devouring my lips. I lapped him up like a thirsty animal. *Please don't stop, don't even breathe.* He broke to kiss my chin, my neck, and he ran his hands down the front of my bodice. I moaned softly, surprising myself. *I have lost control.*

Footsteps sounded in the antechamber. I pushed the king away. He stared down at me with heated intensity. His *valet de chambre* walked in, took one look at us, and walked right back out again.

I sidestepped. I resisted the urge to stroke the anguished look off of the king's face and followed the valet.

Hortense found me in our bedchamber hours later. "The cardinal has returned. You should have heard how he flattered and praised that Mademoiselle." It didn't surprise me. Hortense wolfed down a bowl of green lentil and sausage soup Moréna had set out. "Eat or your stomach will growl during Their Majesties' supper."

But I couldn't.

Their Majesties dined to a harpist's melodies. I stood behind the queen, serving her and Mademoiselle. Monsieur talked to Mademoiselle constantly. The queen mother kept interjecting, trying to get the king to talk. But he was watching me. I could feel it. I avoided eye contact.

He paid Mademoiselle due respect by opening the dance with her in the reception hall.

Then he took my arm and walked me to a corner. "Will you avoid me?"

"Perhaps."

"How am I to take your silence? Don't cut me out before I have a chance to prove my adoration."

His words stunned me. But the joy they brought was quickly stricken by shame. *If the king adores me, Mazarin will only make me abuse him further.* "Like you adored Olympia?"

He blinked, taken aback. "I can't eat. I think of you instead of sleep. Even at Montmédy I thought of you during the fighting. I don't know what to do. Normally I'm handed everything I want."

I glared. "So I am a thing to be wanted?"

"Is it wrong to want you?"

"What happened to admiration?" How easy it was for the king. Olympia, d'Argencourt, and even our gardener's daughter had too willingly fallen into his arms. Did his feelings for me extend no further than they had for them? The thought hurt, then it made me angry. "Go back to studying your siege maps and your battle plans and quit teasing me. You don't know what love is."

"Don't be angry at me because women throw themselves at my feet. Don't assume it blinds me to what's real." He paused for a long moment. "I'll prove myself to you. Give me a quest."

"Like some knight in a novel? Do you think you're Rinaldo?"

"Name it, Armida." His expression seemed anguished.

I longed to trust in him. Courtiers keeping their respectful distance leaned toward us a fraction. Mademoiselle shot a glance over her shoulder. My hand flew to the diamond necklace Mazarin had given me. Mazarin's goal seemed as good as any to keep King Louis from focusing on Mademoiselle. "I'll believe you when you win the title of Holy Roman Emperor."

He turned serious. "As soon as we return to Paris, I will arrange an envoy to Metz. I will accompany Cardinal Mazarin and bribe the Electors myself if I have to." He bowed slightly, then walked away. He nodded to his mother and Mademoiselle, signaled his attendants, and retired. Mademoiselle looked dejected.

I found Hortense, took her arm, and led her upstairs to bed. "But it's so early," she complained.

"We must rest up for our miserable journey back to Paris."

But I didn't sleep a bit. If all the stars and Papa's spirits confirmed I was born bad, then why did I feel so guilty?

CHAPTER 15

There will be signs in the sun, moon, and stars.

— WORDS OF JESUS CHRIST IN LUKE 21:25

When the envoy left Paris for Metz, Venelle stayed with my sisters and me at Palais Mazarin. Autumn fell, and I did not have herbs to harvest on the equinox, no tinctures to mix, no bundles to prepare. Instead we dressed daily and took my pretty carriage to attend the queen mother's afternoon salons at the Louvre.

The envoy returned a failure. When Cardinal Mazarin arrived home, he closeted himself with Colbert. I hid behind an ancient statue of Psyche in the gallery and listened at the library door as Mazarin screamed and raged about greedy German Electors who'd enriched themselves by failing to be bribed. Shame compounded my guilt.

King Louis came to his mother's salon wearing his austere frown again, all quiet dignity. He let me win at cards without waiting for me to flirt in return. He led me in a dance at a ball without leaning too close. He listened intently when I sang an aria for the queen's ladies, nothing like the spoiled prince I'd accused him of being. He didn't speak of our conversation in Sedan. I regretted it too much to remind him. My quest had ended when I'd set his up to fail. Soon Mazarin would realize I was no longer useful.

King Louis came to Palais Mazarin one day, requesting to see me.

He bowed slightly in the reception hall, a noble knight clutching his hat. "I was riding nearby."

My heart thudded wildly. It made me light-headed.

He gestured toward the city. "Olympia's child is due any day." He looked as though he wished to say more.

I nodded, longing to draw near to him. *Neither of us deserves you. Go away.*

He did go. And for an hour I stood in the spot where he had stood and wished things could be different.

M oréna leaned over my bed in the dim light of a mid-December morning. "It is time."

Olympia is giving birth. She dressed me in haste, and we rushed in my carriage to the Hôtel de Soissons so I could serve as her witness.

But I stepped into the hall to the sounds of infant cries. "She called for me too late."

"You don't have to go up," Moréna replied in a huff.

I wanted to see the child, though. When we'd returned from Sedan, Olympia refused to let me join her lying-in. I'd presented a basket of apples, but she'd turned me out of the room saying, "You're no sister, you're a thief." She'd kept the apples.

Now she hadn't summoned me in time for the birth. I climbed the wide staircase to her wing and passed through chamber after opulent chamber. The nurses were washing Olympia's newborn son. He kicked and screamed, pink and healthy, while a flock of doctors stood over him. A midwife tucked fresh silk sheets around Olympia, then carried a bowl of bloody linens away. Olympia reached to me.

I took her hand, sat on the edge of her bed.

She wiped her eyes. "I don't want to die like Victoire."

"Shhh." I tucked her hair behind her ears.

"Please," she whimpered. "Make up the herbs for me like our father taught us. Don't let those damned doctors touch my son."

I placed a velvet bag upon her lap.

She realized it was the herbs she'd just requested. She kissed my hand. "I'm sorry."

"It doesn't matter," I whispered. "We will both do what we must."

I went to the cradle, pushed the doctors aside, and took a great swath of red silk from the nurse. With a quick motion I swiped my nephew into it and carried him to Olympia. The doctors fussed and clucked and flapped their arms. I cooed to the boy and he quieted, trying to focus his newborn blues on my face. I placed him in Olympia's arms, and together we took hold of his tiny hand. We peered at his palm and saw it at the same time: a long and prosperous lifeline. We smiled at each other, and for a moment everything was perfect.

But after Olympia ordered a good dinner for her guests and I'd left her asleep in her bed with her infant son, I went home to Palais Mazarin, where the front doors stood wide open to the cold air. In the hall, the maids and footmen jumped around wildly, yelling and waving brooms in the air, looking ridiculous, trying to shoo out a raven that had somehow gotten inside. I leaned on the doorframe and watched the poor bird swoop from one end of the hall to the other. It didn't matter if they got it out; the damage had been done.

Moréna gasped. "Is this a bad omen in your culture, too?"

I crossed myself. "If you consider the impending visitation of death a bad omen, then yes."

A fortnight later the cardinal summoned us all. I stood in his private study, holding my sisters' hands. The comte de Soissons arrived without Olympia. Philippe entered unshaven. Martinozzi and her husband, Conti, swept in last.

Mazarin gestured for them to close the door. "Alphonse injured his skull while playing with classmates." He struggled to maintain composure. "Physicians removed broken bits of bone to relieve bleeding in the brain. It is no use. Alphonse is dying."

Marianne started whimpering. Hortense held her. I remembered the raven and silently cursed it to keep myself from crying out.

Mazarin went on. "As you know, Alphonse is my heir."

Everyone glanced at each other. We had not known this. Not for certain.

"If he dies, to whom will I leave the management of this great country?" Mazarin looked at the men. "None of you are capable."

The muscles in Philippe's jaw tensed. I didn't blame him for being angry. Mazarin refused to give Philippe responsibilities or offices, a slight that would become more obvious to the court if he were the only remaining Mancini male.

Marianne interrupted. "Marie could. She knows everything."

The cardinal smiled at her forbearingly. "Thank you, Marianne, but Marie is a girl."

My own jaw muscles twitched.

The cardinal went on. "I must defeat Spain before age and infirmity overtake me. To do it, we must first win Naples."

Philippe cut in. "What will you do with Naples?"

Mazarin gave my brother a look that made us all cringe. "If we seize the Spanish territory of Naples, we can eliminate Spain's access to reinforcements. We will meet Condé's troops at Dunkirk this summer with Cromwell's army at our side. Condé will run out of men. We will crush him."

The men in the room glanced at each other. Mazarin seemed to sense what they were thinking. "Don't start casting lots for Naples. Christina of Sweden will rule there. I can control her." Christina had abdicated her throne in Protestant Sweden to become Catholic and had taken refuge in the French countryside. Mazarin could control her because she owed him money.

His Eminence went on. "Conti, you must get information about the movement of your brother Condé's troops. Find out where they get provisions and their number of cavalry." He shifted his stern eye to Martinozzi, who looked like she wanted to flee. "Anne, write to your sister in Modena. She must make her husband move his troops to take Naples." He looked around and barked, "Soissons. You have ties to the House of Savoy. Ensure the duc de Savoy will permit the passage of French troops south through his province to Naples. In the meantime, I will ask Oliver Cromwell to send his ships into the Mediterranean."

Soissons looked confused. "Why wouldn't we send our own?"

The cardinal ignored this. But I knew. France didn't *have* enough ships. Instead, the cardinal had a treasure trove of jewels and gold.

"You could triumph over Spain," said Philippe, attempting to recover from his earlier blunder.

"If I triumph, you all triumph. Hortense and Marianne. You may be called upon to make marriage alliances as your sisters and cousins have done. Can I trust you to submit willingly to betrothals to secure your family's power?"

The girls nodded, and I shuddered.

Mazarin crossed his arms. "If Alphonse dies, we must abbreviate our mourning and participate in the festivities of carnival season. I cannot have you wasting at home. If the nobles or their meddling wives speak against my methods, or if any of them gets word of our secret doings . . . tell me."

The question of his heir remained open. Whom would he appoint as his *successor*? Who would manage my king's affairs when my greedy uncle finally croaked?

He dismissed us with one sweeping wave but called, "Marie. Stay."

I stepped out of line and stood before his desk. "Eminence?" The doors to his cabinet closed softly.

"You mustn't give up hope just because I couldn't buy the German Electors."

Hope couldn't be bought. Nor could trust. "I never had any to begin with."

"You should." He curled the ends of his mustache upward. "If I can beat Spain, we will be the richest, most powerful nation in Europe. King Louis can be great without being emperor. And he has never looked upon a woman with more desire than he does you."

I tried not to believe him.

"You have read my important documents." I started to protest, but he held up a hand. "Do not bother lying. Do you understand my work?"

I glanced at Colbert. His face betrayed nothing, but that man knew everything. "I understand how you line your pockets."

"You confuse greed with preparation. If there is another Fronde, the king must have money enough for troops and provisions. How do you think I quelled civil unrest last time?"

King Louis came of age, and you control King Louis. "You bought the nobles' loyalty?"

Mazarin grinned. "You might say I bought power. The power and glory of France will be my legacy. Now Alphonse will not be present to see my plan through to the end. You are the only Mazarinette capable."

King Louis didn't need to be emperor. He didn't need to rob his people of riches to defend himself against them. He needed to feed his poor, build hospitals for his sick. He could do these things on his own without a greedy chief minister. "I am."

"That is why I will let him marry you if we defeat Spain. You've proven you can guide Louis, and with Colbert's assistance, you can muster the wealth to make him the greatest king."

I ignored the silly flip my heart did. "The queen mother will never allow her son to marry a pagan of minor Roman nobility."

He waved this away as if he had always valued me. "I can influence the queen. Your task is simple. Keep the king. Keep him at all costs."

Colbert opened the door, my signal that the conversation was over.

Moments later I reached the landing at the top of the stairs, where Philippe grabbed my arm. "I can't bear Mazarin's arrogance another day."

"Does that mean you're willing to set yourself against him?"

He looked surprised. "Can you help me?"

"Do nothing yet. If you're willing to wait for the right time, I might have information that will topple the cardinal."

He sagged. "Mamma is dead. Victoire is dead. Death comes in threes. If Alphonse dies, the cardinal will slight me. How long will you make me wait?"

"Until I know what must be done." I turned to my bedchamber, leaving him behind. "In the meantime, pray God allows Alphonse to live."

CHAPTER 16

February 1658

What an unapt instrument is a toothless, old, impotent, and unweldie woman to flie in the aier? Truelie, the devil little needs such instruments to bring his purposes to passe.

— REGINALD SCOT, *The Discoverie of Witchcraft*

Alphonse died. Our uncle declared a two-week mourning and enclosed himself at the Château de Vincennes.

"When our mourning is over, you will go to masquerades with me," said Olympia the next week, checking herself in the mirror of my bedchamber at Palais Mazarin. "And the finest ballet of the carnival season."

"Is King Louis performing?"

She nodded. "You and I have parts in it, too. You will distract my husband while I win back the king. But I must prepare. Come with me."

She was testing me. Pushing me out of the way. "Where?"

"Rue Beauregard. I need a rare ingredient for a love powder." She pointed to a new ring on her finger. With a subtle flick, the jeweled bezel lifted to reveal a little container.

A poison ring! "To visit La Voisin? She practices the black arts!"

Olympia put her fists on her hips. "She's the only one who'd have cantharides, an insect that drives a man's lust."

"There's no need to visit La Voisin," I said. "The Spanish fly you speak of is here at Palais Mazarin. The cardinal keeps a supply hidden in his medicine chest."

She seemed stunned at my knowledge. We avoided discussing *why* a prince of the church possessed an ingredient to drive a man's lust. "I checked. He is out." She moved to the door. "I shall get it elsewhere."

"Olympia, potions will get you in trouble."

She grinned. "No one will suspect me of witchcraft for visiting Ninon de l'Enclos."

"The courtesan? She is imprisoned at the Madelonnettes Convent for offensive conduct."

"The *celebrated* courtesan. Even Condé himself was once in love with her. She was released, and she is bound to have what I need."

Moréna stopped dusting tabletops to whisper close to me. "Might this courtesan still have a memento of her former lover? An old handkerchief or strand of hair I could use in a spell to speed Condé's downfall?"

"I don't practice *malefica*," I hissed.

Moréna shook her head. "No harm will befall him. Condé will be conquered by diplomacy instead of battle. The war would end, and Mazarin might quit meddling in the king's affairs."

Allowing just one spell might be worth it if Mazarin would leave my sisters and me alone. I turned to Olympia. "I'll go with you."

We rode east through the city to the Marais quarter. On rue des Tournelles the houses looked like miniature castle towers, and Olympia knew exactly which belonged to Ninon de l'Enclos. Some of my friend's salons were nearby. "What makes you think she'll admit us?" I asked.

Her footman took our names, and we were admitted immediately. He showed us into a salon decorated with blue and white tapestries and divans covered in yellow taffeta. Upon one of these divans sat l'Enclos. She wore no cosmetics, no jewels, just a simple muslin shift and a green satin undress gown. She did not get up, but studied me with sparkling hazel eyes. "So this is Maximiliane."

My friend Somaize had nicknamed me Maximiliane at our last salon gathering. "I see we have friends in common." I curtsied.

She turned her gaze on Olympia, though still spoke to me. "This must be your sister. I see none of your fire in her, though she has the look of a woman who wants something."

She sees fire in me?

Olympia seemed taken aback. "Indeed. I have it on good authority you possess a certain Spanish fly."

"I possess no such thing. That makes you wrong twice."

"Twice?" Olympia's voice wavered.

"Yes," said the courtesan. "Wrong about the insect and wrong about your authority; it's no good. I wager no one told you such a thing, which means you assumed I use it."

Olympia turned a bright shade of pink.

L'Enclos laughed. "I've heard of this Spanish fly. I never had any need for it. So that makes you wrong a third time." She turned back to me. "You want something, too. But you're changing your mind."

This unusual woman, not beautiful but alluring and witty, was not the type to keep a former lover's handkerchief. Everything about her felt right— the simple grandeur of her salon, her wit, the angle of the curtain letting in sunlight. Her libertine ways had cost her her reputation, yet she seemed secure in the life she'd chosen. "I think I just needed to meet you," I replied.

She smiled. "I'll bid you farewell with a bit of advice. All you need is right here." She tapped a finger to her temple.

The footman ushered us out without another word. Olympia gave instructions to her driver, then wouldn't speak in the carriage. Neither of us had gotten what we went for. I had gotten much more.

I pondered the courtesan's words until I realized we had traveled north instead of west. We rolled through the crumbling towers of Porte Saint-Denis, and I sat up, alarmed. "Are we on rue Beauregard? La Voisin could be dangerous!"

Olympia pulled our two old vizard masks from beneath a cushion as we stopped before a small, weathered house. "You won't let me go in alone." She put the mask on me, damn her, tying the ribbon behind my head. She took my hand, leading me to the front door.

"I regret this whole errand," I said as she knocked. "Let's leave."

The door opened, and a round-faced young woman stared out, appraising our silks and jewels.

Olympia spoke quickly. "I'm to see Catherine Monvoisin, known as the sorceress La Voisin."

"Shush." She glanced behind us. "What do you want?"

"Cantharides," said Olympia, flashing a silver *ecu.*

The woman eyed it, then opened the door. "Come, come." She disappeared into her dark front chamber.

Olympia stepped in. I grabbed her arm, but she shook it off. "We can't be seen on the street," she hissed.

Inside, the smell of rotting flesh and dirt struck me like a blow. The woman poked around a shelf of pots and covered bowls. A central table crowded the room, littered with piles of fingernails, a dish of bones, and jars. The labels read powdered mole, pigeon hearts, coxcombs, potable gold, fat from a hanged man, and infant essence. My stomach roiled. To distract myself, I scanned herbs hanging from pegs on the wall. There was ergot, *droué,* biting stonecrop, hemlock, and human-shaped mandrake root; all poisonous. Olympia nudged me, pointing through a doorway. In the dim second chamber stood a makeshift altar holding crucifixes, chalices, a pyx containing communion wafers, and a wax poppet poked through with pins. Whatever transpired here was sacrilege at its worst. No Mancini would practice such *malefica.* We both took a step back. I felt behind me for the door latch.

The woman turned, holding out a little jar of dead green beetles. "I know a priest who'll hold your love potion over the chalice during communion to consecrate it."

Olympia tossed her ecu on the table. "Just the cantharides."

The woman stepped closer. "A fine lady like you can afford to let me mix a *philtre d'amour* with bat wing, your own blood, and semen of the man you wish to snare."

Olympia flung enough silver coins on the table to pay a scullery maid's yearly wage, then grabbed the jar.

I flung open the door, and we ran to the carriage. We rode south through Porte Saint-Denis with the windows open, but I couldn't rid myself of that rotten smell. I swore I'd *never* again consider casting a malevolent spell for the rest of my life, even if I found a whole lock of Condé's hair. "Promise you won't go back there, Olympia. One day that woman will burn."

Olympia wouldn't answer, just stared at her beetles. I couldn't stop thinking about how to keep her from using them on the king.

* * *

"I adore carnival and I adore masquerades," said Monsieur weeks later, staring across a sea of costumed nobles in the Maréchal de l'Hôpital's reception hall. Olympia, Soissons, King Louis, and I laughed. From our place at the door, we peered through our gold masks across the throng of dancers. Gold and silver ribbons decked the columns, and musicians played furiously in the balcony. We all wore fanciful dress, but Monsieur looked completely natural in a woman's bodice, skirts, wig, and jewels.

Beside him, Mademoiselle waved her feathered fan, cool and regal. "You like any opportunity to flaunt your finery."

The king grinned at the crowd, hands on his hips. "I like wearing this mask so no one ceases dancing for a bow."

He gestured, and our party moved into the hall, folding in with the dancers, bumping each others' shoulders, clapping and kicking our heels. Our clothes swished and rustled in the crush of people. We became a sea of gold and silver, hearts pounding in rhythm to the melody and the movement. We gave ourselves to it, throwing back our heads, spinning, and laughing, until someone finally recognized the king. We tossed off our masks and a roar of cheers arose. The marshal herded us into a private chamber, where a smaller group danced to a new set of musicians. And so, at a ball within a ball, we danced for hours.

At three in the morning, Mademoiselle found a dining room with a collation of cheese and fruits and wine. I poured, and Olympia chugged hers.

The king gestured to Mademoiselle. "Take a chair."

She gasped. "I wouldn't sit in your presence, sire."

The ease of the evening almost seemed shattered. Olympia plopped a chunk of cheese in her mouth and sauntered over to the chair, sinking into it.

Mademoiselle looked scandalized. I laughed and refilled everyone's wine.

Monsieur turned to Soissons. "What will you do with such a reckless wife?"

Soissons raised his glass. "Reckless but prosperous."

"I can afford to be reckless," said Olympia, pointing to her palm. "It says here I would marry a content man and have sons." She winked at her husband, who bowed. "And have a long, happy life."

"You haven't told my fortune," said Mademoiselle.

I gave Olympia a warning look, but she reached across the king's glass to take Mademoiselle's hand, palm up. She studied it for a long while. Too long. Sneaky Olympia.

Mademoiselle yanked her hand back. "What did you see?"

"Prosperity."

Mademoiselle glanced at Monsieur. She might have relinquished the prospect of marrying the king, but I knew Mazarin wouldn't let her marry Monsieur either. "Anything else?"

"If you mean marriage, no." Olympia reclined in her chair.

Mademoiselle frowned. "Superstition."

"Forget this nonsense," said King Louis, reaching for his glass. "Let's go home."

"Shouldn't we wait until dawn?" I snatched the glass from him and pretended to sip. "Paris is dangerous at night."

Olympia stared at the glass in my hand, stunned. I shrugged innocently.

The king looked away from me and walked to the door. "I'll order the coach to move with all speed."

We crowded into Mademoiselle's coach, Olympia giving me looks that could kill. King Louis shouted orders, and we took off with a jolt down the dark streets. Monsieur slipped from the bench; we saw a flurry of petticoats and hairy legs as he righted himself.

Houses sped past, and the king's musketeers fell behind. King Louis just laughed. He kicked open a compartment hidden in the floorboards. It held pistols, shots, and gunpowder. "Wouldn't it be grand if assassins attacked?"

I frowned. "*You* are the one who is reckless."

King Louis caught my serious tone. He tried to grab my hand, but I crossed my arms.

Why is he so careless of himself? Slowly I realized. Cold and alone in my convent cell, I had felt the same. *King Louis is unhappy.*

CHAPTER 17

It was the same at every masquerade and every ballet practice; Olympia fiddled with her ring, and I distracted King Louis more than I distracted Soissons. As carnival season ended, opening night of the *Ballet d'Alcidiane* arrived. We lined our eyes with kohl and slathered our lips with Spanish red. Peeking from behind the stage, I watched nobles and musicians fill the theater at the Louvre, cramming into balconies and packing shoulder to shoulder on the floor. The queen mother and distinguished guests took the front. The flickering lights of two dozen candelabra illuminated their judgmental stares as well as the stage. Lully summoned up the music of his violins.

Olympia, Hortense, and I danced onto the stage in supporting roles as foreigners dressed in turbans. Scarves edged with jingly gold coins hung low on our waists. We twirled, we leapt, and we finished each wave of our arms with a flick of the wrist. Professional singers played the lead roles of the warrior Polexandre and Princess Alcidiane. In three acts, we journeyed from Alcidiane's royal court to a New World and battled a sea monster, demons, and a sorceress.

The king appeared, and a wave of appreciative *ahhs* swept across the theater. The spectators hung on his every move, his lunges and toe points, his expression and his eyes. In the final sequence, he danced a chaconne to baritone verses that rang across the court. "He hardly feels the power of love . . . I doubt he will endure love's yoke."

The meaning struck me. *Ballets de cour* were written expressly for King Louis, and he considered them an expression of himself. I struggled to keep the spring in my step as we made our final leaps to exit the stage. Was the king untouched by love? Servants and costumers bustled backstage preparing the final wedding scene. I ducked into an alcove to hide my face. *I lost my chance with him anyway.*

The music ended, and the audience applauded. I felt a hand on my shoulder.

It was King Louis. "The verses about me aren't true. I do feel love."

I smiled. "You won't suffer its yoke."

"I want to. Please tell me you'll let me. That you won't shy from my kisses."

Everything inside me wanted to pull him close. "A kiss from me is a yoke from my uncle. You could never trust me."

"Trust implies risk." He wrapped his arms around me.

I savored his warmth and the musk of his ambergris perfume. "To love is to risk."

"You won't run from me again." He kissed me softly and I let him. It happened as suddenly as it had before, the rush of urgency and fire that terrified and exhilarated. I couldn't have run again if I'd wanted to.

Someone far away cried out, "Where is the king?"

He broke the kiss but pulled me closer. We held each other, breathing heavily, unwilling to part, understanding the line must be drawn.

Behind us, a page cleared his throat. "Your Majesty, the audience!"

The king pulled me by the hand into the light of the stage. I laughed at the smeared Spanish red on his lips, and he laughed at mine. Olympia stared, astounded. *She knows.* She would be furious. Courtiers threw flowers at our feet. What would *they* think when they found out?

Everyone with access to court followed the king to the Pavillon du Roi for a collation. Mazarin and the queen mother clung to his side as everyone congratulated his performance. The king winked at me from across the chamber. *Tomorrow,* he mouthed. A promise. I slipped away unnoticed.

At Palais Mazarin, Moréna wasn't in my bedchamber to help me undress. A servant pointed to the window. I pushed it open. On the terrace below was a great circle of candles. In the center, a pyre of sweet-smelling herbs went up in smoke. Moréna danced around it, humming, hands raised to the light of the full moon. She'd worked some spell.

"Clean that up," I cried.

She stopped. "Is he yours?"

"On *my* terms. Not because of this."

She grinned, bright teeth shining. "At last!" She hopped around, victorious. "You will live a life of freedom and you will take me with you."

"Hush, fool. Come up at once!"

I pulled the window closed and told myself tonight had nothing to do with Moréna's magic or her drive to be free. My relationship with Louis would be entirely my own. I would brook no more interference. Not from Olympia, and certainly not from Mazarin. If I had to deceive Mazarin, so be it. *Love takes risks.* To truly love King Louis would be to risk *my* very freedom.

CHAPTER 18

Spring 1658

Marie was the best and the wildest of all the Mazarinettes.

—LOUIS DE ROUVROY, DUC DE SAINT-SIMON's memoirs

A huge fire warmed my salon, and half-emptied bowls of strawberries and peas sat alongside platters of fruit tarts upon my table. Monsieur, Soissons, and Conti sat at another table, looking bored while Louis and I huddled on a divan discussing *Jerusalem Delivered*. We sat so close you couldn't slide a piece of paper between us. I treasured every moment of the king's daily visits, savoring his musky ambergris perfume. But Soissons's eyes were on me. I knew he reported everything he saw here to Olympia. The husband was jealous that I'd snatched his wife's lover. If only I could wrap my hair around the king and tie him down with braided flower vines to keep him as Armida had done to Rinaldo.

"Summer approaches," said Monsieur. "The war campaigns will soon begin."

I frowned. The cardinal had tried using these visits to broach his Naples Plan. He'd given up, as I managed to turn every conversation from business to literature.

"Sire," said Conti, "will you inspect Cromwell's troops at Mardyck?"

King Louis glanced at me. He knew I didn't want him going near the troops again. "Don't worry, my mother will follow as far as Calais."

"That gives me an excuse to follow as her lady in waiting. I shall take my own carriage."

"Take whatever means necessary," the king said, standing to go. "So long as you come." He kissed me soundly on the mouth, right in front of the others. He'd managed to avoid the question about the troops.

When he'd gone, Soissons remained. "Olympia wants you to stay behind."

"Why should I?" I wished *Olympia* would stay.

"The king hasn't visited us since Lent began."

"He shows you both favor."

"She wants . . . time alone with him." He clenched his jaw.

I didn't envy Olympia, whose husband would willingly lead her to the king's bed for his own benefit. "What? She wants a turn, as if the king is some plaything?"

He turned ruddy red and said no more.

The court left Paris in a fanfare of kettledrums and trumpets, with commoners waving from every street corner and leaning from every window. Standard-bearers rode one behind the other the entire length of our train, flags snapping in the breeze. Drivers cracked whips, and postilions called, "Ho!" In the rear, coaches packed with servants, cooks, musicians, and artists were followed by wagons of furniture, food, wine, and gunpowder. I had my own carriage, with my own servants and footmen and drivers. Moréna sat where the postilion usually stood, and my postilion rode Trojan. Hortense, Marianne, and Venelle traveled inside with me holding baskets of breads and wines and smoked salmon. A chamber pot was stored beneath one seat. I was not unprepared for *this* journey. We slowly rolled northwest to Calais by way of Amiens. The king rode at the head of our cavalcade and did not allow us to stop.

When the sun dipped into the afternoon side of the sky, I opened my carriage door.

"What are you doing?" asked Venelle.

I didn't answer but called to my postilion, "Throw me Trojan's reins and climb onto the carriage."

He tossed me the reins and scrambled up. Hortense cried, "Be careful, you fool!"

"Mind the door." I stepped out, securing one foot in Trojan's stirrup. "Easy, boy." Holding the pommel tight, I threw my other leg over the saddle. I straddled it perfectly, and my skirts fell neatly into place. I kicked Trojan into a trot.

Gendarmes and musketeers gaped as I passed, and every carriage rang out with cries of shock. "It's that Mancini girl!"

I approached the musketeers that flanked King Louis and slowed to match their stride. One of them was Philippe, who laughed when he saw me.

"Lovely day for a war, Your Majesty," I said.

King Louis never looked more surprised. "You're either wild or mad."

Trojan pranced beneath me, tossing his head, itching for a run. I laughed. "Those meadows are begging to be ridden."

He heeled his horse and took off, breaking through the musketeers. Trojan galloped after him through the fields. Philippe and three other musketeers followed. We scaled outcropping rocks and a winding stream and left the train inching slowly behind. At the top of a hill King Louis stopped, signaling for the guards to keep a good distance. I pulled Trojan to a halt beside the king, and we looked back at the court, now just a thin line in the distance. He jumped off his horse and helped me dismount. We embraced between the horses, kissing until I wanted to fall into the tall grass and have our fill of one another.

"One day," murmured King Louis, "I want to be alone with you."

"That sounds dangerous."

He laughed. We led our horses down the other side of the hill.

"If you must go near the fighting, I want to be with you," I said.

"No. I must go to Mardyck, where Turenne has his headquarters. It is too close to the front."

"Then it is too close for you to go!" I dropped his hand.

He grabbed it again. "Don't be angry."

"You mistake fear for anger."

He brought my hand to his lips and kissed it gently. "I will be careful."

I slipped my hand into my hanging pocket and brought out the white silk pouch hanging from a long silver chain. This time, it contained more than merely blessed rue. It held vervain, the Heavenly Letter on a miniature fold of parchment, and a cross of brown agate. "Wear this around your neck."

He looked skeptical.

"Keep it by your heart. It will bring you back safely to me. Please."

He let me loop it over his head and unbutton his doublet enough to tuck it under his shirt. I stroked his chest. His breathing grew heavy, and he pulled me close. I planted one kiss in the hollow between his collarbones and slowly buttoned his doublet, wishing I could tear the thing to shreds and kiss every inch of him. He propped his chin on the top of my head, and I rested my ear over the sound of his heart.

"Return to me," I whispered. "If this heart stops, *my* life will end."

Philippe interrupted. "Your Majesty," he called, pointing to the cavalcade. It had come around the hill by a bend in the road. "We must keep near the others."

We returned to the train, and I'd extracted no promise from my king.

"You should hear how people talk when you break free riding with the king!" Cardinal Mazarin paced the tiny chamber allotted to my sisters and me in his Calais lodgings.

"I do hear. I don't care."

Hortense pretended to be asleep on the bed. Marianne snored in earnest.

"Don't care that they call you a wild pagan? That you ride like a man? That they can't see what the king sees in you?"

"Jealous spite."

"Their spite will reach his ears and turn his mind against you." He crossed his arms. "I expected decorum. Olympia never behaved thus."

"We never get time alone."

He stepped to me. "So you stole some. What did you learn in your time *alone*?"

"We discuss books and poetry."

"Has he mentioned Naples? Cromwell's troops?"

It was the first time my uncle had questioned me on this score in weeks. Praise heaven I could answer honestly. "No."

He flung his hands out. "Do you want to be queen or don't you?"

His words froze me.

"Find out what he thinks, girl. See if he makes the connection between victory and his ability to choose a wife. If he doesn't, plant the seed." I nodded, and he went on. "Most importantly, make him promise to capture and execute Condé!" He bid me good night so fast, with little more than a wave, that he didn't notice my shock.

Hortense sat up. "Did he say you might be *queen*?"

"Never repeat that."

"The queen mother will tear out her hair."

"Swear, Hortense!"

"You better follow Uncle's advice."

"What do you mean?" I threw open a trunk, hauled out a feather mattress, and tossed it on the floor.

"Know the king's mind and have him firmly in hand. Be certain of his love, or his mother will take you down."

I snatched her pillow.

"Do you want to be his queen?"

I collapsed on my makeshift bed. "All I know is—" I couldn't say it. *I love him.*

As part of the cardinal's household, we didn't have to wait upon the queen mother. But the next morning she summoned us to her lodging anyway. My sisters and I dressed each other quickly. We met Olympia in the queen mother's antechamber.

"There is the wild Mancini," Olympia said quietly. "Step aside and let me handle the king without *scandalizing* the family."

"He is nothing but a prize to you," I said.

She tried to look defiant. "The court is starting to say . . . that you've supplanted me. Did Mazarin promise to make you queen?"

I gasped. A handful of ladies looked our way. Hortense started talking loudly to Marianne to obscure our conversation.

"He tried that with me," Olympia muttered. "Mazarin will use your own heart against you."

I tried to look amused. "I have no doubt he would have elevated you to queen if he could have. But there is a difference. The king never loved you."

She bit her lip. "I need royal favor for my son's benefit."

I put my hands on her shoulders. "You would have everlasting favor if I were queen. For once, give *me* a chance."

Madame de Motteville opened the doors to the queen's chambers, and

Olympia moved to the head of the line of ladies. Olympia said nothing as we dressed the queen and said nothing at mass. She said nothing as we served the queen's dinner and nothing when we played cards. Finally, as the hour we anticipated news about the war approached, Olympia seemed to come to a decision.

She yawned loudly and stretched her arms. "Our queen must be bored to tears!"

The queen mother smiled indulgently.

Olympia grabbed a lute. "My sister must regale us." She handed it to me. "You're the only one here with any talent, Marie. Won't you play?"

I took it with a grateful smile. She nodded and walked away. I strummed chords and hummed tunes to old Italian lullabies. The chamber fell quiet except for my music and the other ladies humming along. Thus, when King Louis crept in, I held the floor. When my song ended, he was first to applaud.

The queen mother opened her arms to receive his kiss. "What news?"

"Cromwell's men joined General Turenne's at Mardyck, six thousand strong. Provisions are in. They move toward Dunkirk to engage within days. I leave for Mardyck before dawn."

The queen mother nodded. "We will be ready."

"No," said King Louis. "Your household will stay at Calais."

She frowned. "You will take your physicians and best musketeers?"

"Of course." He glanced at me. I refused to meet his eye.

The queen mother gave a short nod. "I expect regular dispatches."

He kissed her again. "As you wish."

We played cards until Monsieur and King Louis started discussing ammunition. That's when I ushered my sisters back to the cardinal's lodging on the northern reaches of Calais.

In the hall, maps and charts and muster rolls were spread across half a dozen tables. Messengers came and went constantly. My uncle's command center. "Stay out of the way," he barked when he saw us.

I leaned to Moréna. "Order my equerry to ready Trojan before dawn. I will sleep in my black riding jacket tonight."

"You can't go to Mardyck," said Moréna, for once reserved.

"Nothing in heaven or on earth will stop me from going to Mardyck."

CHAPTER 19

"Nothing in heaven or on earth will induce me to let you come to Mardyck." King Louis dismounted his horse right in front of his cavalrymen and moved toward me in the predawn glow. I'd ridden Trojan from the stables into the ranks before the first trumpet blare.

My feet never touched the ground. His arms encircled my waist, and he tossed me over his armor-plated shoulder. Philippe watched helplessly from the ranks of musketeers. The king marched inside and deposited me on the reception hall floor, skirts in disarray around my ears. I pushed them down, glared, and scrambled to my feet.

He dragged me through the command center, where two sleepy footmen jerked to attention. He kicked open the door to my bedchamber. "Out!" he commanded. In a flurry of sheets and robes, Madame Venelle, Hortense, and Marianne scurried away.

King Louis slammed the door and threw me on a bed. "Stay."

I jumped up. "No!"

He pushed me down, pinned my wrists by my ears. "There is no place to quarter a woman at the front. I share a bunk with General Turenne, you understand?"

"I cannot let you go alone." I fought it, but tears filled my eyes.

"I have men with *muskets*."

I stretched to kiss his chin.

He shook his head. "I—I wouldn't be able to focus, let alone command. I can hardly breathe around you—" He kissed me with a hot fury then, hungry, angry, demanding. He buried his face in my chest. Shameless, I wrapped my legs around him, pulling him closer, anything to keep him, to trap him. But he pulled away. My skirts fell back, and he kissed the inside of my knee.

It felt like fire. "Damn that armor."

He laughed quietly, covering my knee with his hand. Trumpets sounded outside. The cardinal pounded on the door. "Majesty!"

I reached for the handle of the king's saber and pulled it out. I lifted the blade to his neck. He studied me cautiously but didn't stop me. I grasped one of his curly locks and cut it off.

He pointed to the gap between his armor and his neck. My silver chain. "Your amulet goes with me."

Pounding sounded at the door again. "Majesty!"

He rose, sheathed his saber. I stood, but he pushed through the door.

The cardinal looked at my riding habit and shook his head. I hid the lock of hair in my hanging pocket. The trumpets blared, and kettledrums began a steady roll. I flew to the window in time to watch the king mount his horse. He charged to the head of a long line of cavalry, thrusting his arm in the air, signaling the move forward. The thunder of a thousand horses and battle wagons and foot soldiers shook the ground, and my only love disappeared in dust on the horizon.

Mazarin muttered behind me, "Did you convince him to execute Condé?"

Cold-blooded execution seemed a breach of war protocol. Worse than heralding Condé's downfall with witchcraft? "King Louis will do what is right."

Mazarin grabbed the front of my neck, turned me, and pinned me against the casement. "I wanted him to leave intent on spilling Condé's blood. Instead you sent him off with poetry in his head and lust coursing through his veins."

The image of my uncle slapping Olympia in the carriage flashed through my mind. I reacted. I dug into his hand with my nails. I clawed until my fingertips grew slippery with blood. He finally released me, staring at his hand in disbelief.

"He'll do what I ask simply out of love. You should try that sometime."

He covered his wounds with his other hand. "He wouldn't even stay in Calais for you. You overestimate yourself, and you underestimate him."

"I'm going to handle the king *my* way."

He assumed a snide expression. "And your crown?"

I turned back to the window. He left without another word.

Skirts rustled behind me. It was Hortense. "I hope Louis gets Condé this summer, or the cardinal will target *you* next."

"I hope we get Condé for entirely different reasons." I took out the king's lock and bundled it with a ribbon from my own hair. "If Condé escapes, the cardinal will expect me to convince King Louis of the Naples Plan."

"Stay in this château and stay out of the way," Cardinal Mazarin warned us sternly the next morning. "Step one foot outside and you are at the mercy of soldiers."

Venelle, Hortense, Marianne, and I sat in chairs by the front door in the hall and spent our days watching the comings and goings of the cavalry leader, the head of the Cardinal's Guards, and Charles, comte D'Artagnan, reporting for the King's Musketeers. Everyone marched right past us to the command center and reported to my uncle. It infuriated me to think they brought intelligence King Louis might need, yet he was risking his life at the front.

Dining held no ceremony. We took meals in the hall, and the men ate rations in their camps. Tents, shanties, cook wagons, and campfires covered the meadows. Captains drilled regiments in the fields. Men and goods flowed constantly to the front and back. Yet I could not go.

Days turned into weeks. I lived for dispatches. Messengers came flying in on horseback several times a day. They marched inside shouting updates, waving sealed missives in the air. Saying they'd constructed roads to travel the sodden landscape. Saying the stench of last year's bodies rotting in shallow graves permeated everything. Saying the wet ocean air spoiled the soldiers' biscuits. Saying, finally, the Spanish had arrived outside Dunkirk earlier than expected, and Turenne attacked earlier than planned.

I nervously watched my uncle's expression. He pointed to the great map on his table. "If Turenne fails to capture Dunkirk, this fortress in a line of fortresses, he will be left surrounded by the enemy." He pushed a row of tiny model ships close to the coast. "Cromwell's fleet will create a blockade." And that afternoon we heard cannon fire from the fleet echoing down the coast.

At last a messenger rode in, kicking up gravel, running inside before that gravel returned to the ground. "Turenne and Cromwell's forces whipped the Spaniards on the dunes! Dunkirk will be ours."

Mazarin jumped up. "And Condé?"

"On the run!"

I couldn't look at Mazarin. Hortense spoke for me. "When will the king return?"

The messenger shrugged. "After he addresses the troops. A day. Maybe two."

But two days later the same messenger came with a different dispatch. "The king has a fever."

"How bad?" asked Hortense as I clutched my stomach.

"High, and getting higher," said the messenger.

I paced. "What have they done for the king? Uncle, demand a report."

The next day's report said they'd bled my poor king to no avail. The queen mother summoned my sisters and me to join her at mass. All of Calais prayed for the king, and orders went out for Paris churches to expose the Holy Sacrament. Monsieur stayed in his chambers, and a line of courtiers formed outside his door, lips full of flattery for the man who might inherit France.

I sat by the door, weeping, waiting for dispatches. Each day it was the same. *Fever.*

When one messenger refused to speak, I ripped the dispatch from his hands and read it as I ran to the cardinal. "His body is bloated and he has lost consciousness." My voice cracked. "He is near death. Saddle Trojan! I am taking a concoction of senna to the king."

My uncle grabbed the red zucchetto from his head and hurled it on the table. "If you set one foot outside of this château, my men will shoot you on sight."

"If the king dies, I will run straight into your firing squad. At least send a local physician who might be more familiar with this ailment."

He did it to placate me.

I refused supper. I refused to change my gown. I refused to go to bed. I kept to my chair by the open front door and waited, praying over the king's lock of hair.

"Take a bath and eat a proper meal," said Hortense. "At least dry your tears. You're scaring Marianne."

"Tell her a bedtime story. Tell her there was once a girl who loved a king so much she vowed not to sleep until his health was restored."

"You're mad."

In the midst of many tears, I started to feel mad. The messengers all stared at me. I knew everyone was talking about the girl who wouldn't stop crying for the king.

At long last, on the tenth day, a messenger appeared in the distance, waving his dispatch. He dropped it in my hands on the threshold.

"His fever broke!" I ran to the cardinal, waving the report like a woman crazed. "Long live the king!" And I collapsed on the floor in a heap.

CHAPTER 20

No man was ever wise by chance.

— LUCIUS ANNAEUS SENECA

I slept for twenty-four hours straight. When they finally brought the king in on a litter, I had bathed and eaten and sprinkled his bed with rosewater. His men moved around the room, setting up tables of medicines, hanging the royal tapestries, laying out reports for him to read. I knelt by his bed.

When the room quieted, I felt his hand gently stroking my hair. "They tell me you've done nothing but cry."

"I prayed," I said. "That if you died I would follow you."

"I prayed that if I lived, I might never leave your side again."

"And here you are." I kissed his hand.

"Here we are," he said.

There I remained while the queen mother and her ladies, Monsieur and Mademoiselle, my sisters, my brother and his officers, and all the courtiers streamed in to pay their respects to the king and kiss his ring.

The king was weak and thin and had no appetite. I sat by the window and played my guitar and hummed and let him drift off. After the first week he became more alert. By the second week he was humming along. By the third week he was sitting up, gesturing for me to sit by him on the bed.

In the fourth week, Mazarin walked in while King Louis and I were both sitting in his bed, singing and playing my guitar. Mazarin frowned. "Turenne is advancing on Furnes, then Dixmude. By the grace of God, we might even force Gravelines to surrender before the season is finished. But Condé escaped."

I had pondered this issue. The downfall of Condé was essential. Not for Mazarin but for peace, for the king's security, for the French people. "It would be easer to defeat the Spanish if you cut off Condé's access to fresh soldiers from Naples."

"Could that be done?" King Louis asked Mazarin.

Mazarin didn't hesitate. "It will depend on cooperation from Savoy." I didn't like his expression.

The king nodded. "Do whatever it takes. Soon I will be strong enough to ride out with Turenne."

"No," said Mazarin. "You're traveling south to Fontainebleau by way of Compiègne."

The king and I looked at each other. So long as we were together, I didn't care where we went. If away from Mazarin's watchful eye, all the better.

We bypassed Paris on the slow journey to Fontainebleau, where the king summoned me to his chambers every day. "No troops. No siege. No battle. Marie, I will grow thoroughly bored this summer," he grumbled.

I swatted him. "I don't feel sorry for you. Pity me. I have the greater task. More difficult than distinguishing oneself in battle, more arduous than defeating boredom . . . I shall improve your mind."

The king laughed, accepting my challenge affably.

Courtiers stepped aside when they saw me coming with my guitar and my stack of books. I could almost hear their thoughts. *Why in the world does King Louis prefer her?*

The queen mother came straight from hearing mass one morning. "You're looking better by the day, my son." She gave me a grateful smile. "Mademoiselle Mancini, I owe this to you."

Thus I basked in royal favor all around.

When King Louis was at last dressed and strong enough to venture out, it was to my chambers that he came. I showed him history books he'd never heard of, and we covered politics he quickly grasped. He wouldn't touch a pamphlet on astrology but spent hours over a book by Seneca. We talked of what he might do with his power, of building hospitals for the poor, opening a new university, building bridges, and setting up grain stores for times of famine.

I summoned Lully, who brought his musicians, and I ordered up a platter of foods to be kept near the king always. King Louis reclined in an armchair, nibbling oranges from Portugal, while my brother and sisters and I danced for him.

Olympia even brought her husband. "You must have been terrified lest he die and all your royal favor evaporate," she muttered, holding her belly. She was with child again.

"*Favor* be damned," I said, pulling her to the center of my chamber, trying to make her dance and laugh. "It's the *royal* I wanted!"

She did laugh, thank goodness. And the king laughed, too.

"We are so merry without the cardinal," she said. "If only there were some way to live independently from him."

I eyed the king, and plans for Philippe's future formed in my mind.

As the king left my chambers that night, he showered me with kisses that suggested he was very much recovered. "Let's ride in the forests tomorrow," he said. "I want to be in the fresh air with you every day."

"You mean you want to go hunting." I tipped my head.

He grinned. "That, too."

I laughed. "How shall I punish you for trying to fool me?"

"The worst penalty would be to leave me."

I stroked his cheek. "Let us ride and hunt, then, for I'll never do that."

He bowed on his way out. "And you must tell me the details of your uncle's Naples Plan."

I closed the door behind him, remembering my uncle's strange expression when King Louis had approved the plan. Mazarin was up to something, and I dreaded what it might be.

CHAPTER 21

Fontainebleau

Autumn 1658

Trojan pranced beneath me, impatient to burst into a canter. "Wait." We held our ground in a game-park clearing in the forest not far from Fontainebleau Palais.

The chief huntsman had taken the king's best bloodhound to locate a red stag, note the size of his antlers, and initiate the hunt. Five pages each held a dozen leashed hounds that bounded over one another, barking, tugging, dripping saliva. Forty carriages lined the dirt avenue, cleared especially for spectators and the hundred or so hunters riding horseback. The queen mother watched from her open *calèche* with a disinterested frown. Hunting was not for her. But every courtier not at the front attended to make today's hunt the spectacle King Louis enjoyed.

Trojan nudged the king's horse in the flank.

"Trojan," I scolded.

King Louis just grinned, excited. He'd regained his healthy glow, praise heaven.

Then we heard it. The huntsman's great horn-call. *The stag is on the move!* The horn-blowers sounded their brass and ran.

The Master of the Hounds cracked his whip, and the pages unleashed the dogs. *"Halali!"* called the Master. *"Halali!"*

The pack went wild, jumping over each other, tails wagging, noses in the air and noses to the ground. They followed the sound of the horns, spreading out to cover more ground. When we heard their baying cries, we knew they had the scent.

King Louis nodded once to me, then dashed off. *"Tayaut!"*

Trojan hardly waited for my heel and tore after him. The carriages, hunters, handlers with extra packs of hounds, grooms, and quartermasters reeled into motion behind. Trojan put distance between us.

Mine was the only steed fast enough to keep pace with the king. We cut through the trails, following the cries of the hounds as they chased the scent through the woods and underbrush. After hard riding for more than a mile, we came to a crossroad, and the king stopped. The hounds had quieted, and he stood in his stirrups, listening.

Trojan circled him as I put my ear to the wind, soon hearing the distant horn-call. "Westward!" I cried, and trotted before the king. He caught up with me at a handler's building. We halted while the grooms there unleashed a fresh pack of hounds. A slew of hunters caught up with us. We heard the horn-call again, and the dogs gave chase. The trail led us to a stream, where the dogs lost the scent by the bridge.

"The stag must have escaped the hunting grounds," said King Louis. "We should wait for the other hounds to bring it back."

"Our quarry is west." Trojan reared up, hoofs pawing the air. *"Tayaut!"* I called, and let Trojan cross the stream with a glorious splash.

The king followed me. "Westward!"

The dogs soon caught the scent and chased it for miles. At last we heard the special horn-call nearby. We cut through the woods, coming to a clearing by another stream. Handlers kept the dogs back with a signal from their whips so we could watch. The stag stood on the opposite bank, panting, lapping the water, something rarely glimpsed on the hunt. We'd run him to the point of exhaustion, too spent to continue the chase. More hunters found us and some of the carriages rumbled over a nearby bridge. The handlers released the hounds and they splashed across the stream, howling and barking and snapping at the stag until it was surrounded. The Master of the Hunt crossed the stream, took hold of the stag's huge antlers and brandished his knife. That's when I closed my eyes. The horn-blowers sounded a magnificent fanfare. The Master opened the animal's belly and threw out the entrails to feed the dogs to the applause of hunters and onlookers alike.

"You prefer the chase to the kill," said the king.

"The chase is where I excel."

King Louis laughed. "But can you beat me back to the palais?"

I didn't bother answering, just gave Trojan the signal and we were on the trail again. I barely heard the king's musketeers cursing and shouting, trying to keep up with us. I willed Trojan on for miles. *Go, my champion, fly!* When I reached the front curving staircase of Fontainebleau, I couldn't stop laughing. I hopped off of Trojan and kissed and hugged his neck as he panted and huffed.

The king's horse scattered gravel beside us, and King Louis dismounted. "Damn, you're good. What will you demand as your prize?"

"Supper and dancing in the Salle de Bal."

The king turned, ready to give the command. Suddenly he looked shocked. "Where are my pages? My heralds? Have we outrun everyone who could take orders?"

"There is only me."

He circled my waist with his arm. "Are you at my command?"

"Anything." I tipped my chin up for a kiss.

He didn't kiss me. "Do you swear?"

I responded without thinking. "Anything."

Just then the musketeers galloped into the courtyard, trumpeters and pages chasing behind. Servants filtered from the palais, and liveried stableboys appeared. I slipped away from the king and ran up the horseshoe staircase, stopping at the top to peek down. King Louis hadn't moved.

Pages and guards rotated around him. Stableboys took our horses. Breathless courtiers caught up to the king and bowed, offering accolades. The Master of the Hunt bent his knee, presenting the stag's great antlers. King Louis stood amid this clamber for his attention, ignoring it, with his eyes on me. I ran inside to dress for supper.

We dined late, dancing to Lully's violins between courses. We sat by the fireplace beneath frescos of ancient mythological scenes and consumed enough wine to embarrass Bacchus himself. The queen mother and her women retired, and we called for still more wine. The courtiers drank until they could no longer dance in time with the music, and watching them caused fits of laughter.

The king leaned from his armchair and muttered into my neck, "Let me come to your bed."

It wasn't what I expected. "*That* is your command?" I thudded my wineglass on the table, angry at how careless he sounded. How could the king respect me and all my future plans if I gave myself to him too easily?

He seemed stunned. "I could never command your favors."

"I've no wish to flop on my back and give you *favors*. I will give myself to you when you have the *right* to command me. When I am your lawful wife and queen."

He stared, dumbfounded. Then he kissed my hand.

I took it back. "Are you too drunk to understand?"

"You know my feelings."

"Lust isn't love." I stood. "You wanted to discuss my uncle's plan? He will march through Savoy to seize Naples and cut Condé's supply of men so Spain will surrender, leaving you the freedom to choose your queen. Make me your choice, then you can make such commands." I rushed from the Salle de Bal upstairs, turning the corner into my bedchamber.

No candles were lit. The windows stood open, letting light from the full moon spill in. "Moréna, where are you?" A shadowy motion caught my attention. She huddled over something. I went to her, peeked over her shoulder, and gasped at the sight on the floor. She had taken my lock of the king's hair, twined it with a darker lock, and splattered it with blood. A dead toad lay beside it, splayed open. Moréna dug into the toad with a knife, ripping and breaking. Finally she held a tiny, bloody bone in the moonlight.

I knew what it was for. "Make no incantations. I want nothing to do with this."

"It's done. Take this, for you are under chase."

"Never." I grabbed my curls. When had she cut my hair? "I've put this practice behind me."

"Touch this bone to the king's skin, and he'll soon become your husband."

"I'll win him by my own merit, not lust or enchantment, and certainly not because you killed some—"

She grabbed my hands and forced the little bone into them. "I said you're under chase—your uncle comes down from the front even now. He'll trap you in his schemes and set *you* up for the kill."

I knew she was right. Mazarin was planning something underhanded. I needed more than the king to shield me. I stared at the bone in my palm. I ran to the window and hurled it with all my might. "It will be the king's choice. Now clean up this mess."

Next morning there was no trace of blood on my floor. No frog, no bones. Moréna drew me a bath, and I combed through my hair until I found one lock snipped close to the scalp. I scowled. She showed no remorse. After the midday meal, a message arrived from King Louis.

His young page entered my antechamber clutching his hands behind his back. "His Majesty requests your attendance at a picnic."

"Requests," I said. "See, Moréna? My way wins respect."

It was exactly what I'd been waiting for. I donned a rose-colored damask riding gown with the overskirt bustled up in back. My liveried page walked before me, and I presented myself in the bright François Gallery.

King Louis was leaning against the carved walnut wainscoting beneath the stucco-framed fresco of the nude goddess Diana. Mademoiselle, her ladies, and my sisters surrounded the king, and courtiers lined the walls. Everyone turned when I entered.

He strode to my side. "Mademoiselle Mancini. At last." He took my hand, kissed it in front of everyone. He whispered, "Forgive me." With a sweep of his hand he called, "Come! Monsieur is hosting a picnic in the forest."

Half the horses stood saddled outside. The king helped me mount Trojan himself. We led the long ride through the dappled autumn light of a forest starting to turn gold and red.

A ruined stone monastery peeked through the trees, and we came to a rocky gorge. Monsieur and his men greeted us. "Welcome to the hermitage of Franchard," he said with a bow and a flourish. As if on cue, Lully put out both hands and signaled twenty-four of his violinists to strike up their melody.

The king helped me dismount. "Let us explore, for we feast at sunset."

Mademoiselle found a bench in the garden arbor. Olympia and my sisters followed Monsieur down a winding path.

King Louis took my hand. "I want to show you something." He led me through the gorge, where giant rocks soared to the sky. "Look." He pointed to one rock in particular that jutted out. It dripped.

"The weeping rock!"

"Commoners believe this water will heal the sick." He opened his mouth and caught a drop.

"Magic?" I caught a drop in my palm.

"It must filter from above." King Louis gazed up the rocky slopes. He took my hand. "Shall we find out?"

I grinned. Together we climbed, one precarious step at a time, to a wide plateau.

I heard Mademoiselle cry out from the hermitage garden, "The king will break his neck!"

"See." He pointed to a pool of water in a pit in the sandstone. "It must filter through the fissures. Now do you think it's magical?"

"We didn't break our necks climbing up, did we?"

Laughing, he grasped my hands and twirled me in tune with the echoing sounds of the violins. "Lully," he called, "bring your violinists to the top! Everyone must dance atop the cliffs so all France might see us."

We heard a confusion of strings and bows, and half the troupe climbed the rocks while the other half serenaded from below. The courtiers huffed and puffed, slowly making their way up. Monsieur, Mademoiselle, and even Olympia with her pregnant belly scaled the cliff and joined us in dancing a branle.

King Louis noticed the setting sun and stopped. "There is more to show you." He pointed to another crop of rocks beyond the timbers. "Come."

We scrambled down, leaving bewildered courtiers. King Louis led me through the woods past strange boulders in the shapes of camels and mushrooms. He showed me caves filled with roosting bats, moss-covered grottos, and tight rock passages that we squeezed through. He pointed beyond a slope of heather where a pond of still water stood. "The Lake of the Fairies."

I ran down through the heather.

"I guess this means you don't want to see the Gorge of the Wolves?" he called, chasing after me.

At the water's edge I peeked down at my reflection. I hardly recognized the nymph smiling back, with springy dark curls tumbling over glowing skin. I scooped up a handful of fairy water and threw it at King Louis.

He splashed me back. I squealed and ran along the bank until I could safely scoop up more, but he grabbed me before I could toss it. He carried me into the heather and we collapsed in a giggling heap. He kissed my wet hands. "I wrote to Mazarin urging him to take Naples. With luck and Savoy's cooperation, we might be victorious next summer. Then I will prove my love with a ring and a crown."

"Do you mean it?"

He grinned. "I appreciate you joining me upon *request* today, but I prefer the right to *command* you into my bed." I slapped his arm, and he laughed. But then he was serious again. "I'd do anything for you, my Marie."

My heart seemed to soar. "There is the matter of my brother to discuss."

Just then Olympia called from the path above. *"Mon dieu!"*

Monsieur panted at her side.

I sat up. "Is something the matter?"

"Yes," she shouted. "I'm starving! You lovebirds need to come back to the hermitage so we can have supper. Right now."

We laughed so hard we clutched our bellies.

We supped under the red and purple sunset, then rode back to the palais in the royal calashes with dozens of torchbearers. We reclined, gazing at the stars. I pointed to the watery part of the sky. "Aquarius is bright because we're under a new moon. This is a time for new beginnings."

Bats ascended from their caves in swarms, leathery wings dark against the moonless constellations.

"Do you believe the stars predict our fate?"

If the stars are right about me, I shouldn't be here with you. "My father did."

"I don't," said King Louis firmly.

"I hope you are right," I replied.

CHAPTER 22

October 1658

"You wanted to see me?" I clasped my hands behind my back as I stood before the vast table in my uncle's private study at Palais Mazarin. He'd just returned from Calais. The king and I had just returned from Fontainebleau on horseback, to the general rejoicings of the Parisians. I still had flower petals they'd thrown from their windows stuck in my hair.

He shuffled papers, dipped quill into ink, and signed something before speaking. "You were busy in my absence." He looked up. "Interesting that your brother Philippe should be appointed captain of the King's Company of Musketeers while I was not near enough to prevent it."

"Philippe has your old spy Charles, comte D'Artagnan, as his first lieutenant should he need assistance." I'd suggested King Louis arrange it this way to prevent Mazarin from revoking it. "Do you think Philippe incapable?"

He glowered. "I know *you* are not trustworthy."

"The king made up his mind without my influence," I lied.

He pounded the table. "You elevated your brother so you would have someone besides me to depend on. What's next? Will you have the king make him duc de Nevers?"

That was indeed the title I had in mind. I shuddered.

"I wanted to believe you would carry out the plans I set into motion when I die."

"Believe it. I want the king to be great, too." My tone didn't sound convincing. Pretending we had the same definition of "great" had grown too difficult.

He slumped in his armchair. "The king is more taken with you than ever. I take it you haven't spread your legs for him yet?"

I frowned. I would not answer that.

"Do not capitulate." He thumped the table again. "Damn Condé. He charged right through the center of our entrenchments to relieve Dunkirk. We surrounded him, even killed the horse underneath him. But his captain put him on his own horse and sacrificed himself while Condé made his getaway under a shower of musket fire. The bastard."

"Spain will concede when they are unable to conscript soldiers through Naples."

"Oliver Cromwell is dead. Alliances may shift."

"Help Charles the Second reclaim England, then. Charles will keep England faithful to France, especially if you marry him to Hortense." I held my breath.

He waved the idea off as if swatting a fly. "Spain could rebuild their army through Savoy if we don't get there first. I need you to be brave now. Brave as one of our men in battle."

I didn't like the sound of that at all.

"For years Savoy," he said, pointing between France and Modena on the map on his table, "has claimed neutrality. The queen regent, Christine of France, a daughter of Henry the Fourth, has refused to help France. Disloyal snit. The only way she'll even meet with me is if I agree to marry her daughter to King Louis."

"No." I tamped down my panic. "I cooperated. King Louis agreed to the Naples Plan because I pushed it. You said I could be queen."

"Did you forget that Savoy's cooperation was part of the Naples Plan?"

"What is my role in this?"

"Princess Margherita is an ugly little thing. King Louis will meet her." He curled the edge of his mustache. "You must ensure he doesn't like her."

"You expect Savoy to cooperate and grant safe passage for French troops after King Louis *rejects* her?"

"I will seal the alliance. Margherita will be relieved if you do your job right."

"The Savoyard court will think I'm some all-powerful, shrewish *maîtresse-en-titre*."

"Consider this an opportunity to prove your loyalty to me and keep your king." He paused. "Olympia is with child again. Will you force me to use Hortense in your place?"

Not my sweet little sister. I shook my head, stuck obeying the cardinal's orders. Again.

He stacked papers and took quill in hand. "My household follows the king's court south within the week."

"The queen mother's household isn't going? What excuse do I have to travel south?"

"Figure it out."

The next morning, I didn't attend the queen mother's toilette. I stayed abed, sick in mind if not in body, and waited. It didn't take long for King Louis to visit. "What's wrong?"

"You know perfectly well." I reclined on ten feather pillows in a red silk undress gown clasped up the front with rubies.

"Your uncle told you about Savoy."

I clutched the embroidered coverlets.

He saw my frown and slumped. "No matter who I wed, you know you will always rule my heart."

"How can you say that when you want to marry *me*? I won't be your whore."

King Louis rubbed his face with his hands. "My family expects me to take a wife of royal blood. Our position in Europe is insecure. Royal marriage is a political alliance."

I closed my eyes. "We should have discussed these things before."

"You're right. I just couldn't face it." He sighed. "Why can't I have a wife to secure alliances and provide heirs and keep you by my side?"

I sat up. "You swore never to command my heart, and my heart will not share you."

"Think how lonely a political marriage will be for me. Say you won't leave me."

"You are leaving to meet her. Who knows how long you'll be gone? Lyon is a long way south." I cringed. Hinting and fishing was more underhanded than outright lying and cheating.

"I will beg my mother to go so you have an excuse to travel with her household." He took my hand. "You'll come, won't you?"

I had done it again. *Damn my uncle.* "As you wish."

Days later, the entire royal court stood in Notre Dame Cathedral listening to mass, listening to the echoes of the organ, listening to boyish Latin voices rise like the song of angels in four-part harmony, and listening to prayers for the marriage of King Louis and Princess Margherita of Savoy. Anyone not listening gossiped about the marriage behind feathered caps or fluttering fans. A sparrow soared through the nave between the arches of the aisles. We set out from Notre Dame. Outside the birds flew south, the same direction our train traveled, one rumbling coach after another.

The blue cornflower petals the commoners had thrown days earlier to greet the king had shriveled on the paving stones. Now the Parisians threw a shower of sunflower petals. Even with standards, guards, drums, and the fanfare of trumpets in our procession, the people only had eyes for King Louis. His white horse draped in red velvet, his hat topped with a red plume, his head held high, they cheered at the sight of him. They never looked at me, riding horseback close behind him, and they didn't throw mud at the cardinal's carriage. They waved banners and hoisted children upon their shoulders, shouting, "Long live the king!" and "Bring us a queen!" Even they expected a queen of royal blood.

CHAPTER 23

The King, as if inspired by this new devotion to Mademoiselle Marie de Mancini, was always in the best humor—indeed quite gay.

—MADEMOISELLE DE MONTPENSIER'S MEMOIRS

We stopped in a town well past Fontainebleau. We endured the usual welcome harangue from city officials. They thanked the royals for the honor of the visit, then begged us to make ourselves at home.

In the morning, the king's page found me bundled together with my sisters in some drafty room in some crumbling castle. "The king requests Trojan made ready, that you might ride with him again today."

Hortense buried herself deeper under our covers. "But it's raining."

I tossed the covers aside. "Then I shall wear a hat."

King Louis and I rode beyond the hearing of the queen mother's ladies, who had quickly given up riding in the rain and retreated to the carriages. They stretched from the windows, straining to hear our conversation. In a moment of downpour, King Louis took off his wide-brimmed hat and reached between our horses as if he intended to shelter me.

I steered Trojan away a pace. "Sire, do you fear I will melt?"

"I don't want you to take a chill," he said sheepishly, replacing his hat. "Don't be indignant. I forbid you to be indignant."

"Just how do you intend to control my emotions?" I asked, laughing.

He pointed to a distant hill. "I will race you."

I kicked Trojan into a gallop and reached the top of the hill just ahead of him.

He beamed. "I knew you couldn't be indignant if you could beat me soundly."

But he wouldn't be able to mend my heartbreak if I lost him.

At Dijon, city officials gave the keys of the city to King Louis. Courtiers scattered in sumptuous houses throughout, and I was delighted to be assigned lodgings near the king's. The cardinal stopped to inspect our chambers while servants bustled about hanging our tapestries and setting up our furniture.

He swept from room to room, checking everything. "We will be here a fortnight while the assembly ratifies taxes for the king's exchequer. Where is Venelle's room?"

I pointed. "Just a chamber away." Had he assigned her to spy on us?

As he left, I grabbed his arm. "Have you received any messengers from Spain?"

"You will be the first to know." He eyed my hand on his arm.

I removed it. "Conceal nothing from me."

"Look to your affairs and leave me to mine. I must have these Burgundy Estates vote a tax of two million livres."

"That is an outrageous sum!" *He doesn't need it.* I thought of the huge chests of gold at the Château de Vincennes.

Mazarin didn't respond, and I fought the urge to argue.

"Oh, Hortense," I said, fluffing my curls a week later. I glanced in the looking-glass that Moréna held aloft. "I wish we could journey all the time."

She laughed. "Is the king hosting another collation tonight?"

"As he will every night here at Dijon." He spoke to almost none but me, as if I were the only person at the table, in the ballrooms, or at cards.

"What on earth do you talk about for hours on end?"

"The upcoming *lit de justice.* He's outraged that the Parlement here in Burgundy resist coming together." We took pains to avoid any mention of the proposed marriage. I didn't push, and he seemed grateful.

"He hasn't been to the queen mother's table even once. She'll hold it against you."

I dabbed perfume on my wrists. "We visit her every morning after mass, and the king takes me to her rooms to say good night before he walks me home. She's so complimentary. Praising my clothes or my hair, giving me little trinkets."

"That is because she doesn't know your plans."

I tried not to look nervous. "Perhaps she will accept me if she knows the king loves me."

She shrugged. "Olympia sent word that she is returning to Paris instead of continuing to Lyon. Pregnancy makes her unwell. And jealous, I think."

"Olympia will benefit if I prevail."

Hortense sighed. "I hope you become queen just so I don't have to wed that wretched Armand de la Meilleraye!"

The Parlement chamber at Dijon was a miniature of the one in Paris. Magistrates in red robes sat in a square against a backdrop of blue, dotted with gold *fleur-de-lis*. I stood well outside the square with a handful of the queen mother's ladies, watching the king sit tall in his place of honor. The president of the *lit de justice* gave a polite, firm speech suggesting Burgundy was too poor and unprotected to pay for the ruinous war and overgrown government. The cardinal looked stunned. They voted merely three hundred thousand *livres* and concluded the session. The king seemed at a loss for words. The cardinal . . . could do nothing. I grinned. I might not be a bewigged parliamentarian but I, too, intended to show Mazarin the limits of his power.

We followed the River Saône through the countryside, finally crossing it onto a peninsula, the heart of Lyon. To the right ran the River Rhône, and beyond its banks rose a hill with monasteries and the Archbishop's Palais. To our left beyond the Saône, the land was dotted with silk factories and merchants that made the city wealthy. Windows started opening everywhere. People leaned out, waving colorful silk scarves, cheering for the king and his supposed marriage. As the king and I approached the Cathédrale Saint-Jean-Baptiste in the city, the Cardinal's Guards galloped between us. They surrounded me.

"What is this?" called the king.

"Cardinal's orders," barked a guard. "Mademoiselle Mancini must return to her carriage and wait until he assigns quarters."

The guards made Trojan nervous. I let him buck and rear, but they wouldn't back down. Keeping a tight ring, they ushered me toward my carriage. "Philippe," I called to my brother on the far side of the King's Musketeers.

Philippe looked astounded, glancing left and right for some means to help me. But he couldn't break ranks. The procession forced him and the king to move forward. The archbishop arrived, and I lost sight of the king as he helped his mother from her carriage for presentation. The counts of St. John began the formal welcoming harangue.

As I climbed into my carriage, Marianne said, "Flames and fury, are they starting those eternal speeches again?"

I didn't bother answering. After an age, the long train of carriages started breaking up and moving. I hung out the window. The king and queen were headed to the hill across the Rhône, and we were heading deeper into the city. In the opposite direction!

In the Place de Belle Cœur a noble family welcomed us. Silk adorned every wall and window and bed. The cardinal came, as usual, sweeping our temporary chambers, making his inspections.

"Must we stay here?" I asked my uncle, careful to keep the edge out of my voice. "There is room at the Archbishop's Palais, and it's closer to the king's quarters."

He pointed at me. "The Archbishop's Palais is for me and the Savoyard party."

"You've arranged for Margherita to be closer to the king? I don't understand."

"This must start well. Don't make a fuss. They will be here in a few days. You will not go to the fields with the court to meet them."

"That's unfair. What news from the Spanish king? Tell me you've had a message."

"No fuss!" he yelled, and he left in a huff.

CHAPTER 24

I did not fuss when we missed that night's dinner banquet. I did not fuss at having no place in the next day's ceremonious parade. I did not even fuss when the king was surrounded by the officials of Lyon on the third evening's ball.

But on the fourth day, Moréna announced, "The royal households are riding outside the city to greet Princess Margherita."

"Have Trojan saddled." I pinned on a cape.

"You can't ride through the city alone," she cried.

"I won't make it in time if I don't." I rode Trojan fast through the streets, over the Rhône to my uncle's quarters at the Archbishop's Palais.

"I'm coming with you," I said to him, breathless.

A footman helped him into his carriage. "You are staying put."

"You want me to fail," I cried. "Since the moment we left Paris, you have announced this marriage publicly."

Trojan's ears flattened as Mazarin signaled to his tallest footman. The man yanked me from my horse and pushed me into the carriage. My loyal steed reared and kicked the equerries that rushed to surround him.

My uncle slammed the door. "The Savoy marriage is a ploy to force Spain into peace."

"It's a ploy to get rid of *me* so you can have the king's ear to yourself again."

He stood over me. In a frenzy of blows, he brought his fist down on my ribs, my back, my side. I screamed, kicked him, and yanked the door handle. It didn't budge. The guard on the other side held it fast. Trojan whinnied outside. The cardinal grabbed my hair in fistfuls by my ears and pulled.

A fury like I'd never known came over me. *I will let him kill me before I let him see my fear.* I wanted to open his throat with my teeth. Instead I grabbed his ermine cappa magna, pulled him close, and spat in his face.

He released my hair. "You can thank your saints or your stars or whatever it is you believe in that I haven't marred your face or made you bald. I won't show the same grace next time."

I felt no pain. My entire body shook with rage. I put my hand out, pointing at his legs, and whispered, "As you betray me, so shall your body wither and your bones ache."

And that old expression, that vague sense of fear, reemerged. Shadows of it played on his features. Then it disappeared. "Go back to the Place de Belle Cœur and await the morrow. You will receive a summons to a reception here at the Archbishop's Palais." He pounded the wall of the carriage, and the door finally opened. "When I send for you, I will put you before the king. Until then, stay out of sight."

I could hardly mount Trojan for the violent trembling in my limbs. I scrambled up the saddle in a clumsy disarray of skirts and cape. We rode hard through Lyon, getting lost in the winding streets of the city, skirts, cape, and mane flapping wildly. I ignored the strange looks that the flower sellers on the streets shot me. When a shabby man leapt from the gutters trying to grab my reins, Trojan kicked until the man fell back. I rode without fear. I no longer feared the convent. My uncle could banish me, marry me off, he might even kill me. But I refused to fear him. I rode until my limbs stopped shaking, and found myself in a small square. Pigeons scattered, and I halted, searching the skyline for the hill. I kicked Trojan into a gallop in its direction. It took me another half hour to find my way through the city, but I finally arrived at my destination, panting and sore. Twilight began to fall on the royal quarters.

I marched inside, upstairs, and demanded to see Mademoiselle de Montpensier.

"She won't see you," said a footman.

But she entered the antechamber at that moment, riding hat in hand. She greeted me with her usual tall, graceful poise. "I'm just back from the queen mother's chambers. We escorted Princess Margherita into the city. The entire Savoyard party is here except the duc. He won't enter until we grant his branch of the family precedence over ours. Can you believe his audacity?"

"I didn't see the king's carriage outside."

"He is taking the princess to the Archbishop's Palais."

"Do you think he liked her well enough to . . . marry?" I asked, unable to summon the wit to construct something clever.

"He complimented her eyes, and they conversed a great deal." She studied me. "But there is little chance of a marriage happening now. The cardinal just rushed into the queen mother's rooms with a remarkable message from the Spanish king."

Spain. My uncle had been telling the truth! "He surrendered?"

She paused. "Not exactly, but he did offer peace as part of a marriage agreement between King Louis and his daughter, the Infanta Maria-Thérèsa."

Another marriage? I stood speechless.

Mademoiselle stepped to me. "You will have to give up this pursuit sometime. The king must marry the daughter of some great country for the sake of his kingdom." I stared, and she flung out her hands. "I cannot make you understand how royals think."

"Try," I said. "Explain my obstacles."

"We trace our noble heritage back hundreds of years. We have generations of royal blood, descendants of Saint Louis himself."

"Mancini is one of the oldest noble families of Rome. How conveniently you forget that your family tree is littered with two Medici women, decidedly nonroyal Italians raised to queenship."

She sighed. "There is a difference between you Italians and us French. Louis was raised with a sense of duty. We submit to our parents as royals are expected to do. King Louis won't act against his mother's wishes regarding marriage."

"The queen mother adores me."

She shook her head. Of all people, Mademoiselle understood matters of precedence best.

Everything will depend on King Louis alone. "Forgive my outburst." I curtsied deep and stepped to go, but she grabbed my arm.

"Tell me something in return. Would Cardinal Mazarin approve my marrying Monsieur?"

"You killed my oldest brother the day you fired cannons from the Bastille." I slipped from her grasp. "His Eminence says you also killed any chance he'd let you marry *anyone*."

I left her standing agape, relieved that she no longer aimed to wed King Louis. The downstairs hall of the abbey where the royals were housed seemed sparse. Bare. They must have sent their wagons of royal furniture to the Archbishop's Palais to impress Princess Margherita. Part of the farce.

I recognized one of the king's guards standing sentry and went to him. I stared at him as he stared dutifully ahead. "Admit me to the king's chamber."

He folded. "That I can't do."

I whispered, "Please."

He turned, walked through the doorway, and gestured to another door.

I pulled out one of my pearl drop earrings and handed it to him. "See to it I get time alone with the king before his men enter behind him."

The guard refused my bribe. "I'll do my best."

The king's bedchamber seemed dim, so I opened the curtains. Soon I heard a brief exchange with the sentry; then King Louis appeared.

He smiled the warmest smile. "Marie."

I ran to embrace him.

He held me close. "Does this mean you'll forgive me if I marry her?"

"The cardinal never intended you to marry Princess Margherita," I said. "Spain sent an emissary with a letter from the Spanish king. Mazarin is coming here to tell you his conditions for peace."

He smiled. "He's surrendered?"

"No. A peace treaty sealed with your marriage to the infanta Maria-Thérèsa. Mazarin flirted with Savoy only to make Spain feel threatened into a peace. Mazarin knew all along we wouldn't get as far as Naples."

He seemed stunned. "That's too simple. There are too many details, too many territories to allocate."

"My uncle *used* you. He's using me in a worse fashion. He staked everything on my ability to separate you from Margherita so *he* wouldn't look underhanded."

"I cannot believe he would put you in such a position."

"*Us.* He counted on your loyalty to get you to play the believable suitor. He sent heralds announcing the Savoy marriage to the four corners of the earth to ensure Spain would hear of it. Now he waits to see if I will become his scapegoat." I took a deep breath. "Now you have an excuse to assert yourself."

He hesitated. "I have no proof."

Proof? I hid my frustration. "Your mother and Mazarin will take drastic measures to show you don't like Margherita. Tomorrow their actions will be your proof."

"You and I are no closer to wedlock if they have yet another match for me."

"Expose them and claim me."

He stooped to kiss me. I enjoyed him for just one moment, then pushed away. "Tomorrow." I opened the door. The sentry nodded. The king's men in the hall were busy comparing the size of their scabbards, and I left unnoticed.

W hen I finally found my quarters in the Place de Belle Cœur, Moréna had a hot bath waiting.

"How did you know?" I asked. She wouldn't answer. I stripped off my chemise. She didn't seem shocked by the red marks on my skin that were turning to bruises. The water smelled of heavenly spices. I sank into it, and the stiffness in my muscles slowly melted.

"Fetch the St. John's wort tincture," I said.

She fished it from my trunk, but hesitated. "This is all you have."

How long had it been since I'd harvested this herb properly under the sun and sign of Leo? If country healers could be condemned as witches for trying to heal the sick with prayers and poultices, inquisitors would find the effectiveness of my herbal tinctures and decoctions suspicious. I couldn't risk making more. "Pour it in."

The oily red mixture swirled around me like blood. Moréna gave me the bottle, and I gulped the last swig.

"Why treat your bruises? Show the king Mazarin's fury."

The king had asked for proof only hours earlier. "What, show the king I am weak and easily battered? Incite pity rather than respect? I need to show the king my strength if I'm to lead him away from Mazarin."

"Your brother can command the King's Musketeers. Seize the cardinal. France would rejoice."

I shot her a warning look. "The *king* loves Mazarin. He must be convinced subtly, and that will take time. But when I'm ready to tell the king what I know, it will shake the very foundations of Paris."

CHAPTER 25

The next morning I endured Moréna's worst-smelling unguent and facial scrub. We perfumed my hair and curled it into puffs above my ears. Moréna laced red ribbons up the back of a rose satin bodice with great paned sleeves that rested off the shoulder. I wrapped a gauzy rose scarf around my shoulders, gathered it in the front, and tacked it into place with a ruby pendant.

Hortense burst in with a summons from our uncle. "The duc de Savoy will arrive today, though he hasn't yet granted precedence. He wants to meet me in particular! They say he's terribly handsome. You're to report to the Archbishop's Palais this afternoon for a private dinner before his reception. May Marianne and I join you?"

I plucked my linen chemise through the panes of my sleeves until they puffed out prettily. "Why not?" Let them watch and learn.

My carriage stopped in front of the Archbishop's Palais at the appointed time. Hortense jumped out. "Are we late?"

As I stepped down I winced at the tenderness over my ribs, where bruises were rapidly healing thanks to my St. John's wort. Yet the reminder of Mazarin's rage made me regret letting my sisters come. I leaned to Venelle. "Keep Marianne and Hortense close."

Mazarin appeared at the door, that snake in cardinal red. "Come." He ignored my sisters and ushered me up the steps. In the hall, Christine of France, duchesse de Savoy, known as Madame Royale, stood to the left with her daughter. Princess Margherita was short, brown, and plain. To the right stood King Louis with his mother and brother.

Cardinal Mazarin should have presented me to the family from Savoy. It would have been the proper thing to do. Instead, he took me straight to the king.

It was the perfect opportunity to take control of the situation, to guide King Louis away from Margherita and make a show of myself. Just as Mazarin wanted.

Instead, I did nothing.

Mazarin cleared his throat. King Louis looked from Mazarin to Margherita, then to me. He seemed to realize what was happening. I saw a flicker of anger. Mazarin actually looked uneasy. Madame Royale and Margherita glanced nervously at each other. Finally, King Louis made the introductions himself. My sisters crept in, and he introduced them, too. We curtsied low, and the Savoy women tried to look indifferent.

The king took my arm. "Let me escort you to the dining hall and show you the archbishop's fine tapestries along the way." We strolled from the room, pretending to study the sumptuous tapestries. It forced Cardinal Mazarin and the queen mother to chat with Madame Royale. Margherita just watched with quiet dignity.

King Louis muttered, "Did he expect you to break all protocol and make a fool of yourself?"

I leaned in. "I told you he wants to blame me for breaking up the marriage."

The Savoy royals sat on one side of the table, and we Mazarinettes sat at the other. Footmen appeared with great platters, and Madame Royale seemed no longer able to stand the silence. "My son the duc so enjoys hunting the stag, he hunts at every opportunity."

Rather than offer an invitation to hunt, King Louis said nothing.

Madame Royale went on. "He is such a devoted son, so dutiful, so loyal. I dote on him. Whenever he asks for a little money, I give it without inquiring what it's for. He's entirely trustworthy."

The cardinal nodded his approval at this example of conformity. King Louis said nothing. The tension thickened.

"He talks constantly of his desire to meet King Louis for advice on how to train his regiment." Madame Royale giggled nervously. "I think perhaps he should marry Mademoiselle de Montpensier."

Monsieur cleared his throat. "Mademoiselle is scrupulous in matters of precedence. She won't be warm if he continues to refuse to give us the *pas*."

Madame Royale tried to wave this off. "My son is exceedingly proud of his royal lineage—"

King Louis interrupted. "The right to decide a French noble marriage lies with me alone." He glanced at Mazarin.

I dared not look at the cardinal, but I'd made note of the king's words. *The decision to marry is his alone.* My first victory.

Madame Royale took a breath to continue her prattling, but her footman hurried in before she could speak. "The duc de Savoy is approaching Lyon," he cried.

She clapped her hands. "Meet him and see for yourself how worthy a young man he is."

King Louis called my brother, who'd been standing sentinel at the doors the entire time with a tense expression. "Double the troop of musketeers. We'll meet him properly outside the city walls."

Within moments we watched the king and Philippe's troops riding down the street. I tried to keep close to Venelle and my sisters, but that didn't stop the cardinal from pulling me aside.

"You were supposed to take over," he hissed, so close that the curl of his mustache scratched my cheek.

And make myself out to be the wicked mistress. "I must have misunderstood."

"Don't let him fall in love with Margherita. You'll lose your chance."

Liar. "Did you have a message from Spain?"

"Yesterday. The Spanish king offered to negotiate a peace treaty."

"Did he place any conditions upon it?" I watched him carefully.

He studied me, choosing his words. "There are a thousand conditions. It will take months to settle."

He is still pretending I could be queen! But King Louis had seen the cardinal's duplicity. I decided to say nothing. Let the blows come from the king at the right time.

149

* * *

Savoyard and French nobles flooded in for the reception, and the Archbishop's Palais became a crush of men and women stepping on each other's skirts and boots. The queen mother and Madame Royal sat upon a dais, and titled families filtered toward them to pay respects. Mademoiselle and Princess Margherita stood behind their chairs, and Hortense and I stood nearby.

Hortense leaned close to speak under the din of chatter. "Why are you letting the cardinal use you? Complain to the king."

"There is no need for tantrums and demands."

"Taking the noble road." Hortense shook her head.

But I knew better. My intent to make the king a great leader might be noble, but I'd resorted to my uncle's own style of cunning and trickery.

We heard the kettledrums and trumpets sounding the return of King Louis. A great excitement washed through the chamber, and everyone turned toward the door. He entered with a handsome man by his side.

My sister gasped. "Is *that* the duc de Savoy?"

The man rushed forward, nudging lords and ladies aside until they parted. He practically ran to the queen mother and made a show of throwing himself at her feet. "My beloved aunt, I am your nephew Charles Emmanuel, duc de Savoy, and your devoted servant."

The queen mother accepted this overfamiliarity with grace. She embraced him, and the anxious court released a collective breath. "You are most welcome, nephew." She allowed him to kiss his mother's hand, then moved him in our direction. "Allow me to present your cousin Mademoiselle de Montpensier."

The duc bowed. "I've been most anxious to meet you and prove my undying devotion to you."

Mademoiselle curtsied. "Your tongue is full of flattery."

"Had I known how pretty you are, I'd have come sooner."

I'd never seen such a flirt. I tried to catch Hortense's eye, but she was engrossed.

Mademoiselle made a little snorting sound and looked away.

So he turned to my sister. He bowed low. "This must be the famous beauty, Mademoiselle Hortense Mancini. I recognize you by your portrait."

Hortense, who had hardly blinked when King Charles asked for her hand in marriage, now did something astonishing. She blushed. Though she had reached marriageable age, it annoyed me to see men flatter her. Was it her beauty or her favor with Mazarin they coveted?

King Louis approached, standing so close we could conceal our clasped hands in the folds of my skirts. I felt myself relax. Together we laughed at the duc's exaggerated bows as he moved from Hortense to greet the others, then made his way back to Hortense again.

"Your cousin is making an excellent show," I said to the king.

"It is indeed all show. He politely told me he is against my marriage to his sister. Apparently he doesn't trust Cardinal Mazarin." King Louis frowned. "Tomorrow is the reception at the Hôtel de Ville. We will confront your uncle when it concludes."

The duc stirred our circle like a cook tending a stewpot, kissing hands and dallying, jumbling us together like so many boiled vegetables. He managed to displace our order of rank until I found myself standing next to Princess Margherita. I caught her glance at King Louis. For a moment she looked embarrassed, but the expression vanished, and she was all dignity again. *She is pretending to be strong.*

I felt sorry for her. "The king is quite charming."

She smiled lightly. "He was yesterday."

I nodded. "It isn't your fault. There is a reason for his change."

"I'm told that reason is you," she said, without a trace of bitterness.

"Think what you will," I whispered. "But know Cardinal Mazarin received a messenger from Spain yesterday bearing an offer of peace attached to a Spanish bride."

She went pale. "It appears your uncle used us both." Margherita straightened her lace cuffs as if it were a matter of course.

I glanced at my uncle, standing across the chamber, watching everything with a sharp eye. "He won't be using *me* again."

CHAPTER 26

It is double pleasure to deceive the deceiver.

—JEAN DE LA FONTAINE's *Fables, II*

M y sisters and I skipped mass the next morn as usual, but Madam Venelle returned with sensational news.

She plopped down on our bed and started counting off on her fingers. "Madame Royale is mad that King Louis paid no attention to Princess Margherita yesterday. The cardinal is beside himself making excuses for the king's behavior. The queen mother made Mademoiselle yield precedence to Princess Margherita this morning. Mademoiselle is upset. Monsieur and the duc are angry at each other because neither will yield precedence, and rather than resolve it in time for tonight's ball, they've both given up the right to dance! Now the *king* is mad at the duc, especially since Lyon has gone to such trouble to host us." She dropped her hand, dazed.

"What a mess," cried Marianne with delight.

"Wait," said Hortense. She turned from the looking-glass holding skirts and petticoats. After talking to the duc all night, she'd been primping all morning. "The duc de Savoy won't dance?"

Hortense's expression made me laugh. "I think someone is in love with the flirt of Savoy."

She shook her head. "I'm determined not to fall in love. I'm at our uncle's mercy." But she went on holding up different gowns, trying to find the most flattering. I'd never seen her do that before.

Moréna coiled a strand of my hair around a curling rod, and I wondered whether our uncle might see Hortense's feelings as an opportunity to salvage the Savoy alliance.

A multitude of French and Savoyard carriages converged outside Lyon's Hôtel de Ville as the clock tower's belfry struck the hour of nine. Torches lit the façade of the city hall building, where great lengths of red silk stretched from the highest windows all the way to the ground. Fireworks burst over the nearby river, lighting the festive entry. Footmen lined the stairway holding more swaths of red silk over our heads, waving them so we entered under ripples of silken red. We passed through the reception hall to the Court of Honor, where lit braziers lined the perimeter. Banners of red silk draped every balcony, column, and banquet table. I spotted the king standing in the center of it all beside Cardinal Mazarin. Both were frowning.

The court seemed all atwitter. Monsieur pouted in one corner. His beribboned gentlemen pranced around him, trying to entertain him, but he just stood with his arms crossed. Mademoiselle stood in another corner, tall, proud, haughty, surrounded by the biggest gossips. The duc de Savoy and his men joked and laughed in another corner.

All three corners ignored the fourth, where Madame Royale stood sulking. The queen mother put an arm around her shoulder. Their ladies in waiting encircled them, waving fans nervously, ignoring poor Princess Margherita, just paces away, placid and dignified as ever. Then the herald announced my sisters and me. Our names echoed through the courtyard. Heads turned. The queen mother pointed a short, chubby finger at me. Madame Royale burst into tears. The ladies surrounding them gasped. They moved aside, shuffling and jostling, until they encircled Princess Margherita. They patted her, made reassuring faces, and muttered in her ear. *They've managed to blame me.*

Trumpets sounded from the balconies, and footmen streamed in carrying great silver trays of lobsters in lemon sauce, roasted duck dressed with foie gras, dishes of fruit confits, pastry pyramids, shanks of beef, towers of pear and apple tartlets, steaming onion and mushroom ragout, and salads with rolls of cheese and prosciutto. The platters went to every table, and the herald announced, "A collation!"

This signaled to the court that we might take a dish, sample from each platter, and eat standing, since we were in the king's presence. But the king swept his arm over the Court of Honor and said, "Let the courts of Savoy and France sit together." Alas, the factions from the four corners broke, migrating toward the food.

Hortense grabbed my arm. "How can I sit near the duc?"

The duc inched near the king. "Act natural," I said, whipping out my fan.

She fanned herself, walking behind me nonchalantly toward the king's table. I nodded to Mademoiselle's ladies as we passed. They averted their eyes. When we neared King Louis, he pulled out a seat for me. Those who'd been pretending to ignore me now pointed and stared. This amused me. I swept up a little dish of escargot and sat, motioning for Hortense to do the same. She flitted from table to chair, eyes on the duc the whole time.

The duc took notice. As we watched, he turned to Mazarin and gestured our way. Our uncle frowned, shook his head. This made the duc de Savoy throw out his hands and talk rapidly. The cardinal spoke back, and suddenly they seemed to be negotiating, or . . . bargaining.

"What do you think they're talking about?" asked Hortense nervously.

"I thought you didn't care."

"Don't tease," she said. "I've never met anyone quite like him."

The cardinal shook his head and cut the air with his hand. A refusal? Then it struck me. The peace treaty not only made the Naples Plan obsolete, we no longer needed an alliance with Savoy. Poor Hortense.

I took tiny tongs and forks from a footman and fished a tiny snail from its tiny shell. "Remember not to fall in love. As you said, we're at our uncle's mercy." *Hopefully not for long.*

The stir Hortense and I created sent the royal factions, with plates full of food, back to their four corners in higher dudgeon than before— Mademoiselle's ladies gossiping and eyeing me, Madame Royale in tears, Monsieur complaining bitterly, and the duc now frowning in a cloud of anger. They spent an hour thus before Lyon's mayor approached King Louis.

"Your Majesty, would you do us the honor of commencing the evening's dancing?" Everyone within earshot hushed, leaning forward in anticipation. Trumpeters in balconies stopped playing. Violinists paused their bows.

The question of precedence had been half solved that morning when the queen mother made Mademoiselle yield to Margherita. Since the purpose of the ball was to honor the newly betrothed Princess Margherita and King Louis, he should open the dance with her. Would he? Mademoiselle and Monsieur stood to attention. Savoy frowned at Monsieur. Madame Royale nudged Princess Margherita forward. The cardinal shot me a nasty look.

King Louis noticed all of this. Exasperated, he grabbed Mademoiselle and pulled her to the floor. Mademoiselle glowed with pride. The king had asserted her precedence. Madame Royale and Savoy glanced at each other in stunned silence. For them, this proved the king had no intention of elevating Margherita to queenship. Song swelled from the balconies.

Every corner watched agape as the king and Mademoiselle danced the hop steps of a passepied in a line down the Court of Honor.

Except Madame Royale. She advanced on the cardinal. "I will not let you make a mockery of the House of Savoy."

He actually glanced at me, a look full of spite. "If King Louis doesn't love your daughter, let's come to some other understanding."

But the duc de Savoy interrupted. "Any arrangement designed by Mazarin benefits Mazarin alone." He led his mother away.

Hortense looked after him, crestfallen.

The dance ended, and Monsieur promptly swept Mademoiselle into the next dance. Without asking, King Louis took my hand and walked me to the dancing floor.

I spoke so only he could hear. "I thought you were going to wait until we talked to the cardinal to get out of this marriage. You just made it clear to the whole court you'll refuse Margherita's hand."

"Good."

"Look at them talk. They blame me."

"I order you to forget it this instant. Let Mazarin salvage the situation while you and I dance until the stars fade into daylight." He twirled me in a circle until my skirts flared out.

I looked up at the night sky and laughed. "As you wish, my king."

The next morning Hortense leapt from our bed far too early and yanked open the drapes.

"Get back to bed!" I pulled a pillow over my face.

"The duc de Savoy is leaving," she cried.

I dragged myself to the window.

There, in full dress, the duc rode his horse in circles around the Place de Belle Cœur. "Farewell, France," he called. "I quit you without the least regret."

Hortense pushed open the window. Cold air gusted into the chamber. The duc raised his hand to his lips and blew her a kiss. She reached, pretending to catch it. He laughed at that. Then he heeled his horse, galloping off, disappearing beyond the walls.

My sister closed the window slowly. "He asked the cardinal for my hand last night. The cardinal refused. First the King of England, now the duc de Savoy. He berates me for skipping mass, calls me pagan, and corrects everything from my posture to how I talk. Am I so bad?"

I wanted to tell her to ignore the cardinal, to be herself. But that would make me a hypocrite.

"Did you and King Louis confront him last night?"

I shrugged, uncomfortable. "The king seems to have made his point without being direct."

"And so the cardinal's power over you and of me continues. I will never love." She closed the drapes and got back into bed. "Mazarin has taught me to close my heart."

I thought of how the king's affection had brightened my world. "Don't do that." I climbed in beside her.

She turned her back to me. "It is the only way to ensure it doesn't break."

Hortense stayed in bed when I rose and didn't get dressed that evening. I took my carriage to the queen's antechamber alone, where the crowd had dwindled. Most of the Savoy party was already gone.

Madame Royale sat with the queen mother in the presence chamber. Though her eyes were puffy and red, she wore a huge smile. When she saw me, she held out a velvet tray, glittering with diamond earrings and a handful of jewels in gold and black enamel. "I told your uncle such parting gifts weren't necessary, that I wouldn't dream of preventing peace with Spain." She waited for my polite nod before she finally moved on, showing everyone her trophies on her way out, waiting for courteous praises.

Princess Margherita followed her mother, pausing at my side. "She's been crying all morning, a right royal fit. Your uncle had to offer consolation."

"She seems well enough pleased. And you?"

She whispered, "Your uncle gave my mother more than jeweled trinkets. He gave her written promise that your king will marry me if he doesn't marry the Spanish infanta."

Beyond my line of sight, I sensed the queen mother watching. I fought to maintain composure.

Margherita went on, "Get me out of it, if you can. I have no wish to become your uncle's subject. Nor to spend my wedded life groveling for my husband's attention."

I gave her a questioning look.

"When the king is in your presence, his face reveals his complete adoration of you." She moved past. "No wife could rival that."

She and her mother curtsied before backing from the door. I turned to the dais and saw the queen mother studying me. She never wanted King Louis to marry Margherita. She would quash me now. I approached her wishing Olympia and Hortense were by my side. I curtsied.

She didn't smile.

"I am looking for my uncle."

She sighed. "He is busy gathering gold and silver to send with Madame Royale, and he is cursing you for it. It seems you did your job a little too well."

Does she suspect I warned Margherita? "Please forgive Hortense's absence. She was too saddened by the departure of Savoy to join me."

"I imagine you're glad to see them go?" Her glare shook me. She'd always shown me the natural kindness of an older woman to a younger. Now her eyes said she recognized me as a feminine rival. Civility remained, but the tone and expression were meant to cut. In this one glance, I had become a woman.

I wanted to choke her. I wanted to tell her I knew *everything* about her affair with Mazarin. I wanted to scream secrets from the rooftops of Lyon that would damn her. Instead I played her game one better. I smiled an innocent smile, curtsied deeply, and said, "Me? I'm perfectly indifferent and ever at your service."

It stunned her. She recovered quickly, carefully arranging her expression to one of contentment.

It didn't matter if she believed my ruse. I now saw *her* for the adversary she was.

CHAPTER 27

*The queen mother wished to show King Louis the mirror presented to Rinaldo . . .
to draw him from the spell of Armida.*

— MADAME DE MOTTEVILLE'S MEMOIRS

I suffered the queen's antechamber for hours, but King Louis never appeared. Nor did my uncle. I went to bed as melancholy as Hortense. But
in the morn, Moréna opened the window to reveal King Louis on his horse
in the Place de Belle Cœur.

"Feel like riding out of Lyon?" he called up with a grin.

Philippe waved from his place behind the king with three other musketeers.

Moréna dressed me in a hurry, and my equerry readied Trojan. The king
and I trotted through the city, over the Saône, and past the hill to the fields
beyond.

"Race you to those ruins in the distance!" I cried, and heeled Trojan to
a hard gallop before the king could answer. We beat him by an arm's
length. I laughed, breathless. King Louis helped me off my horse, and we
collapsed in the grass below the stone arches of an ancient Roman aque-
duct. He held me, and we didn't care about getting grass in our hair or what
the musketeers thought. Philippe kept them at a distance, and we lolled
together, kissing and caressing, settling into a comfortable embrace, alone
at last.

"Which Caesar do you think had these built?" he finally asked, staring
at the stone arches.

"One that declared himself the greatest of all, no doubt."

He laughed. "One day I will be called a great king. I will expand France and make it wealthy."

I made a *tisk* sound. "Focus on improving Paris; clean the garbage off the streets and line them with lanterns to light at night. Install fountains so your people don't have to drink dirty river water. Greatness cannot be accumulated in a coffer. It pours from here." I pointed to his heart. "And is reflected in how you treat your weakest subjects."

He thought on this for a long while, then changed the topic. "You were right. This escapade with Savoy was designed to force Spain into a treaty."

"It's pointless to seal a peace treaty with a marriage alliance. Your mother was once a Spanish infanta, and she's been no instrument of peace these last decades." I sat up. "You begged me never to leave your side. Cardinal Mazarin will try to separate us."

"I can make him secure peace without the marriage."

"He gave his *written word* to Madame Royale that you would marry Margherita if you don't marry the Spanish infanta."

King Louis sat up. "He wouldn't do that without my consent."

"Margherita told me herself."

He waved me off. "To spite you."

"To warn me." I stood. "*She* sees Mazarin for what he is."

He leapt to his feet. "Are you calling me a fool?"

"Do you want to marry me or not?"

He embraced me roughly and pressed his lips to mine in a fierce kiss. A fire rose within me, and I plunged into him. I ached to make him mine.

Instead I pushed him away. "You take my kisses, my trust, and offer nothing in return."

He grabbed my arm, dragged me to his horse, and with one swift move threw me into the saddle. He mounted behind me and kicked his horse into a hard gallop. Philippe scrambled to grab Trojan, and the musketeers followed. King Louis didn't wait. He drove his horse straight to the hill and the cardinal's lodgings. Pages and guards rushed to greet him, but the king paid them no heed. He pulled me from his horse and marched me inside. Every sentry fell back for King Louis, who didn't wait to be announced.

In my uncle's antechamber, Colbert spotted us and dropped a stack of papers. He called out, "The cardinal is unwell!"

King Louis pushed through the doors to the cardinal's bedchamber.

My uncle sat before a fire with his feet in a basin. He started, and water sloshed. "Majesty." He lifted one swollen foot from the basin and made to stand for a proper bow. *His bones are aching already, I see.*

"No ceremony." King Louis waved him down. "Did you promise my hand in marriage to Savoy if I do not marry Spain?"

The cardinal paused in his half-risen posture. He glanced at me, as if to say, *You call this having control of the king?*

The king went on. "Don't look at Marie with blame in your eyes. What have you to say?"

My uncle fell back into his seat. "Madame Royale must have circulated that rumor to salvage the remaining shreds of Savoy's dignity. Can you blame her? After you treated Margherita so coldly?"

"Your pathetic trick at the Archbishop's Palais proved you wanted Marie to take the blame," said King Louis.

The cardinal held up his palms. "I am only guilty of doing my utmost to protect you. And secure an alliance that will bring you peace, new lands, and riches."

King Louis seemed surprised. "You know I want peace, but I won't marry Spain." He cleared his throat. "I want to marry Marie."

The cardinal didn't seem to know what to say. "Majesty, you do me too much honor."

"It is my right to bestow honor where I choose." King Louis smiled at me. I forgot the tension in the room for a heartbeat, reveling in that smile. He turned back to my uncle and drew himself up to his full height. "So concede whatever terms you must, but write my marriage out of it."

My uncle cleared his throat. "I will do my best."

I couldn't believe it.

"I won't marry Margherita either." said King Louis.

My uncle shrugged. "I never intended it."

The king glanced at me. It had come too easy. I shook my head.

King Louis turned back to my uncle. "Promise you'll let me marry Marie."

My uncle pressed his chair with shaky arms until he came to a standing position, robes falling, half in the water. He bowed. "I would forfeit all I own before standing in the way of Your Majesty's happiness."

King Louis smiled broadly and turned to me. But Mazarin hadn't promised. What could I do? With the cardinal still bowed low in his gouty footbath, I led the king out. Back through the sentries and Colbert standing agape, back out to his horse, where exasperated musketeers waited with Trojan. I dropped the king's hand and signaled Philippe to help me onto my mount.

"Say something," said the king.

"You asked me to go riding this morning. So let us ride. This meeting changed nothing."

"I did what you wanted. Your uncle will clear the way for us to wed."

I settled in my saddle and looked down. "My vow to remain at your side implies I will be loyal and honest. So I will tell you a truth. If you love me as deeply as you say, then the cardinal will be the cause of your greatest heartache."

"How can you speak of your own guardian this way?"

"Because, my love, he is a liar."

"He is clever and cunning, but he wouldn't lie to *me*."

I twisted Trojan's reins around my hand until I thought they would cut right through my gloves. *King Louis isn't ready for the truth.* He was a man to demand proof, and my proof was in Paris. "If I could prove he is deceitful beyond all doubt, would you denounce him?"

He kicked the gravel, startling the horses. "You're right." He mounted and took reins in hand. "We should stick to riding."

Thus, we rode. Every day. Over frosty fields or snowy meadows. King Louis came to our quarters every morning, bursting in while we were still in our undress gowns, sending Madame Venelle into fits of the vapors. He waited until I dressed, then challenged me to a race over the bridges, through the squares, or across Lyon's countryside. He riding with a heart full of faith, and me in possession of a half-victory.

King Louis ordered a collation every evening, saying, "Any excuse to keep you by my side instead of behind my mother's table." And so we never had to endure the cardinal's patient glare at supper, and he no longer had to see the lines of worry creasing his mother's brow as she watched him watching me while they ate.

Every night we danced at the Archbishop's Palais or the Hôtel de Ville. Madame Venelle exhausted herself keeping our late hours and waking early to wait upon Hortense, ill and melancholy since Savoy's departure. Venelle began to quit our night parties early with bleary eyes.

Thus we spent them unsupervised. In the darkest hours before sunrise, when we were full on oysters and honey mead and worn out with dancing, the king followed my carriage home with an escort of Philippe's musketeers. He soon abandoned his horse and climbed into the carriage to kiss me and press against me and put his face beneath my skirts. Oh, the things I let him do to me and the things I did to him! I lost all resolve at the sensation of his fingers moving slowly inside me, moving me to the edge. I could forget everything on those slow rides back to the Place de Belle Cœur. Once, when the ride hadn't been slow enough, I saw that Venelle was fast asleep in her bed, and quietly opened my window so the king could climb inside.

"What are you doing?" asked Hortense hazily.

"Go back to sleep and get some for me," I whispered. "For I shall get none."

We set fire to my bed that night, with his hand over my mouth to keep me from calling out in the height of pleasure. We broke one of my old pearl bracelets, and he crept out, using pearls to silence the frustrated musketeers. My body ached at the loss of his warmth.

When Venelle came into our chamber the next morning, I saw in her expression that she could smell it. She made sure the windows were locked fast from then on. She slept more lightly. She wore herself out checking on us in the middle of the night, groping along our bedsteads in the darkness. Once she tripped on my slippers and fell smack into me. I bit the hand that landed on my face, eliciting a scream that would have woken the dead.

"Stay out," I told her. "Or I'll bite you again."

She grabbed a silk stocking to stanch the blood. "I won't. I can't. Your uncle commanded me."

"To spy?"

"To ensure your safety."

But I knew better.

In the evenings, when we breezed into the queen mother's presence chamber so King Louis could kiss her cheek and she could pay her compliments, I thought I caught glimpses of the Spanish dignitary leaving. One day we stopped in Mazarin's chambers so King Louis could sign some certificate and pick up a little velvet bundle.

"Did you smell foreign shaving water?" I asked as we left. "I swear I caught a whiff of scented Spanish leather."

King Louis shook his head and handed the bundle to me. Inside the velvet folds was a new pearl bracelet. The king laughed at my surprised expression. He whispered that he longed to see me wearing nothing but that bracelet.

Soon, all of my dancing slippers had holes on the bottoms and we had lit every advent candle.

"Why haven't you told him about his mother and Mazarin yet?" wailed Moréna as Christmastide ended. She eyed the open box of wax I used to make lip paints. "I will craft a wax figure of Mazarin and toss it in the river."

"You will not." I closed the box and put it in my *cassone*. "I need the king to develop a sense of independence. I can't make demands and force my will when he must learn to exert himself." But the edge of my worry had dulled from razor to butter knife.

The new year came and went, and we packed for our return to Paris. King Louis waited for me at the city gates, mounted on his horse. I wore my black velvet *justaucorps* trimmed in sable with a huge purple plume in my matching hat. We set out ahead of the long string of carriages for our vast journey home, talking of books and of fêtes we would have before the Lenten season. No other courtier dared brave the late January cold to ride horseback with us. They knew it would have been to no avail, for before we rode out, the king kissed my hand so lords and ladies peeking from heavy leather carriage curtains saw; he had no wish for any company save mine.

CHAPTER 28

Le Palais des Tuileries
February 1659

I held my parchment lace–covered overskirt out on each side and twirled in hop steps in the center of Monsieur's masquerade ball at le Palais des Tuileries. King Louis looked on, one hand on his hip. The gold sequined half-mask he wore matched mine exactly, ending just above the broad smile he wore while watching me. The masks fooled no one but allowed the king to move freely in public. He nudged Lully, who often put aside his violin to dance with us. Now he nodded appreciatively at the glimpse of ankle flashing beneath my skirts. Lully leapt into step beside me on the dancing floor, adding flourish with a flick of the wrist here, or holding a pose a beat longer there. I started to mirror him, and soon we had a crowd of onlookers.

The violinists ended their song. Lully and I collapsed into each other, giggling.

"You must dance in the *Ballet de Raillerie* this season," he said.

I'd been hoping for this invitation.

As we'd reentered Paris at the first of February, King Louis had turned to me and said, "We have but one month until the Lenten season. What shall we do?"

"Have grand fêtes," I'd said. "Banquets, balls, masquerades, and more balls."

He'd laughed. "Then this will be the most spectacular carnival season the court has ever seen." He'd lined up his courtiers at the Pavillon du Roi and issued a command: Entertain us. And so it was that every evening we'd feasted, and every night we'd danced. But every morning, while dressmakers and cobblers streamed in and out of Palais Mazarin to refresh my armament and let Hortense's bodices out at the bosom, King Louis had practiced for this season's ballet.

Mazarin had commissioned it, as usual, but he hadn't given parts to his Mazarinettes. A purposeful omission. Mazarin spent most of his time locked up with Colbert in his private study, outlining demands for the treaty with Spain. Or plotting how best to dispose of me. Would it be the convent? Marriage to some foreign noble, so far away I'd never see the king again? I couldn't know.

Nor could I obtain leverage to prevent my downfall. Every night when I returned home, feet throbbing from dancing, Mazarin or Colbert was in the study, quill scribbling and candles ablaze, blocking access to my uncle's chest of letters. Mornings were the same. When I wasn't home, Moréna always found someone there. Even Philippe traveled back and forth from the musketeer garrisons to work for Mazarin in hopes of gaining a moment to search. I *must* have my proof.

But for now I smiled at Lully, watching King Louis approach from the corner of my eye. "We must ask the king if I should take part in the *Ballet de Raillerie*." Though I already knew what he would say. He'd been scheming ways to get me onto the stage all week.

Lully turned to him. "Sire?"

The king grinned. "Put her in a shepherdess costume and set her to dancing. She'll outshine even me."

Lully feigned a look of surprise. "Outshine the Sun King? Is that possible?" Our crowd of observers dissolved into laughter.

Just then Philippe appeared. He bowed, then took hold of my arm. "Sister, shall we dance?"

The king nodded his consent. My brother led me out, and the courtiers parted. They watched as we began the steps of a sarabande.

I kept my expression passive. "Why would you take me away from the king?"

"Were you able to get to Mazarin's chest of letters?"

"Not for lack of trying. I assume that means you were unsuccessful, too?"

"Mazarin assigns me menial tasks, copying letters or adding rows of sums in ledgers." He sounded frustrated. "They never leave me alone."

"The pressure weighs on me, Philippe. What if Mazarin consigns King Louis to marriage with the infanta before I have a chance to expose his affair with the queen mother? I need those letters."

"It's going to be harder to get your hands on them now."

I didn't like the sound of that. "Why?"

"While you've been twittering around on your toes, our eminent uncle moved to his apartments at the Louvre. To free up space at Palais Mazarin for a particular dignitary to inhabit."

"Tell me this dignitary isn't from Spain." I let my guard down, pausing in the dance.

My brother quickly swept me back into step. "No sense getting upset. Don Antonio de Pimentel *is* here on behalf of King Philip of Spain."

"He'll live at my own house? The humiliation!"

"Pimentel will never leave his wing. He'll be concealed from the court's thousand eyes. Mazarin will come daily to Palais Mazarin to work with him on peace negotiations."

"If our uncle moved his offices, does that mean . . ."

My brother shrugged. "I don't know whether he moved his chest of letters. Everything is in disarray."

It was too much. "How will we ever get them now?" I couldn't breathe. I stopped dancing to grab the fan from the gold chain hanging at my waist. Philippe immediately walked me toward a door. Every head turned to follow us, pointing and talking. "They watch me constantly now. Those thousand eyes are ever upon my skin like twisting blades."

"Hold up your chin and show them you have the dignity to be queen."

I did it, and dropped my fan.

Armand de la Meilleraye appeared out of nowhere with a goblet of watered wine. He must have run for it as soon as I'd stopped dancing. "Can I get you something? Show you to a chair? Are you well?"

Lully and Somaize and the Prince of Lorraine and a few other masked faces gathered behind him, acting concerned. Other curious masked faces appeared.

I was not used to people seeking my favor. I took a courteous sip of the watered wine as King Louis approached. "Perfectly well. Why wouldn't I be?" I held out my hand.

King Louis kissed it right there in front of everyone. "Is anything wrong?"

"My brother told me the most tedious joke about a Frenchman brought before a judge and charged with stabbing someone's dog with his scabbard. The judge asked why he didn't just hit the dog with the *hilt* of his scabbard instead." I paused.

Finally the king asked, "What did the man say?"

"He told the judge that's exactly what he would have done if the dog had been trying to bite him with his *tail* end."

Laughter rose up like a windstorm, and I let King Louis walk me to the floor for the next dance. My brother departed with a knowing look. Though I danced a courante with enough grace to elicit praise from Lully, I couldn't stop thinking about those letters. With Pimentel under my own roof, could I afford to wait any longer to make King Louis overthrow my uncle?

Hours later, we stumbled from the Tuileries carrying half-empty wine bottles to the carriages.

"We shall sssuit you up in the cossstume of a shepherd girl," said Lully, slurring his words. "You shall be the ssstar of the *Ballet de Raillerie!*"

"Can I carry a great crook to hook the king if he ventures too far away?"

Some tipsy old marquis in need of favor interrupted. "Can I play one of your lost sheep?" He fell on all fours and cried, *"Baah Baah!"*

The king laughed so hard he could hardly climb into the carriage.

Everyone standing too close barked the exuberant laughter natural to the shallowest of courtiers. Even drunk, none of them sounded genuine.

I was not drunk. My carriage drove me, sober and determined, to Palais Mazarin. We halted in the court behind the cardinal's carriage and another I didn't recognize. *They are here together.* The moon shone full, making my satin gleam as I mounted the steps three at a time. I considered pausing to invoke the moon goddess to deliver the letters to my hands. What would the stars tell me about my quest? I had ignored their position for so long now I couldn't guess. I was too impatient to stop and slipped quietly inside so as not to stir the servants.

The whole house was still. The gilded clock in the hall read three of the morning. I kicked off my slippers, gathered up my skirts, and crept to the library. As usual, a sliver of golden candlelight spilled from beneath the door. If the cardinal was still here, there was a chance he hadn't moved his letters to the Louvre yet. I put my ear to the door and closed my eyes, making out a muffled male voice, presumably Pimentel.

"Losing their vibrant young Sun King would have been a terrible blow to the French people."

"It's true his recovery was slow," said my uncle. "But he is well now."

"He's grown strong," said the man. "With an appetite for more than the physician's healing broths. He seems to have recovered his appetite for pretty women."

My uncle chuckled. "It is no cause for concern. You can assure your master King Philip that King Louis keeps company only with women I trust."

"But can you trust your *king*? Everyone in Spain talks of the mistress who broke up his engagement to Margherita of Savoy."

Mazarin laughed. "The *mistress* you fear is my own beloved niece." I bit my lips together to keep from snorting at the word "beloved," and my uncle went on. "She does my bidding."

A pause suggested Pimentel's uncertainty. "I hear he wants company with no other. He reads what she reads. He rides in fields where she rides."

"After his grave illness, it was necessary to prove to the French people that King Louis was strong in all ways. He must keep their admiration and faith. I admit I've allowed the relationship to carry on overlong, but it was to a political end."

My fury mounted with each word. Mazarin's skill at exploitation seemed boundless.

"Does King Louis love your niece too much to become another woman's husband?"

"King Louis will wed the woman I tell him to. I will keep the girl only as long as necessary."

"Why keep her at all?"

In my mind I saw my uncle's sly grin. "When you come to the Louvre you will see how every mother slathers her daughter in face paint and stuffs her into low-cut bodices. Every father positions himself near the king waiting for a chance to thrust his girl forward. They would run this country into the ground if I let them close enough to the king to take it over. You will see the purpose my niece serves."

"An alliance with Spain will strengthen the king's position."

There was a thumping sound, as if my uncle were pounding Pimentel on the back. "Exactly, good man! We shall work together to achieve it."

Footsteps sounded. I hid behind a statue of Circe, gathering my skirts, making myself small. The door creaked, and the two men walked out together. Pimentel carried a taper while Mazarin leaned heavily on a new gold cane, no longer light of foot.

I forgot my anger. *They are leaving the offices empty at last!*

"Remain here, out of sight," said my uncle. "We must give gossips no cause for speculation as we draft the preliminary terms of the agreement."

"When we have our draft, you will dismiss your niece?"

"In good time, Monsieur Pimentel," said my uncle as they turned a corner. Their voices faded to echoes and their light disappeared.

There was no time to waste. I grabbed a candle from a sconce and slipped in without touching the door. I shoved the taper into the usual candlestick and went straight to the bust of Julius Caesar for the key. I needn't have bothered. The doors on the bookcase stood slightly open. I scanned the tidy rows of books and found the letter box. *The very same letter box. I'm saved!* I popped the catch.

Empty.

I lit another candle, locked the door, and spent hours dismantling the chamber, searching, then putting everything back. The seal with the letter *S* repeated four times was nowhere to be found. I searched in vain for letters mentioning the queen mother's crimes of treason that made the old king despise her. The physician's ledgers proving the old king had been too ill to sire a child were gone. I tried to find letters addressed to Mazarin in Paris during the year of 1637, but the only sign of his correspondence were scratch marks on the floor where the chest that housed it once stood. At dawn I retreated to bed with nothing.

There, waiting on my pillow like a threat, was the Colonna book from the cardinal's letter box. *Strife of Love in a Dream.*

CHAPTER 29

In important affairs we ought not so much apply ourselves to create opportunities as to make use of those which present themselves.

— FRANÇOIS, DUC DE LA ROCHEFOUCAULD, *Maxims*

I n the afternoon I awoke to the sound of Moréna crushing snail and egg shells with mortar and pestle for my weekly beauty unguent. She would mix them with onion and sulfur and other stinking, secret ingredients when I wasn't looking.

"I don't have time today." I pulled the covers over my head. "I have to think of what to do."

She whipped the covers down and pulled me by the ankle until I had to stand to keep from hitting the floor. "There's a new man under this roof with an aim to wed your king to Spain. So I'll tell you what you do. You get up, you make yourself perfect, and you tell the king everything. And it won't hurt to look beautiful while you tell it."

Defeated, I gave in to her ministrations.

She clucked her tongue at the dark circles beneath my eyes and brushed her foul mixture all over my face. It slowly hardened as I soaked in a rose-water bath. I leaned back while she poured silver vats full of water on my hair so it wouldn't mess up my mask. She buffed my finger- and toenails until my face mask was crispy and fell off in little flakes. She rinsed my face, then rubbed almond paste and lily water in tiny circular motions over my forehead and cheekbones. I brushed my teeth with orris powder and a silver-handled toothbrush while she put drops of belladonna in my eyes to make them bright. She blew handfuls of violet-scented Venetian talc onto my skin, and by then my hair was dry enough to set. The smell of over-heated hair filled the chamber as she moved around me, twisting and rolling long strands, darting back and forth to the hearth to exchange curling rods.

Philippe walked in as she stitched a stiff beaded stomacher over the front laces of my bodice. "Only the empty letter box is here," I said to him. "Mazarin took what we need to the Louvre."

He put out his palms as if to soothe me. "You know I won't give up."

"I'll tell the king everything tonight. But he believes only things he can see and touch."

"Mazarin left the letter box empty as a message. He knows you're searching. What if he burned the letters?"

He was right. Mazarin left the Colonna book for me as a warning. "We have to find *something*."

Philippe ran his hands through his hair, and it seemed he'd aged a decade in the year since our uncle eliminated him as heir. He needed this leverage as much as I did. "The papers in His Eminence's offices are legion. I could search for weeks and find nothing, yet I've not been allowed a single *moment*."

"You have no place in government. No title. No home of your own. No wife and sons. No money. The cardinal will see to it you never have these things unless you help me take him down."

His face turned a ruddy red. "Tell me what to look for. Even if I have to sell my soul . . . I'll find it."

Madame Venelle fussed with Hortense's hair as we rumbled along in my carriage to Bois le Vicomte for the evening's fête, given by the duc de Richelieu, nephew to my uncle's predecessor, Cardinal Richelieu, and a man much in need of royal favor.

"You should have worn it straight, Hortense," said Venelle. "It's a mess of curls. Don't you want to look your best for the dances tonight?"

"Leave her alone," I said, trying to shield her while I could. Hortense had agreed to help me this evening. "This is a private party. Only a handful of people will be there."

Hortense merely shrugged. She hadn't bothered with herself much since

Savoy left us in Lyon. She had resigned herself to her fate as a Mazarinette, which made my heart heavy.

We reached the end of the lane, and I climbed from the carriage first. King Louis spotted me before my slippers touched the ground and met me in front of the château. "Hortense is going to help us break away from Venelle so we can be alone," I whispered.

He glanced at Venelle, who seemed torn between straightening Hortense's wrinkled skirts and catching up with me. "We haven't been *alone* in far too long." He winked.

I pinched his arm. "Not for that. There are things I must tell you." I caught my sister's eye and gave her a little nod.

Hortense immediately put the back of her hand to her forehead and leaned into Venelle. "Oh, I feel faint!"

Venelle ushered her past us toward the château. The duc de Richelieu called for his wife, who cooed and clucked as she examined Hortense. An overeager Meilleraye appeared with both a blanket and a fan. They disappeared inside. King Louis took my hand, and we ran down a tree-lined path. We kept running, laughing, until the path met the bend of a little ravine. We stopped to catch our breath. The sun was slipping beyond the blue-gray horizon. The twilight and the trees, even in their naked winter form, were just enough to hide us from view of the château. King Louis kissed me. I pressed against him, driven by the heat of our run, and we were soon out of breath again.

"We must talk," I said, fighting the urge to draw closer. Even Hortense would soon get sick of playing sick.

He took a deep breath. "Very well, I will resist devouring you. I couldn't help but try."

I laughed. "You can devour me every night in our wedding bed. But there is an obstacle."

"I will cut through this obstacle with my scabbard." He put a hand on the hilt of his sword in a pose of mock defense.

"It will take cunning rather than brawn. The obstacle is my uncle."

He turned serious. "What has he done now?"

"He lies, cheats, bribes, and embezzles, and everyone who understands the governance of France sees it. He and his tainted money are why you weren't elected Holy Roman Emperor. He is why your countrymen revolted in the Fronde wars. He is why Burgundy refused to vote your taxes."

"For all the trouble he causes, he manages to turn things favorably. You have to admit his genius."

"*You* are the king. You alone should rule."

"What would you have me do? Exile him? He is my godfather."

I took a deep breath. "No he isn't."

"I think I know my own godfather, Marie."

"He is more than that. Have you never wondered why your mother trusts him so?"

"He is an able minister." He pinned me with a hard stare. "What are you getting at?"

I shook my head. "Have you never heard the rumors?"

He frowned. "You are not the first woman to fill my ear with sour stories about my mother and His Eminence. I warn you now, each of them failed to supplant him."

A wave of nausea washed through me. I bent forward.

King Louis put his hand on my back. "Marie?"

I understood my reaction—his comment made me jealous. And knowing he had reduced me to a sickly, jealous mistress made me furious. "If you are so willing to sweep me into the category of past conquests, I will call for my carriage." I started for the path. He caught my arm. I tried to pull away, but my hand hit the jeweled hilt of his scabbard. "Ouch!"

He let go. "Did I hurt you?"

We studied the scrape on the back of my hand that would soon make an angry welt.

"Damn it!" King Louis unsheathed his scabbard. He took a few steps and, grunting with the force of his might, hurled it into the stream. The jewels and steel made a glittering twilight arc until it splashed and sank out of sight. He came back, knelt, and kissed my injured hand. "Forgive me. There is no one like you, Marie. None so bright, wise, nor bold." He kept kissing my hand and, like no magic I'd ever encountered, it made the pain melt away. But I still had to tell him.

I raised him up and put my arms around his neck. "They are lovers. Married, some say."

He laughed nervously. "A cardinal cannot marry."

"Priests cannot marry. He was never a priest."

A shadow passed over his features. "Everyone knows a cardinal cannot marry, even if it is not plainly written in law."

"Theirs is a union you won't find documented in a parish register."

He sighed. "I admit, I have heard the rumors from—well, it doesn't matter where I heard them. But that is all they are. Rumors."

"Your mother allowed him to act as your father."

He pulled away. "Because it was necessary. I was so young when my father died and I became king."

"There is evidence that the cardinal is your real father."

He took a few steps away. "Show me."

"He has hidden the proof, but I will find it."

He turned to me, angry. "Do you hear yourself? If what you say is true, I'm no king."

"Were you not anointed with oil and consecrated as king in the *sacre* at Reims Cathedral? The late king, the cardinal, and your mother conspired together to produce a king. You *are* king."

He started pacing with his hands folded behind his back. "Explain."

"Did you know your father had your mother imprisoned for treason the summer before your conception?"

The confused look on his face proved he did not.

"She had written letters full of state secrets to her brother, King Philip of Spain. It enraged Louis the Thirteenth. He wasn't known for his love of women, and he *hated* your mother. But he hated his brother Gaston even more because of his many attempts to seize the crown."

"Gaston would have become king if I had never been born."

"Much as they disliked each other, they shared equal dislike for Gaston. But ledgers show physicians were treating your father for consumption at the time you were conceived. Even had they been able to stand one another's presence, your father's fits of coughing blood, his night sweats, and his weakness would have made physical consummation impossible."

He seemed stunned. "It is true she never contracted his illness, but that isn't enough. She insists the cardinal lived in Rome the year before my birth."

"Correspondence proves he was in Paris. And there are piles of letters written between Mazarin and your mother. All closed with a wax seal of their interwoven initials, encircled by the letter *S* repeated four times. It is a cipher from the Spanish novel *Don Quixote*."

"You read too much, Marie."

"True lovers possess the four *S*'s. *Sabio* for wisdom, *solo* for fairness, *solícito* for affection, and *secreto* for discretion. The Spanish nobility know them. Everyone in the Paris salons knows. They are a symbol of love. Your mother and Mazarin use them as a seal to symbolize *their* love."

He dropped his head into his hands. "I know the symbol. I've seen her use it in her letters to Mazarin."

"They both lied to you."

He looked at me again. "Anointed or not, Europe would move heaven and earth to overthrow me and put Gaston on the throne if they knew."

"Demote Mazarin. Rule alone."

"Without Mazarin, I wouldn't know how to rule."

"I know for certain that you *do*." I grabbed his palm and pointed to the deep solar line running from his ring finger to his wrist. "You will be the greatest king the world has ever seen."

He closed his hand on mine. The evening had grown cold as well as dark. "Let's go back now."

He doesn't believe me. An owl screeched in the distance. "Decide whether or not you trust Cardinal Mazarin's version of your life before he decides the rest of it for you."

We started walking toward the château, where the strains of harps and violins beckoned. In the moonlight I could only make out his profile. Despair and confusion poured from him, and I hated that I had been the one to cause this. He said nothing but held on to my hand as if for life itself.

CHAPTER 30

Jean-Baptiste Colbert visited us too early the next morning, walking in wearing his usual grave expression. "His Eminence inquires as to your health, Mademoiselle Hortense."

Hortense and I glanced at each other. Mazarin must have heard of last night's fake fainting spell.

"Better, thank you," she said.

He nodded. "In that case, His Eminence expects you to attend Armand de la Meilleraye's grand fête tonight."

As Grand Master of the Artillery, Meilleraye kept quarters in the Arsenal. He was no different from every other noble in Paris, eager to please the king by hosting a private party. But while most understood the king wanted entertainments in order to enjoy keeping company with me, Meilleraye only wanted an excuse to draw Hortense near.

Colbert held up a hand to stop Hortense's grumbling. "Meilleraye shows special interest in you. Your uncle commands you to look your best and favor Meilleraye with a dance." He turned to me. "Mademoiselle Marie, your uncle has revoked your carriage."

My breath caught. "Is this some sort of punishment?"

His eyes flicked to Venelle and back. "You may keep your horse. But you may only travel in coaches belonging to His Eminence under orders from Madame Venelle."

My coach, my drivers, my ability to move about freely. Gone. *Because I slipped away with King Louis last night.* I cast Venelle, my uncle's spy, a hot look.

"Don't be cross," she said. "I give them honest reports, that is all."

I noticed her use of the word "them."

Hortense scowled. "You mean you complain about us."

"And Mademoiselle Marie," said Colbert as he turned to leave. "You're to loan Hortense your finest *parure* of jewels for the evening."

My sister sighed. If a sigh could have a tone, hers was that now familiar sense of resignation. "Sorry, Marie."

I waved her apology off. "I'm more sorry for *you*." I opened my lacquered cabinet and retrieved my diamonds.

Venelle rang the silver bell on my dressing table to summon Moréna. "Hortense has nothing to be sorry for." She went around the room, shaking out our sheets and closing bed curtains.

I suppose Venelle had nothing to be sorry for either. She was only doing what my uncle paid her to do. "Tell me, Madame Venelle, did the queen mother say when I might get my carriage back?"

She didn't look up. "No. She gave the impression she never wanted you to have it ba—" She froze.

I grinned, satisfied she'd fallen into my trap. "So the queen mother pays you to spy on us, too."

She turned white.

I didn't revel in my victory. Instead I helped Moréna slather the stinking unguents followed by almond paste onto Hortense's face. Without my carriage I couldn't move safely through the city to my apartments at the Louvre, where I could search for paperwork. I needed Philippe now more than ever.

Hortense's hair and skin shone on our trip east through Paris's evening streets, but she looked more nervous than I'd ever seen her. Venelle must have ordered the driver to take the long route, for we entered the rue Saint-Antoine. The imposing block of the Bastille rose over us. Hortense gaped at its centuries-old towers with its dreaded chambers of torture, the *calottes* and *oubliettes*. Thankfully we turned toward the Arsenal, where a row of cannons seemed less threatening.

"Does Paris really need such a fortress?" asked Hortense.

"Not now that England and Italy are no longer our enemies." Venelle seemed indifferent to Hortense's anxiety. "With the king's marriage, Spain won't be a threat anymore. But where else would we imprison thieves, vagabonds, spies, and traitors?"

I clenched my fists. *Lord, help me to not slap Venelle herself into the Bastille!* But as soon as I stepped out of the carriage, I caught sight of Mazarin limping into the Arsenal with the queen mother. "Why are they here?"

Venelle gave a smug laugh. "His Eminence is the guest of honor."

Hortense ignored what this might mean and managed to hold her head high on our way into Meilleraye's apartments. The place had the heavy stone walls expected of an auxiliary building to the fortress, but the tapestries and Turkish carpets and polished furniture inside gave the chambers warmth. Meilleraye's cousin Madame d'Oradoux helped him play host. They greeted us in the reception hall, kissing our cheeks. Meilleraye lingered a little too close to Hortense for a little too long. D'Oradoux tittered and cooed appropriately, complimenting the pretty crimson of my gown, the elaborate curls of my sister's *coiffure*.

But I had neither eyes for their well-suited apartments nor ears for d'Oradoux's flattery nor patience for the way Meilleraye ogled Hortense. I searched every face trying to find the king's. Instead, I found my brother's.

I curtsied to Meilleraye and d'Oradoux, and left Hortense in Venelle's hands. But Venelle surprised me. She left my sister with that ogler and followed on my heels!

I spoke to Philippe quickly. "Brother, focus your search on letters addressed to the cardinal in Paris during the year 1637."

"One letter seems flimsy proof."

"The queen mother told King Louis that Mazarin lived in Rome then. This will prove she lied, and he will have to question *why*—"

Venelle was beside us before I could finish.

My brother frowned at her. "What, you've been ordered to listen in on every conversation?"

She didn't respond, just plastered a casual expression on her face and clung like a fly on dung. Her eyes darted to where His Eminence stood beside the queen mother's armchair. Both watched us carefully.

"I see you'll be an especially efficient spy this night," said my brother, "with both of your employers present."

As I contemplated clawing Venelle's eyes out, the king's herald called from the door. Philippe and Venelle bowed along with everyone else in the chamber. Except me. I ran to the king, pausing for a quick curtsy, and circled my arms around his neck. A hushed murmur sounded like a breeze through the guests. Shock at my behavior, no doubt, and at the king's acceptance of it.

I ignored them. Louis gestured for guests to act informally. Conversations resumed. Fans waved. And Venelle appeared at my side *again*.

"Madame Venelle," I said, deciding words could be sharper than claws, "I was just telling the king what you told me earlier. About how the queen mother is paying you to spy on my conversations. Nay, my every waking move."

Her eyes widened to two huge balls of fright. "I . . . well . . . she just . . ."

King Louis frowned. "Speak, woman. Is this true?"

Instead of answering, she stuttered, making no sense.

Nevertheless, the king understood. "So it is true." He hooked my arm into his and slowly made his way through the room toward his mother's armchair. Instead of the customary kisses, he gave her a cold stare.

The queen mother actually seemed nervous. "Majesty." She held out her hand.

He didn't take it. "I hear you're hounding someone I hold dear."

She thought carefully before speaking. "Anything a son holds, the mother must first make certain is safe."

A glance at his profile showed he wasn't softening. "Sons learn to judge for themselves."

"A mother must seek assurance for *herself*."

His cheeks flared an angry red. "I presume you won't be dancing." Since she was the highest-ranking woman in the room, it was his duty to offer the first dance of the evening to her. But this was no offer. It was a statement.

She bowed her head; acquiescence. The king led me away before she could speak further.

She stands firm in some battles and submits to the unimportant ones, clever old minx.

King Louis led me to a small clearing between courtiers and positioned himself for a minuet. He winked. *He's going to dance with me instead of some duchess or countess as he ought to.* Together we made light steps to the harp music. Everyone moved back. My brother and sisters, Meilleraye and d'Oradoux, Mazarin and the queen mother, and all the rest watched the king and his Italian inamorata with admiration and awe.

"Don't let her ruin our fun," he said. "Tomorrow morning you come to the Louvre to begin practicing for the *Ballet de Raillarie*. There are memories to be made, my Marie, memories we will treasure into our old age."

I smiled. *Yes, the Louvre.* Might I break away from the ballet long enough to search my uncle's offices?

Then my heart sank, for I realized my anxiety about Mazarin made me miss the love in my king's tone.

"Yes, my love, my king, these memories will delight us." I just hoped we'd be *together* for the reminiscing.

CHAPTER 31

Pour the wine, throw the roses,
Dreaming only of delight,
Time at his own hour discloses
What may be our future plight.

—A POEM BY GUILLAUME AMFRYE, ABBÉ DE CHAULIEU

"Hold up your chin, Marie," muttered Lully the next morning at ballet practice. "Good. Now raise your arms. Bend your wrist, make it light, make it lovely. Like this." He stomped his heel and raised his arms with a flourish of the wrist.

Pierre Beauchamp, the king's ballet master, walked toward us with a disapproving stare. Since my arrival, he'd shown he didn't much care for a late addition to the dance sequences. "Mademoiselle Mancini," he said through tight lips. "Do you know what you are doing? Do you even know my five positions for the feet?"

Instead of answering, I put the backs of my heels together with my toes pointing out in first position.

He looked doubtful. "Second?"

I slid my heels apart. "Third?" I asked, but didn't wait for him to answer. I aligned one foot in front of the other, the heel of the front in the arch of the back. Without asking, I separated them to make the fourth, then brought them together again for the fifth, this time with heels aligned to toes.

Beauchamp's frown disappeared. "Now the *port de bras*."

Holding the fifth position and keeping a strong center line in my body, I moved my arms in a series of graceful sweeps to the front, then the sides, and ended with my hands above my head, arms an oval frame around my face.

"Again, again!" Beauchamp clapped to get everyone's attention. The other courtiers playing village girls, including Hortense, gathered around. "See Mademoiselle Mancini? She keeps a noble carriage of the head. To impress with formal presence, keep your movements simple!"

The village girls murmured their agreement and returned to their stations. They made a semicircle and took a series of crossing steps, sliding steps, and hops. Village girls had no song, no verses, no major role, but eleven of us would perform a pastoral dance interlude.

Stage builders climbed about the scenery, testing paint colors and drapery in the light. Venelle stood in the wings with a keen eye on Hortense and me. Costumers nearby pieced together my shepherdess outfit. Members of the orchestra lined the perimeter, fussing over pages of music and practicing various pieces, making a pretty discordance of differing melodies. King Louis himself stood amid the orchestra, watching me with approval.

"Your costume will be a little too short, to better see your steps," Beauchamp said to me. "Besides, showing a bit of calf gives the men a thrill."

Surrounded by the synchronized motions of other village girls, I followed him in a large circle making full turns, half turns, crossing steps, and jumps. My focus didn't prevent me from noticing Philippe lean into the theater. He shook his head. *He hasn't found the letter.* Feet together, knees bent, jump, circle in, circle out, hop. We repeated the movement in reverse and came to the center. "Then," Beauchamp exclaimed, "finish with a *pas rond!*"

I made the circular motion with my leg and stepped back, and the ladies behind me finished in the same position.

King Louis left the orchestra, pounding his hands together in applause. "You will make a sensation," he said. "We'll perform every night until Lent!" He lifted me up and spun me around. The other village girls giggled, and he led us from the theater to an antechamber where we could rest. Ladies playing the roles of court girls shuffled onstage. We heard the claps and complaints of Beauchamp and Lully as they commenced.

King Louis motioned for us to sit. "You must be tired." He sat next to me on a divan.

All but Hortense giggled and exchanged sly glances. They were familiar faces, daughters of the noblemen who waited in line outside the Pavillon du Roi for an audience with the king. The girls jostled and shoved each other for the divans and chairs closest to the king.

King Louis snapped his fingers. Red-liveried pages streamed into the chamber, each holding several pastel satin-covered boxes.

"What's this?" I asked.

"Village girls deserve a taste of the sophisticated confections offered at court," he said with a wink. The pages handed a box to each of us.

Hortense tossed aside her lid. *"Macarons,"* she cried. She held a white fritterlike bun in her palm. "Mmm. It smells like almonds, sugar, and roses!"

"Mine smell like orange blossom," said another girl.

I bit into one, and the crunchy shell gave way to a cloud of honey sweetness. "And lavender!"

A page handed a box to Madame Venelle. "Oh," she exclaimed, lifting the lid and putting in her hand. "And I am not even dancing in the *Ballet de Raillarie.* Your Majesty is too kind."

The king nudged me with his elbow, and I watched her carefully.

While still smiling at the king, she pulled out not a white *macaron* but a tiny white mouse! If there was one thing in this world Venelle feared, it was a mouse. She took one look at the creature in her hand and howled like an eastern gale. She dropped it into her lap and tossed the box to the center of the room. Venelle gasped for breath, and the other ladies jumped up, fanning her, shaking her skirts, and brushing the poor mouse from her lap. Meanwhile, the lid of her discarded box twitched and tipped off, and out streamed a dozen white mice. They darted and scattered, and the room erupted with screams. King Louis laughed hysterically. Watching Venelle recover her breath to let out yet another curdling scream, I laughed until tears sprang to my eyes. The girls jumped onto couches and clung to one another, squealing and squeaking and standing on one foot so the miniature monsters wouldn't devour them. Pages scurried about like valiant knights in a fairy story, chasing the mice as if they were fire-breathing dragons. Pages hopped over benches and threw up the Turkish carpet. Hortense scooped one mouse up from behind a chair leg and cradled it in her hands.

Venelle finally came to her senses and hushed. She hitched her skirts so high above her gartered knees that the king and I saw bare legs! We bawled with laughter as she took great, jig-jagging leaps on tiptoes all the way out the door. King Louis slapped his thighs, and even Hortense snickered.

I turned to the king and said, "The village girls squeak more than the mice!"

He gasped for breath. "They will squeak themselves to death. Quick, call a priest to bring the *oil* of extreme unction!" The image of a priest oiling squeaky girls with the holy ampulla made us laugh until we clutched our stomachs. Hortense finally gave way to peals of laughter.

The girls calmed down long enough to fill their mouths full of *macarons* and start helping the pages. They ran around with stuffed cheeks, scooping the mice into their empty boxes. I didn't see Venelle return until she stood before us. Though blurry through tears of mirth, her face seemed white as the offensive mice.

The king's joy faded. "Have you recovered already?" he said to Venelle. "I expected you to run to my mother and resign as her spy."

"I have not recovered, sire." She looked like she might burst into tears. "In fact, that is why I came back. I thought the best way to regain my courage would be to seat myself next to a warrior king!" And with that she plopped herself on the divan between us.

We watched the girls and pages collect the last of the mice. I couldn't even be disappointed that I hadn't taken the opportunity to search the cardinal's papers.

A thousand wax candles winked and flickered in candelabra, dropping globs of melted wax on the stage at the Petit Bourbon, where professional dancers performed the *Ballet de Raillarie*. On one side of the floor, a professional Italian singer complained in a bellowing tenor that the French no longer liked Italian music. On the opposite side, a professional French soprano belted that France scoffed at outmoded Italian styles, and France would produce her own music henceforth. The audience, entirely French, murmured and giggled in the appropriate places. At times they let out a proud cheer.

Watching their faces from my hiding place backstage, I understood my uncle's genius. He had funded the entire production. The audience nodded powdered heads, mollified, reveling in being the superior race, oblivious that they were eating propaganda from Mazarin's Italian hands. I looked over the dancers, past the orchestra, and could just make out his face behind the queen mother. He wore a smug grin beneath that waxed mustache.

Colbert sat in the front row. For the first night in weeks, Philippe finally had a chance to search freely. *Please, God, let him find what we need.*

The singers finished their bantering arias and made way for the stream of village girls prancing to their places. I fluffed out my skirts, layer upon layer of bouncy lace. True to his word, Beauchamp had made them short enough to show my calves, shapely in white stockings. Loops of shiny gold ribbons sparkled on my country-brown leather high heels, on my crook, and in my hair. The leather bodice was more like a kirtle. It pushed my breasts up so high my nipples threatened to peek over the edge of my low-cut linen chemise. One misstep, and they would.

We'd performed for the court and nobles all week. Tonight King Louis had opened the theater to the paying public, and it was packed with the bourgeoisie of Paris. I held my crook and my arms out, took a deep breath, and made hop-leap-step turns onto the stage, taking center position. I paused with my staff in one hand and the other shielding my eyes, careful not to cast shadows over my costume. I scanned the audience as if looking for lost sheep. They got the full effect of my revealing outfit. A surge of whispers and gasps punctuated the orchestra's music. This happened every night. It was King Louis's favorite part of the whole ballet.

While I'd lived in the convent, Olympia had danced as a nymph in a ballet wearing a see-through bodice that had gotten her jeered off the stage. Even the nuns had gossiped about it. No one would dare jeer me off the stage.

The orchestra ended the melody, and I made the ending circle of a *pas rond* with my leg. I glanced to the queen mother's private box. She'd spent the week at Val de Grâce to escape the excessive festivities of the final week of carnival and returned tonight just to see this performance. She looked thoroughly scandalized. *What a delight!*

King Louis met me in the wings wearing his gold-threaded costume. "You were perfectly wicked!"

I pinched him. "You loved it."

"Every moment." He leaned in for a kiss.

I pushed him back. "You'll muss our makeup! Besides, you're on."

He groaned. "Very well. Prepare for tonight, for we dine with the queen mother."

"Must we?" He'd been so angry at his mother for hiring Venelle that he hadn't visited her in the week before she left for Val de Grâce. Tongues in every faction wagged about this mark of disfavor.

He walked toward the stage. "We must, for it is her first night back. And I have something to say to her that you don't want to miss."

I watched King Louis dance his part with a twinge of disappointment. It seemed his mother's disfavor was to be short-lived.

The audience roared with applause at the end of the performance. Players and courtiers alike surrounded us on the short walk back to the Louvre. The nobles tried to outdo one another complimenting the king and his favorite . . .

"You were delightful, Mademoiselle Mancini!"

"Our king dances beautifully!"

"*Vive le roi!*"

They tripped over skirts and scabbards in a rustle of silks and high heels clicking on creaky parquet floors. Like a wave, they rolled with us through chambers and galleries, crushing one another against the wall in their haste to get the king's attention, crowding the queen mother's door as it closed behind us.

A cold collation awaited on sideboards. The queen mother sat at her card table with Madame de Motteville playing *bête*. She held her hand out to King Louis, and he bent to kiss it.

I glanced at the gathering of our closest connections: Olympia with Soissons, Martinozzi with Conti, Venelle with Hortense and Marianne, and Mademoiselle with Monsieur. Philippe stood apart. I searched his face for some sign. He nodded.

He found something! I wanted to shout, but instead I curtsied demurely.

The queen mother spoke. "We were just talking of the ballet. Certainly pleasing to the proud Frenchmen. They will talk of it throughout the Lenten season, no doubt. Especially your performance, Mademoiselle Mancini." She eyed me with disdain.

King Louis turned to me with a satisfied smile. "She was the beauty of the stage. Did you see how she held her poise? They will talk until the entire kingdom has heard of her. They will come from far and wide to see her for themselves. Which is why we must dance it again next week."

The cardinal laughed lazily. "Carnival is over tonight. We abstain from such entertainments during Lent."

"This ballet is worth repeating." King Louis used a tone I didn't recognize. "I say we have it."

The queen mother put a hand to her chest. "I've been accused of loving theater too much, but even I cannot condone such extravagance as we approach the anniversary of Our Lord's crucifixion."

The king shrugged. "We're doing it whether you like it or not."

"It's disrespectful!"

"It's happening!"

She turned pale. "You flaunt your disregard for a season designated for abstinence and reflection." She looked away. "I will be forced to return to Val de Grâce for the entirety of Lent."

"By all means," the king said, looking smug, "go."

Their collective intake of breath echoed in the chamber. The queen mother threw her cards on the floor, pointed at my uncle, and spewed a tirade of Spanish. I discerned the words "your fault" and "outrage."

The cardinal held out his hands, trying to calm her. Madame de Motteville fell to her knees to gather the cards, and the queen mother whacked her on the head, saying something like, "Cut it out."

Motteville recoiled. She tried to scramble up but pinned her own skirts down with her feet. Venelle rushed to help her, wincing at the queen mother's shrill tones. Monsieur and Mademoiselle glanced at each other. They each pulled out a fan and watched the scene unfold.

Olympia put her hands on her hips and frowned at me. "This is your doing. Subtlety never was your strong suit."

Philippe hit her elbow, knocking one hand from her hip. "Shut it, Olympia. She's been doing her best in an area where *you* failed."

Olympia put her finger in Philippe's face, but I couldn't hear her words because the cardinal started yelling to make himself heard over the queen mother, who was now standing and red-faced.

Hortense put her hands over her ears and kicked Philippe in the shin. "Just drop the subject, Philippe. You can never win an argument with Olympia!"

So Olympia yanked a strand of Hortense's hair. "Nobody asked the petted little favorite to get involved."

The fracas seemed to make Venelle and Motteville edgy. They stepped on each other's skirts and spilled the cards on the floor again before they finally stood upright.

King Louis observed all of this and actually looked surprised. "Do Italians always argue like this?" he asked.

I shrugged. "Your mother started it. She's Spanish."

"Actually, I started it," said King Louis.

I giggled. "Perhaps you should *end* it before your mother ruptures our eardrums."

Just then she pointed at me and let out a series of words that I would have understood in any language. "Send her back to the convent or marry her off in Italy. She's nothing but trouble."

King Louis caught it, too. "This isn't Marie's fault!"

"Like hell it isn't," yelled the queen mother.

Everyone else hushed. My uncle glanced at me as if to say, *It's over—you're finished.* It rattled me.

I grabbed my king's arm and turned him gently toward me. I whispered, "Perhaps this is insignificant."

"You don't want me to exert my authority?" he asked under his breath.

I glanced again at Philippe, who gave me another nod. *He has my proof. Better to let the king fight this battle when he's well armed.* Mazarin studied Philippe and me carefully. He'd noticed our exchange.

I spoke softly to the king. "Assert yourself on a more important issue."

He nodded, turned back to his mother. "No need to pack, Mother. Marie has no wish to dance in the ballet again. The Louvre will be as boring and bleak as you desire."

She fumed. She must have assumed I enjoyed this, that I considered it a great triumph. But I was no fool. She would have dragged me straight to hell just to put some distance between her son and me, such was the force of hate in her eyes. Together we ate in silence, the most uncomfortable collation I'd ever partaken. All I wanted was a moment alone with Philippe.

* * *

I woke the next day at Palais Mazarin to the sight of Moréna leaning over me. "Your brother is here, but your governess won't admit him."

"Why would Venelle keep Philippe away?" I jumped out of bed. If she was keeping my brother from me, she was ordered to do so. Why would my uncle or the queen mother order *that*? From the top of the stairs, I saw Venelle standing at the bottom with her arms crossed, blocking him. "Philippe!" I called. "Come up immediately, brother. I've been expecting you."

Venelle looked up, surprised.

"Thank you, *madame la gouvernante,*" I said lightly, "for welcoming my brother."

He skipped past while her back was still turned, mounting steps in double stride. Venelle let out a huff. I grabbed his hand and we ran to my chamber, slamming the door.

"Why wouldn't she let you in?"

He frowned. "Same reason the cardinal never left his offices unoccupied. He was *guarding* his papers."

"They know you'll side with me in a family rift. They told Venelle to keep us apart." I grinned. "But everyone dropped their guard last night."

He reached into his doublet and produced a fold of parchment.

I grabbed it. It was Mazarin's copy of a letter he'd sent to the English Ambassador Lord Montagu dated *Paris, September 1637.* "This proves Mazarin was in Paris before the king's conception *and* that the queen mother lied about it. Perfect!"

"The king is feeling frustrated. Now is the time to show him this letter."

I pulled Mazarin's old Colonna book from its hiding place under my bolsters and slipped the letter between the pages. "Now is not the time. You saw how the queen mother reacted when he tried to extend *Ballet de Raillarie* into Lent. Imagine what she'll do when he tells her he wants to wed me."

"I've never seen her so angry as last night when you changed the king's mind with a whisper."

"Angry?" I turned to my toilette table and started stirring crushed coral and grapeseed oil together, preparing face paints like a savage preparing for battle. "That is an understatement. It is no wonder females are so misunderstood with men writing the history books. She has declared *war* on me."

Philippe tensed. "When will you show him?"

"I wish the king would assert himself without me having to wield this letter at all."

"You can't blame the king for requiring tangible proof before taking the drastic measure of breaking with his parents."

I hesitated. "This tactic makes you and me no better than our uncle."

Philippe kicked the leg of my toilette table. The coral face paint mixture sloshed out onto my fingers. "I've been nosing around for you when I could have been working on my poems and songs. Pimentel and our uncle work constantly on the peace treaty. They grow closer to a first draft by the day."

I threw down my mixing spoon. "Our cardinal-uncle promised the king he would keep the Spanish marriage out of that treaty. If he doesn't, the king will be so outraged neither Mazarin nor the queen mother will dare cross him. *That* will be the perfect time."

He thought it over. "Will it be enough?"

I should have pondered that question. Instead I wiped face paint from my hands and said, "Be proud, Philippe. You've discovered the clue to France's best-kept secret."

CHAPTER 32

March 1659

With carnival over, our fêtes and dances were replaced with the long excursions to country fairs, the rides through the farmlands and fields surrounding Paris, and the never-ending supper banquets with platters and trays of fish that marked the Lenten season. Eel, scallops, trout, salmon, and sole. Boiled and braised, baked and basted, with delicate sauces or crusts, topped with sturgeon eggs and offered up in increasingly fanciful silver dishes. At the Pavillon du Roi and Palais Mazarin, at Monsieur's table at the Tuileries or Mademoiselle's at the Luxembourg, we ate fish until we thought we'd sprout gills.

One quiet evening we sat in my chambers before a table of half-eaten truffle pies and *gâteau* cakes topped with cream and fruit. Venelle sewed quietly before the hearth. Hortense and Marianne sat on the floor by the window, drawing the constellations on huge sheets of parchment.

"You're dreary this evening," I muttered to King Louis.

"I've something I hate to discuss in front of the spy," he said.

Venelle stiffened but did not look up from her embroidery.

I tried to make a joke of it. "Why so serious? Are we to be visited by some mighty angel of death?"

"Worse." He sighed. "Don Juan, my mother's nephew, has arrived. My mother greeted him with a feast at Val de Grâce. He will stay a few days before returning to Spain." He leaned back in his seat. "He wants a better feel for Frenchmen's attitudes toward the alliance."

"He will push for the marriage articles in the draft treaty while he's here," I said, leaning forward. "Don't let your mother make promises or assurances."

"I have final say."

I relished seeing him cloak himself in his authority.

He shifted. "The inroads to peace are fresh, fragile. Don Juan will have to be handled delicately."

My relish melted away. "Are you saying you won't protest if my uncle included an article of marriage?"

"I'm saying I want to marry you, my love, but that we must first have Spain's assurance of peace."

Venelle sewed furiously. Hortense and Marianne looked up from their constellations.

I clenched my glass goblet hard. "I'm trying to make sense of this, Louis."

"France's resources are strained. If we remain at war with Spain, I'll have to marry some rich princess from Portugal and use her dowry to pay my troops."

I whispered so Venelle couldn't hear. "You could pay for a dozen wars with the gold Mazarin has hidden at Vincennes."

He shook his head. "He doesn't."

"I'll take you. I'll prove you have the money to protect France." I stood. "Moréna, have the stables saddle Trojan."

"Don't, Moréna." King Louis remained seated. "Marie, if the marriage is in the draft, it won't be in the final treaty."

I fought the urge to overrule him and drag him to Vincennes. "And if it is?" Should I wait until then to show him the letter? "I don't trust my uncle."

He grabbed my hand. "Trust *me*."

And so I did. I trusted him to shield me with his cloak of authority. I trusted him with all my lovesick heart.

The next evening I dressed in my finest *robes de cour* and insisted my sisters accompany me to the queen mother's presence chamber at the Louvre. Venelle begrudgingly agreed. I stepped from Mazarin's carriage and let my skirts of red satin, bustled at my hips and backside, settle into place. The gold-embroidered toes of my high heels peeked out with each shimmery step. The heavy boning of my tight-laced bodice emphasized my slender form and supported the train sewn to the back.

Mazarin's diamonds glittered around my neck, from my ears, and in my hair. Even my sleeves, layers of Venetian lace, were as fine and delicate as Her Majesty's. But the train, made of blue satin and lined with white rabbit fur, mimicked that of royalty. Had it been lined with ermine instead, and the blue satin embroidered with gold *fleur-de-lis,* I might pass for a queen.

Everyone noticed. The king's favor gave me more power than any charm or spell. The throng of lords and ladies crowding the chamber saw me and parted. They divided to create a path they all desired to take—one that led directly to the dais holding the queen mother and the empty armchair where King Louis would soon sit. The usual Mazarinettes stood around the dais in order of rank.

Monsieur stepped from his place behind the king's chair to take my hand. "You must meet my cousin, Don Juan," he said. He swept his arm toward a dark-haired man upon the dais and made the introduction.

Though Don Juan was King Philip of Spain's acknowledged bastard son, he had no right to stand on the royal dais. But royal favor surpassed convention, so I curtsied for him.

He nodded a fraction.

A short person peeked from behind Don Juan to ogle me. Seeing cropped hair and a riding suit, I first took this person for a man, but I noticed the curve of breast and hips as she walked toward me. She also had a curve in her spine, and her eyes looked crossways. She cocked her head in strange directions to get a good look at me. "So this is she, the famed Marie; who hopes one day the queen to be."

Her little rhyme drew laughter from everyone within earshot. I was not amused. I glared at Monsieur.

Monsieur cleared his throat. "This is Capita, Don Juan's infinitely amusing jester."

I chose not to acknowledge her. I passed her to stand with my brother and sisters by the dais to await the king's arrival.

But Capita did somersaults in my wake. She pranced around us Mazarinettes. Hortense looked nervous. Capita circled me the way a cat would a mouse.

I turned to Philippe. "Where is the king? Get him quickly."

My brother hurried out with Mazarin glaring at his back. Capita tugged Olympia's purple silk skirts. Olympia swatted at her.

"Ignore her," I whispered to Olympia.

But Capita heard, and she pointed at me. "This Mazarinette is very proud; sailing through court on a jeweled cloud. But I wonder, Marie; what will you do; when your king abandons you?"

Everyone roared at her bad poetry—the queen mother, her ladies, even my own uncle and all the courtiers who had parted in deference for me only moments before. They all hooted and jeered. Hortense put a hand on my arm. The king's herald called from the doorway.

Face flaming, I fixed Capita with my haughtiest glare. "You think you can see into the future with those squinty crossed eyes? Go back to Spain, you little hunchback."

Everyone looked to Capita. She put both hands over her heart and stumbled to the ground. She did sloppy backward rolls into the throng of courtiers, who leapt out of the way with exclamations. She lost momentum and splayed across the floor at the king's feet.

"What now, Capita?" King Louis said, staring down at her.

She didn't rise. "My infanta bid me lie before you; to proclaim she loves you true."

The king laughed!

Capita scrambled up and made a courtly bow. "The Spanish infanta has no malice nor pride; for a king of your stature she's the one perfect bride."

King Louis scanned the dais until he spotted me. He gave Capita a tight nod. "I bid good evening to the jester who always speaks in rhyme."

She hopped up, landing in a ridiculous pose. "Only when I have the time!"

The courtiers applauded. King Louis walked past her. He kissed his mother but didn't sit with her. He acknowledged his cousins, nodded to the cardinal, then stood beside me. I took his arm with relief.

Capita stood on her hands and walked in circles, holding everyone's attention. "My infanta is light of hair and sweet of heart; a dark Italian miss would tear France apart."

My sharp intake of breath stunned even me. Every single head in the chamber turned toward King Louis. The muscles of the king's arm flexed.

The fool did an awkward backflip, landed with her arms wide, and said,

"For all Marie might pluck and preen; when Louis weds his Spanish queen; Marie will not again be seen!"

King Louis turned to Don Juan. "Your jester doesn't know her place."

Don Juan chuckled. "Ridiculing the vain tends to elicit laughs."

The king stepped to him, stretching to his full height. "You insult me."

Don Juan backed away with his hands up. "Not you. Your Italian mistress. Surely she understands she must disappear once you're married."

I wanted to slap him.

King Louis clenched his fists. "You make me glad I beat you at Dunkirk. Tonight I rejoice in that victory anew."

"Victory? Our war isn't over." Don Juan's confidence seemed to return. "There is life in the Spanish army yet."

The queen mother twisted her thick frame. She gave King Louis the sign to hold his tongue.

King Louis paused. "Your jester's stay at the Louvre has come to an end. I want her on the road back to Spain before first light."

Soft groans of disappointment rose among the court.

Don Juan leaned forward in a small bow, so shallow it screamed of disrespect. "As you wish." He backed away, snapped at his jester, and they both left the chamber. She swayed like a damned monkey with each exaggerated step.

I could not contain myself. "You should have dismissed the don as well," I muttered to the king.

"Don't you understand?" he replied. "This peace is uncertain."

Mazarin heard us. "Now he'll demand to see our outline. I'll have to make reparations. Marie, go back to Palais Mazarin. Stay there, and stay out of this mess."

The king spun on his heel. "Handle it, Cardinal, as is your duty. Quit barking orders at Marie." He pulled me away, calling for his carriage. Everyone scattered. Together we left the Louvre, Venelle hustling close behind.

We didn't speak in the carriage, unable to do so freely in front of the spy. King Louis ripped open the curtains to let in the chilly air. Venelle huddled in her cloak.

He looked at the sky beyond the rooftops and torchlights of the city. "What do your stars have to say about this?"

"You know I don't consult them anymore."

He eyed me.

I understood. "But I watch them sometimes, from the northwest corner of the garden where the shadows help my eyes see them arc across the sky."

He smiled. Venelle just shivered.

After his carriage pulled out of our court and Venelle watched Moréna undress me and tuck me dutifully into bed, I waited for our wing of the palais to fall silent. I donned my fur cloak and slippers, crept noiselessly outside, and ran to the northwest corner of the garden with the hand of fate against my back.

We could hardly see so far from the lights of the palais. But we sensed each other and fell into each other's arms.

"Did you come here to read the heavens?" he asked.

I glanced up and searched for the constellation of Virgo, the virgin. But she had not yet ascended to the early spring sky. Instead I saw a shooting star sweep across the heavens. A sign of change? I chose to believe it meant we would overcome the odds. "You know I came for you."

He ran a hand inside my cloak, feeling my satins. "You'll be cold in this."

"Not with the Sun King to warm me."

"Look at us, forced to meet in the dark. What will happen to us, Marie?"

"You will shine," I whispered, "and darkness will flee."

There, under stars tossed like silver against a velvet sky, our lips met. We held each other as if we would soon be torn apart, fighting to keep our grip. We fell to the ground, wrapped in my fur cloak, and thrust into each other like animals. I fumbled with the ties to his pantaloons until they gaped wide. He groaned, pulled up my chemise, and devoured my breasts, muttering, "You'll be queen, I swear . . . you're the only queen for me." I forgot politics and schemes and lost all resolve. I gave myself to him, dreaming the garden was our marriage bed, where we generated enough heat to force an early spring.

CHAPTER 33

Easter 1659

I pass my days in great delight,
With wise Marie and Hortense Bright.

—PHILIPPE MANCINI, DUC DE NEVERS

E aster morning I stood before the mixing table in my chamber and
tipped a vial of citron into a dish, savoring the lemony scent, then added
powdered pearls and coral. In another dish I combined citron and bismuth
powder. Lent had given way to Easter at last. Tomorrow I would combine
my mixtures with peach flower essence to make Spanish White. As a powder or mixed with pomade, it would add a luminous fleshy-pale glow to
my face and shoulders for the upcoming balls. As I set a pot containing a
block of wax and rosewood oil by the hearth to melt for pomade, Moréna
burst in.

"Your brother," she cried. "He's been arrested!"

"He went to Roissy for Good Friday," I replied. "He will be back on the
morrow."

"He returned early because his companions were eating meat and he
disapproved."

"It was Lent. What's wrong with refusing meat?"

She stared blankly, unfamiliar with Catholic dictates. "Your uncle
charged him with abusing Holy Week and had him seized."

"Our uncle wouldn't—" But of course he *would*. I remembered the look on Mazarin's face as Philippe went to fetch the king for me a few weeks earlier. "Where did you hear this?"

"Our washing women get their lye at the Louvre. The dairymen that deliver milk to the Louvre come here, too. Coachmen talk to guards who talk to scullery maids. They're *all* talking about it."

Then it was true, for servants knew such things first. Without trusty Philippe, the cardinal's old spy D'Artagnan was left in full control of the King's Musketeers. In other words, the king no longer had command of his own men. "Mazarin knows Philippe is helping me." I rushed to my bed and grabbed the Colonna book. I pulled out the cardinal's letter, resolving not to let it out of my sight. "Ready my clothes. And call—" I almost said *call for my coach.*

"You can't go anyway. You'll miss Easter mass." But she must have seen the determination on my face. "Shall I tell the stables to saddle Trojan?"

"Not on Easter Sunday. I'd better take my uncle's sedan chair."

"Mazarin's runners won't carry you."

I fell to my knees and ran my hand along the mattress slats until I found the pouch of pearls left over from my old bracelet. I held them out in my palm for Moréna to count. "This will convince them."

She scooped them into the pouch, then tugged the hem of her décolletage a little lower with a wink. "I'll make sure it does."

She ran out of my chamber, and I stepped awkwardly into a front-lacing bodice. I wrapped the cardinal's letter in a handkerchief, tucked it under my chemise, and yanked the bodice ties tight. From now until the time I was forced to use it, the letter wouldn't leave my body.

One hour, and one jostling sedan ride later, I mounted the stairs two at a time to the Mazarin apartments at the Louvre. I ignored sentries, marched beyond footmen, and elbowed past the valet into my uncle's bedchamber.

He was sitting at his dressing table, combing wax into his mustache and curling it ever upward. He didn't budge. "Ah. Marie. You must have heard of Philippe's arrest."

"Explain yourself."

"I explain myself to no one."

"You know Philippe left Roissy before his companions ate meat."

Mazarin shrugged. "He wrote a licentious song."

"That was months ago, and you laughed when you heard it."

He put away his mustache comb and started slipping a jeweled ring onto each soft white finger. "You've risen too high."

It was both an admission and an accusation. *This whole thing is my fault.* "You know you still hold more power over King Louis than I do. Philippe and I are no threat. Let him go."

"The court sees you in a new silk gown every day, your pretty coach, your diamonds. I must make an *example* of Philippe to prove I don't favor my family too much."

I opened my mouth to say I'd get King Louis to free Philippe but stopped myself. "You bestow *favor* with self-seeking motives. Once I was proud to be your niece, but you've treated me like your marionette."

He put out his hand, now gleaming with his favorite diamonds, and twitched his fingers upward one at a time. As if it were that simple to make his puppet dance.

It sparked anger as if he'd struck me. I walked out.

I went into the Pavillon du Roi in a haze of fury, not seeing courtiers or sentries. I reached the king's bedchamber doors just as they opened. King Louis emerged.

He smiled widely at first. "You're just in time to go to mass." Then he faltered. "What's wrong?"

"Mazarin arrested Philippe on the outlandish charges that he ate meat on Good Friday."

He looked stunned. Taking my arm, he steered me toward the *cour.* "This cannot be. I was counting on Philippe to command the musketeers if you and I had need. Now who can I trust?"

We neared the queen mother's apartments, so I spoke softly. "This means the cardinal is preparing for his next move."

King Louis started to respond, but his mother emerged from her chamber. She began walking with us to the carriages in the *cour.* King Louis fell silent, and I was forced to fall into step behind them.

Monsieur was waiting at the royal carriage. He gestured for us to climb in before him.

The queen mother stopped short. "I didn't realize Mademoiselle Mancini was joining us for Easter mass."

The king guided me into the royal carriage himself. "Of course she is. I wish never to be without her."

The queen mother frowned. The ride to Notre Dame Cathedral was tense and mercifully short. We listened to mass in silence, though I didn't hear a single word. We left the cathedral in procession.

Venelle met me outside in the parvis. "Mademoiselle! Come home with me at once." She followed me, fuming, to the king's carriage.

Right there in front of the cathedral and the French subjects and the queen mother and the long line of carriages, I leaned close to my king, cupping my hand around his ear. "You have to set my brother free," I whispered, then turned to go with Venelle.

He nodded.

Venelle dragged me toward the carriage that had once been mine. "I hope you enjoyed yourself, because that is the *last* time you're going anywhere without me. Honestly, you are almost more trouble than you're worth."

I laughed bitterly. "Oh, I'm sure the queen's and the cardinal's money will inspire you to persevere."

It was she who came to my chambers the next morning to announce King Louis's arrival at Palais Mazarin. She perched herself on my bedstead while Moréna fastened diamond clasps up the torso of my mantua undress gown. The red silk gaped open from neck to floor, letting my white lawn chemise peek through between the clasps, and revealing the outline of my leg under the white lawn with every step.

"You can't wear that," said Venelle as Moréna brushed my hair into curls that tumbled down my shoulders *à la négligence*. "It's too loose."

Loose drapery was intended for indoor wear among family or for portraits, not for receiving guests. Wearing it during the king's visit signified our intimacy. "There's nothing loose about it. I'm wearing a corset underneath." This new garment was boned like a bodice. Moréna had barely slipped Mazarin's letter under it unnoticed with Venelle watching. I shook my shoulders to prove to Venelle the corset allowed no inappropriate jiggling.

She gasped, shocked, but had no chance to protest as I opened the doors for the king.

He entered, smiling at my ensemble. "What, no jewelry?"

Though I longed to talk of Philippe, I laughed lightly. "Help me choose something."

We moved to my jewel casket, turning our backs on Venelle. He whispered, "Philippe's situation isn't good."

Venelle moved closer, skirts rustling.

King Louis heard her. "Madame Venelle, go to the window." He had never issued orders in such a tone. "Go on. Your king is having a private conversation."

She curtsied stiffly and obeyed.

I turned back to him. "I *know* that much."

"He may have to stay there for some time."

"You're the king," I said. "Get him out."

He rifled through my jewel casket, opening little drawers. "Your uncle listed half a dozen reasons to keep him in."

"Exaggerated and falsified."

"I could give Cardinal Mazarin simple orders such as to stand by the window like Madame Venelle, and he would comply. But when I told him to release your brother, he gave me words of assurance and pacification. I paid a guard to disclose Philippe's whereabouts. He is in the Bastille."

I gasped.

"At dawn they transfer him east to the Citadel of Brisach. That is all I could learn."

"Brisach borders Germany. This is exile. Don't let Mazarin send him so far! Give orders to the prison directly."

He shook his head. "The guards, the wardens, the chiefs—they are all in Mazarin's employ."

I stared at the jewel casket. He was right. "Mazarin demands oaths of loyalty. Those who don't comply are removed. Those who do are rewarded."

"If I issue a command, they will consult Mazarin first. How would it look if my own subjects disobey my order? It would emphasize *I'm not in charge.*"

My hand flew to the letter safely tucked out of sight by my breast. Showing it to him now would only punctuate his dependence. I needed him to feel strong, powerful. "You must learn to play Mazarin's game. Buy the loyalty of these guards and chiefs and wardens for yourself. Buy your generals to wield the might of the army. Allow only reverent courtiers to attend you." I could see it all in my mind: every last lackey eager to please the king; nobles vying for the right to hold the king's candle aloft during his *lever.* "It will take time, but you *will* elevate your status. Start by buying the guards at the Bastille."

He toyed with a necklace of small pearls. "Oh, my love. If I had the money, I'd have gone to the Bastille already. I'd have bought you a necklace of huge pearls fit for a queen."

I put my hands on his cheeks. "Don't you listen to a word I say? All the money you need is at Vincennes."

He looked doubtful. "Even if he encrusted Vincennes itself in gold, it is *his* money."

"Philippe could show you ledgers that prove Mazarin took the money from *you* first. This wouldn't be stealing. It would be taking back what is rightfully yours." I snapped my fingers at Venelle and rang the bell for Moréna. "Come! We shall take the king's carriage!"

We raced east out of Paris, the silent king, the grumbling governess, my bewildered maid, and I. We stopped on the drawbridge, and Venelle tried to follow us out of the carriage.

King Louis signaled to his musketeers. "The governess stays."

The musketeers looked askance at each other as if they were trying to decide what to do. King Louis looked at me as if to say, *See?* Oh, how I hated the way Mazarin undermined the king!

Moréna peeked through the carriage door. She'd loosened the neck of her chemise. "The governess stays, and so do I. Let me see your hand." She reached for one of the musketeers. "I'll tell your fortune."

The musketeers gathered around the carriage, intrigued by the novelty of my maid's exotic charm. She could keep them distracted for a time. They forced Venelle back into the carriage, where she flopped on the seat.

We rushed to the gate. "Do you think the guards will admit us?" I asked.

They all seemed stunned upon seeing the king, and they let us pass. It made me nervous. Inside the bailey, the stone donjon towered over us. There were no more guards. We descended the spiral staircase to the vaulted cellars in a flash. The door was unlocked. *Oh no.* I threw open the first great coffer.

Empty.

I took a few steps back. King Louis dropped his face into his hands. I opened another coffer. And another. All empty. Everything gone. I felt light-headed. I reached out for something to steady myself. King Louis guided me to sit on one of the coffers.

"He knew I would take it," I said. "Mazarin hid the money because he is about to send me away. Now you have no control of the musketeers *or* money to intervene."

"All these were full?" King Louis stared at the coffers, which gaped like great coffins ready to swallow us. "What do we do?"

I didn't know. Without the money, everything depended on the king's force of will. Without a regiment, he would have to be cunning. "Now our love is put to the ultimate test." I put my face into his doublet and felt my tears moisten the damask. What did my uncle have planned for me? *The convent? Rome?*

"Don't cry." King Louis stroked my hair. "I will be the king you think I can be. Have faith."

CHAPTER 34

Judicial Astrology may well be lookt upon as a fair introduction to the Diabolical Art . . . a lure to draw the over-curious into those snares that lye beyond it.

—RICHARD BOVET'S *Pandaemonium*

F aith has never been my strongest trait.
    King Louis spent the evening in my chambers at Palais Mazarin, supped with me, read with me, but never said a word about how he would get the money or the army we might need to fend off Mazarin's imminent attack. When he left, I retired. Instead of sleeping, I spent four hours trying to have the faith King Louis had begged of me. Finally, I rose and ordered my sisters to dress.

It took another hour to get permission from Cardinal Mazarin for the use of his carriage to visit Philippe. I'd sent a missive with the request. It was refused.

Venelle had looked relieved. "Prisons are no place for ladies of stature."

So I'd made Hortense pen a second request. Hers was granted. Before dawn Colbert de Terron, cousin to Jean-Baptiste Colbert, had arrived with the cardinal's carriage and a pass to enter the Bastille.

Now my sisters, Venelle, Terron, and I rolled over the freestone streets through the still-dark city. I enjoyed the look of trepidation on Venelle's face. From the rue Saint-Antoine we turned into a narrow passage and came to the *Petit Pont*. Terron showed his pass to guards carrying sharp halberds.

"There is no need for you to follow us in," I said spitefully to Venelle as the guards lowered the first drawbridge. "As you're a lady of *stature*."

Marianne huddled against Venelle. "Do I have to go in?" Her eyes widened as we rumbled over the *pont-levis* and through the second draw-bridge to the inner compound.

"If you want to say good-bye to your brother," I replied.

"Can you promise they'll let us back out again?"

I could not. Marianne curled closer into Venelle's side. Hortense and I left them. There was no time to waste.

The Cardinal's Guards surrounded us. Terron barked Mazarin's orders at the custodian, who jangled a ring of huge keys to open the portcullis. We followed him through countless oak and iron doorways, then climbed one of eight great towers. With walls as thick as carriages, the Bastille seemed impenetrable. Any hope I had harbored of breaking Philippe free evaporated. The place reeked like the sludge of the moats. Hortense covered her face with a handkerchief. The custodian jangled his keys at a final door. He pushed it, and it creaked as it opened.

Tapestries full of the floating sticklike horses and soldiers of two hundred years ago hung from every wall. Carved wooden chests and tables stood in the corners. There was no bed. Philippe lay stretched on a single oak bench in the middle of the cell, face shadowed with stubble. Our skirts swished against the doorframe.

He looked up. "Please tell me you're fools on a visit and not more Mancinis under arrest."

We rushed to embrace him. Tears sprang to his eyes. I hated myself for putting him here.

I sensed Terron enter behind us and frowned. "Won't you let us have a conversation?"

Terron shrugged apologetically. "You may have all the conversation you can manage within ten minutes' time if I am present. Your uncle's orders."

Hortense ignored him and muttered to Philippe, "Do you know he's sending you away?"

Philippe nodded. "Far enough that I won't be able to issue commands to my regiment, yet still within Mazarin's reach."

"How long will he keep you?" asked Hortense.

"Until he can dispose of Marie. He hates us both. He'll keep us apart to keep us weak."

My legs trembled. I sat on the bench with a heavy thud. "So it's true. He is planning on locking me up."

Philippe nodded. "Though I don't know his exact plans."

Below my breath, I said, "I took the king to Vincennes."

"Let me guess," Philippe responded. "You didn't find the money?"

Hortense positioned herself between us and Terron's line of sight.

"Tell me where he hid it." I said.

Philippe shook his head. "He'd never let information like that slip my way."

"What am I going to do?"

"You still have the letter?" he asked.

My hand flew to my bodice, where the letter was safely concealed.

Philippe glanced past Hortense's skirts, then said, "The draft of Mazarin's damned peace treaty will be complete when they finish article twenty-three." He took my hand. "Article twenty-three is a marriage agreement between King Louis and the infanta Maria-Thérèsa."

Hortense put a hand on my shoulder. "You knew this would happen."

I shook my head. "Some part of me was holding on to hope that His Eminence still wished to partner with us."

She sighed. "It will upset the king."

But will it upset him enough to break with his parents for good?

The bells of nearby Saint Paul's Cathedral tolled for the seven o'clock mass. The custodian entered. "We must transfer the prisoner."

Terron stepped toward us. "It is time for us to go, mademoiselles."

I embraced my brother again. "And time will reveal whether I'll replace you in exile or set us both free."

I didn't sleep well for weeks. One night at the end of April I retired early. Instead of wasting fitful hours in bed, I dragged a chair to my window to look upon the moon. Did it shine on my brother, too? Or was he trapped in some windowless corner of his new prison? Without him I felt more alone than ever. *The cardinal is sending me away.* I had nothing but a twenty-year-old piece of foolscap hidden against my skin to save me from being locked up in some windowless cell myself. I hugged my knees and studied the heavens.

Oh, how I miss you, stars.

I pulled a coverlet around myself, feeling my eyes grow heavy, ignoring my urge to read the stars. As I watched their slow glittering dance across the dark, I noticed a shadow touch the moon. I jumped up. The shadow slowly widened. *A lunar eclipse.* I panicked. What did it mean? I had ignored my stars for so long, I hardly knew what they were saying. I leaned from the window and searched for the constellations, finally deciding the eclipse was in Scorpio with Mars in dominion. *This is a bad omen.* It meant flooding, which could cause food shortages and sickness. It suggested war on the horizon. I backed from the window in disbelief. It suggested treasonous activities conducted by powerful men that would cause more to be taken into captivity.

No! I sat back down, watching the shadow slide for hours until the moon shone bright again, as if the eclipse hadn't happened. As if such a powerful message could be forgotten.

H ours later, I woke to Moréna's gentle touch, concern lining her features. The light of a rosy spring sunshine washed over us. My moon and stars had gone to bed.

I knew what I had to do. "Fetch one of my diamond clasps. Then send a summons to Monsieur Somaize. He will help you find somewhere to pawn it."

She looked intrigued, bless her. With her dark skin and servant's attire, she had more freedom to move about the streets of Paris than I ever would.

"He will help you find an astrolabe, a brass disc with a turning dial. And an ephemeris from the year of my birth, a pamphlet of dates, numbers, and symbols. He will know where to buy copies of William Lilly's *Christian Astrology* and *Culpeper's Herbal with Medicinal and Occult Properties*."

She grinned. "Tools to read your stars. But why?"

"To prepare for a time that I might need them."

"I'll get whatever you need."

But she couldn't. The brass astrolabe and books she brought, along with extra gold ecus from the diamond, did much to ease my tension. But after searching all the shops, neither she nor Somaize could find an ephemeris from my birth year. How could I possibly determine what unnamed star my father saw that threatened my hopes for a happy marriage?

So one night, while everyone else slept, I crept to the cardinal's library to fetch my father's book on summoning angelic spirits, *Heptameron*. It went into the false bottom of my *cassone* with the astrolabe and other books, and I prayed no one but me would ever look upon them.

Thinking of article twenty-three and the eclipse made me ill in the next weeks. I took to my bed, and every day my king brought trinkets to entertain me. Decks of cards, a chessboard, even his cook, who mixed rare chocolate paste with sugar and milk over a candle in a special silver pot. The chocolate drink did much to lift my spirits.

One day he brought his mother's favorite spaniel, Frippon, to play. We laughed as the dog bounded over my pillows, making a mess of my coverlets. She attacked my sheet like a beast, pulling it down until my legs were bared. I didn't rush to cover myself, and the king's expression heated. My body ached for his touch. With Venelle at her post by the window, we could do no more than whisper to each other behind the shield of *Jerusalem Delivered.*

"The cardinal is waiting for the right moment to be rid of me. That moment will coincide with the presentation of his draft."

He held my hand. "Don't fret over this."

"Philippe said article twenty-three includes your marriage to the infanta."

"Stop, Marie. I'll find a solution."

"Do you swear?"

He kissed me on the lips.

Venelle stood. "Sire!"

We ignored her. We turned our attentions to Rinaldo and Armida and read their enchanting love scenes aloud, pretending it was us clothed in vines and flowers on a magical island with nothing better to do than bask in one another. It didn't occur to me until later that King Louis hadn't sworn.

CHAPTER 35

June 1659

S pring frosts gave way to summer blooms. The merchants and theaters flourished at the Fair of Saint-Germain. We often went at dusk to shop for goods from the East—dishes of fine porcelain, lacquered caskets, and delicate paper fans. We watched tumbling dwarfs perform and acrobats walk on tightropes. The King's Musketeers accompanied us, with Mazarin's man d'Artagnan at the head in Philippe's place, and Venelle scurrying close behind. Sometimes we'd make a quick turn into the hippocras shops. We laughed at the shopkeepers' astonished faces. The most they'd seen of their king was his profile on the coins in their pockets. They let us sample spiced wines while the musketeers and Venelle ran frantically around the pavilions outside looking for us.

One day in the middle of June we slipped into a jeweler's. While examining different pearls on offer, the king didn't seem his jovial self.

"What do you think of these?" I asked, holding up a strand of pearls slightly bigger than the old ones around my neck.

He shook his head. "Not big enough."

The jeweler looked crestfallen at the notion of losing the sale.

Finally, King Louis said, "Your uncle has granted me a sum without forcing me to tell him what it is for."

"A sum?"

"One thousand pistoles. I wanted it. In case you and I ever need private messengers."

I forgot the jeweler and the musketeers and Venelle. "Why would we need messengers?"

He laughed nervously.

"You're still trusting Mazarin to keep his word!"

"Your uncle is terribly concerned about you."

"He's tricked you into thinking so."

King Louis glanced at the jeweler, who made a hurried bow and disappeared into the back of his store. It was the mark of inherent power, to be able to issue orders with a mere glance. It left us alone.

The king put his arms around me. "A papal nuncio named Piccolomini visited the Louvre today with a letter from Pope Alexander the Seventh."

I tried to step away, but he held me tighter.

"The pope has heard rumors. About us."

"Are you trying to tell me the pope issued you a command?" This time I did break away.

He put his hands on my shoulders. "He voiced concerns about my behavior."

"Then Don Juan and Capita must have gossiped about us to everyone with connections to the Vatican. The Spanish are pursuing the marriage."

"Pope Alexander only wishes to protect my reputation with the other European kings. To secure peace." He looked down, struggling to find his next words. "And since my love for you is plain to everyone, maybe it would . . . be a good idea for you to spend a few weeks at Fontainebleau."

I pushed him. It was suddenly hard to breathe. I managed to eke out the words "You are a royal *fool*."

He pointed at me. "Don't."

I smacked his finger. "You're so used to Mazarin's trickery, you can't even see it."

He grabbed my shoulders again and shook me. "You told me to play his game. Without money and loyal ministers, I'm doing the best I can."

"You don't need *any* minister!"

He released me, anger shadowing his eyes. "You were right. He wants you gone. I've been haggling with him over this for weeks. Happy now?

Fontainebleau is a hard-won *compromise*. If I can't coax you to move quietly, he'll send you to Italy by force. *Italy!*"

We both panted as if we'd been throwing blows. I couldn't respond.

He stepped to me. "I can't live with you so far away."

I let him kiss me. I felt weak, unsure of anything save the purity of his passion in that moment. His erection pressed against my belly, and I wanted us to forget ourselves. But it would be all we could ever have. I had no power, no plan, no means to secure our happiness. Outside of this kiss, would we have nothing? I tore at the neck of my chemise, tugging until I could slip my hand down the front of my bodice.

The king drew back, his expression curious.

I pulled out the letter. "This is something you shouldn't have to see." I ignored the disappointment I felt at handing it to him. "You told me you confronted your mother with rumors that Mazarin is your father, and she insisted he didn't live in Paris the year before you were conceived."

He seemed confused.

"This is a copy of a letter Mazarin sent to the English ambassador. In his own hand, it is marked from Paris, 1637."

He opened it gingerly, read it slowly.

"Proof that she lied," I said. "You must question why."

"Sh-she wants me to believe the king was my father." He slid the letter into his doublet.

"I won't bother condemning their adultery." I tidied my clothes. "They were merely trying to reserve the power of the throne for themselves."

His hands balled into fists, knuckles turning white.

"They have *kept* the power of *your* throne far too long."

He looked so angry I feared he might hit something.

I whispered, "Will you be ruled by liars? Or will you rule?"

He nodded. "I will rule."

I smiled. "Start now."

H e stormed from the jeweler's shop, and musketeers hastened to follow. Venelle and my sisters and I struggled to keep up. Subjects in the pavilions spotted him, gasping and bowing. Mothers pointed. Children clapped. By the time we reached the carriages, a great cheer was swelling in the fair's pavilions. He ordered the driver to carry us fast to the Louvre.

Venelle wisely held her tongue. Hortense eyed me, and I quietly gripped her hand.

At the Louvre, the king barked to his driver, "Fetch the nuncio Piccolomini to Cardinal Mazarin post haste." He gestured for me to follow him up the stairs to Mazarin's rooms.

Mazarin looked up from his vast worktable and frowned.

King Louis cut to the point. "I understand you've completed the first draft of the peace treaty."

The cardinal swept his hand over bound packets of paper on his table. There were more than a hundred, each marked with a different article number and notations of properties, borders, or funds. No wonder it took so long to draft.

"Show me article twenty-three."

My uncle paled. *Ah yes, uncle, you sent Philippe away a little too late.* He sorted through the packets and handed one to King Louis.

The king rifled through it, then held it out to me. "Look, Marie. It is an article of marriage"—he threw the thing on the table so hard other papers fluttered to the floor—"between me and a Spanish cow that your uncle swore he wouldn't attach me to."

My uncle held out his hands,

The king wouldn't let him speak. "All these months you've been laboring on this? I trusted you."

"The Spanish king has expectations . . . I deemed it unwise to surprise him."

"Unwise to surprise *him*?" The king glanced at me with exaggerated shock, then put both fists on the table and leaned toward the cardinal. "Surprising *me* has cost you my trust, my love, and the last of my patience."

The footman announced Piccolomini. The papal nuncio walked in timidly, trying to read the situation. I remembered him from Rome, where his family had been one of the most powerful. Would his Italian cunning preserve him today?

The king stood upright. "Monseigneur Piccolomini! I was just talking to the cardinal here about our Holy Father. It has been some time since we heard from him, hasn't it?"

It was a brilliant move.

Piccolomini eyed Mazarin as if to ask, *What should I do?* Finally Piccolomini replied, "Alexander the Seventh beseeches me to extend his blessings to you in every letter, sire."

Louis was not deterred. "And that last letter was . . ." He waited for the nuncio to bury himself.

Piccolomini answered uncertainly. "A fortnight ago?"

King Louis smiled, a slow, sly grin. "You may go."

The poor nuncio bowed, backing from the room unaware that he had exposed yet another of the cardinal's lies. I wanted to clap and cheer.

Mazarin spoke first. "I thought you would accept the warning more easily if I pretended it came from the pope." He curled his mustache. "In truth, it is your mother and I who think your reputation would benefit from Marie's departure."

The king paced. "Marie is not to be sent away."

The cardinal studied him. "Very well."

Is that all? No quarrel?

The king went on, "Take article twenty-three out of this treaty."

The cardinal stood. "Sire, the marriage is a matter of delicate politics—"

"Then you are the perfect man to extract me." The king leaned over the cardinal's table until the two men stood nose to nose. "For I intend to make Marie Mancini the next Queen of France."

King Louis steered me from the chamber without giving Mazarin a chance to reply. He took me to his carriage, where Venelle and my sisters waited with eyes wide. "Go to Palais Mazarin," he ordered me roughly. "Go nowhere without my knowledge."

Hortense nudged me on the ride home, but I dared not discuss it and tempt fate to reverse my good fortune.

B ut when everyone else was asleep that night, I did tell Moréna. She shook her head. "You should look to the stars. I don't trust your uncle."

"I don't need to," I said. "My king is finally standing firm. You should have seen him!"

"Why did you get the astrolabe and the books if you don't intend to use them?"

"The Queen of France!" I twirled around the dark chamber, ignoring her frown. "I will be the Queen of France!"

CHAPTER 36

I woke the next morning to Moréna's scowl. "The queen mother summons you to attend her *lever*." She laced me up hastily, scowling all the while.

But I was drifting in the clouds, and nothing could make them rain. "One day I will command pretty young noble girls to the Louvre on a whim."

"You'd do better to wipe off that smug grin. She hasn't summoned you for months. She's gotten an earful from the cardinal, and now you're in for it."

I laughed. "You look as if you'd like to poison her!" I paused. "Don't, by the way. Don't poison anybody." And I danced my way down to the carriage.

The queen mother's apartments were the newest and loveliest at the Louvre. I'd always enjoyed the tap-tap of my heels on the marble floors and the shadow I cast on the columns as I passed. *Soon I shall dwell within these walls.* I entered the antechamber, and all heads turned toward me. As usual. But something was different.

Gone were the flattering smiles. There came no admiring appraisal of my gown, my jewels, or my hair. I met the disdainful glare of every noble lady in the room. One little girl, the youngest daughter to the third son of a minor count, actually sneered. She turned to whisper something vicious in the closest ear.

Olympia and Martinozzi caught my eye from their place beside the queen mother's toilette table. They both shot me warning looks.

"You're late," said the queen mother. The women parted so she could get a good look at me. They'd squeezed her into a green silk bodice and skirt. "I suppose I should expect such contempt from one such as yourself."

I curtsied low, remembering too late that King Louis had warned me not to go out. "I beg your pardon, Majesty. Your summons arrived only half an hour—"

She silenced me with a wave. "Don't just stand around," she said to her women. "My jewels! My drapery!"

The ladies in waiting set into motion like a flock of pigeons in an open courtyard, fluttering to the different cabinets for jewels, hairpieces, ribbons, powders, and trains. They powdered her face, plopped a partial wig on the top of her head, and tied green ribbons around her wrists. Motteville fastened a necklace of emeralds set in gold around the queen mother's neck and poked the hooks of matching earrings in each earlobe. Martinozzi stood impatiently waiting for a scarves to be selected so she could fasten it into place with an emerald and gold brooch.

The girl with the sneer brought a tray of scarves to me. One was made of blue satin, the other of gold, shot through with green silk thread. I selected the gold and green and gave it to Olympia. Olympia turned to drape it around the queen mother's shoulders.

But the queen mother wrinkled her nose as if it smelled of dead fish. "How ugly." She shot me a nasty look. "Only someone with no taste would wear *that*."

The ladies snickered.

Olympia rolled her eyes to the heavens.

The girl with the sneer handed the blue satin scarf to Olympia, who managed to wrap it around the queen mother's shoulders. The blue clashed with the green. She looked ridiculous.

The queen mother let Martinozzi secure it with the brooch, then regarded the looking-glass propped on her table. "Much better."

More snickers from the women. In that moment I remembered what Victoire had explained years earlier; *noble blood doesn't make a person noble at all.*

"There is nothing more hopeless than a woman with poor taste," said the queen mother to no one in particular. The ladies murmured agreement. "You cannot teach good taste to a tasteless woman any more than you can teach goodness to a pagan. Or teach a greedy upstart how to keep slanderous gossip to herself. Or how to keep her nose out of business that doesn't concern her."

The ladies seemed confused. They cast each other sidelong glances. But I knew exactly what the queen mother meant.

She looked straight into my eyes. "Thankfully, real queens know how to keep such tasteless women in their place. How to squash them like vermin. How to pack them back to Italy where they belong."

I raised my finger and opened my mouth to issue a Mancini whisper—

The king cleared his throat from the doorway.

The women gasped. I lowered my hand. The rustling of skirts sounded as everyone curtsied.

King Louis walked to his mother. She sat in silence as he planted a dutiful kiss on top of her puffy wig. "Mother."

"My son," she said, averting her eyes.

"You know what else you can't teach a tasteless woman?" he asked.

Nobody breathed.

He leaned to her. "Good manners."

Madame de Motteville dropped a dress pin, and we all heard the gentle *plink* as it landed on the marble floor. The queen mother turned so red I thought she would sweat blood.

King Louis offered me his arm. "My love, I do not think it fitting for a future queen to stand as a lady in waiting."

Everyone but the queen mother watched me put my arm in his and sail from the chamber, still walking on clouds, unharmed by the rainstorm, confident that the Sun King would ever shine upon me.

CHAPTER 37

*The king was passionately enamored of Marie Mancini and, to all appearance, she
wielded over him a power as complete as ever mistress had to sway the heart of a lover.*

—MADAME COMTESSE DE LA FAYETTE,
Secret History

A fortnight later my sisters and I prepared for the biggest fête of the
season. I'd spent an hour soaking in a tub of milk and honey the day
before, and now painted my lustrous Spanish White on my face. I dabbed
Olympia's special red, which I'd finally learned how to mix myself, on my
cheeks and lips. Moréna used wires to lift my hair in puffs over each ear.
Ringlets from each one dangled to my shoulders.

Hortense sat nearby enduring Moréna's facial mask. "Honest to heaven,
this sludge smells worse than dog piss. What do you mix it with?"

My maid chuckled. "You don't want to know."

Hortense jumped up. "It is mixed with dog piss! I knew it." She poured
water from a silver vat into a matching bowl and started splashing herself.

"There's no better beauty treatment," I said, remembering how much I
had detested the stuff at first.

"The cardinal is going to dump me on that zealot Meilleraye regardless
of how I look." She began dressing in the silver lace gown King Louis had
ordered for her. "He's going to be there tonight, you know. The cardinal
told me to dance with him."

I wanted to tell her I'd forbid Meilleraye from entering her presence when
I was queen, that I'd arrange her marriage with the duc de Savoy. But I
needed a crown on my head before I started making promises. "The

entire court and the nobles from the surrounding countryside will be at Berny tonight. Hugues de Lionne is giving this fête in the king's honor."

Lionne was one of Mazarin's ministers, but King Louis had told him firmly that this evening should honor me. King Louis had ordered the bodice and skirts that Moréna cinched me into. All silver tissue embroidered with gold *fleur-de-lis,* its splendor rivaled any court gown. A trained overskirt matched the bodice and parted in the front to reveal gold lace petticoats. My puffy sleeves fell low on the shoulder, paned to show the layer upon layer of fine white lace chemise that ballooned down to my elbows. Moréna secured my sleeves with knots of gold perfumed ribbons. A mirror and my fan hung from gold cords at my waist like royal emblems. The whole ensemble took an hour to put on.

Marianne peeked in from the antechamber. "Olympia has arrived." She pushed the door open wide.

Olympia floated in wearing silver and white. Silver lace adorned her hair, her bodice, and her skirts. She held out a jewel casket. "The king wants you to wear this tonight." She opened it to reveal the Mirror of Portugal suspended in a necklace of diamonds.

"How did you ever get it from Cardinal Mazarin?"

Olympia shrugged. "King's orders."

The deep beauty of the stone mesmerized me, and I didn't press her with questions. She fastened it into place. Hortense placed diamond pins in my *coiffure.* My reflection in the great Venetian looking-glass winked and glittered back at me.

Olympia rubbed a bit of my Spanish White onto my shoulders until they gleamed, then nodded approvingly.

"Perfect," said Marianne, peeking around me to admire my reflection.

I turned. The king had ordered silver lace gowns for Marianne and Hortense. My sisters fairly glowed with excitement. I grabbed their hands, and we made a circle. "If only Mamma and Papa could see us now."

I knew my sisters were thinking my thoughts, of poor Paul, Victoire, and Alphonse, all taken too soon. And of Philippe, in his faraway prison. Even when we were all together as children at Palazzo Mancini on Rome's Via del Corso, we had never been an ordinary family. Each of us had glory and misfortune pronounced in our stars. But tonight, united, we were full of promise. "This could be the start of a whole new life," I said.

We heard a commotion in the antechamber, and a herald called, "Make way for the king!"

Olympia dropped our hands and gathered her skirts. "Your royal chariot is here."

"I thought we were going to Berny in your carriage," I said, puzzled.

But Olympia ushered Hortense and Marianne aside. "We're to follow you and the king."

He entered, and we curtsied. His suit of clothes matched mine exactly, from the silver cloth to the gold embroidery down to the diamond buttons. He put out his hand, raising me up. "My radiant queen." He kissed each of my cheeks.

"Is it me you love?" I asked. "Or do you merely bask in the reflection of the Sun King's rays?"

He chuckled. "If I shine, it is because you lit me from within." He held open his hand.

In his palm was a pair of earrings. Seven round and pear cut diamonds were set in a quatrefoil pattern in each one. More diamonds encrusted the bell caps, suspending the biggest pearl drops I'd ever seen.

"Are these your mother's?"

"Were." He watched as I carefully put them in my ears. "They belonged to Queen Marie de Medici before her. Now they belong to you."

"Jewels for a queen." It seemed fitting that they would return to an Italian for the next reign. As if it were destiny.

"There will be more." He planted a kiss on the tip of my nose. "For you will soon *be* queen."

Past the walls of Paris, the countryside hills gave way to the manicured gardens of Château de Berny. Hugues de Lionne stood on the front steps with an array of courtiers already arrived. He gestured to his trumpeters. A fanfare of cheers and trumpet blasts arose, but the king did not turn to receive Lionne's welcome until he'd taken my hand to help me down from his carriage. Oh, the looks on their faces when they saw us— our matching attire, our diamonds and pearls, and the pinched face of my governess as she scrambled behind us without the king's regard—I would never forget it! These French saw me as too low-born for their king. They hated my uncle and my hot Italian blood. But they curtsied and bowed for *both* of us this night. Because I had the king's arm, I had his ear, and soon I would share his throne.

The king greeted our host, then spoke to me. "Lionne here has promised the most spectacular evening of our lives. Do you think he can succeed?"

"We've had our share of spectacular evenings," I replied with a grin.

"Quite right. Quite right," said the king, leading me past Lionne and into the château.

His subjects wasted no time hitching up their skirts and holding on to their scabbards and hastening after us. We gathered in the shade of hundreds of orange trees to hear Lionne's orchestra give a lively concert while we drank syllabubs. King Louis applauded and said for his retinue to hear, "That was almost as enjoyable as listening to Marie Mancini sing and play the guitar."

The château's little theater could only accommodate half the guests, who jostled and fought to follow us in. I sat by the king in the front row to watch a comedy. We laughed, we applauded, and at the end the king remarked, "Marie Mancini can memorize an entire play, recite the lines of every part, and still pull off the jokes with more flair."

After sunset, in the avenues between the *parterres* of the front garden, Lionne bid his guests to sit for a lavish supper. The queen mother sat with us, her expression impervious. The cardinal kept silent. Don Antonio de Pimentel appeared, causing a flurry of talk at every table. I tried to ignore him, but he sat between Mazarin and Lionne. King Louis insisted I sit at his right hand at the royal table, and he kissed me after the artichoke soup, the orange salad, and again after the duck confit. As we finished sugared almond cakes, the king said, "That was splendid fare, but not so sweet as the taste of my Marie Mancini's lips."

We traipsed through the house to the courtyard that met the canal, and descended the steps into gondolas festooned with torches and flowers. With wine-filled Venetian goblets in hand, and a violinist serenading at the foot of our gondolier, we reclined on blue satin cushions and glided along the canal. Fireworks in gold, red, green, and blue burst overhead, raining their sparkling colors. But King Louis paid no attention.

"Won't you watch the fireworks?" I asked.

This time he spoke for my ears only. "They're far more dazzling reflected in your eyes."

Back in the courtyard, Lionne commenced a ball. The queen mother declined to dance, and King Louis politely opened the dancing with Mademoiselle. Then he gestured for me, saying loudly, "I'll partner with no one else tonight but my Marie Mancini."

The queen mother watched from her armchair with her husband-cardinal and Pimentel standing by, watching our every move. We danced the gigue, the tarantella, the forlana, then we danced them all again in double time. We danced until the black horizon paled to blue with the imminent sunrise.

When we were finally delirious with exhaustion, we stumbled back through the château to the front gardens and the king's carriage. Pimentel's glare was like a hot poker boring into me.

King Louis didn't notice. "Lionne, you were right. This was indeed the most spectacular evening I've ever enjoyed," he said, as everyone gathered to bid us farewell. He spoke for all to hear. "But that is understandable, since I spent it in the company of my Marie Mancini."

He might as well have poured golden honey all over me, his promotion had been so blatant. But to see their faces—those fickle courtiers! They applauded as we climbed into the king's carriage. They congratulated an exhausted-looking Lionne for his successful fête. As Venelle climbed into the carriage behind us, I could just make out in the garden torchlight one face that didn't feign flattery. Pimentel looked like he might breathe fire.

CHAPTER 38

Cardinal Mazarin answered that he was master of Marie, and would stab her to the heart, sooner than elevate her.

—MADAME DE MOTTEVILLE'S MEMOIRS

I'd fallen into bed at dawn, expecting to sleep until after noon. But mid-morning, I awoke to a terrible crash. I sat up, clutching my coverlet to my chest. My uncle stormed through my bedchamber, knocking the dishes and bowls of unguents off my dressing table. They broke and splattered on the floor.

He noticed me sitting up and pointed to the mess. "What potions are you brewing here?"

"They are merely face paints." I leapt from the bed in full alarm. "Facial plasters and beauty elements. Nothing bad, Uncle, I swear."

He poked a manicured finger into a pot of rouge, then sniffed it. "You've become a slave to vanity and pride?"

All the excitement and hope from the prior evening evaporated.

He wiped off the rouge with one of my handkerchiefs, then touched the Mirror of Portugal, resting in its casket on my toilette table. He grinned, then slammed the casket closed and tucked it under his arm. "Search her things."

The Cardinal's Guards swept in, opening trunks and cabinets, shaking out books, and looking into every pot and jar in the chamber. *He is searching for an excuse to confine me.* I tried not to look at the guard rifling through my *cassone.* I bit my lip as he tossed out my linen underclothes. Finally the guard held up a lace garter, saying, "There's nothing here."

Marci Jefferson

Mazarin stepped to me and whispered, "Where is your father's book?"

I struggled to hide my astonishment. *Does Mazarin use my father's necromancy books?* I didn't move, not even to blink. "What book?"

Mazarin moved away and tossed me a *robe de chambre*. "You managed to make a good show of yourself."

I hastily wrapped the robe around myself with new fear of my uncle's power.

Mazarin went on as if he'd never mentioned the book. "Good enough to perpetuate the war I keep trying to end."

"Did you expect me to crawl under some rock?"

"You mistake me, Marie. I knew full well what you would do. And I let you." He laughed, and the sound had a triumphant ring.

I felt a sinking sensation in my gut.

"How did you expect the Spanish dignitary to respond when you started prancing around like the Queen of France? You know the marriage article is in the treaty."

"That article is coming out."

"But it isn't out yet. You've endangered the entire treaty by threatening that single article. Shame on you for making the king seem untrustworthy. Now you'll pay."

"I won't discuss this without the king present."

"This is not something *you* will discuss at all. This is my peace treaty, and my word is final."

The guards finished their search and awaited orders.

Every fiber within me twitched. "You cannot send me away! King Louis will not allow it."

"He won't allow it *yet*." He turned to the guards. "Give her one hour to pack. Deliver her to the Mancini apartments at the Louvre and stand watch. She sees no one without my permission."

"What is this?" I wanted to claw his face.

He shrugged. "It's time I started to keep a closer watch on you, supervise your activities better. I must prove to Pimentel I have you under control. What better way than to bring you into closer quarters with me?"

"But it's also closer to the king's quarters."

"And *all* those courtiers with their watchful eyes. Besides, it will simplify things when it's time for you and King Louis to say farewell."

230

He glanced around one last time, ignoring my shock, then walked out quietly. The guards started filing out.

One barked over his shoulder, "One hour."

Moréna crept out of her alcove.

Alone, we looked at the mess. "One hour, Moréna."

She gave me a meaningful look. "And how long do we have after that?"

I understood. "I don't know how long my *uncle* intends for me to stay at the Louvre. But King Louis will put a crown on my head and make it forever."

Moréna tried to make me use a vizard mask so we wouldn't have to waste time on face paints, but I insisted on showing my face so those *watchful eyes* at the Louvre wouldn't think I hid in shame. I stepped out of the carriage, gazing up at the stone walls and shiny windows, hoping they'd see. Let them judge whether the glint in my eye be one of sorrow or determination. Guards on my right and left ushered me inside the Mazarin apartments like a prisoner with Moréna trailing behind. Footmen carried in my trunks, rolled out my Turkish carpets, hung my tapestries and bed drapery. I made sure my *cassone* went into Moréna's closet, out of sight. I stood at the window, calm as the servants flitted about.

Colbert de Terron arrived as they finished. "His Eminence asked me to remind you that the king forbids you to wait on the queen mother. You are not to wait on her at table. You will instead dine with His Eminence. Any invitations you receive must first be approved by His Eminence. You are not to leave the Mazarin apartments without permission from His Eminence."

"May I use the chamber pot without permission from His Eminence?"

Terron stifled a laugh.

I considered carefully how to handle this man. A young cousin of the powerful Colbert might seize an opportunity to please the king. I let sadness tinge my tone. "Am I to have visitors?"

"Only if His Eminence allows." A flicker of unease crossed his features.

His Eminence be damned! "Surely the King of France need not get clearance from His Eminence before visiting a wretch like me."

He paused. "You would have to find a messenger."

"Would I need a discreet messenger?" I stepped closer. "One willing to speak to the king without going through His Eminence?"

He thought about it, then nodded.

I smiled.

"What should I tell him?" He put on his hat.

"Tell the king to come to me without delay."

Bless Terron, for the king arrived within the quarter hour. He rushed to my side. "Are you well?"

"How can I be well? My uncle said we must separate so he can salvage the peace treaty."

"Pimentel is angry."

"My uncle provoked us into flaunting our love before the court because he *knew* it would anger Pimentel. He says you will send me away."

"I won't."

"Never?"

He smoothed my hair. "Do you trust me?"

I wanted to but found I couldn't say it. He pulled me close. I put my head on his chest, and he rested his chin atop my head.

Moréna's voice sounded from the corner. "My lady!"

King Louis and I started.

The cardinal stood in the center of the chamber. "I knew I would find you here, Your Majesty."

King Louis stepped to him. "By the side of my future queen."

"Her mother and father, God rest them, entrusted her care to me. It is incumbent upon me to make decisions for her regardless of her wishes."

"You must do as your *king* wishes."

"Must I?" The cardinal flicked a piece of lint from his sleeve. "Her presence at court endangers the one thing you have pursued your entire life. Peace."

"The marriage shouldn't have been entered. You said you would take it out."

"King Philip of Spain has too much territory to lose." The cardinal held out his hands. "Without the marriage there will be no peace."

I could stand it no longer. "You don't care about peace, territory, money, or even the greatness of France. This is about you and Condé."

My uncle didn't look at me. "If we don't get our hands on Condé, he will make other enemies for us. We would be at war again."

King Louis made a dismissive gesture. "King Philip should give up territory *and* Condé. He is as good as beaten."

"But he isn't!" Mazarin stared King Louis down. "Do you wish to keep sending your subjects into battle? The strong men and boys who plow the fields so the women and girls have bread to eat—do you wish to keep sending them to their deaths? We must make peace with Spain. And because of King Philip's pride, he cannot make concessions to anyone other than a son-in-law."

I shook my head at Mazarin. "You never intended to make me queen. Even before the possibility of peace, you used me to control King Louis."

Mazarin shrugged. "Think what you will. You're leaving either way."

"You've been lying to me since my birth," said King Louis. "About my father, your love for my mother, my sovereignty. Why didn't you ever tell me you're my real father?"

The cardinal looked puzzled. "I have never wronged you."

"I never should have trusted you," said King Louis.

Mazarin put his hands out again, palms up. "There is none you can trust more than me. My son."

The king stared in utter silence. The anger in his stance melted. Neither man moved on the declaration. It dangled between them like a hangman's noose.

Finally, King Louis took my hand. "If I am your son, I am not the rightful king. I can marry whom I choose for the sake of love rather than country. I choose Marie."

"The boy I raised cannot choose Marie over France."

The king hesitated for a wisp of a second. "I already have."

The cardinal shook his head. "Think it through. If you are my son, then you are kin to Marie. You cannot wed her in the eyes of God without a dispensation from the pope. Obtaining one would reveal your paternity to the world. Parliament and the law would brand you an imposter, a bastard. The people would tear the crown from your head. They would tear your very head off with it. Every greedy noble and monarch in Europe will encroach on France."

"I'll wed her without dispensation." He squeezed my hand hard. "God knows your own marriage wasn't sanctioned."

Mazarin shook his head again. "You'd need more than a dispensation. You'd need permission. From her guardian."

"Grant it, Cardinal. If you ever had an ounce of love for me, grant me her hand in marriage."

Mazarin took two steps toward me. "I would kill her first."

The king and I took a step back. Though I squeezed his hand as hard as I could, it seemed King Louis was slipping out of my grasp. We glanced at each other.

He turned back to the cardinal and said, "Swear you won't send her to a convent."

"Louis!" I cried.

The king ignored me. "We can revise our demands. I'm willing to make concessions if King Philip is not. Swear you won't send Marie to a convent while we remove the marriage article."

The cardinal curled his mustache.

King Louis went on. "I will call off the peace and muster the army for a campaign in the west tomorrow if you do not assure me Marie remains within *my* realm while we work on the treaty."

At last the cardinal nodded. "She may remain in France, but not in Paris. She's leaving."

"To a city of her own choosing."

I pulled his arm. "Louis!" *It cannot end this way!*

"Very well," said the cardinal. He turned to go, calling over his shoulder, "She leaves within the week."

King Louis grabbed my shoulders and whispered low, "I've never seen him this way. He would have sent you to Italy, where I might never find you."

"The cardinal's prediction was correct," I said in disbelief. "He made you send me away."

"I've bought time. I can convince him."

"Once Mazarin gets you to himself he will make you forget me. He'll let you argue your cause all the way to the altar, and it will be too late." I sat on the floor in a heap of silk and tears. "Recruit Condé. Invite him into France with his Spanish troops to overthrow Mazarin."

The king knelt beside me. "Condé would overthrow me in the process, my love."

"Ally with King Charles of England. He'll soon be restored to his throne, and then you will have the might of the English army."

He shook his head, unbelieving.

He'd made up his mind—he had outgrown my influence. But if King Louis couldn't use his power to keep me at the Louvre, would he ever have the power to marry me? "What can we do?"

He took a deep breath. "I'm going to try talking to my mother."

CHAPTER 39

Evil will not depart from the house of him that pays evil for good.

— PROVERBS 17:13

K ing Louis left. I remained on the floor, leaning on the window casement. "The cardinal has bewitched him! Moréna, you must obtain the
king's urine, bake it in a cake, and feed it to a stray dog to break the spell."

"You think I haven't tried?" she asked. "The king's valet is in the cardinal's
pay." She grabbed her birch besom and swept the cardinal's evil residue out
the door. "I could finish him painlessly. A tasteless potion."

"You cannot kill my uncle. We wouldn't be able to live with ourselves."

"I would," she said proudly. "It's no worse than his kind have done to
my people in slavery."

I could easily mention Mazarin's mustache comb, where she'd find stray
hairs to mold into a wax poppet that she could drop in the River Seine.
"Whatever harm we wrought in this life comes back to us. Leave Mazarin
to God."

She went back to arranging my things. I stayed on the floor and watched
a sliver of sky turn from afternoon pink to twilight ink. Would it make
any difference if I brought out all my tools to read the stars now? Perhaps
I shouldn't have resisted using magical elements to attain my desires.
After all, I'd been trying to alter fate.

When the servants came in with supper, Venelle arrived with Hortense
and Marianne.

"We're to stay with you," said Hortense, crouching beside me.

I didn't move. "Venelle must take the other chamber with Marianne. I don't want her in here."

Hortense gestured to Venelle, who moved to the adjoining chamber with no argument. Her job would be easy now.

I clung to Hortense's hand. "Do you remember how to make that charm for protection Papa always made for us? The one of rue and a cross of brown agate?"

She left to find the necessary objects. But she never uncovered a cross of brown agate, and brought a cross of jet instead. I stayed put as she wrote the prayer, mixed the bag, and hung it around my neck. She sat with me until everyone else had gone to sleep and her own eyes drooped heavily. "You must come to bed," she said.

"I won't."

She took me gently by the hand with such a sweet look that I couldn't argue. She led me to bed and tucked herself beside me and held me while I cried myself to sleep.

Venelle and Marianne's chamber had the larger dining table, which is where we broke our fast in the morning. The cardinal sent up servants with asparagus soup and dainty pastries and ham in parsley and butter. Moréna looked terrified when I accepted a porcelain dish full of a prized golden brew from the east called tea. *She's leery.* I loved tea; it smelled heavenly. Then I thought back to all those Italians traipsing in and out of Palazzo Mancini back in Rome, with their stories of poison and the ease of disposing of rivals. I wondered how well I knew Mazarin, a cardinal who'd torn my room apart looking for a book on necromancy. I thought of the look in his eye when he'd said to King Louis, *I'd kill her first.* I shuddered, dropping the porcelain dish. Venelle rushed to clean the mess. I left my food untouched and moved to a chair Hortense had dragged to my post at the window.

A commotion arose beyond my door midmorning. The voices of the musketeers standing guard outside mingled with the king's. The king denounced them angrily, and it was quiet again. I glanced at Moréna, who nodded. She slipped out through the servants' passage to learn what she could. She didn't return for hours.

* * *

"The king has gone from the cardinal to the queen and back again in a rage," said Moréna when she finally returned. My sisters sat in the other chamber for dinner, and Moréna arranged herself at my feet by the window.

"The cardinal will travel to Saint-Jean-de-Luz to meet the Spanish prime minister, review the treaty, modify it, and finally ratify it," she said. "The process will take months. The king and queen mother will accompany him as far as Bayonne, so they will be nearby if difficulties arise. A large portion of the court will go."

"So I can stay at the Louvre?"

She shook her head. "You leave before anyone else."

"Why? What happened?"

She hesitated. "After the king railed at the cardinal for denying access to your rooms, the king went to his mother. He begged her to order the cardinal to grant your hand in marriage. She insisted he couldn't choose you over France. He . . . he threw a fit. Yelling, screaming, and crying, he threatened to elope."

"Really?" I felt a glimmer of hope that faded as its meaning sank in. He was willing to give up France. "I suppose she cursed my name."

Moréna shook her head. "No. She became so alarmed that the king might elope, she followed the king to the cardinal's chamber. She actually urged the cardinal to let you go to Bayonne. To not separate you and King Louis."

"She wouldn't. She hates me."

"She *fears* you. And fears what the king might do if he can't keep you."

"Keep me? You mean as a mistress?"

Moréna nodded. "The queen mother considers it a compromise."

"That is an an insult after being promised a crown."

Moréna looked down. "The cardinal refused anyway. You leave for a city of your choosing in two or three days."

"The king will choose." I turned my gaze back to the window, to the sky.

"You should eat now, my lady."

But I had no stomach for it.

I counted the passing hours by the toll of church bells announcing masses throughout Paris while Moréna roamed the Louvre for news. The king couldn't visit. My sisters urged me to take bread, wine, sips of broth.

Unable to eat, I sat in my chair at the window and waited. They bathed me, tended my hair and nails, and avoided talking. Even Venelle respected the cloak of quiet I'd wrapped around myself. On the third night, the king was admitted.

I tried to stand but had no strength. "My love."

He sat at my feet, put his head in my lap. There were times when that gesture would have set my skin to tingling, and I'd have longed for him to slide a hand up my leg. Now his tears dampened my skirt, and I felt only sorrow. He had failed.

Which meant I had failed. I failed to make him the powerful king he was destined to be. But I knew I was right. He *would* be the most glorious king of all time. I glanced at the stars. Perhaps if I had read them more carefully, I'd have understood his timing better. But I had let fear steal that opportunity, and now it was too late to be part of his life.

"My love," he replied. "Tomorrow you leave for La Rochelle."

"La Rochelle tomorrow, the next day Italy."

"No," he said emphatically. "I know for certain they won't move you, because they agreed to let me come to you at La Rochelle in a fort-night."

"When you are on your way south to your wedding."

He glanced away. "I will not cease trying to eliminate article twenty-three." He removed a velvet bundle from his doublet and opened it on my lap. Out rolled a strand of huge, luminous pearls. "They belonged to my aunt the exiled Queen Henrietta Maria of England. She sold them to me."

Judging by their size and luster, they were worth a castle. "How did you get the money for this?"

"I made the cardinal pay."

What the cardinal had ought to have been the king's anyway. I smiled. "They are lovely, but I cannot wear them. They are fit for a queen."

"You must wear them. We will be together."

I didn't touch the pearls. "My own Rinaldo, you give me this gift, yet you cannot wed me. What is your intention?"

"You've lost faith."

"Don't degrade me by asking me to be your mistress."

He stood and walked behind my chair. As he reached over me to take the pearls from my lap, his lips grazed my neck. "I will never give up." He brought the pearls to rest, cool and heavy, above my collarbone. He knotted their ribbon behind my neck. "You shouldn't either."

CHAPTER 40

Moréna rose before dawn and packed. Mazarin arrived, standing in my doorway with a stream of servants trickling in from behind him like an army of ants. They disassembled my room, carting carpets and furniture down to the wagons.

Mazarin leaned on his gold cane. "Here is how things will be."

"I won't listen." I turned away.

"Because of the hold you still have on the king, I am handling you gently. The more intelligent side of you must know he is the only reason you are still alive."

Bile rose in my throat.

"The king will write you letters. He will visit. He will even tinker with plans to help you escape and elope. You will ignore him. This relationship ends when you leave the Louvre. You will make a marriage alliance of my choice."

I should have let Moréna poison him. "I will not marry another."

"Today is your fall from favor. The king will marry, and you will be an outcast. Be wise. Accept my marriage alliance for you. Salvage the tatters of your life . . . or accidents may befall you."

Another threat? I glanced at his cane. "How is your health, Uncle? Do your bones ache as I warned you they would if you ever hurt me? Does your body wither?"

He only stared.

"As you steal our happiness, so shall you sicken," I whispered. "You shall not live to see France made great."

He turned to go, ignoring my words. "The queen mother insists you should say farewell to King Louis. Find him in his apartments." With that, he limped out.

I stood in the empty chamber until Moréna nudged me. She fluffed my hair and straightened my skirts. "Hurry if you wish to see the king!" She pushed me through the doorway.

My silk slippers made no sound on the stairs, the marble tiles of the gallery, or the parquet floor in the antechambers. My slow steps didn't rustle my skirts, didn't bounce my curls.

Every courtier and noble man or woman living near Paris had come. They clutched together in the galleries and crowded the chambers. They did not sneer. There were no frowns, no whispers. No fluttering fans or haughty looks. I had fallen. I had the king's favor, and I had still fallen. I was like each of them: at Cardinal Mazarin's mercy. Footmen opened both doors to the king's bedchamber. I walked in, and they closed the courtiers out.

The king sat at the table, eyes swollen and red. "Is it time?"

I didn't speak.

He stood and handed me a leather purse of coins. "I have secured messengers and will write every day. Please tell me you'll write back."

I didn't answer.

"I will see you in a fortnight. If I can delay the peace treaty, Mazarin swears he will let you choose your next residence. You are to choose Brouage." He waited for me to answer, and continued when I didn't. "Brouage is by the sea. If Mazarin sends men to take you into Italy, use this money to escape by boat. For God's sake, do nothing to provoke him." He studied my face. "Do you hear me? Tell me you understand."

The doors swung open again. The time had come.

King Louis pressed his eyes, and I knew he was hiding tears.

"Sire," I finally said, "you weep, you are king, and yet I am leaving."

He didn't respond. He slowly lowered his hands. He avoided looking at me but gave me his arm. Together we retraced my steps through the courtiers. This time they lowered themselves, curtsying into satin skirt puddles or presenting their legs and bending at the waist as the king and I passed. We walked to the Cour Carrée, where carriages waited.

From the steps I glanced up at the façade of the Louvre and saw faces peeping down from every window. Mazarin glowered from his carriage. Hortense, Marianne, and Venelle climbed into the one designated to carry us. The world seemed strangely still. As if we were in a painting, no church bells tolled, no birds sang. It was as quiet as a theater full of spectators watching the end of a tragic play.

Tears ran down my king's face. Our eyes met.

What is left to say? I turned, climbed into my carriage, and didn't look back. I put my head in Hortense's lap. We started rolling, and I heard myself cry out, "It is over. I am abandoned."

CHAPTER 41

Take a toad, whip it, and make it swallow arsenic, and then kill it in the silver vessel that you want to poison.

— MARIE BOSSE,
accused witch and condemned poisoner burned alive in Paris in 1679

The rain started falling before we were out of Paris. It fell on the commoners who stood along the road watching our departure. They didn't sling mud. They didn't shout hatred for Italians. They let the rain pelt their hair and their smocks. Did they feel the ache of lovers torn apart? Did they love their king so much that they would have accepted me as his choice? We rumbled past the city gates. The rain no longer fell on people but on meadows and trees and fluffy sheep. We must have stopped at Vincennes, for my uncle separated from our train there. But I was hardly present. My mind, my strength, my whole being had dripped from my body. Venelle complained of discomfort. I felt none. Marianne huffed with boredom. I felt none. Hortense clung to my hand, squeezing it every once in a while in some gesture of affection. I felt none. I could've slit my very wrists and felt nothing.

We made it as far as Notre Dame de Cléry. Town officials gathered us beneath the shadow of the great basilica and the relentless drizzle for a welcome harangue, but I hardly heard. The Cardinal's Guards directed us to the King's House across the street, a long white building in the Italian style.

Moréna arrived to ready me for bed. "My lady . . ." She looked concerned.

"I failed you. I'm sorry."

She shook her head. "I know I'm right about you, but I must have been wrong about the road we would travel."

I wanted to assure her we would find some new means of gaining the freedom she deserved, but no words would come.

"When did you last eat?" she asked.

I crawled onto the bed, looking forward to being alone. "I don't want anything."

"Nonsense. Your uncle sent his cooks, and I'm fetching them up."

She was gone before I could protest, and returned within the quarter hour with a silver dish of ham broth. She propped herself behind me and put it to my lips. The savory and sweet hit my tongue, and my stomach growled for more. She fed me the bowlful, and that was all I could take. "Thank you," I whispered.

She blew out the candle and settled on the floor pallet. I lay motionless, wishing I hadn't eaten, too exhausted to get up and purge myself. I didn't want to sleep. I wanted to waste away into nothing until my soul could separate from my body and fly up to the heavens, free from the cares and the sorrows and the rain and the disappointments of this life.

I could not wake up. Hortense's voice came as if my ears were underwater. She said I had a letter from the king. A great long letter with the king's seal, brought by his private messenger. I fought to sit up, but my limbs were heavy logs. It alarmed me. I tried to speak, to order them to read the letter, but my voice would not sound. I tried to scream! But my body wouldn't obey. All I managed was a flicker of my eyelids, long enough to see Moréna and Hortense leaning over me. One of them shook me, but then everything went murky and soundless for a long time.

Thoughts drifted in the darkness. Had I died? Had I made my wish come true and sent my soul soaring to the heavens? I searched frantically for the stars, but there was only black expanse. I waited an age for my father's shadowy phantoms to grab me, but they never came. I felt heat and looked for hell's fire, but I was still drifting in obscurity. Once I thought I saw my mother's ghost. Voices seeped through saying "fever," "don't move her," and "don't tell the king."

But I wanted to tell the king. I struggled to scream, "Fetch the king!" But I couldn't, and fell into the darkness again. How long could I linger?

Hands lifted me. Opened my mouth. Put something tangy and warm on my tongue and rubbed my throat. A voice said "poison," and I welcomed it. If only it would speed my release.

I saw red that hurt my eyes. I opened my lids and the red gave way to bright white. It took several blinks, but I soon made out a chamber. I was on a strange bed, and Hortense sat in a chair beside me.

"My lady!" cried Moréna. She dropped a heap of linens and rushed to me.

Hortense jumped up. "Drink this. You must drink, Marie."

I tried to ask her what it was, to decline if it wasn't the poison that would end this suffering, but my lips only twitched.

They took it as consent and shoveled the liquid in. "It is broth from our own cook this time," said one of them. "We mixed it with *orviétan*."

An antipoison.

The next time I opened my eyes it was dark, with the dim flicker of a candle on a nearby table. Hortense was gone, and Moréna slept on the floor. There had been a letter. I looked around, seeing none. Hadn't someone said the king wrote me a letter?

"M—" But my voice sounded like air.

In the chair where Hortense had been, there sat a flask. Was it the poison? The antipoison? My mouth felt like a dry creek bed, and I didn't care what it contained. I was obviously on the mend. It took every ounce of resolve to reach out and grab the flask. Could that hand be mine? So thin and trembling? It obeyed and brought the flask to my lips. Watered wine poured out, wetting my face, pooling on my tongue. I swallowed what I could before I passed out.

A great commotion went up in my chamber. A basin scraping the floor. Pots clanging. Female voices. I opened my eyes. Venelle carried my feet while someone hoisted me by the armpits, dragging my limp form out of bed. They lowered me into the tub, and my chemise floated off my skin to the surface of jasmine-scented water.

"She is awake," Hortense said. She appeared beside me with bowl and spoon in hand. I opened my mouth for the soup she fed me.

Venelle massaged and stretched one of my legs. "You must get well, child."

How long had it been?

Moréna poured water over my hair and scrubbed my head. It felt luxurious.

"We thought he killed you!" blurted Marianne. She handed a vat of water to Moréna.

"Hush," said Venelle. "It was just a fever." But the look on her face spoke of uncertainty.

Hortense said, "After Moréna fed you that ham broth, our uncle's cook disappeared. You wouldn't wake up."

Marianne refreshed the vat of water from a pot in the fireplace and handed it to Moréna again. "The king went raving mad when he learned you were ill. He accused the queen of poisoning you. Everyone heard him."

Venelle gestured for Marianne to be silent, then spoke gently to me. "The cardinal sent a message saying you must get well. He comes today to check on you himself. He is bringing his physicians."

I laughed, and each of them paused. "His Eminence doesn't want me *well* any more than he wants me on the throne."

They stared, probably more shocked that I could speak than at what I'd said.

"Well, wash me and feed me. I've lost the battle, but I've no wish to give him the satisfaction of my death."

King Louis had sent two dozen letters over a fortnight. I read them slowly, savoring his words of longing, hope, reassurance. He stayed at Chantilly so the court wouldn't see his tears. When he learned they'd been concealing my illness from him, he rushed to his mother at Fontainebleau and accused her of trying to kill me. He informed Mazarin that if I died or disappeared, he'd figure out a way to confiscate Mazarin's property. He'd signed each letter:

Do not lose faith in he who truly loves you,

L

But it was over. Wasn't it? Perhaps it was just the weakness in my body from prolonged illness, but I had no strength for faith. I slept, and in the evening awoke to sounds of the officials welcoming Mazarin outside. I shoved the letters under my pillow.

He came to my room leaning heavily on his cane. "You are awake."

I grinned. "And alive. Sorry to disappoint you."

He frowned. Oh, how he hated me. "You must write to the king at once."

"Must I?"

He paused. "*Yes.*"

I looked about. "Where are your physicians?" There was a pause. "You brought no physicians because you know my *illness* was no illness. What did you learn from your collection of occult books besides poisons? Your enemies would love to know."

He looked away. "You talk nonsense."

"I talk from a position of advantage. If I don't write, the king will come here, and I will tell him things. The king will prove himself his own master, and you can't have that."

"Write a neutral letter of reassurance, or I will put Olympia in his bed."

I blinked. "What?"

"She knows how to blur his judgment. She will confuse and arouse him with her potions and destroy what he feels for you."

Had I not been lying down I might have fainted.

"Write. My courier will take your missive to the king at dawn." He left.

I closed my eyes. Could I persevere? If I could send a private message warning Louis against Olympia, I could confirm the accusation of poisoning since the cardinal brought no physicians. Hadn't Louis given me money to hire messengers? But he had also advised me not to provoke Mazarin. The fatigue crept in before I could work it out.

I wrote King Louis a neutral letter of reassurance just before dawn.

CHAPTER 42

The cardinal stayed with our party, but I remained in my chambers. Venelle stretched and massaged my legs every day. Moréna bathed me. Hortense fed me. I slowly regained my strength. But not enough to face the cardinal. I would surely lose any battle with him.

When I could again endure travel, we resumed our journey to La Rochelle by way of Chambord, where we stayed a few days at Gaston, duc d'Orléans's, deserted château.

I did not like the Château de Chambord. With its keep and huge corner towers, it was certainly beautiful. Gaston had done what he could afford to restore it, but it still crumbled and echoed like a forgotten lover—a reminder of Gaston's defeat that punctuated my loneliness. Marianne and Hortense ran up and down the double-spiral staircase designed by the old master Leonardo da Vinci, and I sat by the door, staring down the walk toward the moat.

If the cardinal hoped our travels would stop the king's letters, he was disappointed. Private messengers arrived almost daily. If they missed a day, they came the next day with *two* letters. One day the messenger brought a total of five letters of five pages each and a miniature portrait of His Majesty.

"He sent Marie a picture of himself?" asked Marianne, breathless from her race down the fancy staircase.

"It's a marked sign of favor," Hortense answered.

I tucked in into my bodice close to my heart. His Majesty's love was the only thing that kept it beating.

By the time we reached Poitiers, my uncle started showing outright alarm. "How many letters did the king send you today?" he asked, bursting into the bedchamber I shared with Hortense. There was no castle to house us here, only the *hôtel* of some minor nobility who'd welcomed us with looks of pity.

"Only two," I said.

"What does he say?"

That he feels dead without me. To only use private messengers. That I can trust Colbert de Terron. To keep faith in him. "Nothing."

"There are too many reports from Paris and Fontainebleau about the many messengers going back and forth. Do not write a reply for three days," he said, wincing with pain as he walked out. "And use *my* courier!"

"As you wish," I called after him.

I sat to write my reply immediately and sent the letter by private messenger.

My only king, without your letters I think I might have died,
and daily I think I do die a little for want of your company,
but your words, your writing, they are my sustenance, and I
imagine they are an extension of you, as I put the letters to my
face and almost feel your caress, which is the only thing I long for
in this world, and the one thing that gives hope to the heart that
swears she will never lose faith, the one that is entirely yours
for as long as the stars shine in the heavens,
M

Within days our households prepared to separate. The townspeople of Poitiers gathered outside to witness the spectacle of our glittering carriages, the repacking of wagons that had only been unpacked days before, and armed Cardinal's Guards amassing on the road; my traveling prison. The cardinal's carriages pointed south for Bayonne, where the king's court would join him. My train would head southwest to La Rochelle.

Trojan stood harnessed to the team of horses that would pull my carriage. Before climbing in, I fed him oat cakes from my pockets and stroked his nose. "My poor steed," I murmured. "One day we might race the king again." Just then I caught sight of Moréna standing among a clutch of commoners in the street. She spoke to a man wearing a turban, handing him something that flashed in the morning sun. She gestured toward me, and the man turned. He was Arabian. But he left, disappearing in the crowd. Moréna climbed into a wagon, and I forgot it.

Mazarin handed my sisters into our carriage with congenial parting words. But to me he hissed, "Don't write so much to King Louis. Let his heart mend."

"As you wish."

"And you will use my couriers?"

I smiled. "As you wish."

He studied me for traces of deception, but I kept my expression plain.

And in the carriage I drafted in my mind what I would write to the king as soon as we arrived in La Rochelle.

L a Rochelle functioned under our uncle's direct governance and his appointed intendant, my friend Colbert de Terron. We arrived to a cannon salute in mid-July. Terron and the city's municipal authorities spoke a formal welcome harangue designed to impress. I felt myself grow tired in the sun as they droned on.

Terron stepped away from the authorities, holding a red velvet canopy aloft to shade me. He glanced over his shoulder before he whispered, "Your uncle appointed me to keep watch over you. But the king charged me to be your particular servant."

I grinned. God praise the king.

Villagers illuminated the town with torches and bonfires to celebrate our arrival. I wrote a letter by candlelight late into the night.

"What else could you possibly have left to tell the king?" asked Marianne, a little too curious.

"That I have met his secret agent and that I will be queen or die." Then I clamped my mouth. Though a wisp of a child, Marianne could be wily.

* * *

In the morning, Venelle came to my chamber before I could get my missive to Terron. "You've written a letter," she said.

I eyed Marianne, who rushed to hide behind Venelle's skirts. "Of course I haven't."

Venelle scowled. "I know you wrote, and I know you intend to send it through a secret agent. I insist you send your letter through the cardinal's courier. Don't wear yourself out with a fuss in your weakened state. Come, give me the letter."

I wanted to yank Marianne's hair. "If you wish me to write a letter for the cardinal's courier, I shall." I sat at my table. I wrote a bland letter to the king that I knew Venelle would copy for Mazarin. I gave it to Venelle.

She scurried out with it.

I sat and wrote another, explaining the decoy letter.

Hours later Terron came for his daily supervisory visit, and I slipped both real letters to him. "What news?" I asked.

"King and court have set south from Paris," he said almost apologetically. "But I'll get these letters to the king wherever he is."

Days later, I received a letter from the king that contained one of Mazarin's letters. The cardinal called me a liar. Unworthy of love. Ambitious. Greedy. He threatened to send me to a convent in Italy. But the king assured me he hated the cardinal for his ill treatment of me, and promised to tell him so.

Venelle stormed into my chamber that night. "Have you sent the king secret messages?"

I stared blankly.

"I should have known." She looked exasperated. All the care she showed nursing me back to health disappeared. "The cardinal says there are diplomats in Flanders, Germany, Paris, and Madrid wagging their tongues about your affair with the king. They speak of nothing but the stream of messengers he receives and how he does nothing but read and write letters all day long."

I smiled. "Fault belongs to the cardinal and queen mother for separating us. Tell them that next time you send your reports."

"You are not to leave this room. You shall receive no messengers."

"You *cannot* prevent a messenger from the king coming to me."

* * *

The next day a dusty messenger from the king stormed into my room, stomping mud and carrying a packet of letters. Venelle tramped in after him, red as I'd ever seen her. She stood in the corner, wringing her hands, while the road-weary messenger caught his breath. The old spy could do nothing about it. The packet contained more letters Mazarin had written to the king. King Louis bid me to read them and judge what we ought to do next. So, I read.

Mazarin was outraged. Mazarin was ill. Mazarin was delaying his journey to the Pyrenees, where final negotiations were to take place.

"Hortense!" I cried. "Everything is delayed. Their trip, the negotiations, even the marriage."

Venelle looked helpless. The messenger looked shocked.

"All is not lost," said Hortense.

Beaming, I sat to write my response.

> My darling king once promised to visit the one he loves so that
> her soul might be nourished, and now would be the time,
> for that soul languishes like a flower without her Sun King.
> The more you push to break your marriage article, the more
> I begin to hope, and the more I fear my uncle, and so I urge you,
> my love, to send our friend in prison some means to escape
> and come to my aid, for a time might soon come that we have
> need of his protection. I beg you never to forget the one
> who loves you,
> M

CHAPTER 43

August 1658

The king even went on his knees before the queen mother and the cardinal to obtain their consent to his marrying Marie Mancini.

—MADEMOISELLE DE MONTPENSIER'S MEMOIRS

The court lumbered south slowly, and Venelle received messengers from the queen mother within weeks. They issued orders to deliver me to Saint-Jean-d'Angély for an audience with the king. I put Moréna through a frenzy of preparations.

"None of your gowns fit anymore," grumbled Moréna as she pinched an inch of loose silk around my ribs.

"It doesn't matter," I said. "He will be there, and he will take me with him to the Pyrenees, where I can stop this marriage."

She looked skeptical, but I ignored her.

I urged our driver to make haste. We spent a night in Surgères and arrived at Saint-Jean-d'Angély the next midday. The very next morning, one of the king's musketeers arrived to announce His Majesty's arrival was imminent.

I stood in the doorway of the Abbey Saint-Jean-d'Angély with my sisters and Venelle waiting behind. The monks, who had opened their abbey and presented a rich supper, loitered in the courtyard, eyeing me curiously.

Everyone knew. The town talked of nothing else. We'd been given the usual welcome harangue and every show of respect. The townspeople treated us like princesses of the blood. *They know I might yet become their queen.* It bolstered my spirits.

The thunder of his entourage sounded before we saw him. The monks scurried out of the way, and city officials rushed from the guildhall. He galloped through the gates. An armed musketeer on each side, horses lathered into a sweat, they halted in a shower of gravel. I ran out. He leapt from his saddle and swept me into his arms. *At last!* The officials blurted a brief welcome, and the king gave them a polite nod. They knew he didn't want to see them.

We walked into the abbey, where Venelle and my sisters curtsied. "Your Majesty," they chanted in unison.

I gestured toward the reception room, and the king led me inside. Venelle moved to follow, but King Louis turned. He said not a word, just stared her down. The musketeers marched into the hall, the sound of their metal spurs causing Venelle to jump. King Louis closed the door in her face.

"My love," he said, cupping my chin. He looked thin; the angles of his face seemed sharp, more lined.

"My king."

He smelled of dust from the road and the countryside winds, but I didn't care. We moved toward a divan and fell into a heap of heated kisses. There were a thousand questions, but I wanted him more than I needed answers. He made me weightless; everything faded when we touched. "Your mother and the court?" I asked, suddenly nervous.

"Two full hours behind me. I wanted you to myself as long as I could manage."

And he made those two hours the most memorable of my young life.

We were asleep on the floor by the time Moréna slipped into the reception room. "The court approaches, my lady. They are at the city gates."

She snatched up lace, stockings, garters. We'd made a pallet of our clothes and lay stretched in a sunny spot under the window. Moréna didn't flinch at the sight of our naked bodies tangled together, just helped us dress.

I clung to King Louis. "This might be the last—"

He put a finger to my lips. "We must make her welcome you back into the court. She has softened to our plight. You'll see."

The sounds of the city officials making their welcome harangue to the queen rose outside. Moréna assured me my hair was perfect, and King Louis opened the doors.

Venelle studied our appearance, fanning herself. Hortense and Marianne gaped at us. There was no time for explanations. The monks outside in the court offered the abbey, and the queen mother walked in at the head of her ladies.

She looked me up and down. To my astonishment, she bore not a trace of her old animosity. And though there wasn't an angle in her round face, she, too, seemed more lined with worry. This separation had drained everyone. I myself was too weak, too worn, too worried to shoot her defiant looks. I dipped low before her. So low that my legs lost their strength. I caught myself with a hand on the floor.

"Rise, Mademoiselle Mancini," she said. "I'm weary and will retire. I've traveled long so we all might have this brief respite." She moved toward her wing, and her train moved with her.

Except Martinozzi and Olympia. Martinozzi embraced me. "Take courage," she said, then followed the queen.

Olympia smirked. "Take all the courage you want, sister. It's nothing weighed against the great anger you've sparked in our uncle. He's charged me to tell you just how many burning coals you've heaped upon your own head. You must come to my rooms for supper."

I opened my mouth to make some excuse, but King Louis cut me off.

"No," he said. "I forbid Marie from supping with you, Olympia. I will sup with the queen, and so will you."

She grinned, careless. "Whatever you wish, sire. But what you don't let me make her see, our uncle will make her see in time."

"Get out of here, Olympia." He put an arm around my shoulders, walking me toward my wing. We settled at the table in my bedchamber, where my sisters sat on the floor playing marbles, with Venelle watching from the adjoining chamber.

I felt a nagging discomfort. "Does Olympia accompany you in your train?"

He nodded. "Forget Olympia. My mother finally understands the force of my feelings for you. Convince her to let you join us in the Pyrenees. The Spanish will see the affection Pimentel saw between us and will withdraw the marriage article themselves."

"But the peace?"

He looked away. "Perhaps Spain will want to carry through with it."

"And if your mother refuses to let me join her?"

He stared. I could see he had not allowed himself to consider it.

"Think of every scenario. Have options for any eventuality. You are a warrior. You know this. You also know traitors attack from within. Beware of Olympia."

He frowned at Olympia's name. "All Europe knows that if ill befalls you again I will tear the peace treaty into little bits. If you cannot join us, you will wait at La Rochelle, and I . . . will pressure Mazarin to make more concessions in the peace treaty."

It isn't enough. "Threaten to remove him from office! Be king."

He sat back. "I *am* being king, with as delicate a touch as possible. Threatening to remove him will make him withdraw to Italy and he will take you with him."

I pulled him gently to me again. "You're right. Forgive me. What news of my brother's release?"

He merely shook his head. "If the cardinal tries to seize you, flee to the seaside citadel at Brouage. Use the money I gave you. Make promises in my name—anything necessary to secure yourself. Keep a hired boat at the ready. It will take the cardinal too long to prepare a sea pursuit. Just don't leave France. If he locks you in a convent in Italy, I won't be able to force your release."

My head dropped, and I turned his hands over to stare at his palms. I traced the solar line that had inspired much hope in me. "You are destined for greatness." I rubbed my thumb across the heart line that I'd chosen to ignore. Extending from the mound of Jupiter beneath his index finger to the mound of Mercury under his pinkie, it was as weak and wavy as my own. I put my right palm beside his left and saw that our fate lines didn't match. I didn't want to admit what those lines might mean.

He laced his fingers in mine, pressing our palms together. "No fortune-telling. We'll write our own destiny, you'll see."

We spoke no more of our future, and for an hour tried to discuss books and music. Neither of us could keep up the dissembling, and finally we just sat together, quiet, still.

K ing Louis stayed with me until two in the morning, when I made him go to his own chambers for fear of upsetting his mother. He returned to my rooms at dawn, where we sat together before a table that the monks loaded with cheeses, fish, eggs, fruits, and peas and an arrangement of sunflowers. We were too anxious about the upcoming meeting to eat.

Midmorning, we had word that the queen mother had heard mass and was prepared to leave. The king walked me to her antechamber. "You must curtsy when you ask. Stay low," muttered the king.

I nodded, feeling weak, and he ushered me in.

The women stopped what they were doing to curtsy.

King Louis called out, "Mother, my favorite has a petition to make of you."

The queen mother turned from her table to face us.

I dipped low, this time commanding my legs to hold firm. "Most Gracious Majesty," I said, "with a humble and broken heart, I beseech you, please allow me to follow your court south so that I might be present for the upcoming celebration of peace." I didn't stand; I didn't even look up. The room was silent. I knew her answer before she spoke.

"Since it is clearly what my son desires, I admit I would allow you to follow me." Everyone held their breath. "But first you must get permission from your guardian."

I stood, keeping my eyes downcast. Her answer was as good as a refusal.

"Mother—" started the king.

"Sire," she said, interrupting, "even I cannot overturn her guardian's rights over her."

I gathered my skirts and curtsied quickly, backing from the chamber, then fled to my rooms. The king's shouts seemed to shake the very walls, but I didn't comprehend a word.

The queen mother's train left within the quarter hour. Without me.

King Louis came to my chamber, red-eyed and hoarse. I felt blown apart, as if I had taken a musket ball to the chest. Marianne stared at us for a long while. Hortense cried. Even Venelle seemed forlorn. Finally Marianne bawled earnestly, something I'd never seen her do. I soaked the king's doublet with my own tears. I didn't know how long we stood together.

"I cannot bear to say good-bye to you again, sire," I heard myself say. "Please . . . go." I led him to the entrance hall and out the door.

"I won't give up. Remember my instructions." He kissed me on the mouth, warm and lingering, before the gathered monks and townspeople.

I tasted his tears. The only sound was Marianne's wails rising above the courtyard. He got on his horse and tore off like lightning around the corner, musketeers galloping after. The world went black, and I had a faint sense of hitting the ground.

CHAPTER 44

We returned to La Rochelle, and the king's letters streamed in, two a day. Marianne didn't bother spying anymore. I had Hortense read them aloud.

"He says the cardinal is furious about Saint-Jean-d'Angély. Olympia complained that you and King Louis spent hours alone in the reception room before the queen arrived. She suggested you did more than talk." She gasped. "The cardinal is making arrangements to send you to the Benedictine Convent of Santa Maria in the Campo Marzio quarter of Rome!"

I sighed. "Shall I placate the cardinal?"

Hortense looked confused. "Didn't the king tell you to flee?"

"We just need a little more time." And a little push to make Mazarin show his vile side. I moved to my table and wrote Mazarin a letter full of reassurances that I would obey him, that I trusted him to decide my future, and that I would never write to the king again. Lies, all. Then I dipped my quill into ink and wrote to the king, confessing love and adoration in the most affectionate terms.

I gave the cardinal's letter to his courier.

Then I slipped the king's letter to Terron, saying, "This letter should fall into the wrong hands."

"Are you sure?" Terron asked.

It would cause a firestorm. "I am."

* * *

D ays later, Venelle paced my chamber like a caged cat. "Cardinal Mazarin has both of your letters." She didn't catch me hide my smile. "He calls you the most deceitful woman ever to live and breathe. He wrote to tell King Louis so in a scathing letter." She stared at me. "Marie, I really would rather not be forced to travel all the way to *Rome!*"

She shouldn't have admitted that.

K ing Louis sent me the scathing letter a week later. The cardinal had actually called me uncontrollable, ambitious, contrary, unreasonable, and worse, claiming I possessed not a single good quality. I read it to Hortense.

She frowned. "An ambitious woman makes weak men feel threatened."

"The cardinal says he will resign and take me to Italy himself." The final gauntlet.

"What did the king write back?" asked Hortense.

"He wrote Mazarin with rebukes for treating me harshly." I looked both letters over. "But that is all the king shared."

"Is *this* what you were hoping for?"

"My only choice was to force the matter or run." Now either the king would send for me, or the cardinal would come for me.

T hat night I made my sisters drag my bedstead to the window so I could watch the hills. My very skin crawled. Half of me wanted to run to Brouage, and half of me wanted to run straight to the king. But I stayed. I waited. And I watched the dark horizon.

The king's messenger rode down the hills at midnight. He was alone, guiding himself by a torch he held aloft. I leapt from my bed and met the man at the door. He handed me a short letter, panting. I read it while running back to my chamber.

> Your uncle offered his resignation if I didn't give final
> instruction in the matter of article twenty-three. I told him to
> be gone if he wished. Then, to prevent him from sending agents
> to accost you, I aimed to placate him by ordering him to keep
> article twenty-three with a postponed wedding date. It was an

attempt to borrow time and be neatly rid of him, which re-
bounded in ways I failed to foresee. He altered the date, pretended this was my consent, then signed the article as if I had
approved it. He dispatched an embassy to Madrid with the
official offer of marriage before telling me. My love, I beg you to
forgive me, for in trying to trick the man into letting me have
you, he has signed my freedom away. I am beside myself, nay, I
would rather fall on my sword than go through with this, and I
beg you to tell me what you would have me do.

L

I didn't drop to the floor and cry. I didn't rage and tear out my hair. I
grabbed the bell and rang it like hell for the servants. I called for Hortense
and Venelle, Moréna and Marianne. Everyone ran in at the same time.

"Pack essentials. Call up the carriage. Do not wake Terron. We leave for
Brouage immediately."

Venelle put out her hand. "It is the middle of the night. Besides, we go
nowhere without the cardinal's permission."

I must have looked frightful, all skin and bones in my shift, clinging to
that letter. "The cardinal has bested me. He has the king's marriage pro-
posal signed and dated, and my security has dried up fast as the ink he
used to forge the king's signature."

Venelle waved me off. "He is your uncle. He wouldn't hurt you."

"Clearly you haven't known many Italians," I said. "The cardinal has what
he wants. He no longer needs to be good to me in order to appease the
king. He will come for me. We flee for Brouage or *you* will be disposed in
Rome with me."

It took Venelle only a moment before jumping to action, packing and
dressing.

I flashed gold coins to the servants. I promised them payment to conceal
our destination from Mazarin's men and follow us to Brouage with our
belongings in a week. Moréna dragged my *cassone* to the courtyard. I
ordered the coachmen to harness Trojan at the head of the team.

"Please," begged Hortense, hugging a frightened Marianne as the driver
whipped the horses into motion. "Wake Terron. They'll never let us enter
the citadel of Brouage alone."

"We mustn't make our uncle suspect Terron. He is my only link to King Louis."

As we raced south of the city walls, we spotted torchlights moving down the hills toward La Rochelle. Venelle gaped in amazement, but I leaned from the window and screamed to the coachman, "Drive like the devil himself is at your back!"

CHAPTER 45

The coachman knew the way. We reached the salt marshes of Hiers-Brouage well before dawn, and the white walls of the citadel loomed along the moonlit bay. Lights gleamed from the watchtowers.

Hortense studied the angular demibastions of the hornwork and said, "There's no way in." She looked back the way we'd come, but I knew we hadn't been followed.

I called to the driver, "Take us along the bay side to the Royal Gate."

Hortense and Venelle exchanged doubtful looks, but the driver found the narrow archway tucked into the shadows of a curtain wall, and we soon halted. Our coachman pounded on the gate while we climbed from the carriage.

At last a door within the gate opened and a bearded man appeared, looking us over. The clink of keys hanging from his belt marked him as governor. "Be gone! We're in the service of His Majesty, and we don't welcome guests."

Our coachman held his lantern aloft so the man could see me clearly.

I smiled. "But you will welcome me, for I come in His Majesty's name."

The bearded governor squinted. "Who are you?"

"My name is Marie Mancini."

The man's eyes widened. *So it is true. Everyone, even in the farthest reaches of France, knows of me.* He rubbed his face, considering. "Cardinal Mazarin's niece."

I shook my head and tossed him a gold ecu. "Today I am His Majesty's guest. He will pay you and your men to house and protect me and my women." I gestured to Venelle and my sisters. "But you're to keep your fortress closed to Cardinal Mazarin."

He weighed the gold in his hand. "Never thought I'd see the king's woman at these gates."

The king's woman. Not queen. Not mistress. "What I am remains to be seen, sir, and depends on whether I have your protection."

He nodded, stepped back. "Welcome to the citadel of Brouage."

Soldiers showed us to quarters built for my uncle's predecessor. Damp and unused, they were mostly unfurnished. While the soldiers dragged in floor pallets, I sat at the cold hearth and wrote a letter to the cardinal.

"Why write to him when we've barely escaped him?" asked Hortense.

"We are protected here, though not for long. The only way I can hope for better terms from the cardinal is to submit."

"Does that mean you've truly given up?"

I held my quill over the foolscap and considered it. "I don't know."

O ur servants arrived days later with Terron in the lead. The governor of Brouage asked my permission before admitting him.

"When the Cardinal's Guards didn't find you at La Rochelle, they left quietly," Terron said to me as servants unpacked tapestries and carpets and bedding. "They feared a pursuit would be too public. You should have told me of your plans to flee."

"I couldn't implicate you because I need you to help free my brother. I'm not certain how long I can hold out here without reinforcements."

Terron shook his head. "Philippe won't be released until the king is safely married, and that wedding has been postponed until spring."

It was what I suspected he'd say, but I had to hide my disappointment.

"Word has gotten out that you're here," said Terron, tossing a packet of letters on the table. Most were to me from the king. Some were to Hortense.

"Tell Meilleraye to stop writing to Hortense. He may send his requests for her hand to the cardinal." I paused. "I wrote to Mazarin agreeing to end my affair with the king."

Terron seemed stunned. "The king is desperate to hear from you. You could still elope."

I felt my soul rise up to the notion. *Elope!* "The king won't risk losing his kingdom for me."

Terron leaned close. "He is making plans to marry you in secret. You could sail from Brouage to Bordeaux to meet him. Will you do it if he sends for you?"

"If we elope, what will happen to the peace treaty? Tell me the truth. What does your cousin Colbert say?" I glanced at Venelle, who cast us a glance from where she stood unpacking linens.

Terron hesitated. "Without the marriage, there will be no peace."

Why am I hesitating? "Forgive me, Terron, I must think it over."

CHAPTER 46

The city of Brouage was mostly contained within the walls of the citadel itself, and it bustled with business. The market stalls and shops, run by soldiers and their wives, sold goods fresh off ships in the port. Venelle let us explore within the walls on our own, affording a confined sort of freedom. People went about their business and let us alone.

Few farms dotted the marshy horizon, but fishermen bobbed on the ocean, shell fishers dug on the shore, and men worked the interlocking salt ponds, raking damp salt beds and shoveling dry salt into barrows. New merchant ships drifted in and out of the port daily, sailing in from exotic eastern lands, trading for salt, and embarking to sell their treasures to the colonies of New France and Canada. Venelle let me ride Trojan down the shore and back once a day, instructing the soldiers to observe me from the watchtowers.

I lived for those rides—the salt spray in my face, the rush of the ocean falling into rhythm with the cantor of Trojan's hoofs. It was the only time I felt at peace.

I kept my word to my uncle for once. I didn't write to the king. For weeks I ignored the hollow sick feeling inside. I lost myself in the seaside rides and refused to give Terron an answer. The king's letters arrived every day as his court crept south, finally settling in Provence to await the outcome of Mazarin's negotiations. The weather cooled. Gradually the tone of the king's letters changed from desperate to angry to pleading. Reading them robbed me of all hard-won peace.

"What is that?" cried Venelle at the doorway of our chambers after we'd been at Brouage a month.

Terron's voice sounded. "A gift from the king to Mademoiselle Mancini." He bent to deposit his bundle on the floor. It bounded across the chamber in my direction.

"A puppy!" I cried, scooping the little fur ball into my arms. She licked my face and hands. "Is she from Frippon's litter?"

"Indeed. Just weaned." Terron smiled proudly.

The leather collar around her neck had a silver plate engraved with the words *I belong to Marie Mancini.* I felt my heart both swell with joy and ache with longing. "Then I shall call her Frip."

Terron knelt beside me as I inspected my new spaniel. He blocked Venelle's view with his body and slipped me a letter. "You still haven't given your answer."

Ah, but the king hadn't *sent* for me, either.

I reached into my hanging pocket and tossed Terron a different sort of letter, one Olympia had recently written to me. "Tell me why I should believe the king loves me when he has fallen into Olympia's clutches."

He looked the letter over. "The queen mother must have put her up to sending this."

"Do you deny it?" I asked. "Can you honestly tell me the king doesn't frequent her chambers, dine every meal with her, dance with her, and play cards with her for hours as she claims? Have they rekindled their affair?"

He hesitated. "I . . . I have heard rumor of it. He even offered her the position of *dame d'honneur* of the new queen's bedchamber."

I watched Frip gnaw the hem of my skirts. "The king keeps me hanging on to hopes, plying me with love letters and gifts, all while continuing his slow march to the marriage altar. He doesn't want me for his wife. He thinks he'll make me his mistress." I took a breath. "But I am no Olympia. I won't be his mistress."

"Your uncle finalized the last of the articles of his peace treaty, though it won't be ratified until the wedding. He is retiring to Provence with the court to wait."

"The court will talk of my downfall. What humiliation."

Terron leaned close. "Once Mazarin and his guards get to Provence, it will be more difficult for the king to arrange an elopement. Act. Tell the king you are prepared to meet him in secret."

I shook my head. "Did my uncle tell you he offered to arrange a marriage for me? He suggested Lorenzo Colonna, prince of Paliano, Constable of Naples, the preeminent nobleman of Rome." This match would finally ally France and Naples. A new Naples Plan that made me bitter. "Though I would prefer someone like the Prince of Lorraine so I could remain in France."

Terron stood to go. "Decide. Before it's too late."

Terron left, and I peeked at the king's letter. He longed to hold me, to kiss me, to receive a letter from me. He didn't send for me. He was waiting for me to act. I knew King Louis couldn't fulfill his destiny as a great king without peace. Did I really want to be the cause of death, destruction, pillaging, food shortages, and heartache for the poor French, whom my uncle had already extorted? Letting Louis marry Spain would heal his nation . . . though it would break his heart.

I carried Frip past the bastion fortifications and demilunes of the citadel, down to the shore. I walked beyond the busy port of Brouage until it looked like a harbor of model ships. I passed the interlocking salt ponds, where men stopped raking to watch me. I settled on a dune and thought for hours. Herons hovered on the breeze, and shorebirds poked the wet sand with their long beaks. Frip fell asleep in my lap, and I imagined my many cares washed away by the ebbing tide.

Though I had taught him much about how to be a noble king, my work in King Louis was not yet complete. *But I am afraid to elope.* Hadn't my father predicted I would leave my husband? Sunset brought Venelle and the soldiers out to find me. I wondered, whether I married King Louis or not, was I was destined to hurt him?

CHAPTER 47

November 1659

Compacts and contracts of witches with devils and all infernal spirits or familiars are but erroneous novelties and imaginary conceptions.

—REGINALD SCOT, *The Discoverie of Witchcraft*

A week later, Marianne smacked her lips, eyes wide with delight as she handed a coin to the old sailor who ran a bakery within the walls of Brouage. In exchange, he handed her a few sugared candies from the holy land he'd traded for at the port.

She popped a *nebât* into her mouth. "Mmm!"

"You spend all your money on sugared candy," said Hortense. "You're going to get a stomachache again."

Marianne wrinkled her nose at Hortense. "Marie will give me more money." Had I been in the mood, I'd have laughed. I'd discovered how to keep Marianne from reporting my every last word to Venelle; she was cheaply bought.

Venelle had become so comfortable with our explorations within the walls of Brouage that Marianne could gorge herself on sweets every day. Today we strolled toward the little church for mass for wont of anything better to do.

But Hortense stopped at the opening of an apothecary shop. "There's something I need."

Curious, I followed her. Marianne trailed behind us, content with her candy. The scent of spices and tang of tinctures permeated the air. Hortense poked around the shelves, studying labels, swirling jars of liquid, and occasionally uncorking bottles to take a sniff. Finally she grabbed a jar of dried bugs and held them out to me, triumphant.

"Cochineal," I said. "Are you going to make rouge?"

She grabbed a block of wax wrapped in parchment, shaking her head. "It is for my lips. Isn't it time I started dressing the part of a fine lady like you and Olympia?"

I studied my sister. When had she gotten so tall? Her breasts bulged at the décolletage of her bodice. Her face had lost its youthful chubbiness, and her skin glowed with vitality. I thought of Olympia's special red and searched the shelves. I grabbed a bottle of rosewood oil. "This will soften the wax, which is what you want for lip paint. And it will balance out the rather nasty taste of the powdered bugs."

"Will you teach me how to make it?"

"You know I will."

She grinned, taking her prizes to the shopkeeper. Marianne counted out the candies in her hand, making sucking noises and ignoring us. I scanned the shelves, studying the many powders and dried flowers. As I turned a corner, I spotted a man in a turban. He grinned at me. The Arabian from La Rochelle. How did he get into Brouage?

Moréna!

"Tell your fortune?" His French was heavily accented.

I shook my head. "I know how to read palms."

"You read the stars, too." He reached into the front of his tunic and withdrew an old astrological almanac. "But not your own until now." He handed the booklet to me.

I stared at the numbers *1638,* then rifled through the pages. At last. An ephemeris from my birth year. A plan materialized. A way to find the answers I sought.

The man leaned in. "I can cast it for you."

I studied him. "Thank you, but I must use my father's methods. They were . . . unconventional."

He gave me a slight bow and left the store. I gave him time before following.

"What did you find?" asked Hortense, cradling her parcel.

"You know me," I said, tucking the book under my arm. "Always one to find something boring to read. Let's not go to mass today. We should go back to our quarters and start mixing that lip paint."

And prepare to redraw the horoscope I never should have burned.

I made Moréna undergo preparations with me. She balked at going to church. She shot me bored looks during mass. For nine days I made her receive the priest's blessing.

No one noticed I was fasting. I ate so little normally, and by moving food around on my plate enough to distract my sisters, I got away with just taking water for three full days.

I sent Moréna out for extra candles and kidskin parchment and a clay pot and clean white linen while I studied the book Mazarin coveted, *Heptameron.* She went daily to the docks looking for a ship trading sandalwood powder. I drew Solomon's star on the kidskin parchment and took it with me into confession. I managed to unburden myself of pride and vanity without giving the priest too much to gossip about, then swiped holy water from the baptistery font when he wasn't looking.

On the ninth day of daily mass, the third day of fasting, the sixteenth of November, I felt my hunger no more. Excitement coursed through my limbs. I packed a sack and told Moréna we would leave at midnight.

When the hour arrived, I donned a white linen gown and a heavy cloak with a hood that shadowed my face. Moréna pulled the sack from its hiding place beneath the bed. But not quietly enough.

Hortense sat upright. "Marie?"

"Lie back down," I said.

She didn't. "You're going to conjure, aren't you?"

I'd assumed that she wouldn't notice, that she'd been too young when our father had prepared for conjuring to recognize what I'd been doing. I didn't answer.

"Don't go far from the citadel. A storm is blowing in from the west." She lay back down and pulled the covers over her head.

We hurried out. Moréna paid the soldiers standing guard at the Royal Gate and told them only to come after us if we didn't return by dawn. The ocean air felt heavy. A wet breeze from the west dampened our skin and made it glisten in the waxing moon. Moréna carried a lantern, and we walked past the marshes, beyond the quiet docks, into the salt beds I'd come to know.

I put the sack at Moréna's feet. I took out my ink, quills, paper, and almanac from 1638. "You know what to do," I said, and knelt to re-create my nativity.

With the foolscap on the salt bed and the waxing moon as my light, I drew a large square, with a smaller square inside it. In the space between them, I drew zigzagging lines until I had twelve triangles, the twelve signs of the zodiac. I consulted the ephemeris and found the true place of the sun on the twenty-eighth of August. It was in the sixth sign, the house of Virgo. I found the hour and minutes in the Table of Houses and drew the sun symbol in the sixth triangle. Working up the houses and down the columns, I tracked hours and minutes and plotted every planet. I went through it again to note each planet's degree, then sat back on my heels and studied my work.

It was much as I remembered. With Saturn well dignified in the house of Aquarius, I would be imaginative. The lunar node called Head of the Dragon was in Sagittarius, which meant happiness for me. Jupiter in Scorpio made me tenacious. Venus, well dignified in its own house of Libra, indicated my attractiveness, suggesting I might be the cause of jealousies, and that I valued my freedom. My Virgo housed three whole planets, including Mercury, well dignified and almost too strong, making me so intelligent and gifted in the art of divination, it might actually cause my downfall. Mars was not at all dignified in Leo, making me willful. With my moon on the cusp of Leo, I could be hot-tempered. Venus reinforced this in the west, masculine angle.

Had my mother considered me too smart for my own good? Too willful to be corrected? So gifted I might be dangerous? I had tried to take control of my own fate. Perhaps the world wasn't ready for such a woman.

"Did you find it?" asked Moréna.

"Not all of it." I ran my finger over the house of Libra. The mysterious planet my father had noted there, the one indicating I'd leave my husband, simply didn't exist. Could he have been wrong? "My father must have consulted the angels."

For the first time, Moréna seemed hesitant. "So you're going through with it?" She had started a fire in the clay pot and arranged my sandal-wood powder, holy water, and kidskin with Solomon's star.

I nodded. The position of the moon indicated it was now the first hour of the Lord's Day, more than a week before the autumnal equinox. To call upon the hour's ruler, the archangel Michael, I needed to begin. Moréna took my cloak, and I kicked off my satin slippers. I stood barefoot in the salt bed wearing nothing but white linen. I grabbed a walking stick Moréna had left in the fire and studied the charred, smoking tip. Perfect for draw-ing on the crusty salt bed.

"How do you know what to do?"

I smiled. "I watched my father." The necromancer. And I'd prayed every day of my fast that his method would conjure only good spirits.

Now I walked a circle, nine feet in diameter, dragging my stick, drawing a ring. I drew another circle about a hand's-width inside it. Then a third inside that, and then a fourth. In the outermost ring, I wrote names I'd memorized from the lists of *Heptameron*. The angels of the air for Sunday, *Varcan Rex—Tus—Andas—Cynabal*. The next ring was the real work. I wrote the name of the first hour of Sunday and its ruling angel, *Yayn—Michael*. Then I drew Michael's sigil from memory, with its sharp angles and crosses. The angel of Sunday was again *Michael,* and his ministers, *Dardiel—Huratapal*. I wrote the name of autumn, *Ardarel,* and the angels of autumn, *Tarquam—Guabarel*. I poked my writing stick in the fire for a moment, then used it again to write the sign of autumn, *Torquaret,* then the names for earth, sun, and moon in autumn, *Rabianara—Abragini—Matasignais*.

Heavy clouds rolled over the ocean, and I felt myself growing tired. In the innermost ring I wrote four of God's divine names, *Adonay—Eloy—Agla—Tetragrammaton,* and drew crosses between them. Finally, in the center of the circle I drew a great cross. On the east side I wrote *Alpha,* and on the west, *Omega*. My stick had grown faint again, so I stepped out of the rings and shoved it deep in the fire, stirring the embers. Moréna tossed more wood into the flames. I quickly drew four Solomon's stars, one on each side of the fire and two opposing them on the other side of the circle. I looked at everything I'd done and grabbed Moréna's hand. "Come into the circle with me. Whatever you do, don't step out."

Her voice sounded nervous. "I thought you were calling on your God's forces of good."

"I am." I took up the flask of holy water, arm muscles shaking with fatigue. "But some of these angels might have fallen, and one never knows if demons might respond to the call."

I poured holy water into my palm and began committing sacrilege. I threw handfuls on the fire, the pot of sandalwood powder, and the kidskin parchment, reciting the fiftieth Psalm. "Purge me with hyssop, Oh Lord, and I shall be clean: Thou shalt wash me and I shall be whiter than snow." I sprinkled holy water over my entire circle. "*Asperges me Domine.* In the name of Adonai, the Living God, and Ruler for generation upon generation, Amen."

I walked my circle, stopping in every quadrant of the cross to pray, "Father have mercy on me, make appear the arm of thy power." From the center of the ring, I tossed the sandalwood powder into the fire. It popped and hissed and released its musky sweet smoke into the air. I knelt and called the name of every angel I'd written in the rings. The words rose to the heavens with the smoke. I stayed on bended knee out of reverence and exhaustion and cried, "Being made in the image of God, endued with power from God, and made after his will, I adjure and call you forth! Appear before this circle in a fair human shape." I stared into the sandalwood smoke, which swirled and danced as gusts swept in off the ocean.

I stood and threw the last of the sandalwood on the fire. I turned as I called an angel from each direction of the fourth heaven. "Aiel from the north. Uriel from the south. Gabriel from the east." Finally I turned west, to the ocean and the incoming wind, and raised my hands. "Anael from the west!"

The western wind rose.

"What's happening?" called Moréna over the rushing sound of the winds. She crouched behind me, holding her turban.

The parchment with Solomon's protective star tore from my hands. Were the angels coming? I struggled for breath. "Come without delay and make rational answers unto all things I shall ask of you!"

The gale roared in my ears, and I fancied it was the collective voice of all the angels in heaven. The strength of the wind pushed my body, and I fell to the salt bed, clawing the crosses I'd drawn into it, clinging to hold my ground in the circle. Sparks scattered from the fire pot. The smoke stung my eyes and seemed to enter my very mind. The musk of sandalwood filled my lungs, and I coughed out my questions, voice lost in the wind. *Angels, tell me what to do.*

Lightning split the sky, and thunder shook the earth. I heard something as the rains blew in. It was not so much the roar of angel voices, but the still cry within my heart that I'd refused to listen to all along.

The right thing to do is let him go.

We returned to the citadel in silence well before dawn. Hortense had a fire crackling. She asked no questions, just helped us change our wet clothes. When warm and dry, I wrote a letter to my uncle submitting to the marriage alliance he intended for me.

CHAPTER 48

Paris
June 1660

Paris was at its best in spring, before piss-filled gutters became too pungent in the summer sun, and when winter branches in the courtyards were outlined with green buds. Birds fluttered overhead, nesting in every eave, their cheerful twitter making me forget my grief for a moment. Only a moment. In the six months since I'd cast my magic circle and decide to give King Louis up, I had thought of him each day.

On this particular sunny day, I walked in the Gardens of the Tuileries with Prince Charles of Lorraine as we'd become accustomed to doing. We talked amiably of the weather and the variety of flowers emerging from the ground. Sometimes we talked of the potential size of my dowry or whether a marriage between us might gain him enough favor to help reclaim his family duchy from the crown. We even talked of how I'd prefer to marry him and stay in France rather than marry Colonna, my uncle's choice, which would move me to Rome. But we only discussed this if Venelle was out of earshot.

Today Venelle walked several paces ahead of us with Marianne on her arm, occasionally glancing back. Several paces ahead of them walked Hortense and Meilleraye. That man talked of nothing but his adoration for Hortense and his zest for religion, which bored her thoroughly. Mazarin had not yet responded to Meilleraye's latest request for Hortense's hand. Praise God.

Lorraine cleared his throat beside me. "Would it pain you to discuss the king's recent marriage?"

It had happened at the beginning of June. I had done my best to avoid the celebrations in Paris and tedious descriptions of the ceremony and of how seventy-five horses were required to carry the new queen's lavish household.

"It grows easier," I replied.

Lorraine went on. "Soon after I requested your hand in marriage, Mazarin entered an article in his peace treaty to restore certain disgraced nobles to favor. Now that the treaty is ratified, my uncle the duc is out of prison. He is blocking our marriage because—well, he wants you and your uncle's favor for himself!"

I almost laughed. "This means Mazarin opposes you both. He knows I'll refuse to marry an old man; thus he keeps your family's duchy for the crown."

"I'm sorry for it. You and I get along quite nicely," he said, bewildered. "Really, I'm quite shocked at the move your uncle made."

This time I did laugh. "How can you be surprised? My uncle said he opened negotiations with you six months ago."

"He never did."

"Exactly. Because he wants me to marry Colonna so he can send me to Rome. He controls me as he controls my brother and sisters and the king. Do you know when my brother was released from prison? The moment I agreed to give up King Louis."

"Is it so bad?" Lorraine loosened the cravat at his throat.

I smiled grimly. "You heard Mazarin tried to imprison Colbert de Terron for smuggling letters between the king and me, but do you know how Mazarin found out about Terron?"

Lorraine shook his head.

"Because Mazarin paid a spy in the king's household . . . the king's own valet!" Terron had narrowly escaped, saved at the last minute when the king ordered Mazarin not to arrest him. "Mazarin is like a sorcerer," I said bitterly. "He will find a way to make me marry Colonna."

* * *

I n our chamber at Palais Mazarin weeks later, Hortense was attempting to distill jasmine. She watched the bottles and tubes bubble over her flame. She'd become rather clever at concocting beauty elements.

Marianne bounded in. "I've a letter from Philippe," she cried. We sat on my bed while she summarized. "Condé gave up his best château in exchange for the king's pardon, then was forced to beg our uncle's forgiveness on bended knee." We each knew how vital the moment must have been for Mazarin and how he must have gloated. He'd conquered with diplomacy rather than battle, just as Moréna once predicted. Marianne went on. "The court is slowly traveling back to Paris. He complains of the agonizingly slow pace." She paused to smirk. "And he wants to know about Olympia's new baby."

I shrugged. "We will have to confess we haven't been to visit our newest nephew." Olympia had returned to Paris for the birth a fortnight earlier. I just didn't have the stomach to face her.

Marianne gasped. "Philippe describes how the king took a detour to Brouage. He watched the king shed tears in the room where Marie slept."

I grabbed the letter. Philippe went into great detail about how King Louis slipped into melancholy while walking the shores I'd walked. It had alarmed the cardinal. I looked up from the letter to see my sisters staring at me.

I remembered my conversation with Lorraine in the park, when I'd told him how deftly the cardinal controlled us all. "Now Mazarin will stop at nothing. He will find a way to make me *want* to go to Italy."

T he next week we packed freshly cut herbs, which I'd finally managed to plant in the pottage garden behind Palais Mazarin, a bottle of Hortense's new jasmine perfume, and a box of *nebât* into a basket for Olympia. We reported to the Hôtel Vendome.

The footman at the door looked apologetic. "His Eminence summoned her to join the court at Fontainebleau."

But the comte de Soissons called cheerfully from the inside hall. "Come in! I'll take you to the nursery to see my newest son."

We entered the nursery, and the firstborn, Little Louis, bounded to me, trying to climb my skirts. "Maah-ree," he said, practicing my name to the best of his three-year-old ability.

It made us all laugh, and Marianne rewarded him with a *nebât*.

"Where is your little brother?" I asked.

He pointed to the wet-nurse, suckling the one-year-old Little Philippe. Little Louis was too preoccupied with his *nebât* to show us the newest brother.

Soissons took us to a cradle, pulling a coverlet back to reveal the baby. "We named him Louis-Jules."

Despite all she'd done, seeing Olympia's boys made me proud.

Back in the carriage, Hortense asked, "Why would Mazarin bother with Olympia now? So soon after the birth and with the king safely married?"

I sighed. "Because the king still loves me, and the cardinal can't stand the thought of me regaining influence. Just wait. We'll soon find out how Mazarin has employed Olympia against me."

CHAPTER 49

Queen Maria-Thérèsa feels great jealousy when she sees the king making new demonstrations of love to Mademoiselle Marie Mancini and would like her to leave France as quickly as possible.

—PAPAL NUNCIO MONSEIGNEUR CELIO PICCOLOMINI
IN A LETTER

The summons arrived at the end of July. We were ordered to Fontainebleau to pay our respects to the king and his new queen. The moment I'd been dreading. We dressed in our finest court attire and rumbled south along the River Seine to the Fontainebleau I'd once adored, shining green in all its summer glory.

The Cardinal's Guards took us directly to the François Gallery, where Olympia, wearing new diamond hair combs, stood behind King Louis. His skin seemed sallow, with dark circles under his eyes. I felt a rush of worry for his health but tamped it down. The cardinal, standing behind the queen mother, shocked me. His hair had grayed, and he stooped over his cane, making himself seem inches shorter.

Where is the new queen? I curtsied, my sisters dipping behind me in unison. We held our low pose.

The king finally cleared his throat. "I see you've returned to court."

I rose, feeling my hands tremble. "I wish to heartily congratulate Your Majesty on the happy event of your marriage."

The king frowned. My sisters remained silent behind me. Venelle hadn't even entered.

The queen mother's eyes flicked to her son and back to me. "We decided you shouldn't meet Queen Maria-Thérèsa yet."

So this is a test. To see whether Olympia had effectively turned the king against me.

"You can meet my queen this evening," King Louis said to me. "The cardinal invited us to sup in his apartments. You may serve my queen her supper."

The queen mother beamed. I felt the color drain from my face.

Olympia snorted with laughter. "Welcome back to court, sister."

Mazarin had paid her to play this role. I ignored her. "Your Majesty, being assigned to serve her comes as quite a blow."

He straightened abruptly. "So did your betrayal."

I forgot the others and spoke to King Louis in my old way. "You engaged yourself to be married and started an affair with my sister but accuse *me* of betrayal?"

He stood. "You know I delayed my marriage for your sake. Entertaining Olympia was a ruse!" Olympia huffed, and the king ignored her. "I waited for you to—" He stopped himself before revealing too much. "Then I heard of your fascination with the Prince of Lorraine, how you love him, how he visits you."

Olympia had fed him lies. I glanced at her, and she grinned back, full of pride and glittering with Mazarin diamonds.

King Louis waved his hand dismissively, and I curtsied, backing from the room, kicking my skirts back with each step. When the doors closed, I spotted Venelle. "Call up the carriage. We're going home."

Before she could go, the doors swung open again. The cardinal emerged. "That was very good, Marie."

I hated him for making poor Louis suffer! "You orchestrated this like one of your court ballets."

My sisters shrank back. Venelle disappeared. I doubted she'd call up the carriage.

Mazarin curled his mustache. "Whatever do you mean?"

"You didn't have to humiliate me."

"I will do what I must to ensure you wed Colonna. You will leave, Marie. Leave France to me and leave King Louis to Olympia."

"Look at yourself. Your plots and deceptions have cost you your health." I studied him. The pristine red robes couldn't hide his frailty. I whispered quietly, "I warn you, inflicting pain upon me while I am already defeated shall cost you your life."

"Go upstairs." He ignored my warning. "You *will* serve the queen at my table tonight."

I took each of my sisters by the hand. We turned without being properly dismissed and marched up to our apartments to await supper.

That night a herald announced Their Majesties at the appointed hour. I stood against the wall like some overdressed footman. As they entered, I couldn't help studying the woman who'd taken my place. Short of stature and a bit plump, she wore magnificent clothes. The dark roots of her blond hair showed her servants had forgotten to rinse it with lemon juice. Her skin was white as cream. Though her cheeks were rosy, it wasn't a youthful blush but a rash, as if she were sensitive to whatever unguents she used to lighten her complexion. She was no beauty, but I couldn't stop staring. Her chin jutted forward, making her lower lip seem large, as if she were chewing her thin upper lip. Her eyelashes had been plucked to prevent the buildup of ceruse powder on her lids, which made her blue eyes seem unnatural. She said nothing and looked at no one. Mazarin stood shakily from his seat, and King Louis made a show of insisting he sit and rest. The king ignored me completely.

His Eminence had never served a more delectable table. The footmen carried in platters of vegetables and fruit compotes and *bœuf bourguignon*. I set each dish before the queen. Her Majesty's misaligned jaw didn't hinder her eating. She shoveled down every bite, chomping with gray teeth while the king and the cardinal discussed opening a university, a hospital, a grain store. *My ideas!* The queen gulped so fast she swallowed air, which came back up in little burps. *How does he kiss that jutting mouth?* She made no conversation. She showed no interest in anything whatsoever. He would be bored with her within months. I wondered if she even knew who I was.

The supper lasted an hour, yet felt like a year. As the cardinal made farewells, I assumed they would leave without addressing me.

But at the door, the queen muttered to the king in Spanish. "I can't believe this is the woman you thought you loved. She's so . . . dull." Then she glanced at me for the first time. She turned to the cardinal and laughed with disdain.

The king and my uncle froze. They knew I spoke Spanish better than either of them. My uncle had failed to introduce me as a family member, and she hadn't spoken *to* me. Therefore it would breach etiquette to address her.

I didn't care.

I curtsied as if her rude words *were* our introduction and spoke perfect Spanish. "Welcome to France, Your Majesty. I hope all the kindness you bestow on subjects such as myself will be returned to you in equal measure."

She looked at King Louis, blinking her lashless lids at him. *She doesn't even realize I insulted her.*

I glared at the king, daring him to punish me. How could he place this simpleton over me? Anger flashed in his hooded eyes as it used to do when he was mine. And for a moment he *was* mine, staring me down. I imagined what it might be like if he dragged me to the next chamber to rail at me, where I could kiss the anger away. But he steered his queen out. The doors closed on their backs.

"That was too bold," said the cardinal. "Watch your tongue when you serve the queen."

"I've no intention of serving her again." Today had proven things could never be the same. "I'm going back to Paris first thing in the morning." I walked toward my bedchamber.

"Go. Hide your face while you can," he said. "But when the royals return to Paris next month, you *will* serve her every single day. Or marry Colonna and move to Italy."

I paused.

"Just think. The whole court will watch you serve the queen in all her official glory while Olympia services the king in private. Your sisters will marry and be raised above you in rank. You will inherit none of my fortune. You will age in disgrace."

"I don't want to go all the way to Rome. Let me stay here with my sisters in peace."

"If it's peace you want, you will go."

August 26

The next month, the queen mother summoned my sisters and me to the Hôtel de Beauvais to watch Queen Maria-Thérèsa's formal entry into Paris.

Every lady remotely connected to the queen mother's court elbowed every other for a place at the windows. Watching the spectacular procession streaming through the Porte Saint-Antoine was like watching theater on a grand scale. I found I couldn't endure the heat and the crush of perfume-doused women. I had to separate from Venelle and my sisters.

I spotted Princess Henriette Anne, King Charles of England's sister, and stood behind her. "Congratulations on your brother's restoration to England's throne." He had finally recovered his crown, just as I'd predicted.

She looked at me with huge, innocent eyes. She'd been crying. "Thank you, Mademoiselle Mancini. Forgive me if I seem sorrowful."

I tried a smile, but the commoners' cheers from the streets sparked too many memories. I needed distraction. "Are you anxious to return to England?"

"Goodness no," she said. "I . . ." She leaned in to whisper. "It's just that I always thought this would be me." She pointed to the rows of prancing horses, musketeers, the Hundred Swiss, noblemen in jewel-encrusted doublets, and the king himself dressed in silver and red with the Mirror of Portugal gleaming from his hat. The crowd roared as the new queen's chariot came into view.

I laughed uncomfortably. "You mean, you thought *you* would be queen?"

Her cousin, a chestnut-haired girl named Frances Stuart, put a comforting arm around Henriette Anne. I could see this quiet beauty was destined to break hearts. "It was her mother's greatest wish," she said.

The princess nodded. "My mother groomed me for queenship. I—" She squeezed her eyes and tears slipped out. "I was your uncle's second choice. If only my brother had been restored a bit earlier, it would be *me* riding in the queen's chariot today."

I told myself it didn't matter. I looked out at the queen rolling past in her gold and diamond dress, shimmering like sunlight on water. *With his new lands and all this wealth, King Louis is now a step closer to his own vision of what a great king ought to be.* I felt dizzy. I stepped away from the window and looked around, hoping for a chair. Or a door. Instead I spotted the queen mother. She stood in the center of the largest window, and instead of watching the cavalcade, she watched me.

The triumphant smile she wore brought back all the pain. It had never really been just between us, but she gloated all the same. I walked out without seeking proper dismissal. It didn't matter. She'd achieved her purpose in summoning me.

W hen I finally made it to the carriage, Moréna lifted my hair and fanned my neck. I bit my lips to keep from crying.

Hortense climbed in behind me. "Did someone insult you? Forget them. You have your sisters."

I waved my hand. "It's the memories—knowing I worked so hard for something I never could have had."

Moréna shook her head. "You still love him."

Lip biting was no longer enough. The tears spilled. I clung to Hortense. "Cast my feelings for him out!"

"What?" She looked at Moréna, confused.

"Please," I begged, choking on sobs. "Do what Ovid suggests in *Remedia Amoris* and speak ill of the king to me. Whisper in my ear commands to forget him."

"I don't know—"

"Do it," said Moréna, pushing Hortense toward me.

She leaned in, my Mancini sister, and whispered horrible things about the king. She reminded me of his broken promises and his affair with Olympia. She called him too lofty, too proud, too shallow to love deeply. Undeserving. Unkind. Unavailable. And whether it was some power in her Mancini whisper or merely my belief in her, my sobs slowly died away.

T hat evening Moréna brought me a tonic of balm and chamomile. I sat at my writing table and composed a one-line message for the cardinal.

"What is that?" asked Moréna.

"It isn't in the form either of us expected, Moréna, but it is an alternate path to freedom. Another chance. A fresh start." I looked at the sentence. *I will marry Colonna.*

She looked away. "What did you hear from your angels that night in the circle?"

We had never talked of it. In truth, I'd heard nothing more than the roaring winds and the call of my own heart. Though I certainly *saw* something with clarity: myself, clinging like a fool to the ground in a windstorm, desperate for answers, when I knew my affair with Louis had been doomed from the beginning.

"That wisdom is accepting our fate when we cannot forge our own."

CHAPTER 50

Early 1661

That autumn His Eminence allowed me to retreat to Palais Mazarin. I lived quietly while Hortense and Marianne attended court; I read, drew horoscopes, and charted the stars. I memorized the Colonna book, *Strife of Love in a Dream,* and told myself marrying into such a family would bring me joy. I took Frip on long walks in the gardens. Still a puppy, she tasted every flower, every shrub, and when winter's chill arrived, she chewed every frosty leaf.

Though my uncle was still negotiating the terms of my marriage, Constable Colonna sent the Marquis Angelelli to me to act as his ambassador in the new year. Angelelli, with his perfect manners and immaculate clothes, stayed a time at Palais Mazarin.

Angelelli explained my future role as Colonna's constabless. He described Palazzo Colonna on Quirinal Hill, discussed Colonna's yearly trips to Venice, and talked of Colonna's passion for art and music. He explained Italian customs and manners, and I didn't have the heart to tell him I remembered them perfectly well. He spoke of Colonna's charm and good looks, his wealth and his power. "He believes you might have a gift for divinity," he said to me one day as we walked in the cold gardens, wrapped in furs.

I stopped walking. "Did he cast my horoscope?"

Angelelli nodded. "He finds your gift most intriguing. Constable

Colonna has an interest in all manner of things." He glanced at me. "I tell you this so you might feel at ease when you meet him."

Was he assuring me I would be permitted to be myself?

When Angelelli left, I put Frip in a basin in front of the fireplace and hummed while giving her a bath. Poor Frip shivered and groaned the whole time.

"My lady," said Moréna. "Are you . . . humming?"

I grinned. Perhaps I began to look upon my future with a measure of hope.

The queen mother never summoned me to wait upon her. But one morning in the new year, Olympia, as *dame d'honneur*, summoned me to attend the new queen's morning toilette.

Hortense snorted. "Olympia can stuff her summons."

"You don't have to go," said Marianne.

I thought it over. "I've nothing to be ashamed of."

I proudly wore the pearls King Louis had given me and presented myself at the Louvre. I ignored courtiers who searched my face for signs of humiliation.

Olympia opened the bed curtains. Queen Maria-Thérèsa sat up, surrounded by layers of white lace linens and pillows, rubbing her hands together, grinning like a child. "That is a sign King Louis lay with her during the night," someone whispered. The women nodded approvingly, muttering congratulations. They prepared a basin to wash her nether regions, and the queen announced in Spanish that she intended to spend the day in her bedchamber.

"All day?" I asked the nearest lady. "Does she read? Pray?"

The woman shrugged. "She just . . . sits around."

Did Olympia think this display would upset me? The queen's legs were stubby. King Louis had adored my long, slender limbs and the way I wrapped them around him energetically. This woman struggled to scoot herself off the bed. The queen called her priests for a ceremonial communion to sanctify her nocturnal activities. She asked the Lord to bless the night's coupling with a pregnancy. She prayed to the Virgin Mary for a son. I knew she would do her duty and bear as many as she could manage. Indeed, this was her sole purpose in life.

Olympia looked at me knowingly from across the *prie-dieu,* and I understood. She'd summoned me here to show me this woman's position was not necessarily one to envy.

Philippe held a scrap of foolscap when he sat across from me at our dinner table at Palais Mazarin the next month. He frowned, crumpled it, and tossed it on the floor. He'd moved back into his wing and allowed d'Artagnan to manage the musketeers so he could write his poetry and songs. Mostly he neglected to shave and spent time grumbling about Mazarin's refusal to find him a rich wife.

"Brother," I said, "is there any news from our uncle about my marriage negotiations?"

Philippe looked up. "Mazarin sent the final terms to Rome for Colonna to sign at the end of February."

So, it will happen. My marriage negotiations had progressed apace with Mazarin's failing health. He'd become so weak he'd moved from the Louvre to Vincennes for rest.

Philippe rubbed his scruffy chin. "The old man's illness is serious this time. Colbert is having him sign a flurry of papers."

He didn't have to say what he was thinking; *Mazarin won't make him heir.*

I threw a chunk of bread at him. "Cheer up. At least he made you duc de Nevers. Rich women will fall at your feet."

Philippe grinned. "We failed to beat Mazarin, but at least we tried. We mustn't harbor regrets."

I changed the subject. "What have you heard for Hortense?"

He looked away, reluctant to answer.

"Don't tell me he's signed her over to Meilleraye?"

Philippe nodded.

He's done it. Of all my failures, this was the worst. I rose. "I'm going to Vincennes."

At Vincennes I tried to pretend I didn't remember my last visit, when I'd been so sure I could hand all the cardinal's gold over to King Louis and discovered it was gone.

This time, with the cardinal in residence, tapestries lined every wall and carpets covered the floors. Men from every walk of life packed the chambers and halls. Bankers and noblemen, churchmen, even shopkeepers waited for an opportunity to petition a weak yet powerful man. Priests and doctors came and went from my uncle's bedchamber.

I spotted Colbert. "Is it true about Meilleraye?"

He gave a curt nod and led me into the cardinal's rooms.

My uncle lay upon a massive carved ivory bed. The red silk and velvet tapestries hanging around him and covering his frail body were the most luxurious I'd ever seen. Everywhere I looked was a painting by Titian like the *Pardo Venus,* portraits of old French kings, marble gods, bronze and silver statues, vases of jade and rock crystal, and inlaid Italian cabinets.

"Eminence," I muttered.

His lids fluttered open. He studied me hard, mentally acute as ever, trapped in this decaying body. "What do you want?"

I stepped forward, pulling a silver flask from my hanging pocket. "They tell me your heart is weak, so I brought you this tonic of hawthorn." Perhaps I felt guilty, for all my harsh predictions of his failing health had come to pass.

He closed his eyes. "Marie, I wouldn't drink something you mixed for me if it were the last drop of liquid in this world."

I stood there, holding my unwanted gift. "Thank you for sending the marriage documents for Colonna to sign." He didn't respond. "They tell me you intend to wed Hortense to Meilleraye."

A faint smile played on his lips. "Yes, and she'll get the bulk of my fortune when I'm gone."

He thought this would anger me. I'd long given up hopes of receiving any material sign of this man's esteem. "I beg you, Uncle, not Meilleraye."

"I'll make a new title for him, duc de Mazarin. They'll be richer than anyone in France."

"He is fixated on religion. He's a zealot."

The eyes opened again. His gaze bore into me. "I wish I had a zealot for each of you Mancini pagans. Go. Leave me in peace with the knowledge that at least my fair Hortense goes to someone who will steer her right if I die."

I slammed my flask down on a table. I'd taught King Louis strength, but this man had taught him selfishness. In the doorway, I paused. "Finalize your business and say your farewells, for you *will* die, Uncle. I warned you hurting me would kill you."

He sat up, started coughing.

I left without looking back.

Hortense's wedding took place that week at Palais Mazarin. The cardinal could not rise from bed to attend. The Mazarinettes gathered in the chapel. The duc de Mercœur brought Victoire's children. Martinozzi waddled in with a great, pregnant belly, and Conti never left her side. King Louis brought his queen. He didn't speak to me.

Meilleraye couldn't tear his eyes off my sister the entire ceremony. He hardly ate the supper I ordered. He sat at the head of the table in his new home, for most of Palais Mazarin now belonged to him, and watched his bride's every move.

Olympia stayed to help Marianne and me prepare Hortense for bed. She hummed one of Mamma's lullabies as she mixed Hortense a tea of chamomile and raspberry leaf.

"I can't believe I'm saying this," I said to Olympia while Marianne undressed Hortense, "but I'm glad you're here."

"Of course you are." Olympia patted my cheek and moved to straighten the bedcovers. "No one can resist having me near."

I had to laugh.

Hortense trembled when we slipped a thin lawn chemise over her head. "What should I do?"

"Just do what comes naturally," said Olympia flippantly. "It won't hurt for long!"

In the morning, Hortense asked for a pouch of witch hazel and yarrow to put between her legs, and St. John's wort for bruises around her wrists. God forgive me for wishing I'd killed the cardinal instead of letting him sell Hortense to that bastard.

CHAPTER 51

Cardinal's Guards and church officials came to Palais Mazarin at midnight the next week to tell us His Eminence Cardinal Jules Mazarin had received Extreme Unction. They carried us to Vincennes in case Mazarin might wish to offer us a final blessing.

Hortense and Meilleraye, Marianne, Philippe, and I stood in the cardinal's antechamber with Olympia and Soissons, and Martinozzi and Conti. Servants scurried about, hanging black satin over walls, closing curtains, lighting sconces. Priests came and went. At two in the morning, Mazarin's valet emerged from the bedchamber. He crossed to the gold clock in the antechamber and stopped it.

"Does that mean he's dead?" asked Hortense.

"Finally!" cried Olympia.

Philippe heaved a sigh. "Thank God."

Meilleraye frowned. "Can't you Italians at least pretend some remorse?"

"Certainly," I said. Then I looked at Philippe and burst out laughing.

Marianne, always one for a good joke, cupped her mouth, leaned forward, and yelled toward hell, "Sorry you're dead, old man!"

Meilleraye looked scandalized.

We laughed so hard we had to hold our bellies, especially poor pregnant Martinozzi. But when a herald appeared in the king's livery, a hush fell among us.

King Louis entered. His gaze settled on me. "Is he gone?"

I nodded.

King Louis looked away. "My deepest condolences." He left as abruptly as he had appeared.

I felt compelled to follow. In the empty reception hall, I called after him. "Your Majesty."

He paused, looked back. Of all of us, he might be the only one who felt real grief.

"I'm sorry for your loss," I said softly.

He shrugged. "He prepared me as best he could."

"What will you do now?"

He looked puzzled. "You mean, who will I appoint to replace the cardinal?"

"You intend to replace him?"

"I need a chief minister."

I shook my head. "You have the knowledge and ability to rule." I took his hand and traced the solar line he'd pretended to doubt. I whispered so no one would hear, "Don't let grief for your father cloud your judgment. Take control of the government quickly. Start your glorious reign." I dropped his hand and stepped back.

He blinked, glanced at his hand. "You're right. This is, in a way, what I've always wanted."

I smiled.

"You look well." He paused. "I've missed you."

I hardly knew what to say. "I am going to Rome."

He swallowed hard. "I wish you every happiness."

Silence seemed to swallow us up. I heard myself ask, "Was it Olympia who told you I was in love with the Prince of Lorraine?"

He looked away. "Yes."

"Lies," I said. "She lied at the cardinal's command."

"She . . . you . . ." His voice trailed off.

"I'm glad you are allied with Spain, that France is finally at peace. But I want you to know I never lost faith in you. I just lost the fight." It was the one thing I'd wanted to say to him for over a year. The words died in the empty chamber. I curtsied quickly, and ran back to my family.

* * *

We swathed Palais Mazarin in mourning black, then threw the biggest fête it had ever seen. Since protocol dictated we could not go out, the whole family came to stay. We strolled the gardens in the evenings, supped at overladen tables, and played cards late into the night. Martinozzi and Olympia brought their sons and fought over everything—which beds their children should get, which cousin should bow first to the other. Eventually Conti and Vendome told their wives to hush, and poor Venelle and Marianne had to take over care of the children.

Hortense showed us a chest inlaid with gold, silver, and mother of pearl that Mazarin had left to her. She opened it, and gold pistoles spilled out across the table, rolling to the floor. A fortune. She left it open. We all took handfuls from it at a time, and lost them just as quickly to one another at the gaming table.

Meilleraye participated in all of this with a reluctant expression. I never asked permission to order the cooks to bring up feasts fit for an emperor. Nor did I ask whether I could bring in my old musicians, or if we could use the reception hall for dancing. I ordered the servants to keep Meilleraye's glass full of a sweet, special wine I'd selected just for him. I might even have laced it with a tincture of chasteberry and skullcap to weaken his member so he'd be unable to abuse my sister once we'd all gone to bed.

One night, when I was on the verge of losing one thousand pistoles to Olympia in a game of *bête,* King Louis's herald presented himself in our reception room. Each of us froze, handfuls of cards and coins poised in midair. Our violinist stopped playing.

The king walked in alone, as in the old days, and looked around. "Colbert says we can't get burgundy at the Louvre because the storerooms at Palais Mazarin buy it all up." He grinned.

Hortense grabbed a bottle of burgundy from our table and poured him a glass as she walked over. "Whatever you find at Palais Mazarin is yours, Your Majesty." She handed the glass to him, then curtsied.

King Louis laughed. He tipped back his head to gulp the wine in one swig, and we threw down our cards and coins to continue the game. The king dragged another chair to the table . . . beside mine.

Olympia dealt him some cards. "The Spanish woman bores you?"

"Italians have always been more fun." He studied his hand.

"What will you wager, sire?" I asked.

He patted the front of his doublet. "It seems I have no money."

We all chuckled and snickered.

Olympia swept an arm over Hortense's inlaid treasure chest. "That's because every ounce of gold our uncle stole from France through the years is right here!"

Everyone laughed uproariously. Even the king.

"You'll have to win it from us if you want it back," I said.

"But don't worry," cried Hortense. She grabbed a fistful of gold and crossed to the window. "What you don't win, we'll return to the people!" She tossed it all to the courtyard below. She'd done this before.

All except Meilleraye jumped up and ran to the windows to see the exhibition. The gold coins bounced, chinking and clinking and rolling in the courtyard below. Servants and guards and footmen and kitchen maids and equerries ran from every corner of the palace into the courtyard, scrambling after the money, fighting each other for it. Olympia cackled and threw down another handful.

We cheered them on, clapping, and even the king struggled to control his glee. Finally he turned to the violinists. "Play a courante!" And so we danced with our wine and we gambled with our cards and threw away our money.

King Louis returned for more cards and dancing the next night, and when the candles gutted in their sconces, we all played hide-and-seek in the dark chambers. King Louis and I pretended to ignore all that had happened between us and made merry with the others until the sun came up. We did it again the next night, and every night the next week. So what if the king tried to touch my hand under the table a few times? I always moved away. When I found myself alone with him in a dark chamber during one of our wild games after midnight, I ran out. For over a month we Mazarinettes had never been so lively, so carefree, and so high in the king's favor. I didn't want to spoil it. But one night King Louis and I danced in the reception hall while everyone else was getting drunk on cognac.

"Don't go to Rome," he whispered. He took a long whiff of my hair.

The dance steps required that I step back. As I did I said, "You once made me feel worthy of a queen's crown. Don't degrade me now by asking me to be something less."

There was nothing he could say to that.

CHAPTER 52

Early May 1661

One month later, I woke in the afternoon earlier than usual, dressed, and gave Moréna instructions about which gowns to pack and which to discard. I intended to take her on my journey without asking permission from Meilleraye, the new owner of Palais Mazarin and everything in it. For all he knew she belonged to me anyway, and with me, she would be free.

When Philippe arrived, I was waiting.

He bowed. A courtesy, since I was about to embark on a new role as a constabless.

"Has it come?"

He held out a fat packet of parchments, wrapped with red ribbon and secured with Constable Colonna's great red wax seal. "Colonna's uncle, the Archbishop of Amasia, brought them this morning. Everything seems to be in order."

I released a great breath. Colonna had taken his time signing the marriage documents. But Rome was a long distance. A few days earlier a messenger had assured me the party with my papers would be here. Now the time had come.

"You'd better go tell King Louis," I said.

"No need. The Archbishop of Amasia went from here to present himself to King Louis and request the ceremony take place as soon as possible."

Etiquette prevented nobles from marrying without the sovereign's permission. I stared at him. "And?"

Philippe shrugged. "You know how people gossip. Some say Colonna will make you rich if you go, but that King Louis will make you richer if you stay." He waited for me to reply. When I didn't, he went on. "The king has summoned you to the queen mother's apartments at the Louvre."

"Why must I go to the queen mother's apartments?"

"Because the queen cries at the mere mention of you, and if the king received you in his own apartments, it would only upset her more."

I crossed my arms. "Did the king give the Archbishop of Amasia no answer?"

Philippe rang the bell to call Moréna. When she appeared he said to her, "Dress Marie well." Then he turned back to me. "The king's answer is going to depend on you."

I wore gray silk, simple but lustrous, and all the king's pearls. It was the first time I'd shown myself at court in months. The courtiers in the queen mother's apartments seemed to be waiting for me. Painted fans started fluttering as soon as I appeared. I ignored them as I always had. Both doors to the queen mother's bedchamber opened to let me enter.

The queen mother sat at the window, clearly unhappy. She said nothing. King Louis stood behind her. As I walked in he rushed to me, and the queen mother moved to her adjacent music room.

"Marie," he said, "don't marry Colonna. Choose a Frenchman and stay at my court. Marry the Prince of Lorraine if you like."

"Through Colonna and me, you have your alliance with Naples. The documents are signed."

"I will destroy them, find some legal means to dispute their terms. There is nothing to prevent us from being together now."

I pulled my hands away. "That isn't what Mazarin wanted for you. It isn't what I want."

"Marie, I had no choice but to marry."

Can a man be forced to do something he doesn't secretly desire? I looked away. "You altered my heart the day you let me leave the Louvre."

"I didn't understand then." He grabbed my shoulders. "Stay and help me become the king you foresee."

"And subject myself to the whims and humiliations of being a mistress? Mazarin would have tried again to kill me if he thought I would resort to it."

"I would protect you." He held the sides of my face.

"Our fates . . . they won't allow us to be happy together."

His hands fell to his sides, but he didn't back away. His face was so close to mine he might have kissed me. He might have kissed me and made me forget everything. "You are the one who encouraged me to lead. How can I be true to your own vision of me if I let you go?"

"Because you want what is best for me. In Rome I will be a legitimate princess."

"How do we end *this*?" His lips came so close to mine that I could feel his warmth. I remembered how passionately he would devour me, and wondered how things might be if I just let him.

Instead, I threw my arms around his shoulders and put our cheeks together. I tipped my head back and squeezed my eyes shut. "With dignity."

He pulled me to him, and it wasn't possible for two people to hold each other any closer. He dug his fingers into the small of my back until I thought he might tear into me. Then, gradually, I felt his struggle to rein himself in, master his passion. Acceptance made it no easier to let go.

"I wouldn't trade a moment, Louis. Not for a thousand years with a hundred princes would I trade my days with you at Fontainebleau."

He laughed a little. "Or our nights in Lyon."

We separated enough to rest our foreheads together. I forced myself to grin. "I'll never forget how many races I beat you on horseback."

He tried a smile. "I'll always remember how you shone like gold that night at Berny, the brightest part of my life."

"Call me cousin, stand at my wedding, send me to Rome with your blessing."

He took a deep breath and, finally, stepped back. "No one will rule my heart as you did."

My throat ached with the effort of suppressing sobs. I smiled, hoping to show him all the tenderness I felt for him. His expression crumpled, and I knew I would lose control if I watched him cry. So I curtsied. My tears splashed silently on the floor. I kicked my skirts behind me and backed from the chamber. He didn't try to stop me.

* * *

The next morning, enthusiasm lit Moréna's ebon features. She sorted out tools to assemble a blood-filled chicken bladder for me when the time came. She hummed while packing my herbs and tinctures and my forbidden books for our journey to Italy, where I might practice with them openly, study the stars, and be myself for the first time in my life.

Hortense laced me into a bodice covered in my small share of the Mazarin diamonds. Olympia pinned diamonds and pearls to my sleeves and my neckline, and Marianne slid pearl and diamond combs into my hair. I wore the king's pearl necklace and earrings, which I had vowed to wear every day, and my family escorted me.

We appeared as we had so many times before, we Mazarinettes descending on the Louvre in our uncle's extravagant carriages with enough plumed horses to drive an army. We alighted, each in our shimmering silks and jewels, our guards and men of rank in rows. King Louis met me, dry-eyed, at the door of his private chapel. I took his arm, stone-faced, and pretended I felt the strength I showed.

The Archbishop of Amasia arrived, leering at me and smelling strongly of ale. He stood as proxy for the Constable of Colonna. King Louis stood witness. An exchange of vows was made and a mass was said. Never had a wedding been so stoic. Never was I so grateful for Olympia, who, in her charming, authoritative way, led us through crowded chambers to the Mazarin apartments, where we dined. Afterward, the king presented me with a *tabouret,* saying, "To my beloved." Now considered a foreign princess, I could officially sit upon the little stool in royalty's presence. Thus I sat alongside him with his expressionless queen and his tight-lipped mother while Mazarin's favored men streamed in with gifts. My family members carried the conversation, and King Louis and I glanced silently at one another across the chatter.

He had not ruled my heart as he claimed I'd ruled his. But he had helped me understand how to set my own heart free. *I will always love you for that,* I wanted to say. Now the time for words had passed.

My sisters and I uttered no farewells upstairs. We had borne separation before, and distance wouldn't diminish my memories of the glory we'd shared in Paris.

With Philippe and Olympia on one side and Hortense and Marianne on the other, I walked for the last time down the stairs of the Mazarin apartments into the sunlit Cour Carrée. I kissed each of them quietly before I took the king's arm. He walked me to the carriage where the Archbishop of Amasia awaited. A throng of courtiers stood along the walls, ever watchful.

"Was it only two years ago that we parted in this very spot?" I asked.

He grinned, eyes filling. "You made a remark. That I wept and, though a king, I was letting you go. I will always regret that moment. Now I understand, yet I cannot make you stay."

I put a hand over my heart. "The better part of me does stay." I moved my hand, placing it over his heart.

He grabbed my hand, clung to it, searching my face.

"Take courage," I whispered. And I knew he'd learned strength from the pain we'd endured.

There was a flicker of disappointment. Then he nodded, and he said loudly enough for onlookers to hear, "Destiny, which is above kings, has disposed of us contrary to our inclinations. But it will not prevent me from giving you proof of my esteem in whatever country of the world you might be."

His words caused gasps in the crowd, even little cries of pity. Then King Louis took my hand from his chest and bowed over it, kissing it softly.

When he let go, we both turned without another word. I climbed into the carriage, and he marched back into the Louvre. The Archbishop of Amasia pounded the door, signaling the driver to move. We lurched forward and a hundred musketeers trotted into place, surrounding us so I could not see out. I wouldn't have been able to see a thing anyway through the tears that finally fell.

Madrid
February 1689

Just look at the four Mancini sisters: what wandering star rules them!

— MADAME DE SÉVIGNÉ in a letter

The hour had advanced from late night to early morn at my *casa* in Madrid while Olympia and I reminisced about Paris.

Olympia had nearly emptied a bottle of wine, and now packed Virginia tobacco into a long, slender clay pipe. "Do you regret it?"

"I regret losing the king," I said. And I often wondered if he'd felt torn in half the rest of his life as I had. "But I do not regret leaving."

She nodded. "You would have hated being his mistress. He isn't constant to any of them for very long."

I had known it would be so. His palm lines had warned me. "When King Louis didn't have the strength to make me his queen . . . it changed us."

"He was never truly happy again." She blew smoke rings into the air. "Oh, I tried. Heaven knows every woman at court tried her utmost to please him. Any pleasure he found was fleeting, gilded by his new palace at Versailles and ceremony, tedious pomp, nothing substantial. I often think he spent so outrageously to fill the void you left. You'd hardly recognize Paris with all the changes he made, all clean and lit up at night."

I stared past the smoke to the window. The dark sky paled with the imminent sunrise.

Olympia watched me carefully. "You do regret leaving."

I shook my head. "I threw such glorious pageants and parades with

Colonna in Rome and never had such fun as during our carnivals in Venice. No palazzo was more opulent than ours, with our opera and our artists. Colonna granted my every whim."

"Why did you leave Colonna? You caused more scandal in your escapades to escape him than you ever would have as the French king's mistress."

I'd worn ermine in Rome, dressed myself as the sorceress Circe, the goddess Venus, and the witch Armida for portraits and parades. I'd published my own astrological books, patronized opera singers and painters. I'd been myself, but never truly free. I crossed my arms. "He's a murderer."

She gaped.

"Don't look so surprised. He *is* Italian. I might have overlooked it . . . if he hadn't tried to murder *me*. He wanted me for my gifts, but he didn't realize how strong I'd be. Colonna decided he wanted a less stubborn wife, and I decided I wanted to stay alive." Olympia said nothing. "King Louis kept his word. Everywhere I roamed since leaving Colonna, the ambassadors and nobles knew the king supported me. It enabled me to stay one step ahead of my husband's assassins. But that is a story for another day."

Olympia put aside her spent pipe, and we walked through my front hall.

"Men think they can beat and mistreat wives," Olympia said with a frown.

She meant poor Hortense. I was glad I hadn't been in Paris to witness Meilleraye abuse her, grateful she had escaped him, and delighted when she moved to England. Her old admirer King Charles had showered her with gifts, shared her bed, and used his reclaimed crown to shield her from Meilleraye. "Hortense came to Rome and helped me run away from Colonna. You should have seen her in men's breeches, a pistol in each hand, ready to kill anyone who tried to stop us."

Olympia laughed. "You should have seen Marianne and me at the witchcraft trial in Paris a few years ago. The Chambre Ardente was draped in black, alight with torches and candles. The tribunal charged Marianne and her lover with poisoning her husband. She walked in with her lover holding her right hand and her husband holding her left. The charge couldn't stand!"

Philippe fared best. With a rich wife and houses in Rome and Paris, he helped us when he could. Each of my sisters had not only paid the price for our family name, but for taking control of our own destinies. "Our stories are told in broadsheets all over Europe. Women talk of us. They see how we defend ourselves, liberate ourselves, and wonder if they ought to do the same."

Olympia snorted. "Nonsense. The world will call Hortense a king's whore and Marianne a pagan."

I laughed. "You're the poisoner."

She pointed. "You're an astrologer!"

We leaned on each other, shaking with silent laughter.

Finally Olympia embraced me. "You carry the loss of the king's love within you. I am sorry for my part in it."

I nodded.

"You shared a prediction with me tonight," Olympia whispered. "So I leave you with one of my own. One that will lighten your heart. A messenger. Shortly after dawn you will know you were never forgotten by the man to whom you gave your heart."

I gave her a questioning look. She turned, disappearing into the carriage. I was too tired and too sad to pursue it. I watched the carriage disappear down the street. *Lord, keep her safe.*

I returned to the parlor and collapsed on the divan. Moréna brought me a cup of hot Spanish chocolate. I finished it just as the sun touched the terracotta tiles of Madrid's rooftops. That's when I heard the carriage. I stood.

Normally I wouldn't receive visitors at this hour. But Olympia's prediction rang in my mind.

Moréna entered the parlor. "It is the French ambassador." She straightened my skirts and smoothed my hair.

I nodded. "Show him in."

Comte de Rebenac, the French ambassador to Madrid, presented his leg and bowed, sweeping his hat so low it brushed the floor. "Constabless Colonna, you are gracious to admit me so early in the morning."

"Stand, sir, for I am most anxious to hear you."

He gripped his hat nervously. "I come in the name of His Royal Highness, King Louis the Fourteenth of France. Because he considers you his cousin and because of the esteem he holds for you, he bid me to warn you of measures being taken against your sister Olympia, the comtesse de Soissons." He spoke softly. "The Spanish Guard is preparing to arrest her and charge her with poisoning the Spanish queen. Some suspect her of witchcraft."

I relaxed. "Thank His Royal Highness for this generous warning. I am aware of the situation and have taken necessary precautions."

He seemed stunned. "How did you know?"

I glanced out the window to the brightening sky, where my stars had faded for the day. "I have my sources."

He nodded, but seemed hesitant.

"Is there something else?"

"Indeed." He pulled a fold of black velvet from his waistcoat pocket and handed it to me."

I didn't open it. "What is this?"

He cleared his throat. "A message," he said. "One so delicate the king dared not put it to paper, but rather entrusted it to me. He bids you to take my next words as if they were from his own lips."

My breath caught. I sat abruptly.

The poor man cleared his throat again. "It has been a goodly number of years since your relationship with the king ended. He bids you to know that he still thinks of you every day. When constructing a palace, he considers your tastes. When he hears the most moving music, his thoughts turn to how you used to dance. When he reads something interesting, he longs to discuss it with you."

I slowly opened the folds of velvet. There in the morning sun, a frame of diamonds sparkled like so many precious memories. Within it was a miniature portrait of the king himself. To receive a portrait of the king was a symbolic mark of favor.

"He says no other woman can beat him in a horse race. He will never return to Lyon, for he would feel the loss of you too acutely. He cannot live at the Louvre because your image haunts every chamber. He rules in a manner that he hopes would make you proud."

I held the portrait aloft so my tears wouldn't stain it. He didn't look the same, but he had aged well. Neither of us was the same. We could not go back, but we would always treasure what we had shared.

"And, my lady, above all, he wanted me to tell you that yours was the brightest star he ever had the privilege to love."

King Louis XIV is known for having a string of beautiful mistresses, yet he never expressed such an outpouring of emotion for anyone other than Marie Mancini. Some historians believe she was the one true love of his life. None of the numerous letters they wrote to each other were preserved. Every mention of Marie in the king's memoirs was removed, though some were known to exist. Only they knew what really transpired between them that would cause Marie to leave France rather than accept the opportunity to become his mistress.

There are no fictional characters in this novel, though some liberties were taken where facts were unknown. For example, historians consistently call Marie's father a necromancer, and though I couldn't uncover the primary source of this claim, I incorporated it because of other indications that the family embraced mystical ideas. Contemporaries did record that Marie's father was a great astrologer who had discovered an evil star in her horoscope. This horoscope has never been found and cannot be accurately redrawn because we do not know the time of her birth. Her horoscope in the novel was based on a birth time of noon with loosely applied precepts from William Lilly's seventeenth-century publication *Christian Astrology*. I was unable to pinpoint an "evil" star. The "unnamed star" that suggests Marie might leave her husband in the novel is actually Uranus, which hadn't yet been discovered by astrologers and was unfamiliar to Lilly. Marie herself wrote books on astrology, refers in her memoirs to having premonitions, and was known to costume herself as mystical characters. No one can know to what extent Marie practiced magic if at all, so I only put books into her hands that an Italian necromancer-astrologer of noble blood might reasonably have access to. The maid Moréna's personality and heritage were largely fictionalized, for little is known about her other than the color of her skin and her inability to enter convents due to her religion. The witch known as La Voisin may not have been practicing the dark arts at the time of Marie's fictional visit to her home. But Olympia did visit her, and details illuminated in those scenes came to light years later in the Affair of the Poisons. The theory that Cardinal Mazarin was the Sun King's biological father is debated by historians. Author Anthony Levi makes a fair case for it in his book *Louis XIV*. The bold and brilliant Mancini sisters embarked upon too many adventures to detail in one novel. To anyone wishing to study Marie's story in further detail, I recommend starting with the indispensable *Hortense Mancini and Marie Mancini, Memoirs,* edited and translated by Sarah Nelson, and *Five Fair Sisters,* by the late H. Noel Williams.

ACKNOWLEDGMENTS

The enormous task of completing this novel would not have been possible without the constant and complete support of my husband and our patient children, and I am immensely grateful to them. Gratitude goes also to my mother, for always being there; my trusty agent, Kevan Lyon; editor Toni Kirkpatrick, who always makes me smile; publicist Katie Bassel, whose reliability enabled me to focus my energy on this project; Thomas Dunne, for coming up with the concept that inspired this novel in the first place; keen-eyed copyeditor India Cooper; author Sara Ann Denson, whose advice and insight I hope never to be without; my circle of friends and family—I would be lost without you; Julianne Douglas, for researching countless French resources at my every whim; the Allen County Public Library, for its vast resources and for Nancy Saff's assistance with difficult research; author and Mancini expert Elizabeth Goldsmith, Ph.D., for reflections on the Mancinis and for her wonderful work *The Kings' Mistresses*; and finally Marie Mancini, for having the courage to stand up for herself in a world that did not yet value women.